Kill McCoy

A novel by

Michael Greer

Kill McCoy

Manuscript edited by Kit Campbell kittheeditor@gmail.com

Cover designed by Rickhardt Capidamonte. capidamonte@gmail.com

Cerro de la Silla y Obispado photo by Valdez Lopez.

Night Sky photo by M. Barrison

Dedication

For my awesome daughters, Stephanie and Jaclyn.

Chapter 1

Las Vegas, Nevada

Javier Cedillo blinked his eyes as the Nevada Department of Corrections van emerged from the underground parking garage of the Regional Justice Center into the bright Las Vegas sun. As the black and white van turned right on Casino Center Boulevard and headed north, the NDC officer in the passenger seat, a bald, burly African-American in his fifties, plucked a radio mic from the dash and advised the High Desert State Prison dispatch center that the prisoners had completed their hearings at the criminal court and the unit was returning to base.

Javier settled back in his seat and watched the street ahead carefully. His fellow prisoner, a young white man with long brown hair seated next to him, tried to get comfortable, but their hands were shackled to chains around their waists and the seat belts pulled tightly. Comfort did not come easy. The officer driving the van, a lean Latino in his forties with short hair and a mustache, rolled up his window and turned on the air conditioner. The early June heat was already intense.

As the van sped north Javier scanned the traffic through the metal screen barrier that separated the prisoners from the NDC officers. He stretched his legs and flexed his shoulders to keep his muscles loose. To his right, the other prisoner closed his eyes and leaned his head against the side window.

"Don't get too relaxed," Javier whispered in lightly accented English.

The prisoner glanced at him briefly with a curious look then closed his eyes again. Javier smiled and looked straight ahead. He saw the driver glare at him in the rearview mirror before returning his attention to the street.

At Bridger Avenue the driver made a left under the green light and headed west. The noon-day traffic was light in this part of downtown, with most traffic congestion further to the east around the government buildings and the Fremont Street Experience. *That was good,* Javier thought as they passed the rear of the Golden Nugget Casino on the right.

Just ahead a yellow GMC pickup turned right from First Street and proceeded west in front of them. The truck slowed as it approached Main Street and came to a halt at the crosswalk. As the van stopped behind the truck, a sudden impact rocked everyone inside as a vehicle behind them slammed into the rear bumper.

"What the hell?" the driver yelled as he laid on the brakes to keep from hitting the truck in front of them.

"I don't believe this shit!" the passenger said in an aggravated voice, one hand still against the dash. "Can you see who it is?"

"Looks like a woman driver in an old red Buick," his partner replied, his eyes on the side view mirror.

"Okay, keep an eye on her while I call it in," the passenger said as he reached for the

radio mic. "You guys okay?" he asked, looking back at the two prisoners.

"We're good," Javier replied. His cellmate nodded in agreement.

"Aw, shit, she's pregnant," the driver muttered out loud.

Javier looked back and saw a red-haired Latina, about eight months pregnant, walking slowly forward from the open door of her car. She suddenly placed one hand against the front fender and then crumpled to the ground clutching her belly.

"Damn it, she just went down!" the driver shouted. "Call an ambulance, she's probably hurt," he told his partner as he opened the door and got out.

Javier watched out the metal-screened side window as the NDC officer approached the fallen woman and kneeled beside her. He placed one hand under her head and the other under one shoulder. As he gently raised her up, the woman's right hand suddenly appeared from behind her back holding a small Glock with a suppressor attached to the barrel. She placed the end of the weapon under the officer's chin and pulled the trigger twice. Blood spurted from his throat and drenched the front of his green uniform as he slumped to the pavement.

"I think your partner needs help," Javier told the passenger officer who was just placing the radio mic back on the dash.

The man looked at him, then got out and walked around the front of the van. He stopped briefly to look at the truck in front of them. The two male Latinos inside looked back, apparently unsure whether to get out and help. The only other cars around were vehicles passing by on Main Street.

The officer continued to the driver's side and quickly stopped as he saw his partner on the ground, his head in a pool of blood. He drew his sidearm and pointed it at the woman who was standing over the downed officer, the Glock still in her hand.

"Drop the gun!" he shouted. "Put it down. Now!"

The woman stared at him for a moment then leaned over and placed the weapon on the ground.

"Put your hands up and turn…" the officer screamed before his words were cut short by three bullets hitting him in the back. He staggered forward and fell to the ground.

Javier saw the driver of the GMC truck walking forward with a suppressed Glock extended in both hands. He stopped over the black officer and fired another round into the back of his head. The truck passenger appeared beside him armed with an AK-47 assault rifle. The driver said something to him, then reached down and removed a ring of keys from the dead officer.

While the other man and the woman took the dead officers' guns, the driver opened the van's driver-side door and stepped inside. He looked at Javier through the metal screen.

"Soy Jesus. ¿Está listo para ir?" he said in Spanish, identifying himself as Jesus and asking if Javier was ready to go.

"Of course," Javier replied in the same language, "get me out of here."

The man tried two keys before he found the one that opened the cage door. Stepping inside, he used another key to remove Javier's handcuffs and the chain around his waist.

"Whoa, dude, what the hell is going here?" the white prisoner asked from his side of the bench seat, a look of suspicion and alarm on his face.

"I'm taking an early release," Javier told him as he stood up and moved to the door.

"Yo, can I go with you?" the young man asked, holding up his cuffed hands.

"Sorry, *gringo,* you'll have to stay," Jesus said then raised his Glock and shot the prisoner between the eyes. His head snapped back and he slumped down in his seat, his eyelids fluttering softly. Thick, red blood began flowing down his face.

"Vamonos!" said Javier.

The two men exited the NDC van just as a dark blue utility van pulled alongside and stopped. The woman pulled open the side door and hopped inside, followed quickly by Jesus, Javier, and the gunman with the AK. The driver, a male Latino in his thirties, gunned the engine and sped around the corner onto Main Street headed south.

"Here, put these on," said Jesus, handing Javier a paper bag containing a pair of blue Nikes, Levi jeans and a red t-shirt. Javier peeled off his orange jumpsuit and quickly put on the civilian clothing.

"This is Lita and Flaco," said Jesus, pointing to the woman and her partner. "You won't see them again until you return to Mexico."

"Thank you for your help," said Javier.

"No problem, *jefe*," said the woman, now minus her red wig and the prosthetic belly that had made her look pregnant. About thirty, her raven hair was cut short above her green maternity top. Her dark eyes had an intense, piercing look. The short, skinny man with the AK nodded his agreement with Lita.

As the van moved along the street, Javier studied Jesus closely. About his own height at six feet tall, he had a lean but muscular build. His dark hair was cut close in military style and he was clean shaven. He wore a black t-shirt and black cargo pants. A long cut scar ran across his right forearm and another scar ran down his right cheek just in front of his ear. His most intriguing feature was his eyes. Midnight black, they were the most vacant and lifeless pair of eyes Javier had ever seen. A sense of cruelty emanated from the dark orbs. He looked exactly as his brother had described him.

"The plan worked well, Jesus," Javier told him.

"Yes, good planning and a good team. We've been working on it for four months."

"How did you know they would take this route?"

"We followed you from the prison this morning. It was predictable that they would return the same way and all of our assets were in place."

"We're here," the driver said before Javier could reply.

The van stopped and Jesus opened the side door. Stepping out, Javier saw that they were in the parking lot of the Las Vegas Premium Outlet Shopping Mall just off Grand Central Parkway. The van was parked in front of the Eddie Bauer store. Shoppers were coming and going all around, but no one paid any attention to them. Javier knew they had successfully evaded the police.

A white Cadillac Escalade pulled up next to the van and a middle-aged Latino in jeans and a gray t-shirt got out. He shook hands with Jesus and gave him a cell phone.

"This is Roldan," said Jesus. "He will take you to California so you can oversee the mission there. I will complete the next operation here and then I must return to Mexico. We are at war with the Sinaloas and your brother needs my help."

He handed the cell phone and a slip of paper to Javier. "This is a disposable. It has thirty minutes. You can call your brother and then throw it away."

"Very well, and thank you. I will see you when I get home."

Jesus nodded then he, Lita and Flaco walked to a tan Ford Expedition in the next parking row, got in and drove away.

"Shall we go, *jefe*?" asked Roldan.

Javier nodded and moved around the Escalade to the passenger seat, a noticeable limp in his stride. As Roldan drove out of the parking lot, Javier dialed the number on the paper Jesus had given him. A voice answered on the second ring.

"Javier?"

"Yes, Fidel, it's me."

"It's good to hear your voice again, *hermano*."

"And yours as well, *hermanito*. It's been too long."

"Yes, it has. I just talked to Jesus and he told me everything went well."

"Yes, you have a very competent man, my brother."

"He's the best. When you get home, I'll tell you all about him and our operations here."

"I look forward to it after we are done in California."

"When you arrive, you will meet Raul, the head of my team there. Our asset in Las Vegas has provided the information we need and Raul has a plan ready to execute. You can assist. In the meantime, Jesus will finish the operation in Vegas."

"And after that?"

"When you get home with our prize, we'll make our final plans."

"What is that plan, Fidel?"

"We get our revenge, *hermano*. We kill Jack McCoy."

Chapter 2

The spray from the jet ski in front of him washed over Jack in a cooling mist as he sped across the surface of Lake Mead. Greta looked back at him and laughed as she maintained a ten-yard lead on her Kawasaki Ultra 300 LX. The machines' powerful four-stroke engines moved them across the water at maximum speed.

Jack could see the cove they wanted on the shoreline to their right and guided his jet ski in that direction. He yelled at Greta to follow and she pulled alongside him as he headed for the narrow opening in the rocks. They cut the engines when they reached the shore and let the jet skis glide up onto the sand.

Jack hopped off and untied a cooler, a Mexican serape and a pistol case from the seat behind him. Greta removed a backpack stuffed with towels and personal items from her seat and walked with Jack into a sandy cove about sixty yards across. To the right, a rock wall rose a hundred feet high and hung over the sand, providing a wide stretch of shade. To the left, the wall dropped until it met the sand and the slope continued uphill for another fifty yards.

"Over here," Jack said, pulling Greta toward the shade under the wall. There he spread

the serape on the ground and set the cooler down on it.

"Ooh, I like it," said Greta, looking back at the narrow opening in the rocks. "No one can see us from the water."

"Yeah, lots of privacy," Jack replied, an impish grin on his face as he kneeled down to open the cooler.

"I know what you're thinking, buster," she said, leaning over and putting her arms around his neck. "Actually, I was thinking the same thing," she whispered in his ear, "but right now I want to go for a swim."

"Okay, I guess lunch can wait," he said, closing the cooler lid and pulling her to her feet.

As he stood up, the cell phone hanging on his blue swim trunks began ringing.

"I told you to turn that thing off," Greta said, a scolding look on her face.

"You know I can't get away from work. Go ahead. I'll be there after I take this."

I am a lucky man, Jack thought as he watched the shapely blonde in the yellow bikini head for the beach. He pulled the cell phone from its waterproof holder and checked the caller ID. It was Noah Walls, one of the sergeants on the Clark County Sheriff's Department SWAT team that Jack commanded.

"Yeah, Noah, what's up?" he answered.

For the next five minutes, Jack listened as Walls explained the reason for the call. When the conversation ended, he stared straight ahead, a frown line creasing his forehead and his mind distracted by the information he'd just received. After a minute, he dropped the phone on the cooler and headed for the water.

Jack swam out to join Greta about twenty yards from shore and they spent the next half hour swimming, diving from rocks along the beach and enjoying the cool waters of the lake.

When fatigue set in, they returned to the shade under the cliff and dried each other off with warm towels. Greta opened the cooler and set out sandwiches, salads and cold sodas on the serape.

"What was the call about?" she asked as they tore into their lunch.

"Noah called to update me on the prison van escape that happened downtown day before yesterday."

"That was terrible. Those poor officers from the prison. I feel so sorry for their families."

"They also killed a prisoner. Seems the guy they broke out of prison was someone I arrested when I worked Narcotics back in '86."

"Really? Do you remember him?"

"Just vaguely. His name is Javier Cedillo. He was in his early twenties, but already an enforcer for the Colombian drug cartel boss who ran things in Vegas back then. When we took them down, he pulled a gun and I shot him in one leg. Left him with a limp. We also arrested a crooked cop who was helping the Colombian. One of the detectives in my unit was passing information to them. I put a wiretap on him and we caught him on tape. He got twenty years, and Cedillo and his boss got life sentences for drug smuggling and murder for killing one of the boss's rivals in Henderson."

"Do they know who broke him out?"

"Noah said the Homicide guys are still working on that. They think it's one of the Mexican drug cartels, but they're not sure who. The Mexicans took control of the drug smuggling after the Colombian cartels were decimated by the government there in the '90s. He probably has links to one of them.

"He stabbed a prison guard at High Desert four months ago and just got a preliminary hearing the day he escaped. They think the whole thing was a setup from the beginning. He stabbed the guard so he could get a trip to criminal court and his people on the outside could set up an ambush on the van that brought him there. Makes sense. The cars left at the scene were all stolen and they can't find the guy who hired his lawyer."

"You think he might come after you?" she asked, a worried look on her face.

"I doubt it. He's probably in Mexico by now, enjoying his freedom," Jack assured her.

"Well, just be careful out there," she said as she helped him put away the empty soda cans and leftovers.

"Always," he replied as he laid back on the serape and admired the tanned beauty kneeling next to him. "You ready for another swim?"

She threw her right leg across him so she was sitting on his lap. "I had another exercise in mind," she said with a mischievous smile.

"Did I tell you how much I like your bikini?" he asked.

"Which part do you like the best?"

"What do you mean?"

"The top or the bottom?"

"I'm not sure," he replied, smiling up at her, his hands on her hips.

Greta reached up and untied the strings holding the top around her neck. She then reached behind her back and did the same.

"What do you think now?" she asked as she dropped the yellow top to the ground.

"Oh, yeah, the top is much better," he replied as she leaned forward and kissed him.

The sun was just setting as Jack gunned the engine of his BMW R1250 motorcycle and sped out of the Callville Bay Marina. Greta, stuffed backpack strapped over her shoulders, sat behind him, her arms clasped tightly around his waist. They wore helmets, and jeans and t-shirts had replaced their swim suits.

Forty minutes later they pulled into the driveway of Greta's two-story house in Las Vegas's Spanish Trails neighborhood. Inside they found her eleven-year-old son, Adam, and his teenage babysitter doing his homework in the family room.

"Mom, Jack! How was the trip to the lake?" Adam shouted, jumping up to greet them.

"Great. We had a good time," Greta told him. "I hope you didn't give Karen any trouble," she added.

"He was just fine, Ms. Landers," the teenager said with a chuckle. "We had fun."

"I'm glad to hear that," Greta said as she dug her purse out of the backpack and paid the young lady. As the teen left to walk to her nearby home, Greta continued cleaning out her pack while Jack answered questions from Adam about their day at the lake.

"Damn, I think I left my bikini at the marina," Greta suddenly exclaimed.

"I saw it on top of the pack," Jack told her.

"I have the bottom, but the top is missing. It must have fallen out along the way."

"Don't worry, I like that one so much I'll buy you another one just like it," he told her as he got up to leave.

"I'll hold you to that," she said as she put her arms around his neck and leaned up to kiss him goodnight. "We should take more weekdays off together," she continued. "I like spending Wednesdays with you."

"Me too. Today was fun. Are we still on for dinner with Frank and Linda on Saturday?"

"Absolutely."

"Okay, I'll call you later."

Jack said goodnight and went out to his motorcycle. As he put on his helmet, he noticed an old Chevy pickup with a small trailer parked a few doors down the street. The trailer was loaded with lawnmowers, weed trimmers and other yard service equipment. Though common in the neighborhood, Jack thought it was a little late for lawn workers to be out. Maybe they were collecting payment.

The streets were quiet as he headed for home. Three blocks away he was approaching Tropicana Avenue when he noticed a yellow cloth on the other side of the street. Jack veered across the lane and stopped beside the object. As he suspected, it was Greta's bikini top. Chuckling to himself, Jack retrieved the swim suit and headed back. She would be happy to see this again.

A few minutes later, he was approaching Greta's house when he saw the old truck and trailer parked in her driveway. A black SUV was parked at the curb, blocking the truck. Jack cut the headlight and engine and the blue roadster coasted to a stop in front of the house next door. He studied the situation for a moment. Greta's lawn service usually worked on Saturdays. They could be here for another reason, but she hadn't mentioned they were coming tonight. And what was the SUV doing there?

Jack's gut told him something wasn't right. He stepped off the bike, removed his helmet and opened the right saddlebag on the seat. From a black pistol case, he retrieved his Professional model Springfield .45 and two spare magazines loaded with bonded hollow points. Jack put the pistol and magazines in his waistband and slowly approached the house.

The SUV was unoccupied. Walking up the driveway, Jack could see the words "Manny's

Lawn Service" stenciled in white letters on the door of the pickup. The cab was empty and the driver's side window was rolled down. A streetlight at the curb allowed him to see spots of blood on the steering wheel and dash. Jack quickly crouched down, drew his Springfield and flicked off the thumb safety. He pulled his cell phone from his belt and dialed 911. He identified himself to the dispatcher and described the situation at Greta's address. He requested two patrol units be dispatched to the location.

Jack moved to the garage door and peered around the corner and up the walkway to the front door. The lights were still on inside, but he couldn't hear any sounds. Tactically speaking, Jack knew he should wait for the backup units to arrive before attempting to enter the house, but the life of a woman he cared for a great deal was very likely in danger. He was deciding what to do when he heard something that decided for him: the muffled sound of a gunshot inside the house.

Chapter 3

Crouching low, Jack ran to the front door and kneeled below the peep hole. He paused to listen but heard no further shots. He turned the brass knob and the door unlatched. Springfield in his right hand, he slowly pushed inward with his left and crept forward until he was just inside the entrance. The rubber soles of his Tony Lamas made little noise.

To his front against the right wall lay the body of a Latino in his forties. His nose was bloody and the red liquid soaked his denim shirt. His vacant eyes stared upward. The lawn service guy. To his left front, he could hear voices in Spanish coming from the family room. Ahead and to the right he could hear muffled screams from Greta on the second floor and a man shouting at her.

Closest threat first, Jack thought as he moved around the corner of the alcove, and came face-to-face with a short, shaved-head Latino with a Beretta pistol in the waistband of his knee-length khakis. Tattoos covered his arms and his neck above a blue jersey, and he held a beer bottle in one hand.

Over the man's shoulder Jack could see two more similarly dressed and tattooed thug in the family room, one sitting on the sofa and the other putting a CD in Greta's wall-mounted stereo. Before the gangster in front of him could move, Jack glided forward and snapped a hard Hapkido front kick into his crotch, his boot driving the man's testicles deep into his groin.

A loud guttural scream filled the room as the gangbanger dropped the beer bottle and fell to the floor, clutching his ruined genitals. Jack quickly snatched the Beretta from the man's waist and threw it behind him, then moved forward to confront his two companions.

"Manos arriba," he yelled in Spanish, telling them to get their hands up.

For a moment neither moved, both frozen by the shock of what had just happened. Then the heavyset one on the sofa rose up, clutching a sawed-off shotgun in one hand. As he swung the weapon around, Jack extended his Springfield in a modified Weaver stance and fired a double tap into the thug's chest. The big bore slugs drove him backward over the sofa and to the floor. The shotgun fell from his hands and blood soaked his white t-shirt.

Jack immediately turned to the second man, a teenager actually, near the stereo and saw him pulling a stainless-steel revolver from under his green t-shirt. As he raised the gun in his right hand, Jack lined the big dot front sight of his Springfield above the gunman's hands and pressed the trigger once. The .45 roared and a big hollow point blew the young thug back against the stereo and dropped him to the floor.

Jack ran up, grabbed the revolver from the youngster's hand and stuck it in his belt. The teen bandit was hit high in the chest but was still alive, moaning and gasping for breath. Before Jack could move, he heard a muffled pop behind him and a bullet whizzed past his right ear and hit the opposite wall. Over the ringing in his ears, he heard Greta scream his name.

Whirling around in a crouch, Jack saw Greta and another shooter on the second floor landing above the entrance to the dining room and kitchen. The man held Greta around the neck with his left arm and had a Glock in his right hand. Jack ran to the front entrance and took a position behind the inside wall. He didn't see Adam and hoped the youngster was safe.

Behind him the thug he'd kicked was still groaning and rolling on the floor, hands clutched to his groin. *Not a threat.* Peering around, Jack saw the man holding Greta in front of him move down the stairs, his Glock extended toward Jack.

Greta's pink t-shirt was torn at the neck and hanging down her shoulder. She was bleeding from a cut on her lip and one eye was swollen. She clutched at the gunman's arm with both hands. Springfield at the ready position, Jack watched them descend the stairs.

"Turn her loose and drop the gun," Jack shouted in Spanish as they reached the lower floor. "Your buddies are down and you're finished here."

"Get out of the way, cop, or I'll kill her," the thug replied in English.

Jack wondered how the guy knew he was a cop, but that wasn't important right now. He raised his weapon and stepped out in front of them barely ten feet away.

The man was about thirty, average height and heavy. He wore jeans and a blue t-shirt. His head had a buzz cut and both arms were heavily tattooed. The number "thirteen" was tattooed in the center of his forehead and blood seeped from scratches on his right cheek. He held the muzzle of the Glock at Greta's temple.

"Put the gun down and you live," Jack told him. "You hurt her and I will kill you."

"You ain't killin' nobody, cop," he spat. "I got the cards here. You don't wanna see your woman dead, you better back off."

Jack wondered why the guy had not already fired as an idea came to him.

"*Vous me fiez?*" Jack said, asking Greta in French if she trusted him.

She nodded her head, her eyes wide in fright.

"Okay, when I say 'now,' I want you to go faint and collapse," he continued in the same language.

Greta nodded her understanding.

"What is that shit?" the gunman screamed. "You try anything with me, cop, and I'll blow her damn brains out."

Jack took a deep breath and set the dot sight of his .45 on Greta's hairline. He placed all of his focus on the threat in front of him. Long experience with violent killers like this one had taught him how to tune out distractions and how to control his fine motor skills under stress.

He let out half a breath and said, "*Maintenant!*"

Greta closed her eyes and collapsed straight down. Her weight pulled the gunman's arm down and exposed his entire head. Before he could react, Jack pressed the trigger on his Springfield. The 230-grain slug hit him in the forehead directly between the one and the three and dropped him like a marionette whose strings had been cut.

Greta scrambled away from him and fell into Jack's arms. He held her tightly as he watched blood and brain matter flow out of the dead gangster's shattered head.

"Lieutenant, are you here?" came a woman's voice from the open front door.

Still holding Greta, Jack turned and answered, "Yeah, we're in here."

A moment later a female deputy came around the corner of the entrance, her Glock forty at the ready position.

"We have a shooting here," he told her, holding up his badge and ID case. "There are five down, all inside. Three are dead and two injured." He pointed toward the shooter at the bottom of the stairs and the other three in the family room. "Tell dispatch we need more units, paramedics and Homicide detectives. And tell them to notify the sheriff that I'm involved."

"Yes, sir, on it," the deputy replied, reaching for her hand radio and going to check on the bodies.

Just then a male deputy came into the room, pistol in one hand. He relaxed when he saw Jack. "Holy shit!" he said, taking in the scene. "Lieutenant, are you okay?"

Jack nodded and repeated what he had told the man's partner. "Tape off the entire house at the street," he added. "It's all a crime scene."

"Jack, I need to check on Adam," Greta said, suddenly pulling back from him. "They tied him up and put him in the guest bedroom downstairs."

"Okay, make sure he's all right and stay with him until I come get you."

She nodded and headed for the rear of the house. Through the front door he could hear patrol cars stopping outside and sirens in the distance. He looked around and shook his head in wonder.

"What the hell is going on here?" he asked himself out loud.

Chapter 4

It was near midnight and the scene around Greta's house was one of controlled chaos. Jack and Sheriff Frank Martines stood in the front yard watching as crime lab technicians worked on the lawn service truck and the black SUV parked in front. Patrol deputies knocked on neighbors' doors looking for possible witnesses.

Police cars filled the street in both directions. Paramedics had already left the scene and a coroner's van was double parked at the curb. Four Homicide detectives had responded to investigate the shooting. Some residents had come out in their bathrobes and pajamas to watch this rare occurrence in their neighborhood.

"Jack, do you have any idea why these MS-13 gangsters would target your girlfriend and her son?" Martines asked.

"I don't, Frank," Jack told his boss and old friend who was off duty and had come to the scene in jeans and a tan Polo shirt. A red baseball cap covered his salt and pepper hair. The two had known each other since they were classmates in the sheriff's department academy.

The stocky Martines had commanded SWAT's parent unit, the Support Services Bureau, until last year when he ran for Sheriff after the incumbent retired. Jack, a wealthy property and business owner himself, had rallied the Las Vegas business community in support of Martines and he had won handily. The new sheriff had responded immediately upon hearing what had happened to his friend and SWAT commander.

"I do know something isn't right about this whole thing," Jack continued.

"What do you mean?"

"The banger who attacked Greta knew I was a cop and I had never seen the guy before. He also had a chance to shoot me at one point and he didn't take it."

"Well, you do look like a cop and maybe he was just afraid to start shooting."

"Maybe, but how do you explain the lawn guy? They obviously used him to get inside Greta's house, but how did they know he was her gardener? There's something going on here and I don't think it's about Greta."

"Chad and his guys will find out," Martines said, referring to Lieutenant Chad Meyers, the Homicide commander who had also responded to the scene.

At that moment Meyers came out of the house, followed by two deputy coroners with the bodies of the dead gangsters strapped to gurneys. Another van had already removed the body of the dead gardener. As the dead suspects were loaded into the van at the curb, Meyers spoke to Jack and Martines.

"Sheriff, we're about finished in the house, but I'd like to keep it secured until we interview Ms. Landers and her son. We might learn something from them that brings us back here."

Earlier Jack had escorted Greta and Adam out the back door and around the house where a paramedic had treated Greta's battered face before a patrol deputy took them to the Homicide office downtown. They would be interviewed there when the detectives finished at the house. Jack would accompany Meyers to the office to give his own statement.

"That's fine, Chad," Martines told him. "Tell the scene commander what you want and he'll see to it."

"Roger that. Jack, are you ready to go?"

"Yeah, Chad. Sheriff, I'll talk to you tomorrow," Jack told Martines.

"Okay, Jack. As of tonight you're on paid leave pending the coroner's ruling on the shooting. We know what it will be, but you know the routine."

"Yeah, rules are rules," Jack replied.

While Meyers drove, Jack used his cell phone to call Ana Lopez, his housekeeper and close personal friend, for the second time that night. He got her voicemail again. He tried her cell number with the same result. *Not like Ana*, he thought. Jack's gut was gnawing at him again and he didn't like what it was saying.

When Jack and Meyers arrived at Homicide Division, they found Adam sitting in the coffee room with the detective who had interviewed him. He jumped up and ran to Jack.

I didn't cry, Jack," the boy said confidently. "I was scared for Mom, but not for me, and they couldn't make me cry."

Jack looked down at the youngster and put one hand on his shoulder.

"I didn't think they would, Adam," he said. "I've always thought you were a brave young man and tonight you proved it. You make me proud, and your mom as well."

"He gave us a very good statement about what happened at the house," the detective told Jack. "He's a smart young guy."

"Yes, he is," agreed Jack.

Just then Greta and another detective came out of an interview room nearby. Adam ran to his mom and they hugged each other tightly. After a moment Jack joined them. Greta's eyes were bloodshot, the left one blackened and swollen; her lower lip was cut at the corner and her left cheekbone was bruised. She had exchanged the ripped t-shirt for a green top before leaving the house.

"Are you going to be okay?" he asked.

"In time," she said, looking up at him, one arm around Adam. "Right now, I don't feel so good."

"You shouldn't. You just went through a horrific experience and you have a right to feel scared and upset."

"Jack, I just don't understand why this happened. Who are those men and why did they come to my house? I've never seen them before in my life."

"We don't know and there are a lot of unanswered questions about this whole thing. The detectives here are some of the best in the business and they will find out."

"I feel so bad about Mr. Zamora. He was such a good man, hard-working, dedicated to his family, and they shot him down right in front of me."

Her tears were flowing again and Jack took her in his arms. Adam looked up at them.

"The killers are part of a vicious street gang that has members all over the country. They are heavily involved in the drug traffic ring and they have no regard for innocent life. I've had some experience with them right here in Vegas." He paused a moment before continuing. "I'm just glad we've been practicing your French."

Jack had learned French while in Europe with the U.S. Army in the seventies and spoke the language with his late wife, Gabrielle, a native of Paris, France. Greta had taken French in college and the two often spoke the language to improve her fluency.

"I know. You saved my life and I'm so grateful," she told him, her arms around his neck.

"Do you and Adam want to come home with me tonight? I have plenty of room."

"That's really nice of you, but we're going to stay with my mom and dad. I called them when we got here and they're waiting downstairs now."

Greta's parents had moved to Las Vegas from California during the last year and lived in a large house in Henderson.

"All right. I have to give a statement before I go home. I'll call you tomorrow."

"Jack, I don't know if I can even go back to that house."

"I understand. We can talk about it later."

Jack asked a detective to escort Greta and her son down to the lobby to meet her parents. As he watched them go, he was filled with sadness and anger over what had happened to them, and he couldn't shake the feeling that he was somehow responsible. He didn't want to consider the consequences if that turned out to be true.

The detective sergeant who interviewed Jack was highly skilled and his statement took less than an hour to complete. When they finished, Lieutenant Meyers took Jack back to the crime scene. The house was still taped off and lab techs were removing the gardener's truck and trailer and the black SUV. A few neighbors still stood in their yards watching the process. Meyers parked behind Jack's motorcycle.

"I'll be sleeping in tomorrow, Jack," the Homicide boss told him as they got out, "but I'll call you with an update as soon as I get back."

"That's fine, Chad," Jack replied as he straddled his bike and snapped on his helmet. "Call when you have something."

Twenty minutes later Jack pulled up to the gate of his hacienda-style residence on Raven Avenue in the southwest area of Las Vegas. The five-acre estate was surrounded by a five-foot adobe wall and had horse corrals on one end. His housekeeper lived in a smaller structure behind the main residence. Jack had lived here almost twenty years and had raised two kids in the house.

He clicked the remote on his key chain and the metal gate slid back to allow him entry. Another button raised a door on the attached garage and Jack pulled inside. It was 2:00 a.m. and he was tired. He hoped his arrival wouldn't wake Ana. He was still concerned that she had not returned his calls.

The entry from the garage took him through a laundry room and into the kitchen. He froze in place when he stepped into the room. The refrigerator door was wide open, as were two cabinet doors. Some containers from the refrigerator were on the island counter. Jack knew Ana would never leave the kitchen in that condition.

He stood still, listening for any sound or movement in the house. He heard nothing. Homicide had taken his Springfield for ballistics testing and he didn't have his Kimber backup. Jack hated being unarmed. He carefully moved right and down a hallway to his den.

Inside the spacious room he noticed his desk had been rifled through and some papers were on the floor. The computer was still on top and a nearby TV had not been moved. Looking around, he noticed his Japanese Samurai sword was missing from its wooden rack against the far wall. The katana had been a gift from his friend and martial arts instructor, Danny Kim. The shorter Wakizashi version was still on the rack.

Jack moved to the two gun safes along the nearest wall and punched in the number code for the padlock on the larger one. He took a Wilson .45 ACP and three loaded magazines from the top shelf then closed the door. Jack decided he would first clear the house then check on Ana in the back.

Moving across the room, he entered the hallway again and stopped to listen. Hearing nothing, he slowly moved to the dining room and saw that area had not been disturbed. He eased along the wall to the door that connected to the family room. Peering around the opening, he saw that the room appeared normal.

He decided to check the front door to see if that was where entry had been made. His .45 at low ready, Jack stepped across the room and around the corner of the foyer. The sight that greeted him sent his senses reeling. Stretched out on the floor, feet toward the front door, lay the body of his beloved friend and confidante, Ana Lopez, in a large pool of blood. The most horrifying part of the vision before him was the sight of her head in the center of her chest, facing the door.

For a moment Jack couldn't move or even breathe. The unreality of the scene had frozen him in place. Finally, he took a deep breath, stepped forward and kneeled as close to the body as possible without stepping in blood. She lay on her back with her arms pulled behind her as though her hands were tied. He noted how the muscle fiber and nerve tissue of her neck showed a smooth, even cut. The spinal column gleamed white in the center. Cleanly severed. Now Jack knew why his sword had been taken.

Jack stared at the woman who had been such a big part of his life for the last sixteen years, the woman who had helped raise his kids and tutored them in two foreign languages, the woman who had been there for him and the children when his wife was killed by a hit and run driver four years earlier. She had helped get them through that terrible time. His hands shook and his eyes became moist as memories flooded his mind.

After a few moments, Jack calmed himself and shifted his position so he could see her face better. Her eyes were open and glassy and her face was bruised and bloody from cuts on both cheeks. Strangely, her auburn hair looked perfectly coiffed. It was the white playing card protruding from Ana's slightly parted lips that drew Jack's attention.

Placing his fingers on the edges, he pulled the card out so he could examine it. And for the second time that night he was shaken right down to his core by what he saw. The image on the paper card was the head of a black jaguar, and below it, in black letters, were the Spanish words *los tigres negros*, the black tigers.

Jack was stunned by the image, which he hadn't seen in almost thirty years. An image connected to a brutal war in a jungle combat zone from another time. Now, here it was again. In his home, on the body of his dead friend. Once again, it seemed his violent past had come back to haunt him. And this time the people he loved were paying the price.

Chapter 5

Jack watched as the coroner's van pulled out of his driveway and turned right onto Raven Avenue. It was 5:00 a.m. and the first ray of dawn could be seen in the eastern sky. He stood in front of his house with Frank Martines, who had once again responded to the scene upon hearing that Jack's friend and housekeeper had been murdered. Police cars filled his driveway and lined the street outside.

"Jack, do you have any idea what the hell is going on tonight?" Martines asked. "First Greta and her son are attacked as soon as you leave their home, then Ana is killed right here in your house before you even get back.

"I don't know, Frank," Jack told him in a tired voice. "It does look that way, but I'm damned if I know who or why."

"That card you found on Ana's body. Any idea what that's about?"

Jack had decided not to say anything about the card and its connection to his past. The idea that a calling card nearly three decades old could be related to the events that had just happened was too incredible. The people connected to that image and time were all dead. There

had to be another explanation. He would wait and see what the investigation revealed before he considered that part of his past.

"I'm guessing it's some kind of logo or symbol for the people who did this. Probably a gang thing. If the MS-13 who attacked Greta also did this, it could be something they're using as a means of fear and intimidation."

"You may be right," Martines agreed, "but it sure looks like a message."

"Jack, Sheriff, would you come in?" said Chad Meyers from the corner of the house. "We're ready to view the tape."

Meyers had come straight to the house when he received Jack's call and had brought in additional detectives to assist. The sheriff's department overtime tab was climbing high.

They followed Meyers along the side of the house to a patio area where sliding glass doors led into the kitchen. Passing lab techs who were still dusting for fingerprints, they moved on to the den where a computer tech named Carl was sitting at Jack's desk. When the first detectives arrived, Jack had told them about his video surveillance system and how it might have recorded the killers.

Two years earlier Jack had installed a high-tech digital video recorder surveillance system at his house. High resolution bullet cameras posted around the outside of the property and dome cameras in every room except the bathrooms recorded 24/7 when turned on. The video was stored in a digital hard drive inside a wall safe in the den. Carl had transferred the last twenty-four hours of recorded video to a DVD.

"Carl reviewed the outside and interior video and found the time when the killers arrived," Meyers told them as they stopped at Jack's desk. The two Homicide detectives, a male and female team, stood behind Carl.

"He integrated the video recorded on the outside cameras and the interior video onto a single DVD from the time the suspects arrive until they leave. The video shows them clearly. There are six total with one in charge and giving the orders. Their faces are visible and easily identifiable. It also shows the murder, Jack, and it's brutal. Are you okay with seeing that?"

Jack looked at Meyers for a moment before answering. "Yeah, Chad, I'm good. Go ahead."

Meyers nodded at Carl, and the technician inserted a DVD into Jack's computer and clicked on a link that appeared on the screen. A moment later came the image of a beige van at the front gate, followed by a close-up of the driver. A Latina was speaking into the intercom, but the surveillance system did not include audio and her voice could not be heard. A few seconds later the gate rolled back and the van drove forward and stopped at the front door. Large black letters on the side identified the vehicle as belonging to Valley View Cleaners. Jack recognized it as the cleaning service that picked up and returned his and Ana's dry cleaning once a week. She would not be suspicious of the van.

Ana, dressed in a white blouse and tan pants, came out and approached the vehicle. The van's side door suddenly opened and five men jumped out and surrounded her, two grabbing her by the arms. One of the men, older than the others and apparently in charge, walked up to Ana and struck her across the face, opening a gash on her cheek.

Jack winced as he saw his friend sag briefly from the blow before recovering. The man shouted commands and the others pulled Ana inside and into the kitchen where the apparent leader began questioning her while the others ransacked the cabinets and refrigerator.

The female with the group disappeared toward the den. Ana shook her head at the leader and shouted something at him with a defiant look on her face. jack smiled to himself knowing his old friend was a proud and dignified woman who would never submit to scum like this one.

The man responded by slapping her across the other cheek, inflicting another cut that leaked blood. Ana spit at him and kicked out with one foot, narrowly missing his leg. He stepped forward and struck her in the stomach with his right fist, doubling her over. Jack clenched his jaw and his insides boiled as he watched. The son-of-a-bitch was building up a lot of payback. He noted that the man moved with a fluid grace and his strikes had the motion of someone trained in martial arts.

The man said something to the two holding Ana. One of them pulled a flex cuff from his pants pocket and tied Ana's hands behind her back as the boss left the kitchen. The next image showed the leader in the den talking to the female who was looking through Jack's desk. He looked around briefly then walked over to the gun safes against the wall. He tried the handles on each one before turning and walking to the rack holding Jack's samurai swords. He removed the katana and pulled the twenty-seven inch blade halfway out of its bamboo *saya*, or sheath.

After inspecting the sword for a moment, the leader turned his head and said something to the female at the desk before pushing the katana blade back into the sheath and returning to the kitchen. He spoke to the two holding Ana and all of them left the kitchen and appeared next in the foyer.

One man stood behind Ana holding onto her arms. Another stood next to him while two others went outside. The leader and the female stood a few feet from Ana, their backs to her, with the woman whispering in the man's ear. Jack studied him closely. While the others were typical Latino gang members with shaved heads, dressed in jerseys with short, khaki pants or jeans, this man wore a black t-shirt and black military BDU pants and boots.

He was clean shaven and his dark hair was cut military style. Jack had noticed a cut scar across his right forearm and another one down his right cheek close to the ear. The others were all heavily tattooed with the number thirteen prominently displayed on arms and faces, but the leader sported no visible tattoos.

As Jack watched, the female moved back and the man turned and looked up at the dome camera over the doorway. He smiled slightly and lifted the katana, his right hand on the ebony grip. Jack stiffened involuntarily, realizing what was about to happen. A look of sheer evil seemed etched on the man's face as he pulled the katana from the sheath and gripped the handle with both hands.

For a moment he simply looked at the camera, the satanic smile slowly fading. Suddenly, he pivoted on his left foot and swung around in a smooth, graceful arc, the katana fully extended. The man holding Ana's arms stepped back a second before the blade struck the left side of her neck and sliced completely through in the blink of an eye. One moment Ana was standing there, eyes open and defiant. In the next she was gone, her body dropping to the floor, her head following closely. Thick, red blood spread across the tiled entrance.

Jack thought he was prepared for what would happen, but he still shuddered. His stomach turned queasy and his hands balled into fists so hard his fingers hurt. The others turned their heads and looked away. The male detective excused himself and ran for the bathroom. Jack walked to the only window in the room and looked out at the backyard area and the low mountains to the west. He wasn't sure which of the emotions he felt would prevail:

the white, hot rage that burned deep in his veins, or the sadness that threatened to tear out his very soul.

"We'll get the bastards, Jack," Frank Martines said as he walked up and placed a hand on his friend's shoulder. "We won't stop looking until we find them, no matter how long it takes or how much it costs."

"We'll probably find the four bangers pretty quick," Jack replied in a tight voice. "They're just local street scum he hired for muscle. But that son-of-a-bitch and the woman aren't from here. They have no fear of being seen or caught and you won't find their prints or photos in any database. They're back in Mexico by now and finding them will take an act of God."

"We'll send their photos to the Federal Police in Mexico and see if they can help. We might get lucky."

"Maybe, but don't count on it. You know how things work down there."

Just then a patrol sergeant came to the sliding doors and spoke to Martines.

"Sheriff, the press is hammering us for a statement," he said. "Do you want me to handle it or do you want to talk to them?"

"I'll take care of it, Sarge. Just give me a minute and I'll be right out."

"Will do," the sergeant told him.

"Frank, can you delay a bit on releasing Ana's name?" Jack asked. "I need to call my kids and her family in New York.'"

"Don't worry. Take all the time you need. I'll tell them we'll release the name when family has been notified."

"Thanks," Jack told him as Martines turned to go out and meet the press at the front gate.

"We're going to be here for the rest of the day, Jack," said Chad Meyers as he walked up and stopped next to him. "You need some sleep. Do you have a place to go until we're finished?"

"Yeah, Chad. I'll get some things from my bedroom and feed my horses before I leave."

"Okay, I'll call you when we're done. We'll get with the gang unit and go through their data base for local bangers. The MS-13 gang in Vegas isn't that big. We can find them pretty fast. The dude who killed Ana is something else, though. I expect he's somewhere beyond the reach of the law."

"I think you're right, Chad."

Jack excused himself and went to his bedroom to gather some clothes and personal effects. On the way he considered Meyers' comments and decided he was wrong. The son-of-a-bitch might be out of the country and beyond the reach of Nevada state law, but he wasn't beyond the reach of Jack McCoy's law.

Chapter 6

The beeping of the digital alarm clock finally broke through Jack's fatigue-induced slumber and brought him out of the darkness. He reached over and switched off the alarm. 7:00 p.m. Damn! He'd slept ten hours, and felt like he could use another ten. Getting old sucked. There was still a slight buzzing sound in his ears from the gunfight inside Greta's house, but he could hear okay.

He'd checked into the luxury suite at the Bellagio after leaving his house that morning. The first thing he'd done was call Ana's sister, Mona, in New York City. She was the youngest of two sisters and a brother living in the city where all had been born. Ana's parents had long ago passed away.

It had been a painful conversation and Mona's husband came on the line when she could no longer talk. He told Jack they would notify the other siblings and fly to Vegas when the coroner's office released Ana's body.

Jack's next calls had been to his kids, the first to his son, Brian, at West Point. The twenty-one year old had completed his second year at the academy and was in summer session. An information officer had told Jack that Brian's platoon was on training maneuvers in the field. The officer said he would get word to him there was an emergency at home and that he should call ASAP.

Jack's next call was to his daughter, Brigitte, in Palo Alto, California. She lived in a condo there and attended nearby Stanford University Law School. She had completed her first year and was taking a summer class. She also worked part time as a clerk in a law firm. The call went to her voicemail and he left a message to call right away. Jack knew they would be crushed by what had happened. The two had grown up with Ana in the household and considered her family. He dreaded the coming talk with them.

Jack made his way to the bathroom and took a long, hot shower. Feeling refreshed, he put on jeans and a t-shirt and ordered a room service dinner. While he waited for the meal, he checked his cell phone for messages and found two from Greta and one from Viktor Tarasov, his good friend and the former sergeant of SWAT's Blue Team. Vik had been promoted to lieutenant three months earlier and re-assigned to patrol. He was now the graveyard watch commander at Northeast Area Command. Both Vik and Greta had found out about Ana's murder and had tried to reach him. He was about to call Greta first when his phone rang. It was Chad Meyers.

"Hey, Chad. I was hoping to hear from you. You get some rest?"

"Yeah, Jack, I'm caught up a little. I just talked to my sergeant and he filled me in on what's happened since this morning. I wanted to give you an update."

"Good. What can you tell me?"

"The Gang Crimes Bureau had photos of the four bangers at your house and they've picked up three of them already. The fourth has hit the road for California. He has family in L.A. and we've contacted LAPD to help us find him.

"They didn't have anything on the older dude giving orders. The lab techs didn't get any decent prints at your house, so we sent the security tape photo to the FBI and the PFD, the Ministerial Federal Police, in Mexico City. We're hoping they have his mug in their databases."

"Has anyone talked to the bangers yet?"

"They tried, but all four lawyered up right away with PDs. Wouldn't say a word. We had better luck with one of the suspects from Greta's place. It wasn't the dude you kicked in the nuts. One of my teams went to the hospital to see him and he started screaming at them. Seems he has a ruptured scrotum and may not be having any fun with the ladies for a while, if ever."

"What a shame," Jack replied in a sardonic voice.

"Yeah, ain't it?" Meyers said with a chuckle. "But here's the good part. The kid you shot is gonna make it and he's been talking his head off."

"That's interesting. What has he told you?"

"He's just sixteen and was jumped into the gang a couple of months ago. No affiliation before that and he's not hard core yet. His mother didn't even know and has been all over his ass to cooperate with us.

"He told my guys that the military-looking dude in black came to them last month and hired them to make the hits on Greta and Ana and also to help with the take down of the NDC van downtown. He said the guy didn't talk much about himself, but another banger told him the guy works for the Gulf Cartel in Mexico. He also gave us some info you aren't going to like."

"Okay, I'm listening."

"The guy told them their targets were close to a cop with the sheriff's department and his boss wanted to send him a message. He described you and said if they found you there when they made the hit, they weren't supposed to hurt you, just try to get away. His boss has other plans for you. Jack, this wasn't a hit on Greta or Ana, these assholes are after you."

There it was. What he had suspected all along. Someone from his past had come back bent on revenge for something he'd done in another time, and he had no idea who it could be. But it didn't really matter. He, Jack McCoy, was responsible for what had happened to his friend and the woman he loved and her son. How did he live with that?

"There was something else," said Meyers, drawing Jack away from his thoughts. "My guys found a card like the one you found on Ana in the pants pocket of the banger you killed at Greta's house. The one who used her as a shield. Are you sure you don't know what it means?"

"I don't, Chad. I told the sheriff it's probably some kind of new symbol for the gang."

"What about the cartel boss? Any idea who it could be?"

"No. When I worked Narcotics in the '80s, there were a lot of Mexicans involved in the sales and distribution here, but the boss was a Colombian. I put a case on him and his enforcer in '86 and sent them to prison, but he died five years later. His hired gun was the one who was broken out of the prison van the other day. When the Mexicans took over in the '90s, I was in SWAT."

"Well, you pissed off someone in the dope world somewhere along the way. If you can think of anything, call me. I doubt we'll get much more from the kid. He's pretty low level and just did what they told him. He only saw the Mexican twice at a vacant house in North Las Vegas they used for the meetings. He said there was a woman there on one occasion and she's probably the one we saw on the tape. I'll keep you posted. By the way, you can go back to your house now. Let me know if you need any help cleaning up the foyer."

"Thanks, Chad, but I can handle that. And thanks for the update."

Jack sat for a moment and thought about what Meyers had told him. His mind wandered back almost three decades, to the time of *los tigres negros.* He didn't know how, but his gut told him the cards were connected to the events of that time.

Jack gathered his things and went downstairs to check out of the hotel. A few minutes later, a parking attendant brought his silver Ford Explorer to the front entrance. It was dark outside, but the early summer heat still lay like a blanket across the city. On the way home, Jack stopped at a Wal-Mart and bought bleach, ammonia and sponges for the cleanup job at his house.

An overwhelming sense of sadness settled over him as he pulled through the gate and into his garage. Ana would no longer be there to greet him when he came home. No longer there to engage in their lighthearted banter or entertain him with the family piano. To help ease the strain from a hard day at work. He was going to miss his old friend greatly.

Jack took his things inside, then went out to the corrals to feed and water his horses. All three were gathered at the far end, but hurried forward when they saw him. His Arabian gelding, Dancer, whinnied and nuzzled his chest. The Arabian's two companions joined him and made it clear they were ready for dinner. Just being around the animals lifted Jack's spirits and he took time to rub them down after putting out hay and filling their water tank.

Back inside he spent the next hour cleaning the kitchen and the large bloodstain in the foyer. When he finished, a faint shadow from the stain remained and Jack knew he would have to replace the tile. But that could wait.

Jack checked his cell phone, but there were no messages from Brian or Brigitte. He hadn't expected to hear from his son yet since he was training in the field, but he'd thought Brigitte would have called by now. He would try her again in the morning.

Jack sat at the counter with an iced tea and stared at his phone. It was late, but there was another call he needed to make. After a few moments, he dialed the number and Greta answered on the second ring.

"Jack, I've been worried sick," she said in a frantic voice. "I heard the news about Ana. They didn't give her name, but I knew it was her. Are you okay?"

"No," he answered. "I will be, but it will take time."

"Jack, I'm so sorry. What happened? Who did this? Why Ana? I just don't understand."

Jack hesitated a moment, collecting his thoughts, not wanting to explain, but knowing he had no choice. Slowly, in a heavy voice, he told her what had happened at his house and what the Homicide detectives had learned from the young hoodlum he'd shot in her home. He left nothing out. There was a long pause before she replied.

"The people who did this are after you? Who, Jack? Why?"

"That's the hard part. I just don't know. You may have been right at the lake. It could be tied to the man who was broken out of the prison van. Maybe he's out for revenge. It doesn't seem likely, but it's all I can think of."

"What are you going to do now?" she asked.

"I'm on leave until the shooting investigation is over, but I'll give the Homicide guys all the help I can to try and solve this mess. Ana's family will be here in a few days and I'll help them return her body to New York for burial. I'll go to the funeral."

"Have you told the kids yet?"

"No, they haven't returned my calls yet. I don't look forward to that. What are you and Adam going to do now?"

"Lieutenant Meyers called earlier and told me they're finished at my house. I'm going over in the morning to look at things and decide what to do. I'm not sure yet."

"I can meet you there and help with any cleanup you want to do."

She paused for a moment, and her voice sounded strangely distant when she spoke.

"Okay, if you'd like. I'll be there about ten."

"I'll see you then," he said before ending the call. He next dialed Vik Tarasov's cell number and the call went to voicemail. He left a message saying he would call back later. A heavy sense of foreboding settled over Jack as he thought about the conversation he'd just had with Greta. Something had changed. He wasn't sure what, but he didn't like the feeling it gave him.

Chapter 7

Jack was up at 7:00 a.m. and on the street in running shorts and shoes a few minutes later. He hadn't run in three days and was feeling a little dull and lethargic. The sun was up and the temperature was still in the eighties, so he pushed hard and finished the three-mile course in twenty minutes.

Back at the house he cooled down while putting fresh oats and water out for his horses. Inside he checked his cell phone and e-mail but found no messages from his son or daughter. Now he was concerned. Not so much about Brian, but he should have heard from Brigitte by now. He called her cell number and got her voicemail again. He left another message telling her it was urgent and to call soon.

Feeling rested from his run, Jack went into his home gym for a workout. He started with a fifty-set round of sit-ups, push-ups, and chin-ups then moved to his weight machines and barbells. An hour later he was drenched in sweat and had a solid burn in his arms and shoulders. Jack enjoyed the hard workouts that had given him a better body than most men half his age.

He sat on a bench to run a towel over his face and finish off a bottle of cold Evian. He was still worried. Brigitte should have called by now. His gut was screaming at him that she would call...if she could. He was thinking about calling the Palo Alto PD for a welfare check at her condominium when his cell phone rang. It was Brian.

"Hello, son. I was hoping you would call soon."

"Hey, Dad. I just got in from the field a little bit ago. They told me I had an emergency at home. What's going on?"

Slowly, Jack described the events of the last few days. His voice cracked slightly when he reached the part about Ana. When he finished, there was a long silence.

"Dad, I don't know what to say," Brian finally said in a strained, quivering voice. "This doesn't seem real. Ana gone? I can't believe it. Why?"

"There's a lot I have to tell you, Brian, but it would be better if you were here. Can you come home on leave?"

"Yeah, I can get emergency leave for a week, or maybe longer. I'll talk to my platoon leader and try to get a plane out today if I can."

"Okay, call me with the schedule and I'll pick you up at McCarran. I've called your sister but haven't heard from her yet."

"All right, I'll call when I have the flight schedule."

Jack broke the connection. He felt better now that he had talked to Brian. Breaking the news about Ana had been hard and her death would have a lasting impact on both of his kids. It would help them to grieve together.

Jack decided he would give Brigitte a few more hours to return his calls before contacting the Palo Alto police. His workout finished, he showered and shaved, then dressed in Wranglers, boots and a red t-shirt with a Park City emblem on the front. A short-barreled Kimber .45 ACP rode in a belly band holster under the t-shirt. In the kitchen he fixed coffee and toast while he called the SWAT office. His new sergeant, Steve Mendez, answered.

Mendez had replaced Vik as the sergeant of Blue Team. He and Jack had worked together when Jack was Blue's sergeant and Mendez was an entry man on the team. He was a good SWAT man and Jack's first choice of sergeants to fill the empty slot.

"Hey, Steve, Jack here. Just checking in for an update."

"Hey, boss, good to hear from you. You doing all right? We were really sorry to hear about your girlfriend and housekeeper."

"Thanks, Steve. It's been rough, but I'll get there. Everything good at your end?"

Mendez brought Jack up to date on SWAT's missions and training operations and the schedule that Noah Walls, the senior sergeant, had outlined for the next two weeks. Jack told him he would not return to work until Homicide had finished their investigation of his shooting and the coroner's report was issued. He told Mendez to call him if he or Walls had any questions about the team assignments.

His calls finished, Jack got into his Explorer and headed for Greta's house. It was Friday morning and traffic was fairly light. Ten minutes after exiting Tropicana he pulled up in front of her house. Greta's blue Lexus was parked in the driveway.

"Hey," she said upon opening the door for him. "Come on in."

She was dressed in jeans and a blue tank top and carried a cleaning rag in one hand. Jack noted that the pool of dried blood from the dead gardener still stained the tile at the front entrance. He followed her into the family room where she pointed out the bloody carpet and bullet holes in the walls.

"I called a biohazard company and they're going to send a crew over to do the blood cleanup. When they're done, I'll hire a contractor to patch up the holes. Might take a few days and we'll stay at my folks until it's done."

"Tell them to send me the bill. I brought this on you and I'll take care of it."

"That's not necessary, Jack," she replied, brushing back her short hair with both hands and looking away from him. "I can handle it."

Jack caught a sharp tone in her voice and he noticed her eyes were red and watery. She had obviously been crying.

"Okay," was all he could say.

"I just put on some coffee," she said after a few moments. "Would you like some?"

"Sure," he told her and then followed her into the kitchen.

"How's Adam holding up?" he asked as she poured coffee into a large, white cup with a Rebels logo.

"He's a little quiet. I think he'll be okay in time. Kids rebound faster from something like this than adults."

"He's mature for his age. I think he'll cope with it okay. He has you and his grandparents to help him with it."

"Have you told your kids?"

"I spoke to Brian earlier. He didn't say much, but I know he's hurting. He's flying home today or tomorrow. I'm still waiting for Brigitte to call."

Greta sipped her coffee and gazed out the kitchen window. She remained quiet. Jack thought he knew what was bothering her and decided to confront it head on.

"If there's something you'd like to say, just tell me what it is."

For several moments she didn't say anything. Finally, she looked at him.

"I may not see you for a while. I need to think about things and figure out where this is going."

Jack didn't reply right away. In his heart he'd known what she was going to say.

"Are you not happy with where we're going?" he asked after a short silence.

Greta dabbed at her eyes as new tears began flowing. Jack pulled a Kleenex from a box on the counter and gave it to her. She dried her cheeks and looked at him.

"Jack, Adam and I were nearly killed by thugs who were sent by someone who wanted to get back at you for something," she told him in a trembling voice. "Someone out of your past, a violent past that keeps coming back to hurt you. Last year it was that Russian from Laos with those bikers and hired killers. Who is it now? You don't even know. They were going to kill us, Jack, and you don't even know why."

Greta's voice cracked with pain and anguish now. She wiped away more tears as she stood up and walked to the window. Jack remained silent, waiting for her to finish. Her arms crossed, she turned back to him and continued.

"You saved us, Jack, but it was pure blind luck that you came back to the house. And a good man was killed before you did. And then others went to your house and killed a woman who was like family to you. Good people dead because someone wants revenge against you for something you did long ago."

She hesitated for a moment, gathering her thoughts.

"How many more are there like that out there? People you sent to prison or whose relatives you killed in war or in the line of duty? Jack, I'm in love with you and I hoped we could make a life together. Now, I don't know if that's even possible. If it was just me, I could accept it. I know you would keep me safe. But Adam is my only child. I can't stand the thought of losing him, and I would always worry that some killer with a vendetta against you might target him.

"I'm not a violent person, Jack. I know it's been part of your life in war and as a cop, but you're a good man and when you have to be violent it's for the right reason. I just don't know if I can live with that if it's going to put me and my son in constant danger. I don't know what to do. I guess I just need to think about everything."

When she finished, Jack didn't say anything for a minute. He knew there was nothing he could say that would make her feel better.

"I don't blame you for feeling this way," he finally said. "You're right; I am responsible for this and it causes me nothing but pain and misery to know I nearly got you and Adam killed. I still don't know why this is happening and I wish I could say it will never happen again, but, the truth is, I can't say that. We can't escape our past, Greta. Good or bad, it's always there.

"The last thing I want is to hurt you or Adam. I'll do whatever is necessary to keep you safe and if that means not seeing you again, so be it. You take the time you need to sort this out. When you do, you know where to find me."

With that Jack turned and left the house.

Chapter 8

When he arrived home, Jack retrieved his mail from the box at the front gate then pulled into the garage. Inside, his telephone showed one message from Vik Tarasov but none from Brigitte. His worry level increased and he decided to call the law office where she worked and the Palo Alto police for a check on her residence.

A clerk at the law office told him Brigitte had not come to work that day and had not called in. That was unusual for her and a supervisor planned to stop by her condo after work to check on her. A desk officer at the police department took his information and told him a patrol officer would be dispatched to check on her welfare. If there was no answer, they would call and advise him.

Jack knew something was wrong and he was sure it was tied to the events of the last few days. Whoever was after him would go after his family, and his daughter was an easy target. If the Palo Alto PD did not locate her, he would be on the next flight to San Francisco. He would call Brian and tell him to be careful until he and Brigitte returned.

Jack fixed a light lunch and thought about his talk with Greta. He felt burdened with guilt and wasn't sure their relationship would survive what had happened to her and Adam. He didn't want to lose her, but he couldn't blame her if she decided it wasn't going to work.

Lunch over, he cleaned off the kitchen counter and decided to visit Danny Kim at the Fighting Den to spar a few rounds with one of his boxers or MMA fighters. The thought was interrupted by a voice on the intercom announcing a Fed Ex delivery at the front gate. Jack let the driver through and he pulled up to the front door. The small, thin package showed no return address and was not something Jack had expected.

He signed for it and returned to his desk in the den. It was then that he noticed the Mexican postmark from the previous day. Now alarm bells were going off and his pulse quickened. He pulled a Benchmade folding knife from a sheath on his belt and used the four-inch blade to open the top. An unmarked DVD fell from the opening. Jack picked it up by the edges and studied it. After a few moments, he opened the disc drive of his desktop computer and dropped it in place.

In a few seconds the disc booted up and an image appeared on the screen. It was the face of a male Latino in his thirties. He was clean shaven and had short, dark hair and a small mole on his chin. His face looked like it had been through a meat grinder. A white bandage was taped across a bruised, swollen nose and his left eye was blackened and swollen nearly shut. A deep cut marked his lower lip. His face was contorted in a malicious grin.

The camera slowly pulled back to reveal the man was naked and was lying on top of a naked woman. And he was having sex with her. The woman didn't move and Jack couldn't see her face until the camera moved around the man's shoulder and focused on her at a different angle. It was then that Jack's world fell apart. The face was that of his daughter, Brigitte.

Jack's breathing nearly stopped. He felt a pounding in his temples and his heart thudded like a jackhammer in his chest. His vision was suddenly cloudy, and he looked away and wiped at his eyes as though he could make the images disappear. After a moment he took a deep breath and looked back at the screen.

Brigitte's head lolled to one side and her open blue eyes had a vacant stare. Saliva leaked from one corner of her mouth. Both cheeks and her right eye were black and blue and there was a gash over her right eyebrow. Blood oozed from a split upper lip. Brigitte's shoulder-length blonde hair was matted and tangled. Jack noted her pupils were constricted and the look on her face told him she had been drugged, probably with an opiate to keep her sedated.

As he looked at his daughter's face, Jack's shock and horror was replaced by a boiling fury welling up inside him. A burning rage to kill every son-of-a-bitch who had touched his daughter. As the violent anger seared his soul, the camera moved back to hover over Brigitte and the leering, battered face of her rapist, and a man's voice came from the screen.

"Hello, Jack McCoy. I hope you're enjoying this little movie I sent you," the voice said in American English with a very slight Spanish accent. "As you can see, your daughter isn't getting much out of it, but I can assure you the man on top of her certainly is. She's the one who messed up his face like that. You trained her well and she fights like a demon when attacked. A true McCoy daughter."

Jack felt a surge of pride knowing Brigitte had fought her attackers and had made one of them pay the price. He'd made sure both of his kids were prepared to deal with the physical threats the world presented. His daughter had earned a black belt in Combat Hapkido and had also trained in Aikido and Judo. The man on top of her was the recipient of that training.

"However, she was no match for five men," the voice continued, "and, in case you were wondering, she is no longer in California. I'm sure you're also wondering why this is happening, why she was taken, why your friends in Las Vegas were attacked. Don't worry, you may be puzzled now, but you will understand soon enough.

"I have waited a long time for this, McCoy. You don't know me now, but you knew me once. When you see me, you will know why this is happening. I'm going to give you a time and location to present yourself. If you do not appear, the next package you receive will be a box containing your daughter's head. I look forward to continuing this conversation face to face. For your daughter's sake, Jack McCoy, don't disappoint me."

The voice continued on long enough to give him the time and place to appear in person. The time was midnight in four days, and the location was Monterrey, Mexico.

Jack put his Dell laptop on the kitchen island, opened the disc drive and set the DVD in place. Before closing it he looked up at the four faces gathered around him.

"When you see this," he told them in a tense, drawn voice, "you'll understand what's been going on the last few days and why I asked you here this evening. You'll also understand why I need your help."

To his left stood his son, Brian. Jack had picked him up at McCarran International Airport that afternoon. Their reunion had been welcome but quiet and somber. Brian's two-hundred-pound, six-foot-four-inch frame was lean and hard after two years at West Point, and his blonde hair was cut military short. His blue eyes reflected the hurt and sadness caused by Ana's death.

Jack had described the events of the last few days and how the investigations were still underway. When Brian had asked about Brigitte, Jack just said she hadn't called yet and he had more to say about the situation after some friends came to the house later that day. Brian was curious but didn't press his father for more details.

One of those friends standing next to Brian was Frank Martines. Jack was about to embark on a formidable effort to save his daughter's life in a foreign country. An effort that would likely result in lives lost, maybe his own, and could lead to complications for the sheriff's department if his identity became known. He wanted his old friend and boss to understand why it had to be done.

Across from Martines stood Viktor Tarasov. The big, brown-haired Russian had been a *Spetsnaz* officer in his homeland before immigrating to the United States and taking a job with the Clark County Sheriff's Department. When he applied for SWAT, Jack helped bring him into the unit. Like Jack, Viktor was multi-lingual, and the two men were veterans of military Special Forces units. Their common background had led to a close friendship and Viktor had fought at Jack's side the previous year when an old enemy from Vietnam had re-appeared and tried to kill Jack with teams of hired gunmen.

Next to Viktor stood the fourth man in the group. Gary Barnes was a fellow Vietnam SOG veteran and had spent twenty-five years in the Army's Special Forces before retiring to work as a paramilitary operator in the CIA's Directorate of Operations. After six years of hunting terrorists, he left to start his own private security business and shooting school in his home state of Oregon. Gary had helped Jack and Viktor in the fight against

Jack's old enemy, who was also a Russian diplomat, the year before. When Jack had called his old friend with the news about Brigitte, his goddaughter, Gary immediately got on his private business jet and flew to Las Vegas.

Jack closed the DVD drive and waited as the disc booted up. After a few moments, the face of Brigitte's rapist filled the screen. Jack said nothing as the camera moved and the voice began repeating what he had already heard. Instead, he watched the reactions of the men around the island.

The most visibly distraught was Brian as he watched what was happening to his sister. He remained silent, but his lower jaw clenched and his face contorted in emotional distress at the image on the computer screen. The shock and revulsion on his friends' faces quickly changed to raw anger as the video played to its finish and Jack closed the computer.

"Now you have a better idea what's going on," he told them. "I don't recognize the man's voice, but you heard him; he's someone who's come back on a vendetta, and he's using my friends and family to get to me. I don't know who's behind this, but I'm going to find out and I will do whatever it takes to save Brigitte's life."

"Dad, where is she? How do we find her?" Brian asked, the worry clear in his voice.

"She's probably in Monterrey, son, and the only way to find out is for me to go there and meet this guy."

"I know you have to do this, Jack," said Frank, "and I wish I could go with you. As the Sheriff of Clark County, I have to tell you to let the Mexican police take care of this, but I know that won't end well for Brigitte. So I'm speaking as your friend. Just tell me what I can do to help and you've got it."

"I appreciate the support, Frank. I don't want any bad press for the department, but in case things go bad for me, I'm leaving a letter with my attorney that will make it clear that this was a personal decision and had nothing to do with the department."

"Jack, this asshole is setting a trap for you," Viktor told him. "If you just walk into it, you're dead and so is Brigitte."

"I know, Vik, but I don't have much choice. I don't know where else to start. This guy knows me, but I have no idea who he is. He's probably in the drug trade and working for one of the Mexican cartels."

"Jack, you can't go down there alone," said Gary. "You need a plan to take this guy down and find Brigitte, and you need backup."

"I have a plan, Gary. And you're one part of that backup."

"Okay, and who's the other?" replied Barnes. Then a slight smile crossed his lips. "Is it who I'm thinking?"

"Yeah, and he's already there."

Chapter 9

Mexico

The city of Monterrey sprawled out in front of Jack as he topped a small rise on southbound Highway 85. It was 11:30 a.m. on Monday morning. He'd left Nuevo Laredo earlier that morning after stopping at a Mexican immigration office to get a tourist card so he could travel past the border. He'd still made good time on the heavily traveled road.

It had been five years since Jack's last visit and the traffic congestion was worse as he entered the suburb city of San Nicolas de Los Garza and Highway 85 became Avenida Universidad. Cars and trucks, mostly American made, passed him on both sides. Just ahead he saw the exit sign for Avenida Juan Pablo and eased into the right lane.

Jack exited and drove east until he came to the Hampton Inn two blocks down. He drove his 2000 Jeep Cherokee into the parking lot and stopped near the front entrance of the two-story, red-brick building. He'd paid cash for the tan, boxy, sport model in Nuevo Laredo the day before and, although a little beaten up on the outside, it drove and handled well.

Jack retrieved a suitcase from the backseat and went inside to register. He'd chosen the Hampton Inn because it was frequented by Americans coming to the city on business and he wanted to blend into the transient population.

Several people, both Latino and Anglo, milled about in the spacious lobby, some reading newspapers, others engaged in conversation. In one corner Jack heard a man speaking in German on his cell phone. Monterrey was also popular with European business people. He approached the front desk and a young female clerk with short, dark hair greeted him in fluent English.

"Good afternoon, sir. Are you registered or would you like a room?"

"My name is John Dixon," Jack said, giving her the name on his phony passport, "and I think you have a room for me."

The clerk punched some data into her computer and looked up at him.

"Yes, Mr. Dixon, I show you staying with us for three nights. Is that correct?"

"Yes, unless my business plans change."

"I understand," she replied with a big smile. "Just let us know."

After registering Jack went up to his room on the second floor. The suite had a king bed and a kitchenette in the front room. He dropped the suitcase on the bed and went into the bathroom to freshen up after the long drive from the border. Twenty minutes later he emerged, feeling better and ready for the next leg of the trip.

Jack removed his passport, tourist card and a prepaid cell phone from the suitcase. He opened the phone and dialed a number to another prepaid cell.

"Hey, you there yet?" asked Gary Barnes at the other end.

"Just got in," replied Jack. "I'll head out shortly. You here?"

"About thirty minutes out. Call me when you know something."

"Will do."

Jack broke the connection and dropped the phone on the bed. Barnes would be checking into the Crowne Plaza Hotel in downtown Monterrey and would wait there for news from Jack about the next step in their plan.

As he dressed in fresh clothes, Jack thought about the last two days. After showing the video to Brian and his friends, they had spent the rest of the day and Saturday forming a plan to find and rescue Brigitte. They'd come up with different scenarios, but Jack finally realized that if there was any chance to save Brigitte's life, he had one option: make the meeting demanded by the voice on the tape.

But he would do it on his own terms. Unknown to his enemies, Jack had allies who would help him do what was necessary to save his daughter. Allies like Gary and Viktor who, like Jack, had long experience with brutal, violent men. And he had another ally, one already in Mexico and who would be key to a successful operation against the kidnappers.

They had decided that Jack and Gary would go to Monterrey. Viktor and Brian would remain behind and wait for word from Jack. If needed, they would join him in Mexico. Jack wanted Brian to stay in Las Vegas no matter what happened, but his son had been adamant that he would go with Viktor if they needed help to rescue Brigitte.

Jack had strongly mixed feelings about that. Brian loved his sister and wanted to help get her out of a bad situation. He would also be an asset to the effort. Brian was a crack shot with both pistols and long guns and he'd just completed two years of excellent military training. What he didn't know was combat. Brian had chosen a military career and he would gain that experience soon enough, but Jack was uneasy about putting his son's life at risk. Now, unforeseen events might give him no choice. In the end, Jack would let his son make that decision.

Frank Martines couldn't go with them, but told Jack he would assist in any way with logistics and, if they got into trouble with the Mexican authorities, he would pull all of the political strings at his disposal to help them out. Frank was well-connected with the governor and both Nevada senators, and Jack was glad to have him on their side.

Jack and Gary decided they would fly to Laredo, Texas in Gary's business jet and cross the border on foot. In Nuevo Laredo they would purchase separate used vehicles for the drive to Monterrey. Once there they would stay in separate motels as the plan progressed. Jack didn't think he was being watched, but decided not to take any chance that his enemies could see that he was bringing help.

They would not take their cell phones or laptops. Jack didn't want to leave an electronic trail for the cartel or the Mexican police to follow in case things went bad. They would use prepaid cell phones and buy two-way radios there if necessary. They would need weapons, but the country was awash in illegal guns and it shouldn't be hard for two experienced operators to acquire the weapons they needed on scene. However, Gary would see that they didn't go entirely unarmed.

Gary called his wife, Brenda, at their home in Bend, Oregon and told her about the situation. He also told her that he needed some of his "special stuff." Brenda loaded those items on a plane used by their security business, White Star Security Group, and a pilot for the company flew it to Vegas on Friday night.

As a Delta operator in the U.S. Army for fifteen years and a paramilitary in the CIA's Special Activities Division, Barnes had surreptitiously acquired many tools of the trade during numerous missions around the world. Tools that included phony passports and other documents, both foreign and domestic, that he used on the covert operations he still occasionally conducted for his former employer.

Jack knew the Mexican cartels had corrupt government officials on their payroll and they would likely know if Jack and Gary entered the country together using their true names. To prevent that, Gary used his special equipment from Bend to prepare phony U.S. passports and driver's licenses for all of them. The passports didn't have the RFID chips now embedded in official U.S. passports, but they would withstand cursory inspections by border officials.

On Saturday morning Jack had gone to his bank and withdrawn one hundred thousand dollars in cash from his business account. He left half of that with Viktor and Brian and the rest he and Gary would use for vehicles, equipment and to ease their way through Mexican bureaucracy if necessary. That evening Jack went into his den, sat down at his computer and wrote letters to the important people in his life.

Letters to his family in Kentucky, to close friends in Las Vegas, and to his attorney explaining why he had gone to Mexico. Another he wrote to his business manager explaining what had happened and that she and his attorney should help settle his estate. A final letter, the hardest to write, was addressed to Greta.

He explained what he had done, that he had failed and that he hoped his daughter would survive. He told her that he loved her and apologized for the grief and anguish his past life had brought on her. He asked her forgiveness and wished her a long, happy life. Jack signed the letters, put them in one of his gun safes and gave the combination to Frank Martines.

Now, dressed in denim wranglers and a yellow t-shirt with a Jackson Hole, Wyoming logo, Jack sat on the edge of the bed to pull on a pair of brown Noconas. He remained there for a moment, pondering the events that had brought him there. Why? Who? Was the calling card from another time the answer? It didn't seem possible, but he couldn't discount it.

Whatever the reason, *it no longer matters*, he thought as he pulled on a black cap with the SOG emblem on the front and headed for the door. The kidnappers would kill his little girl if he didn't comply with their demands and he was here to ensure that did not happen. Any father who loved his children would move Heaven and Earth to keep them safe. Jack McCoy would move Hell itself to save his daughter's life.

Chapter 10

Back on Avenida Universidad, Jack headed south. Monterrey was Mexico's third largest city with a population of three million. It was the largest production and trade center in the northern part of the country and was often called the "Sultan of the North." It also had several colleges and universities that produced a highly-educated population.

To the south Jack could see the Sierra Madre Oriental mountain range against the skyline. To the southeast rose the Cerro de La Silla, or saddle hill, called such due to its distinctive shape at the top. On his right was La Huasteca, another craggy peak where people went to climb and hike. All around Jack could see new buildings and commercial centers under construction. The city was still growing.

To his left front, Jack could see the Faro de Comercio rising from the Grand Plaza in downtown Monterrey. He and his late wife, Gabrielle, had shopped in the plaza on his last visit.

Like Vegas, Monterrey was also hot in the summer. The temperature was near one hundred and Jack had turned on the Jeep's air conditioning. Avenida Universidad turned into Calle Alfonso Reyes and Jack noticed that most of the streets in the area were named after people. A short distance later the traffic began slowing and soon came to a crawl.

Ahead Jack could see the flashing red lights of a police roadblock. As he drew nearer, he could see a military truck on the right shoulder with several soldiers in green uniforms in the rear bed. All were armed with assault rifles.

On the left of the two-lane street was an armored vehicle with a .50 caliber machine gun mounted on top. Several more soldiers stood nearby, watching the traffic flow past. Parked near the armored vehicle was a black Ford F-150 with the *Policia Federal*, or Federal Police, badge emblem on the doors. Four Federal Police officers stood in the street checking the car in each lane as it stopped.

Dressed in blue/black uniforms with pants legs bloused inside black boots and helmets with goggles on the front, the officers carried Glock pistols on their belts and H&K MP5 submachine guns at port arms. *Looks like the drug war is getting serious,* Jack thought as he pulled forward and stopped for inspection.

"Buenos Dias," said the officer, greeting him in Spanish before asking for his destination and reason for being in the area. Jack presented his passport, tourist visa and a phony business

card Gary had printed up that showed he was a representative for a business computer company in Laredo, Texas. He told the officer in fluent Spanish that he was en route to a meeting with a Mexican business partner.

The officer seemed curious about his Jeep having Mexican license plates and Jack told him he found it easier to travel with a vehicle purchased in the country. The officer nodded and, after inspecting the vehicle registration and the Jeep's interior, motioned him forward.

Jack continued south until he came to Calle Padre Mier where he turned right. After four blocks and two more turns, he came to his destination at the corner of Melchor Ocampo and Ponciano Arriga: the headquarters of the *Policia Federal,* the Mexican Federal Police.

The three-story, gray granite building was an imposing structure and the largest one on the block. The second and third-story windows were plated with bulletproof glass and those on the first floor were covered with metal grates. On the west side was a large lot for the federal police cars, now surrounded by a high fence with concertina wire at the top.

Jack found a parking space on the street one block away and walked to the front entrance of the police building. Also new was the sandbagged barricade at the front doors. Federal officers armed with MP5s stood in front, checking identification as people entered on business. Others stood at each corner of the building. Off to one side was a mobile taco stand where customers stood around eating lunch.

Jack presented his passport and the Texas driver's license Gary had fabricated for him. He told the officer he was in town on business and had stopped by to visit an old friend who worked in the building. When he gave his friend's name, the officer looked at him with raised eyebrows and sized him up. After a moment he told him to wait nearby while he made a call.

Jack bought a cup of coffee at the taco stand and sat down on a low retaining wall at the far edge of the front entrance. He knew the phony name he'd provided would confuse the man he had come to see, but he hoped the description the officer would provide would make him curious enough to come down and check it out.

Sipping his coffee, Jack watched people enter and leave the building. A few minutes later he saw a familiar figure, dressed in a Federal Police uniform, come through the front door and stop at the checkpoint. The officer who had checked his papers spoke to the man and pointed to where Jack was sitting. Jack dropped his coffee cup in a nearby trash can, stood up and walked forward a few paces. Slowly the man walked toward him. As he drew nearer, a wide grin split his features.

"Jack, *mi viejo amigo!* he shouted, calling Jack his old friend as he hurried forward and the two men engaged in a hearty *abrazo,* a warm, backslapping hug.

"Marco, *que tal, amigo?*" Jack replied, asking his friend how he was doing. "It's been a long time," he continued in Spanish.

"Yes, it has, too long," Marco replied, taking a step back but keeping his hands on both of Jack's arms. His eyes narrowed slightly as he continued. "It's great to see you again, but what is this name you gave the officers in front?"

Jack's smile disappeared and his countenance took a more serious tone as he faced an old friend and one of the finest men he had ever known.

Marco Leon-Valenzuela was the commander of the Monterrey office of GOPES, *Grupo de Operaciones Especiales,* the Special Operations Group unit of the Mexican Federal Police. GOPES was similar to the FBI's Hostage Rescue Team. It conducted hostage rescue operations, counter-terrorism and counter-narcotics missions and apprehended highly-dangerous criminals. Since the Federal Police were charged with investigating drug trafficking, GOPES biggest job now was hunting down the leaders of the drug cartels.

The forty-nine-year-old Leon-Valenzuela had served with the Federal Police almost thirty years and with GOPES for the last sixteen. He and Jack had met at a SWAT operations seminar in Houston, Texas eleven years earlier. Jack was the sergeant of Blue Team at the time and the two men hit it off right away.

Marco was impressed with Jack's fluency in Spanish, although he was just as fluent in English. Jack learned that his Mexican counterpart had lived with relatives in Brownsville, Texas for six years and attended high school and community college there before returning to Mexico to become a police officer.

The men had stayed in touch and Marco had brought his GOPES team to Las Vegas to train with the sheriff's department SWAT team. Jack introduced Marco to Gary Barnes and Viktor Tarasov. Jack's friends were both fluent in Spanish and had twice traveled to Monterrey with him to train the Mexican SWAT men. Marco even took his team to Bend, Oregon once to train with the Special Forces operators at Gary's shooting school, White Star Training Group.

Jack and Marco had visited each other often over the years and had last spoken by telephone the previous year. With the increased drug trafficking and the rise of the Mexican cartels, their visits had become less frequent and Marco's last trip north had been to Gabrielle's funeral four years ago. Jack knew his friend had become extremely busy, and it showed.

Lines creased his forehead now and there were crow's feet around his eyes. His short, salt-and-pepper hair was showing more salt than when Jack had last seen him. A new scar, what looked like a bullet crease, cut the skin of his clean-shaven, lower right jawline and side of his neck. Hazards of the trade, Jack knew.

But the man was still in great shape. At five-eleven and a muscular 190 pounds, Marco was a little bigger than the average Mexican. And, like most SWAT men, he maintained a rigorous workout regimen that kept him in good fighting shape.

"It's great to see you, too, Marco," Jack replied. "I just wish it were under different circumstances."

"This isn't a social visit, is it?" Marco asked, his own face taking on a more serious look.

"No," said Jack, "but I'd like to find a more private location to talk."

"No problem. I was about to go to lunch. There's a place nearby where we can eat and talk in private. That okay?"

"That sounds good."

"By the way, do you mind if we speak English?" Marco asked in that language as he led the way to the front of the building. "I don't get to use it much anymore and like to practice when I can."

"Sure, if you like," Jack told him.

Marco stopped at the barricade and told the inspecting officer that Jack was with him. The officer nodded and they stepped through the front door. Marco led Jack through the front lobby and down a long hallway on one side, passing other police officers and civilian employees going about their work. The place seemed busy.

After two more turns, they went out a double glass door and into the parking lot Jack had seen on the way in. The lot was filled with SUVs, sedans, utility vans and SWAT-style assault vehicles. Marco went to a black Ford Explorer with the Federal Police emblem on both doors and motioned for Jack to get into the passenger seat. Marco drove out of the lot and turned north on Melchor Ocampo.

Two blocks later he turned into the parking lot of the Hotel Plaza de Oro. Marco parked in front and Jack followed him inside and to a small restaurant called the Café Paris. The hostess greeted Marco with a hug and kiss and he asked her for his special table. Jack was pleased to see that the lunch crowd in the French-themed eatery was light as the young lady seated them at a rear table away from other customers.

A waitress approached and engaged Marco in some lively small talk and took their order for drinks. Jack could tell he was a regular there. When she left, his old friend looked at him.

"Okay, Jack," he asked. "What brings you to Mexico?"

Chapter 11

Jack told him everything, beginning with the ambush of the NDC van in Las Vegas and ending with the video of Brigitte. Pausing only when the waitress brought their drinks and lunch, he held nothing back. He also described his tentative plan to rescue Brigitte. When he finished, the look on his friend's face was one of utter disbelief.

"Jack, I don't know what to say," Marco told him. "I'm just stunned. Ana is dead and they have Brigitte? And you don't know who? Could it be this Cedillo guy from Vegas?"

"I don't know, Marco. It's probably someone connected with one of the cartels here and it could be him, or maybe someone else I arrested when I worked narcotics. I just don't know."

"And the card with the jaguar doesn't tell you anything?" Jack knew Marco knew the origin of the calling card left on Ana's body.

"It doesn't. That was a long time ago in another country. Everyone I knew then is either dead or somewhere else. I think it's just another group using the same name."

"You may be right," said Marco. "There are a lot of narco groups here now and many have special names for themselves."

"I need your help, Marco," Jack said, looking his old friend in the eye. "I have Gary and Vik, but we need someone who knows the city and the drug scene here. I want to do this the right way, but I don't know who I can trust, except you. That's why I'm here."

Marco took a sip of his iced tea and looked around the restaurant. After a moment he set the glass down and looked at Jack.

"Things have changed a lot since your last visit here, Jack," he said. "Mexico is not the same country it was five years ago. I told you some about it on the phone last year. It's even worse now. Since the drug cartels took the smuggling routes from the Colombians, they have become a plague on the whole country."

"Who are they, Marco, and how do they operate with such impunity?"

"The three biggest groups are the Arellano Felix organization in Tijuana, the Sinaloa Cartel in that same state and the Gulf Cartel here in the east. There's also La Familia in Michoacan, but they don't have much clout yet. The Gulf is in control from here up to Matamoros and down in Tamaulipas and Veracruz. They are constantly at war with the Sinaloas for the best smuggling lanes across the Rio Grande. And, Jack, they are brutal beyond description."

"I've seen stories about the killings," Jack said, "but I suspect they're much worse than reported."

"You have no idea, my friend. I never knew some of my own people could be so vile and ruthless. Mexico has always had a drug trade, but it was mostly small time smugglers of heroin and marijuana that was grown here. Not a lot of violence. Now, with the cocaine, it's a multi-billion dollar business and it's attracted every cutthroat and outlaw in the country.

"They're merciless, Jack. They not only kill each other, they will kill any innocent who

gets in the way. And they don't just kill their enemies; they torture them as lessons to others. They cut off their heads, disembowel them, burn them. They will kill their family members, even the children. And they won't hesitate to kill any police who try to stop them."

"Is that why the military is involved now?" Jack asked.

"Last December President Calderon sent Army units to every area where the cartels operate, but they haven't had much effect. The 8th Division is here and in Nuevo Laredo and the people aren't happy. They don't like the road blocks and the firefights that break out between the troops and the cartel gunmen."

"That's made your job harder, hasn't it?"

"My GOPES unit is charged with finding the leaders of the Gulf Cartel and bringing them in. Over the last year we've had twenty-two gun fights with various factions of the cartel, including their enforcement wing, the Zetas. They've killed three of my men and wounded four others. Six months ago they put this new mark on my jaw and a bullet in my left leg. They're a nasty bunch of scum."

"The Zetas?"

"They're deserters from the GAFE army unit. You know who they are?"

"Your army's Delta Force guys, right?"

"Yeah, the *Grupo Aeromovil de Fuerzas Especiales,* or Special Forces Airmobile Groups as you call them. They're highly skilled in weapons, small-unit tactics, communications and intelligence gathering. They even train with your Special Forces Groups in the States."

"So how did they end up working for the cartels?"

"Money, Jack. The leader of the Gulf, a guy named Osiel Guillen, hired them a few years ago to be his personal bodyguards, and then, as more joined him, he began using them to fight the Sinaloas. They have the right skills and they're good at eliminating the Sinaloa *sicarios,* their hired gunmen. Guillen pays them as much in one week as they made in one year in the Army, so the ones with no honor or integrity were easily lured to the drug world."

"I can see why," Jack said. "How many are there?"

"Not more than thirty or so. The problem is the Gulf has over four hundred *sicarios* working for the Zetas. They're just common street scum and killers, but the Zetas organize and train them and they've become pretty efficient. Guillen is in prison now and about to be extradited to the U.S., but he has lieutenants here who help facilitate the flow of drugs from the entry points in the south up to the border. They have their own Zeta commanders who make sure the drugs get past the Sinaloas and across the Rio Grande."

"Do you know who they are? One of them could be behind these attacks on me and Brigitte's kidnapping."

"The Gulf boss in Monterrey is a guy named Pablo Monroy y Cavazos. We identified him last year and got a warrant for him six months ago. That's when I got my new scars. When we went for him, he had thirty guns around him. We killed eight and put six more in the hospital, but he got away and he's been on the run since."

"Did someone else take over?"

"We think he has a lieutenant here who's running things in his absence. His name is Ernesto Jimenez and he lives in a compound in Santa Catarina on the west side of town, but we can't tie him to the cartel. On the surface he's just a wealthy businessman and he does own a couple of manufacturing companies here along with hotels, car dealerships and a lot of real estate. But we've had informants tell us Jimenez runs the show in Monterrey. The trouble is those informants disappeared and we had nothing to corroborate their statements.

"We're not even sure he's Mexican. He may be from Central America or even the States. Our organized crime unit handles the drug investigations and we assist them in gathering intelligence, but our main responsibility is taking down the ring leaders when we get warrants. Some forensic accountants in the OCU tried to trace his money, but they didn't get far and our investigators haven't been able to pin anything solid on him."

"I don't recognize the name, but that doesn't mean anything. You have some good people in the PF, Marco. How is it they can't get anything on the guy?"

"He's insulated, Jack. He has the kind of money that can buy off nearly anyone with power. Cops, politicians, the military, he has them all in his pocket. You know how things operate down here. The drug money has just made it worse. He runs in high circles in Monterrey and around the state and we can't get close to him.

"In the last year, two PF undercover narcs tried and both were found beheaded under an overpass on 85. Three months ago my new boss, the district commander of the PF in Monterrey, ordered us to stay away from Jimenez unless we have solid evidence that he's guilty. That's what we're up against."

"Marco, if this guy has Brigitte, I need to know, and time is running out."

"I know, Jack, but Jimenez is untouchable. He has bodyguards everywhere he goes and his compound is heavily guarded. It's said that he has another place further back in the hills to the west that has even more security. Getting to him won't just be tough, it will be nearly impossible."

"When you have nothing to lose, Marco, nothing's impossible. Tell me about his bodyguards."

"I've only seen them a couple of times, but they're a hard-looking bunch. Some are as big as you or bigger. There's a rumor he has a chief enforcer who's a real nasty son-of-a-bitch. They call him El Bruto and he has a reputation as the most merciless killer in the drug trade. I don't know anyone who's seen him so we don't know what he looks like."

"Sounds like he could be the dude in the video."

"Yeah, he could be and that's not good."

"I think the best chance I have of finding Brigitte is to make that meeting tomorrow night. And that brings me back to you, Marco. You're my friend and I trust you. I hate to say it, but I wouldn't go to anyone else on the force here."

"I understand, Jack, and it bothers me to agree, but you're right; you shouldn't trust anyone else with this. The cartels buy cops and politicians like you and I buy groceries. I trust the people I work with but very few others. Over a dozen PF officers in the Monterrey district have been arrested in the last year for helping the cartel, some of them high-ranking people. A lot of local and state officials here have also been caught taking bribes. It's a damn mess, Jack. You don't know who to trust anymore."

"I know that makes it tough for you, but can you help?"

Marco hesitated a moment, looking around and seeming to contemplate his answer.

"Yeah, Jack," he finally replied. "Of course I'll help you find Brigitte. There's just one thing I haven't told you yet."

"What's that?"

"I'm not a cop anymore."

Chapter 12

Brigitte McCoy sat up on her mattress in one corner and looked around the large room. Early morning sunlight streamed through a window to her right. The blinds were open and she could see metal bars on the outside. She could hear the sound of running water through an open door to her left. Nearby a stereo on a dresser drawer played soft Spanish music.

Eight other young women, mostly Hispanic, sat or lay on mattresses scattered around the room. They were dressed in a mix of underwear, nightgowns and casual clothes. Some were applying makeup or brushing their hair. Others simply stared into space with a forlorn look on their faces. None of them spoke and, except for the music, it was strangely quiet in the room.

Brigitte looked down and saw that she was naked under the red cotton blanket that covered her. A thin, white sheet lay across the mattress underneath. Her head hurt and she felt a little groggy, but she could now think more clearly. *What happened to me?*

Her last clear memory was of being attacked by several men outside her condo in Palo Alto. It had been dark when she got home and the men had come out of nowhere when she got out of her car in the parking lot. She remembered fighting back when they grabbed her and then things went black.

Brigitte vaguely recalled riding in a vehicle and the sound of men's voices in Spanish. She was moved from one vehicle to another at least once and she was always in darkness. She also remembered a man with something on his face cursing and slapping her.

Brigitte's entire body ached, especially her face, and she felt sure she had been raped. She was also certain that her fuzzy memory was a result of being drugged by her kidnappers. She could think better now, but she still didn't know how long she had been in this place. She also felt hungry and a little weak. Ten feet to her right a young Latina with long brunette hair sat on a mattress in jeans and a red bra. She was folding clothes and putting them on a small stand next to her mattress.

In a hoarse, creaky voice, Brigitte said in Spanish, "*Me llamo Brigitte. ¿Como se llama usted?*" She was telling the woman her name and asking for hers.

The brunette looked up at her with dark, hollow eyes but said nothing.

"Who are you and what is everyone doing here?" Brigitte asked again in Spanish.

The woman raised her head again and looked around the room, then back at Brigitte.

"Me llamo Tina y somos las putas del cartel," she said, telling Brigitte her name was Tina and she and the others were the drug cartel's whores.

Now it became clear what had happened. She had been kidnapped by drug runners, probably a Mexican cartel. But why? How would they know about her in Palo Alto? Did they just kidnap American women at random and bring them here as sex slaves for the cartel outlaws?

She was about to ask her roommate more questions when the front door opened and a man and woman entered. They looked around for a moment, then continued across the room and stopped in front of Brigitte. The woman was in her late thirties, short and a little overweight. She had dark, shoulder-length hair pulled back in a ponytail and was dressed in blue jeans, boots and a white blouse. Her eyes had a cold, callous look as she glared down at Brigitte.

The man was of medium height and stout build, had short hair and wore jeans, a green western shirt and lizard-skin boots. A holster on his belt held a short-barreled Glock. It was the man's face that drew Brigitte's attention. White tape covered a bruised, swollen nose. His left eye was black and purple and a deep cut with stitches marked his lower lip. A mole dotted his chin. Brigitte was sure she had seen the man before but couldn't remember where. He held a brown shopping bag in one hand and looked down at her with a sneer on his lips.

"I'm told you speak Spanish," the woman said in a harsh voice in that language.

"*Si,*" Brigitte replied, nodding her head.

"Good. That will make things go easier. You will be here a while so I brought some personal things you will need. Go in the shower and clean up. You look like shit."

She nodded at the man and he dropped the shopping bag on the mattress.

"Where am I and why did you bring me here?" Brigitte asked.

"My boss will see you later and he can tell you if he wants you to know."

The woman and her male companion then turned and strode out of the room. For a moment Brigitte sat still and looked around. The other girls averted their eyes when she glanced at them, clearly too frightened to offer comfort or solace. Holding the red blanket around her, she picked up the shopping bag by the handles and walked to the shower room door.

On the far wall she saw a row of water faucets for showering, but it was wide open with no privacy. To her left, at the far end, were several toilet stalls with doors. The wall to the right was lined with mirrors and sinks. The whole place looked like a converted gymnasium.

Two women stood in front of the mirrors with towels wrapped around them. One, a Latina, was drying her hair while the other, a blonde Anglo, applied makeup. Neither woman acknowledged her presence. Brigitte stepped over to one of the sinks and opened the shopping bag. Inside were two smaller bags on top of a set of clothing and shoes. One contained toiletries and the other one held makeup and feminine products.

Looking in the mirror, Brigitte understood what the hard-looking woman had meant by her appearance. Her hair was dirty and tangled in knots. Both cheeks and her right eye were bruised and swollen and a cut over her right eyebrow was still raw. Her upper lip had a small cut at the right corner. The image of being slapped around had not been her imagination.

Brigitte left the blanket at the sink and stepped under a shower head with soap and a bottle of shampoo. For the next fifteen minutes she scrubbed and soaked under hot water until she felt halfway decent again. The women were gone when she finished and she was alone at the sinks. She put iodine on her cuts and applied a small bit of makeup. Now she looked a little more human.

Her clothes included a bra and panties, a pair of black jeans, a yellow blouse, and a pair of gray Nikes with cotton socks. The jeans and blouse were a size too large, but the Nikes were a good fit. After dressing Brigitte checked herself in the mirror. As she studied her image, tears began flowing down her cheeks. She felt used and violated at having been raped. A feeling of rage and helplessness she'd never known before. She knew women who had experienced the crime and had wondered how they dealt with it mentally and emotionally. She never expected it would happen to her, but now here she was. And she felt ashamed and degraded.

Brigitte dried her eyes and gathered her thoughts. She couldn't focus on that right now. Her immediate concern was simply staying alive. The young women in the other room had endured the humiliating experience over and over. If they could survive it, so could she. And she could count on one thing the others probably could not: her father.

The man she loved with all her heart and whom she still called daddy with great affection. She knew he would find out where she was and come for her. And God help the bastards who had taken her when he found them. For now she had to push the emotional trauma out of her mind and concentrate on staying alive until that happened.

Feeling better now, Brigitte returned to her mattress and sat down to dry her hair. As she looked around, Brigitte noticed that all of the women were very attractive and a few were quite young, probably teenagers. The others were no older than her. The blonde from the shower room was sitting on a mattress near another Caucasian with brown hair. They were speaking in accented English.

Brigitte shook out her hair then walked over to the pair and kneeled next to them.

"You're not Americans, are you?" she asked in English.

The two glanced around nervously then looked back at Brigitte.

"No," said the blonde. "My name is Michelle and I am from Marseille, France. This is my friend, Sophie. She is from Amsterdam. We are, were, studying Spanish at the Monterrey Institute of Technology."

"What happened?" asked Brigitte. "How did you end up here?"

"We went to a nightclub with some Mexican friends one night. We met some guys there and we were just dancing and having fun. The last thing I remember is feeling dizzy and then I woke up right here in this room with Sophie.

"Some men came in and one told us we now belonged to the cartel. He told us our job was to have sex with his men and if we refused or tried to escape, he would have us killed. If we cooperated, we would be treated well, given some money and be released after one year."

"That was five months ago," said Sophie, speaking for the first time in a soft, nervous voice. "We haven't been allowed to call or write our families or anyone else. They must be worried sick about us."

Tears began flowing down her cheeks and she covered her face with her hands. Michelle put a hand on her shoulder to comfort her. Before Brigitte could ask another question, the door opened and three men came inside.

One of them was the man with the bandage on his nose. Another was tall and heavyset with collar-length hair and a thick mustache. Dressed in black boots, black pants and a black shirt, he projected an air of menace. But it was the man standing between them who stood out.

Late thirties, short, well-groomed hair and clean shaven, he stood a little under six feet and had a fit, medium build. Dressed in gray chinos, a white sport shirt and expensive black loafers, he was quite handsome. The three men walked to where she sat with Sophie and Michelle and Handsome looked down at her.

"You look much better," he said in American-accented English. His voice was smooth and cultured. "How are you feeling?"

Brigitte stood up and faced him. At five-feet, nine inches, she was nearly as tall as her kidnapper and looked directly into his dark brown eyes. Brigitte McCoy had inherited her father's strong will and fearless personality. She had never faced a situation like this, but she was determined not to show this bastard any fear or deference.

"Like I want to kick somebody's ass," she said in a tight voice. "Maybe it should be yours."

To her surprise the man burst out laughing. The big bodyguard glared at her and stepped forward, but his boss held up a hand and he stepped back.

"Bravo!" he said with a wide smile. "You are certainly Jack McCoy's daughter. Not only do you fight like him, you are just as fearless."

"You don't remember, do you?" he continued. "When my men took you in California, Paco here was with them." He pointed to the bandaged-nose man next to him. "You broke his nose with one of those karate kicks you do so well. You also broke two ribs on another man. I'm just glad I sent five of them."

That gave Brigitte a bit of satisfaction. She was glad her father had taken her to Danny Kim's martial arts gym for training when she was nine. She was proud of her black belt in Combat Hapkido and junior belts in Aikido and Judo. Though it hadn't been enough to overcome the odds against her, she'd made them pay a price.

"Who are you and how do you know my father? Is he the reason you brought me here, and where am I?"

Now the man's features hardened and his eyes held a coldness that belied his congenial manner. "You are in Monterrey, Mexico. I knew your father a long time ago. I even liked and admired him once. More importantly, I trusted him."

"What happened to change that?"

"He betrayed that trust and caused me a great deal of grief."

"He wouldn't do that. My father's a good man."

"But he did, and now it's time he pays for that betrayal. I sent him a video of you and Paco here, one that will enrage him and make him come for you, bent on vengeance. When he does, you will learn who I am and why you are here. Until then, make yourself comfortable. You will eat well and if you need more personal items, tell Camila, the woman you saw before. Until my business is done with your father, you will not be molested by my men. After that…we'll see."

As the man and his guards turned to leave, Brigitte called out to him and he stopped to look back at her.

"My father will come for me," she told him with a defiant tone. "You can count on that."

"And when he does, what then?" he asked, a flippant smile on his lips.

For a long moment Brigitte just looked at him with a searing glare. Finally, in a strong, unflinching voice, she replied, "May God have mercy on your soul."

The man's smile disappeared and he turned and left the room.

Chapter 13

"Actually, I'm retiring, Jack," said Marco. "After twenty-eight years I've had enough of the corruption. It's one thing to fight the bad guys. Like you, I've always enjoyed that. But when you can't trust the people you work for and they won't let you do your job, it just seems useless.

"You know we've always had a certain level of official venality here; a few dollars will get you out of a speeding ticket or, if you want a building permit faster, just pad the inspector's fee a little. *La mordida,* or the bite, as we call it. That's just how Mexico has always operated. I don't like it, but it's just been part of our system.

"Now with this new drug thing and the kind of money it's brought in, our whole country has been turned upside down. Five months ago my previous commanding officer was fired when PF investigators discovered he was taking bribes from the Gulf bosses. They found two million dollars in checking accounts in the Bahamas. I didn't like the guy and suspected he was bad. Too many of our operations had been compromised and I knew it wasn't the men in my unit. He's in jail now, but I expect he'll buy his way out.

"The new district commander, my boss, is Cesar Beltran. He's under the Monterrey Regional PF Commander. He's a gutless political appointee and we can't make a move without him looking over our shoulders. I just decided it's time to let someone else take on the fight."

"What does Alma think about that?" Jack asked, referring to Marco's wife.

Marco took a sip of tea and hesitated before answering. "I haven't told you, have I? She left me, Jack. A year ago, just after we last talked by phone. She moved back to Guadalajara."

"I'm sorry, Marco. I didn't know. Was it the job?"

"Yeah, she'd been after me for years to leave. She was tired of the long hours and the low pay. She was mostly tired of the violence, and I can't blame her. She probably did the right thing."

"How did the kids take it?" Marco had two sons, one a captain in the Mexican navy and the other a lawyer in Mexico City.

"About like you'd expect. It's been tough, but they still talk to me."

"So what's your status right now?"

"I'm using up my vacation time until my last day two weeks from now. I'm just in the office today for some admin stuff. My replacement has already taken over the unit. His name is Carlos Ayala-Meza and he's a good guy."

"It sounds like you can't offer any help on an official basis," Jack said.

"No, Jack, and that's just as well. If I go through official channels with this, word will get to the people who have Brigitte and you don't want that to happen. We'll have to deal with this off the books. That means some risk for us, but it's the best way."

"Marco, I appreciate any help you can offer, but I don't want to get you in trouble and this thing could go bad."

"I know, but don't worry about that. Getting Brigitte away from these scumbags is worth any trouble it might cause me. And if it does, I still have a few friends in high places. We'll start with the meet you're supposed to make tomorrow night. They're setting you up for your own kidnapping and, if the person behind this knows your background, he'll send a lot of guns to make sure it gets done. We need a plan to deal with that."

"Yeah, and I wish we had more help. Just you, me and Gary may not be enough."

"I know someone who might help us, but even with four, we'll still be outnumbered. I'll be in the office until this evening, but you and Gary come to my house tomorrow morning about nine and we'll work up a plan to do this."

"That sounds good, but I can't ask anyone else to risk their life for me, Marco."

"Don't worry, the person I have in mind will be happy to help us. You'll see what I mean tomorrow."

"Okay, and thanks, old friend. You were my last hope and it means a lot to me."

"Jack, if I were in your position, you would be right there with me, all the way."

"Yeah, I would," Jack said, raising his glass. "To old friends and old times."

Marco raised his own glass. "And to Brigitte's rescue. *Salud, amigo.*"

At 9:00 a.m. the next morning, Jack turned his Jeep south off Highway 40 onto Hidalgo Boulevard in Santa Catarina, a Monterrey suburb of 250,000 residents and the city Marco called home. Gary Barnes sat in the passenger seat. Both men were dressed in jeans and Polo shirts. Neither had detected any surveillance during their separate trips to Monterrey and Jack felt it was now safe to travel together. Still, they weren't armed and would take proper precaution.

Each constantly checked the rear traffic in their side-view mirrors and scanned the area for potential threats. Jack made three decoy turns and stopped twice to check for surveillance vehicles before he was satisfied they were not being followed.

Back on Hidalgo Boulevard, Jack continued south two more blocks before turning west on Avenida Colosio. A retail area soon gave way to a middle-class residential neighborhood of ranch style and two-story cement homes painted in pastel colors. The homes weren't large, but were well-maintained. Trees and bushes lined the curb along the street.

After two more turns, Jack stopped in front of a white, single-story house with a large Mexican white oak in the front yard. Marco's PF Ford Explorer was parked in the driveway and an older, yellow Audi sedan was parked behind it. Jack remembered the house well from prior visits. It was where Marco had lived for the last fourteen years.

A small alcove shielded the front door from the sun and rain. Jack knocked and, a moment later, Marco, dressed in black jeans and a white t-shirt with a PF logo, greeted them with a big smile.

"Right on time," he said in English, pulling the door back and motioning them inside.

"Didn't want to be late for this," said Jack.

"Marco, great to see you again," said Gary. "*¿Que tal, amigo?*"

"I'm good, Gary, and it's great to see you also," Marco said with a strong *abrazo* for his old friend. "Let's go back to the kitchen so you can meet someone."

Their boot heels clacking on the tile floor, Jack and Gary followed him through a cozy, well-furnished living room, past a small dining room and into a large, airy kitchen that smelled of coffee and fresh-baked pastries. A large oak table with four chairs sat under a window against the far wall. In one of the chairs sat a woman holding a cup of coffee in one hand and a piece of *pan dulce,* or sweet bread, in the other.

"Jack, Gary, I want you to meet my good friend, Maria Elena Cisneros de Lozada," Marco said in Spanish. "Elena is a member of the ATF, the *Agencia Federal de Investigation.* She's actually suspended right now, but we'll get to that in a moment. She doesn't speak English, so we'll keep the conversation in Spanish."

"No problem," both men said in that language as the female agent set down her coffee and bread and stood up to greet them.

"Very pleased to meet you, Agent Cisneros," said Jack as he sized up the woman and offered his hand.

Mid-thirties, about five-seven and a hundred thirty-five pounds, she had a fit, athletic build with curves in all the right places. Shoulder-length raven hair, brown, almond-shaped eyes, and an olive complexion gave her a sultry, exotic look common among female Mexican movie stars. The only blemishes on her smooth skin were a small half-moon scar at the corner of her left eye and a short one on her bottom lip. Dressed in blue jeans, a black blouse and white sandals, she presented an attractive package.

"Likewise," she replied, shaking hands with the two men, "and call me Elena."

"Very well, and we're Jack and Gary," said Jack.

"Have a seat, guys, and we'll get acquainted," said Marco as he poured coffee into cups and placed a basket of pastries on the table next to a laptop computer.

"Elena was with the Highway Police for five years and went to the ATF when President Fox organized the unit in 2000," continued Marco as Jack and Gary sat down. "As you know, the ATF is the investigative arm of the Federal Police and Elena's done a lot of high-level investigations of the Gulf Cartel leaders in the state of Nuevo Leon. She's put a lot of them behind bars and you'd think that's a good thing, right? But she has one problem."

"Let me guess," Jack offered. "She can't be bought."

"Exactly right," replied Marco as Elena blushed slightly and sipped her coffee. "In a business where badges are bought by the handful, she tells them to go straight to Hell. And that's earned her a lot of enemies. Six months ago she and her team started investigating Ernesto Jimenez. Two months along they were making progress when their commander told them to stand down. Elena's a sergeant and the team boss and she didn't take that well. She continued the investigation on the side, but someone gave her up and she was suspended for insubordination. Her commander is doing an internal investigation now to try and fire her."

"You were getting close to Jimenez?" Gary asked her.

"Yes, one of my men had gone undercover and was hired as security at his compound. He had taken pictures of Gulf bosses visiting there and had recorded some of the other guards talking about escorting shipments of cocaine to the border. Two weeks after he was hired, his body was dumped in front of our office. He'd been tortured and his throat cut. The only people who knew he was working for Jimenez were me and my commander."

"Did you confront him?" asked Jack.

"No, I decided to keep digging and find evidence that would tie him to Jimenez. I wanted the bastard to pay for what he'd done. He found out what I was doing and suspended me. Now I can't do anything and my man's wife is a widow and his two kids are orphans."

"There's another reason why Elena wants to help us," said Marco.

Jack and Gary looked at her and Marco nodded for her to continue.

"I was married to a lieutenant with the Nuevo Leon state police named Hector Lozada.

Three years ago his team went to search a farmhouse west of here and they were ambushed by Gulf Zetas. He was tortured badly and shot in the head. I didn't even recognize him."

"Elena, I'm sorry to hear that," said Jack. "You've suffered too much in this drug war already. You don't even know me, but you're willing to risk your life for me. That's very noble of you, but I can't ask you to do that."

Elena didn't say anything for a few moments. She glanced at Marco and took a sip of coffee as if gathering her thoughts. Finally she looked up.

"Jack, Marco and I have known each other for many years. He's told me often what good friends he is with you and Gary. He's says you're both good men and he is ready to give his own life if necessary to save your daughter. My husband and I never had children. I still miss him. He was a good man and he deserves justice for what was done to him.

"I can't fight these damn narcos officially now, but I can still fight. The place they want you to go is the most dangerous area in Monterrey. Marco and I know it well. You will need all of your training and experience to survive there. And you need all of the help you can get. I can shoot, I have a black belt in Taekwondo and I have extensive training in SWAT and small unit tactics. I'd like to help rescue your daughter, and you owe me nothing for that."

Jack liked this woman. She had a rare kind of courage and fortitude. He didn't want to risk her life, but he found it hard to turn down someone so determined to fight evil. And it was her country.

"Okay, if you want to join us, I can hardly say no. You do have experience we can use and if Marco wants you along, that's good enough for me."

"That settles it," Marco said. "We have a lot of work to do, so let's get busy with a plan to bring these bastards down and get Brigitte home."

Chapter 14

The streets here look different at night, Jack was thinking as he turned his Jeep off Calle Colima and moved west on Avenida Jacinto. Less traffic and fewer people out at this hour. Still, he was under no illusions. This was a volatile and dangerous area for an American to travel alone.

La Colonia Independencia was Monterrey's oldest and poorest barrio. Located on the southern edge of the city on the south bank of the Santa Catarina river, the neighborhood was a congested mess of small houses and apartments stacked together on the hills overlooking the river and a dreary-looking commercial area along the dry riverbed.

Earlier in the day Marco and Elena had taken Jack and Gary for a tour in Gary's van. Hidden from view in the back, Jack had been amazed at the destitute poverty of the area. Gang graffiti covered the walls of every shop and cinder block wall, and many small stores were vacant and boarded up, some burned out. The streets were filled with potholes and many were only dirt.

Most of the traffic lights didn't work. Half-naked kids ran along the broken sidewalks and sullen-looking teens in baggy trousers stared defiantly at passersby. Packs of stray dogs fought over scraps of food and braying burros nipped at anything green in the vacant lots.

"The Gulf owns this neighborhood," Marco had told them. "They moved in a couple of years ago and provide all the drugs the local dealers can sell. They bought a lot of the small businesses and help the locals financially. They own the law here, too."

Marco had explained that the Monterrey city police, known as the *Policia Regia,* did not come into the neighborhood except for a major incident, and then only with an army escort. The officers who did patrol on occasion were on the cartel's payroll. The presence of the Federal Police would often bring out crowds of protesters throwing rocks and bottles until the officers completed their business.

To the north Jack could see an impressive skyline of high-rise apartment buildings, office towers and other symbols of a wealthy, industrial city. The neighborhood here made South Central Los Angeles look like Beverly Hills.

Two blocks ahead Jack saw his destination. On the southwest corner of Jacinto and Mesa Boulevard several retail outlets and small shops ringed a large commercial lot. Some were vacant and the others were closed now. The largest building sat at the rear and over it rose a glittering neon sign of a golden palomino horse reared on its hind legs. *El Palomino Cantina* flashed in smaller lights under the horse's legs.

Jack turned off Jacinto into the lot and found a parking space near the front. The lot was dimly lit by overhead streetlights and Jack could see that most of the vehicles there were older cars and trucks. The voice on the video had instructed him to come to this bar today at midnight, go inside and sit down at a table. He was to come unarmed, with no cell phone, and to wear a t-shirt tucked inside his pants. He would be contacted inside.

Marco had told Jack that the Palomino was a Gulf Cartel bar where the *sicarios* came to drink and unwind when not running drug shipments or fighting the Sinaloa Cartel. Some of the locals also hung out here, but most of the patrons were cartel gunmen, not innocents.

Jack knew his enemies expected him to simply turn himself over to them tonight. But that would mean certain death for him and Brigitte and that wasn't going to happen. He didn't have a gun, but he wasn't completely unarmed. As instructed he'd worn a black t-shirt tucked inside tan BDU cargo pants. On his feet was a pair of deadly Blackhawk combat boots.

Six years ago Jack had tested for his 4th degree black belt in Combat Hapkido in Seoul, South Korea. While there he had gone to a shoe shop in the suburb city of Seongnam patronized by members of the South Korean Army Special Forces. The South Koreans were highly-skilled martial artists and the shop owner would insert steel plates in the soles of their boots to give them an edge when they went on combat missions across the DMZ. The heavy boots could break bones and crush organs. Jack had bought a pair of Blackhawks with the steel plates already inserted. He'd never used them but expected that might change tonight.

Jack got out, locked the Jeep door and stood for a moment, looking around. The night air was heavy with humidity and, in the distance, lightning signaled an approaching storm. A stench of sewer decay rose from the nearby riverbed. Jack scanned the lot but saw no guards or spotters. As he moved toward the bar, two male patrons came out and walked drunkenly past him to an old pickup.

The Palomino was a one-story building with large front windows on each side of a single wooden door. Lights advertising beer and liquor flashed in both windows. The door was adorned with a large sign for Jose Cuervo tequila.

Inside, Jack stopped to let his eyes adjust to the large, gloomy interior. In the center space were several tables and a small, wooden dance floor. About half of the tables were occupied and two couples were dancing to loud *narco corrido* music blaring from overhead speakers. To his left front was the main bar, where several patrons were seated on round stools.

Two bartenders were busy serving them and two female servers carried drinks to the table customers.

On the other side of the table and dance area were three pool tables, all occupied. Along the right wall was a row of video game machines, and at the corner a hallway led to the bathrooms. The walls were decorated with Mexican movie posters and pictures of popular singers and actors. On the wall behind the bar was a life-size image of *La Santa Muerte*, a skeleton dressed in robes and carrying a scythe. The Holy Death saint of the narco traffickers.

Jack moved around the center space area and took a seat at an empty table on the edge of the dance floor. Here he could watch the bar and the other tables. The customers were a mix of young and middle-aged with a few more men than women. Jeans and western shirts were the dominant attire. A few of the women cast furtive glances at him, but most paid him no attention.

The dance music stopped and the two couples returned to their tables on the other side of the floor. A Lola Beltran love song came over the speakers. Jack saw a man at the far end of the bar watching him intently as he pulled a cell phone from his belt and began talking.

Shouldn't be long now, Jack thought as the man finished his call then flagged a passing server, said something to her and pointed toward Jack. The young woman came to his table and asked in a nervous voice if he wanted a drink.

"*Una Dos Equis, por favor,*" Jack told her. A minute later she returned with the cold beer. He dropped a fifty peso note on her platter and told her to keep the change. Jack sipped his drink and observed the bar's male customers. Most looked like ordinary working men, but a few had the hardened features of narco gunmen. The man who had placed the call and still watched him was one of those. Jack sipped and waited.

Gary Barnes watched the bar through the rear window of his van. He'd seen Jack pull into the lot and go inside. Since then patrons had come and gone, but so far nothing had happened. A rumble of thunder came from the south and lightning flashed through the windshield. The storm was getting closer.

Gary didn't like that he had no communication with Jack, but it couldn't be helped. They had no high-tech communications gear and hand-held radios wouldn't work in this situation. They had gone over possible scenarios at Marco's house earlier that day, but realized they had little choice but to react to their enemies when they arrived. Gary was confident because he and Jack had been doing this for over thirty years. Still, the unknown worried him. Murphy's Law always showed up at the worst time.

He checked the H&K USP .45 on the seat next to him. The compact model had an eight-inch Gemtech suppressor attached to the threaded barrel and an eight-round magazine filled with hollow-points. On the floor was an H&K G36 assault rifle with a 30-round magazine. The 5.56mm weapon was fitted with an EOTech red-dot reflex sight.

The pistol was Gary's, one he had acquired on a mission in Lebanon ten years earlier with his CIA SAD unit. The G36 was provided by Marco. During the planning session, the GOPES team leader had shown them a weapons cache in a metal shed behind his house. Marco had acquired a lot of enemies and continual threats against his life. He had his official arms, but had also made a habit of taking selected weapons from the sites of gun battles with the narcos for when he retired. He had several assault rifles and handguns. The cartels were a great source of military-grade weapons of war.

It was hot inside the parked van. Gary took a swig from a water bottle and poured some over his face. When he looked up again, he saw two dark Chevy Suburbans and a Ford extended cab pickup pull into the lot and park. Through a pair of 7x35 Bushnells, he saw ten men and a woman unload from the vehicles and head toward the bar. Five of them were armed with rifles. He took a prepaid cell from his pants pocket, dialed a number and let it ring twice before disconnecting.

Through the window he saw two of the narcos take up positions outside the front door while the others continued inside. The two guards were armed with AK-47s. *Okay, Jack,* Gary thought as he stuck the .45 in his waistband, *I hope you're ready. The party is about to start.*

Inside the Palomino, Marco Leon-Valenzuela felt the cell phone clipped to his belt vibrate twice then stop. The signal from Gary.

"They're here," he said to Elena, seated next to him at the table. "Time to move."

They had entered the bar earlier and determined that the people coming for Jack were not there yet. Marco went into the bathroom, called Gary on his cell and told him to send the pre-arranged signal when they arrived. They then ordered drinks and began dancing to blend in with the crowd. They had watched Jack enter the bar while they were dancing and sit down at a table across from them. Like the other patrons they paid him no attention. It was highly unusual for an Anglo to be there, but the regular customers knew this was a narco bar and his presence was probably tied to the business. They knew better than to get involved.

Elena picked up her purse and she and Marco moved toward the bathrooms. They stopped in the alcove separating the two rooms. "We'll meet here after they check the stalls," Marco told his partner. "Come out ready for business."

"Roger that," Elena told him.

Marco passed two men coming out the door of the men's room and saw that he was the only one there. He moved to the last stall and went inside. He pulled the door halfway open, then stepped up on the toilet and leaned against the wall. He was hidden from view unless someone pulled the door all the way open. In the ladies room, Elena would be doing the same.

Marco expected the narcos to run out all of the customers before they accosted Jack, and they would probably check the bathrooms to be sure. He hoped it would just be a cursory look, but was prepared if a gunman found him there. He pulled a Glock Model 21 .45 ACP from under his red guayabera shirt and held it by his right leg. They had planned as well as possible. Now all they could do was wait.

Chapter 15

Jack watched as Marco and Elena got up and moved toward the bathrooms. A minute later he saw a woman and several men come through the front door and gather near the bar. Three of the men were armed with assault rifles, two AK-47s and an AR-15. The others had no visible weapons.

The woman spoke to one of the men and he moved behind the bar while the others spread out around the tables and near the entrance. A minute later the music stopped and a man's voice came over the speakers announcing that the bar was closing early. Everyone immediately got up and hurried toward the door without a glance back. In moments the place was empty except for Jack and the *sicarios* who had come for him.

The two with the AKs went toward the bathrooms while the woman and the other men moved to stand around the dance floor just feet from Jack. They stared at him with malevolent looks, but said nothing. A moment later the two AK men returned and stood behind and to Jack's left. One of them gave the woman a signal.

Jack studied the group of thugs facing him. Most were short to medium height and dressed in an assortment of jeans, khakis, work shirts, and boots. Most had mustaches, beards or goatees. Two of them stood out. Both were taller than average, lean and muscular. They were clean shaven and dressed in black t-shirts and cargo pants. These two would be Zetas, Jack guessed.

And there was the woman. Early thirties and about the same height as Elena, but more slender. Smooth features with short, black hair and dark, intense eyes. Dressed in black fatigue pants, boots and a blue blouse, she looked all business. She looked exactly as she did in the video when she helped kill Ana.

"You are Jack McCoy," she said in Spanish. Her voice was strong, smooth and husky.

"I am," he said, also in Spanish, looking her in the eye without the slightest hint of fear or intimidation.

"Your daughter is waiting," she replied. "Let's go."

Jack said nothing and did not move from his seat.

"I've been ordered not to shoot or cripple you, *gringo*," she told him, "but my men will beat you into submission if necessary."

Jack pushed his chair back and stood up. He took a step to his right to clear the table. The five unarmed men moved closer and faced him in a half circle on the other side of the dance floor. The two with the AKs were still behind and left. The one with the AR stood beside the woman. One of the Zetas moved within arm's reach and took a pair of handcuffs from behind his back.

"Turn around and put your hands behind you, *gringo*," he said in a sarcastic tone.

Jack judged the distance between them and the man's stance. Legs spread slightly, the left one forward. The other four were behind and on either side of him. Jack made mental calculations of each one's position. He'd fought multiple opponents before but only in sparring matches. Now he needed to fight just long enough to stall and distract them. His daughter had fought five and lost. But Jack had two things she didn't: superior skill and 227 pounds of hard-packed muscle.

Jack turned and put his hands behind his back. When he sensed the man step toward him, he twisted on his left foot, bent forward at the waist and drove his right foot rearward in a classic Hapkido back kick. The steel-soled boot impacted the man's right leg just above the kneecap and snapped it like a dry tree branch. The gunman screamed and dropped to the floor, clutching his ruined knee.

As Jack had expected, the downed man's black-clad partner was the first to move forward in a fighting stance. Jack dropped his right foot to the floor then pivoted on the sole and swept his left leg in a roundhouse kick to the side of the man's head. The Zeta tried to deflect the blow with his hand, but Jack's heavy boot landed with a thud on his right temple and crushed the side of his head. The Zeta dropped straight to the floor, already dead.

Jack dropped back to a crouch just as a third attacker crashed into him in a running charge that took both of them across the table where Jack had been seated and to the floor with the long-haired, mustached killer on top. He was strongly built, but he was no match for the man he'd tackled.

As his opponent leaned forward and drew back a fist, Jack pushed him back with his left hand then raised his right leg and hooked his heel under the man's chin. With a powerful thrust backward with his leg, he brought the gunman to the floor. Jack quickly twisted around, put his right arm around the man's head and rolled to his left. From the corner of his eye, he saw the last two gunmen dancing around him looking for the chance to land a kick or punch. The two AK men had also moved closer and raised their rifles.

Jack pulled the man's body across his own, arm lock still in place. He rose to one knee then pulled back with all of his weight and rolled in a violent spin to his right. His opponent's cervical spine snapped and his body went limp.

Jack released him and rose to a kneeling position, ready to engage the last two *sicarios.* At the same moment he heard the crack of gun shots and saw the two AK men twisting from the impact of bullets. His last two opponents whirled around and pulled handguns from under their shirts. To his right, the AR man stepped forward and leveled his rifle at Jack's head.

Marco tensed as the *sicario* pushed the stall door back slightly then turned and walked out of the bathroom. He waited a minute before stepping down and going to the door. Pushing it open slightly, he saw Elena in the alcove, a Glock Model 26 9mm in her right hand. He stepped out and the two of them moved down the hallway where they could hear the sound of fighting. Marco peered around the corner then quickly ducked back.

"Two with AKs, their backs to us," he said to Elena. "Another with an AR on the other side. Jack is on the floor fighting. I'll go left, you go right."

Elena nodded, a tense look on her face, and raised her Glock to the ready position.

On Marco's signal they moved around the corner and toward the group of gunmen at a fast walk, six feet apart and guns leveled. At twenty feet they both opened fire. Three slugs from Marco's .45 struck the AK man on the left in the center of his back, sending him spinning around and to the floor. Elena also fired three times, hitting her target in the neck and back of his head. The gunman tumbled forward, his AK falling from lifeless hands.

At the same time, the two men standing over Jack whirled around and pulled guns from under their shirts. Marco pumped three rounds into the chest of the one on the left and dropped him to the floor. Elena double-tapped the shooter on the right and he fell to one knee. He grunted loudly and tried to raise his pistol, but Marco and Elena fired again and blew the gunman to the floor. They looked up in time to see the gunman next to the woman step forward and aim his AR at Jack. Before he could fire, muffled pops sounded behind him and he stumbled forward over a table to the floor.

Gary watched as customers came streaming out of the bar and hurried to their cars. Soon the lot was nearly empty. The two guards remained at the door. Gary grabbed the dark poncho he'd brought along and pulled it over his head. Next he pulled a black watch cap low to hide his brown hair. He left the G36 on the floor and ducked out the van's side door.

As he walked toward the bar, he stopped to pick up a discarded half-full beer bottle in his right hand. Nearing the door, he adopted a drunk's staggering gait and raised the bottle to his lips to hide his face. At ten feet one of the guards shouted at him that the bar was closed and to go away. One held his AK with one hand at his side, the other had his slung over his shoulder.

With his left hand, Gary threw the poncho over his right shoulder Clint Eastwood style, dropped the bottle to the ground, and raised his H&K to eye level. His first bullet hit the guard on the left in the center of his forehead, dropping him like a rock. His next round struck the other guard in his right eye and blew through the back of his head as he tried to unsling his AK.

Shots sounded inside the bar as he pulled the bodies away from the entrance and ran through the door. Thirty feet away the woman and a man with an AR-15 stood among some tables near the dance floor. On the other side of them Marco and Elena both fired at a gunman on one knee, blowing him to the floor. A few feet away, Jack was crouched on his knees.

The man with the AR moved forward and raised his rifle. Gary locked his arms in a Weaver stance and fired three rounds into the *sicario's* back, driving him over a table and down to the floor. The woman whirled around, saw she was cut off and raised her hands in surrender.

Jack saw that all of the gunmen were down. The Zeta with the broken leg was still moving and groaning on the floor. The woman stood with raised arms. The smell of gunpowder fill the air and, except for the ringing in his ears, it was suddenly quiet. He rose to his feet and looked around to make sure there was no one else in the bar.

"Check the bodies," he said to Marco and Elena then turned and walked toward the woman.

"Jack, look out!" Elena shouted behind him and an instant later came three gunshots. Jack spun around and saw the Zeta with the broken leg falling on his back, his shirt open and a small

Beretta pistol in his outstretched hand. Elena lowered her Glock, smoke still rising from the muzzle.

"Thanks," Jack told her. "I owe you one."

"*De nada,*" she replied. It was nothing.

Jack turned back to the woman. Gary stood behind her with his H&K leveled.

"You okay?" Jack asked his old friend.

"I'm good," Gary replied, "but we'd better hurry. They might have backup in the area."

Jack nodded then patted down the woman for weapons and removed a cell phone clipped to her belt. He was glad she'd survived. She seemed to be an important part of the narco's command structure. Maybe they could trade her for Brigitte.

"They're all dead," Marco told him as he came up and handed over a pair of handcuffs. "Try those on her."

Jack cuffed the woman's hands behind her back then went behind the bar, grabbed a towel and tied it around her eyes. They retrieved the three rifles and took all the money they could find on the dead *sicarios.* Gary and Marco pulled the dead gunmen outside into the bar with the others then hustled the woman out to the van.

Elena drove Jack's Jeep while Marco took the van with Jack and Gary in the rear with their prisoner. They had survived the first encounter and now had a possible bartering chip for Brigitte. Jack knew their next move would be a crucial step in the quest to save his daughter's life and find out who was trying to kill him.

"Congratulations, *gringo*," the woman said as they moved along the darkened streets of Independencia, a light rain beating against the windshield. "You win this round, but you have no idea what you've done."

"You want to tell me?" he asked.

"You will see soon enough," she said, "and not even God can help you now."

Chapter 16

An hour later they reached their destination. The small house sat in a slight depression about one hundred yards south of Avenida Ruiz Cortines. The area was semi-rural with homes scattered on both sides of the road. A dirt road led from the street to the front yard. An old Dodge pickup was parked in the driveway. A dim light was on in the front room.

The others stayed in the vehicles while Marco went to the front door. A minute later a man appeared in the lighted doorway. Five minutes after that Marco returned to the van.

"We can have the place until noon tomorrow," he told Jack and Gary.

The house was in a remote location and belonged to an old friend of Marco whose son he had rescued from Gulf Cartel kidnappers two years ago. The man was grateful and willing to do any favor Marco needed.

Fifteen minutes later the man came out with a small bag, got into the pickup and drove away. The men and Elena took their prisoner inside and gathered in the small kitchen. The owner had told Marco they were welcome to any food or drink in the house. While Marco put drinks and snacks on the table, Jack sat the woman down at the table, opened her cell phone and checked the speed dial list. The first number showed no name or reference.

"Your boss's number?" he asked her, holding up the phone.

"Try it and see," she told him, her dark eyes staring at him defiantly.

"Okay, I will."

Jack copied the number on a piece of paper then took his prepaid cell to make the call. He didn't know if the cartel had tracking devices on their people's phones, but he wasn't taking the chance and would not use that phone. A low male voice answered on the second ring.

"*¿Si?*"

"I have your woman," Jack said in Spanish. "I'll trade her for my daughter."

There was a short pause before the man answered.

"I underestimated you, *gringo*," he said in accented English. "I was told you were good, but you have surprised me. Is she okay?"

"She's fine, for now," Jack replied in English, "but not if you hurt my daughter."

"What do you want?"

"An exchange. Tomorrow. You choose the time and location."

"Agreed, but I'd like to speak to her first."

Jack put the phone to the woman's ear and told her to say something.

"I'm okay, Jesus," she said.

"Give me the location," Jack said putting the phone back to his ear. He wrote down the information the man gave him and told him to bring only one of his men.

"Okay, nine a.m.," Jack repeated. "Don't be late."

"*Gringo*, if you touch a hair on her head, I will cut out your heart and have it for breakfast," the voice told him.

Jack hesitated a moment before answering.

"I'm guessing she's more than just another gun in your chain of command," he said.

"That's right. She's my sister."

Brigitte stood in front of the bathroom mirror in her jeans and a bra brushing her hair and applying makeup to hide the cuts on her lip and eyebrow. Her bruises were fading but still visible. Physically, she was better now, but still felt the sting of humiliation from knowing she'd been raped. But she was determined not to let that distract her. She had to stay strong and calm and be ready when her father came for her.

She returned to her mattress in the living area and put on her blouse and Nikes. She had just put away her toiletries when the front door opened and two men came inside. They walked to where she sat and stood over her. One was the big guy who had come in before. The other was new.

Late thirties, six feet tall, lean and hard looking. He wore black clothing and had short, military-cut hair. His dark, expressionless eyes and scarred cheek gave him a menacing look.

"Stand up," he told her in accented English. "We're going to meet your father."

Brigitte's heart jumped and she felt a sense of joy tempered with fear. She'd known he would come for her, but she also knew these violent, dangerous men would not give her up easily. She couldn't worry about that. Her father would have a plan and she had to be ready.

Brigitte stood up and the big man cuffed her hands behind her back. They led her out of the room as the other girls watched and wondered if she would ever return.

Jack stopped the van fifty yards from the trash dump and parked facing the entrance. It was 8:30 a.m. and no one else was present. The dump was in a hilly area near the small pueblo of Villa Garcia about twenty-five miles northwest of Monterrey. When Jack showed Marco the directions provided by the cartel man, his friend told him he knew the area.

He said the location was state-owned land but was used by locals to dump garbage because of its remoteness. He had once chased a carload of narcos into the dump to arrest them. He added that it was also only a few miles from the compound of Ernesto Jimenez. Marco knew a spot where he and Gary could cover Jack in case things went bad, but they had to get there and set up before daylight.

Jack agreed and Marco and Gary left in the Jeep to get there in time. Elena remained with Jack to assist with their hostage. They had slept in shifts until daylight. After a quick breakfast, they moved out to arrive before the cartel men.

Jack looked at the low hills around them and spotted one about three hundred yards away where Marco had said they would set up. It was covered with brush and small trees and had direct line of sight to the dump. He knew they were in place and watching them now. If they spotted any cartel men, they would call. The storm from the night before had moved out and the sky was clear. They had done all they could to prepare. Now they waited.

Gary looked through the Redfield 3x9 variable scope mounted on his Springfield-Armory M1A .308 caliber rifle. The gun was part of Marco's weapon's stash from his house. He told Gary it was sighted dead on at 200 meters. Marco's laser rangefinder put the distance from the hill to the van at 327 yards, so Gary made minor adjustments to account for the drop at that range.

Eight feet to Gary's right, Marco lay with an H&K G3A3 7.62mm, mounted with a Zeiss 3.5x10 variable scope, also from his private stash. Though not as accomplished a sniper as Gary, he was an excellent shot. Both men felt confident that they could cover their friends well at this range.

They had reached the dump at 3:00 a.m. and gone off road to reach their location. They'd left the Jeep at the bottom of the hill and now lay on top, well hidden in the thick creosote brush and scrub pine around them. They'd seen no one else in the vicinity and slept in shifts until Jack arrived in the van. The meeting time was close and they were on full alert. Like Jack, now they waited.

At 9:05, Jack saw a black Hummer come into view down the dirt road and continue slowly until it stopped thirty yards from the van. Tinted windows hid the occupants well.

"They're here," he said, alerting Elena seated in the back with the woman.

Jack got out and helped her take their hostage out the back door, then move to the front of the van. Elena stood behind the woman with one hand on her collar while the other held the muzzle of her Glock to her head. Elena had exchanged her club clothes for black fatigue pants, tactical boots and a green blouse.

Jack stood a few feet to one side. He was now armed with a Glock Model 34 9mm he'd taken from one of the dead gunmen in the bar.

The driver's door of the Hummer opened and a familiar figure stepped out. He walked forward and stopped ten feet from Jack and Elena. He wore a Beretta 92F 9mm holstered on his belt. For a moment he didn't speak, his eyes moving between his sister and her captors.

"I'm glad to see they didn't hurt you, Lita," he finally said.

"*Estoy bien, hermano,*" she replied. I'm fine, brother.

"You killed some of my best men, *gringo*," he said to Jack, switching to English. "I owe you for that."

"Not as much as I owe you," Jack replied. He felt an overwhelming urge to shoot the son-of-a-bitch between the eyes for what he had done to Ana.

"I understand," Jesus replied, a slight smile on his lips. "Who knows, perhaps I'll give you the chance to repay that debt. But right now we have to settle this."

"Did you bring my daughter?"

Jesus raised his left arm and signaled. The rear passenger door of the Hummer opened and a big man with long hair, a heavy mustache and dressed in black stepped out and pulled a handcuffed Brigitte with him. He held a stainless-steel pistol to her head.

"Daddy! I'm okay," Brigitte shouted at him.

Jack's breath caught and he felt a lump in his chest upon seeing his daughter. She looked to be okay, with maybe some bruising on her face. He felt hopeful. Maybe this would work out.

"Hang tight, sweetheart," he shouted. "We'll get you out of here."

"You ready to do this?" he asked Jesus.

The cartel man stepped forward until he was only five feet from his sister.

"I'm very disappointed in you, Lita," he told her. "Ten good men, two of them Zetas, all dead now. And you have endangered my patron's entire operation. Do you understand what this means?"

"Yes, Jesus, and I am very sorry," she replied. "The *gringo* had help. Professionals, and they were good."

"But you still outnumbered them."

"I know," she said, averting her eyes, an embarrassed look on her face.

"I have asked *la Santa Muerte* for forgiveness. I now ask you."

Lita looked at him for a moment then replied in a strained voice. "I forgive you, Jesus."

"*Gracias, hermana,*" he said. Thank you, sister.

In the next instant he drew his Beretta and shot his sister in the forehead. She dropped to the ground, blood spurting from the bullet wound. Elena stepped back, a stunned look on her face. Jesus holstered the pistol and turned to Jack.

"Now we start again, *gringo*," he said. "I'm sure you have friends nearby with rifles aimed at us. Call and tell them to stand down or I will have Diego kill your daughter."

Jack said nothing for a minute, his mind still processing what he'd just witnessed. But he knew he had no choice. He pulled the cell from his belt and dialed.

"Marco, you saw what happened. Stand down or they'll kill her. You know what to do."

Jesus reached out and Jack gave him the phone and his Glock. Elena handed over her cell phone and weapon. Jesus pulled his own cell and dialed a number.

"You can come in now," he said in Spanish, then put away the phone and stood back.

Five minutes later a second Hummer and two Ford Expeditions sped up the road and skidded to a halt in front of them. Fifteen men with assault rifles and combat gear unloaded and spread out. Jesus ordered one of the SUV drivers and another man to take Brigitte back to the compound in the white van. He told the Hummer driver and five others to stay with him and the remaining men to go search the hill 300 yards away for possible snipers.

"Daddy, I knew you'd come for me," Brigitte shouted as the two men dragged her to the rear of the van. "I love you," she added just before they tossed her through the side door. Jack shouted back that he loved her as well.

"Okay, *gringo*," Jesus said as the van pulled away. "You had no idea what you were doing when you decided to take on the Gulf Cartel. Now I'm going to show you."

He signaled and Diego put flex cuffs on Jack and Elena and blindfolds over their eyes. They were placed in the back seat of the Hummer then Jesus took the wheel and pulled away from the dump, followed by the second Hummer.

"That is one evil son-of-a-bitch," Gary said to Marco as the Hummers pulled away and the SUVs with armed gunmen moved toward them.

"Yeah, but we can't do anything about that now. We need to move before we end up like his sister."

The two men picked up their rifles and ran in a crouch through the brush and down the opposite side of the hill to the Jeep. Ten minutes later they were driving away as fast as the terrain allowed. Gary knew the rough ground would slow the SUVs and they had time to get away before the gunmen reached the hill.

Now they faced a new problem. Both Jack and Elena were prisoners of the narcos and he and Marco were on the run. They had no official backup and few resources. They needed to hide and come up with a new plan. Gary knew one thing. He and

Marco would not leave their friends to these jackals. Jack had told them what to do: keep fighting.

Chapter 17

After a long ride on mostly bumpy roads, the Hummer came to a stop. Jesus had been on his cell phone for much of the way. Jack wasn't sure what he was talking about, but someone seemed to be waiting for him. A scanner in the front broadcast a continuous string of traffic from police cars.

The doors opened and Jack heard Jesus talking to someone near the front and voices in the background. After a few moments, the passenger doors opened and rough hands pulled Jack and Elena from their seat. Their captors guided them forward a short distance and forced them to their knees. A moment later the blindfolds were removed.

Both Jack and Elena blinked their eyes against the bright morning sun. Twenty yards in front of them, a man in a desert camouflage army uniform with his hands tied behind his back kneeled on the ground, flanked by two AK toting *sicarios*. Thirty feet to their right was a woman of around forty years of age, two boys about eight and ten, and a pretty teenage girl of fifteen or so.

Three SUVs and a pickup truck were parked beyond them under a row of Mexican sycamore trees. Around them stood a dozen armed gunmen. The location was bare, rocky ground with only scrub pines for a hundred yards in every direction. Low hills could be seen in the distance.

Jack heard the Hummer driver's door close and a moment later Jesus walked past him to the kneeling man and spoke to the gunmen standing over him. He then walked to where the woman and children were also kneeling on the ground. He pulled the teenage girl to her feet and walked her to the group of men around the SUVs. Two of them put her in one of the vehicles and drove away with her. The girl's mother cried and moaned as they left the scene. Her two sons watched, their faces frozen in fear. Jesus returned to stand over the kneeling man.

"*Gringo*, meet Lieutenant Colonel Gustavo Benitez," he said in a loud voice. "Colonel Benitez is a logistics officer in the 8th Division of the Mexican Army. For the last two years he has helped my employer acquire some very fine military weapons that give us an advantage over our enemies. And he has been well compensated for that.

"This mutually beneficial relationship came to an end when the colonel decided to sell us out to the Sinaloas. Last month he gave us the location of a temporary depot of automatic rifles and machine guns. I sent fifteen men to seize the weapons. They did so and as they were leaving, they were ambushed and killed by a large force of Sinaloa gunmen.

"I just found out that the Sinaloa boss in Monterrey paid the colonel half a million dollars to sell us out. Today he pays for his transgression. I want you to see what happens to those who betray the Gulf."

Jesus waved his right hand and two more gunmen joined the two standing over the colonel. The four of them put the officer face down in a prone position and held him to the ground facing his family.

"Flaco, my blade," Jesus shouted to one of his men in the second Hummer. A door opened and closed and a skinny *sicario* of medium height, about twenty-five years old, walked forward carrying a Japanese katana sword.

He handed the sword to Jesus and returned to stand behind Jack and Elena. Jesus held the elegant weapon up for Jack to see, then grasped the black leather handle and pulled the blade from its wooden sheath. He stuck the sheath under his belt and walked to stand behind the kneeling woman and her two sons.

Colonel Benitez began begging Jesus not to hurt his family. His wife sobbed and wailed for mercy for her sons. The younger boy began crying and his brother told him not to show fear. Jack was impressed with the youngster's courage. He and Elena looked at each other, both sick with the knowledge of what was about to happen.

With another wave of his hand, two more gunmen joined Jesus and pulled the Colonel's wife to her feet. As they held her firmly, Jesus stood behind her sons, extended the katana and waved the blade back and forth. Sunlight glinted off the steel blade and gold circular hand guard.

With a quick, fluid movement he twisted to his left and swung the blade with great force in a downward sweeping motion to his right. Without stopping he spun around and swung the blade again in a downward arc and to his left. Horrendous, agonizing screams filled the air.

Colonel Benitez began struggling to escape his captors while shouting obscenities at the top of his voice at Jesus. His wife screamed a high-pitched shriek and dropped to her knees, wailing and sobbing. The two men holding her stepped back and Jesus again swung his katana in a long, circular arc. The wailing stopped. He removed a handkerchief from his back pocket and wiped the blade clean, then returned to stand over a sobbing Colonel Benitez.

"That was for your treachery, Colonel," he said as he put the katana back in its *saya* and kneeled down to look him in the face. "My computer techs are returning the money you took from us and your daughter will join the stable that services my men." He paused a moment as Benitez screamed an obscenity and tried to lunge at him.

"Yes, your hatred for me is almost too much to bear," he continued with a low chuckle. "Don't worry. Very soon you will have an opportunity for retribution."

Jesus stood up and moved to stand in front of Jack and Elena. He nodded and the men guarding them pulled both to their feet. Jack looked at the merciless butcher in front of him and at the carnage on the ground a few feet away. What a twisted sense of irony that this man was named Jesus. Now he understood the depth of inhumanity these narco killers represented.

He had dealt with evil men before and had seen this kind of moral depravity on other occasions. He'd been able to intervene once and stop the slaughter. Now, all he could do was watch helplessly and hope he survived long enough to make things right for the victims. He looked at Elena and saw tears rolling down her cheeks.

"Are you shocked, *gringo*?" Jesus asked. "I know your background and, like me, you have seen much brutality in war. You should understand these things."

Jack didn't want to acknowledge this primitive brute, but he couldn't restrain his rage.

"I've known war, Jesus," he said, spitting out the name like a foul taste in his mouth, "and scum like you wouldn't last five minutes on a battlefield. It's not a place for hyenas who murder women and children."

"You don't know this war, *gringo*," he said, a slight smile parting his lips, "but you will learn. Right now it's time for you to learn why you are here."

He barked orders at his men and Jack and Elena were blindfolded again and shoved back inside the Hummer. As they drove away, Jack moved his right knee sideways until it touched

Elena's leg. She pushed back to let him know she understood. They were in this together... until the end.

The Hummer slowed then sped up for another hundred yards before slowing again and stopping. Jack could hear voices and other activity all around, but nothing he could distinguish. He and Elena were again dragged from their seats and guided along by hands on each arm. He could tell they were inside a building now. There was a faint smell of food cooking and they passed the sound of a TV or stereo before they went down a set of stairs. A door opened and they were led through and sat in chairs.

The blindfolds came off and Jack saw they were in a large, sparsely decorated room. A few generic paintings hung on the walls, but the only furniture was the two chairs in which he and Elena were seated. Ten armed *sicarios* stood around them. Jesus stood near a window to their right, talking on his cell. After a minute he hung up and walked across the room to open the only door. A moment later two men walked through that door and the violent upheaval in Jack's life took another turn.

Kill McCoy-Greer   144

Chapter 18

Brigitte sat on her mattress, dabbing at her eyes with a tissue. She hated to cry in front of the other girls, but seeing her father again and knowing he too was now a prisoner was more than she could bear. He had come for her and his rescue effort had failed. Watching that man shoot his own sister had shaken her right down to her core. She'd never known such evil. Still, she had hope. Her father had long experience with bad people. If anyone could beat such overwhelming odds, it was Jack McCoy.

The door across the room opened and two men came in, dragging a mattress behind them. They took it to a spot near Brigitte and dropped it on the floor. Behind them was another narco thug pulling a teenage girl by one arm and holding a large bag in his other hand. He led her to the mattress, pushed her down on it and dropped the bag next to her. He then turned and left without a word.

The girl lay on her side and covered her face with both hands. She wore a thin white blouse, blue jean shorts and sandals.

Her chest heaved with sobs. Brigitte got up and sat on the edge of the girl's mattress. She patted her shoulder with one hand to console the youngster and after a minute the sobbing stopped.

Brigitte asked the girl for her name. For a moment, she didn't reply, then she slowly sat up and said, "My name is Abella."

For the next few minutes, they talked quietly and Abella told her what had happened. A few of the other girls in the room joined them to assure the teen she was not alone. Brigitte didn't say so, but she suspected the girl's parents and brothers were no longer alive. For now, she and the other women would act as her family. She also knew why they had brought her here. Brigitte would try to protect the young woman, but she prayed her father could get to them and put down these violent savages before the worst happened.

Jack recognized the slightly taller one. He'd last seen Javier Cedillo at his trial for murder and drug trafficking in 1987. Months earlier his narcotics team had arrested Cedillo, his boss and a crooked cop, one of Jack's own men, at a drug stash house in Las Vegas and Jack had shot the narco enforcer in his left leg when he pulled a gun. The wound had caused nerve damage and left him with a pronounced limp.

He was older now but looked fit and healthy. He'd gained some muscle from weight lifting. His short hair and trim mustache were still dark. His creased jeans, boat shoes and black Polo shirt fit him well. What puzzled Jack was his striking resemblance to the younger man next to him.

About five-ten or eleven, clean shaven, and dressed in tan chinos, a white shirt and a pair of brown Berluti slip-ons, he was the image of casual elegance. His good looks and athletic build no doubt made him attractive to the ladies. Jack couldn't place him, but he looked vaguely familiar.

The two men walked forward and stopped a few feet from Jack and Elena. Cedillo glared down at Jack with barely concealed hatred. The other one looked at him with curiosity.

"Jack McCoy, it's been a long time," the younger man said in cultured, American-accented English. "I'm guessing you don't remember me. Not surprising since I was just a kid the last time we saw each other. I'm sure you remember my brother, Javier. He remembers you well. His leg hurts every time he thinks of you."

"I've thought of little else for over twenty years," Javier snarled down at him in a hoarse, grainy voice. His English was fluent but had a more distinct Spanish accent.

"Yeah, I can imagine," Jack replied. "You've had a lot of time on your hands."

Cedillo lunged forward and swung a fist at Jack's face. Jack leaned back in time but it still scraped his left cheek. Cedillo's brother grabbed him by one arm and pulled him back.

"Easy, *hermano*," he said. "You will have your revenge, but not so fast."

"*¿Quienes son,* Jack?" said Elena from her chair, asking the identity of the two men.

"Ah, Sergeant Cisneros, don't think I'm ignoring you," replied Cedillo's brother in Spanish. "I just need to catch up on my history with your friend McCoy." He moved closer and looked down at her. "You're quite attractive for a cop. It's too bad you're on the other side. I could find a place for you in my organization."

"How do you know my name?" she replied.

"Your boss told me all about you. He was quite upset that you wouldn't stop your investigation of me. Now he's going to have you fired. When he does, I can offer you a much better position."

"Not interested."

"In that case, I'll turn you over to Jesus's men," he said, pointing to his enforcer behind

them.

"If one of your diseased dogs touches me, I'll rip off his dick and shove it down his throat," she spat back at him.

"A woman with spirit," he said, laughing out loud. "I like that. Maybe I'll keep you for myself."

"Have I jogged your memory yet?" he asked, turning to Jack and reverting to English. "I thought the calling card we left at your house would have done that, but apparently not. Maybe this will help. I'm known here as Ernesto Jimenez, but my real first name is Fidel, and I'm not Mexican. I'm Nicaraguan."

For a moment, Jack was incredulous at this revelation, but then the reality hit him as he stared at the man's face and knew it was true. Still, it was seconds before he could reply.

"Fidel Jimenez? Little Fidel? From Matagalpa?"

"Yes, McCoy, Fidel Jimenez, the son of Rodrigo Jimenez de la Fuente, Nicaraguan Army officer. The man you killed for doing his job."

"Your father was killing innocent people, not doing his job," Jack replied after a pause.

"My father was fighting for his country," Jimenez shouted, his nostrils flaring and anger sparking in his eyes. "He was killing the enemies who wanted to overthrow his government. You were there to help him, not oppose him. You certainly weren't supposed to kill him."

"You weren't there, Fidel. You didn't see what your father was doing."

"I was ten years old, McCoy. I worshiped my father. He was everything I admired then. So were you. Do you remember what I asked you the last time we saw each other?"

Jack looked away for a moment, his thoughts going back almost thirty years to a time and place of chaos and political turmoil. To a young boy who looked up to him and asked him to look after his father.

"Yeah, I remember," he said.

"I asked you to take care of my father because you were going on a dangerous mission. You were a great American warrior who came to help my country fight the communists and I trusted you to watch over him. The next day my father's commander told my mother that he was dead. Killed in a battle with the insurgents. I never saw you again and it wasn't until later that I found out you were the one who killed him.

"They never explained why. Just that you killed him because he was shooting some Indian communists. We took my father's body to Managua for burial. A few months later, the communist Sandinistas took over the government and my mother moved us to Miami.

"Javier and I really took to American culture. The clothes, the food, the music. I guess you could say we fell in with the wrong crowd. It was the eighties and Miami was awash in cocaine. The Colombians ruled the drug world then. They called them the Cocaine Cowboys.

"Javier began working with the Medellin Cartel in Miami and they moved him to Las Vegas to protect the boss there. That's when we found out about you. He realized who you were after you arrested him. You didn't recognize him because he was older then and he'd taken our mother's maiden name when we immigrated here.

"He went to prison and I took his place working for the Colombians, but in the '90s I realized they would soon be out of power. The Colombian government was cracking down and the Mexicans were moving to take over the distribution routes. I began making connections with them and soon worked my way into the Gulf Cartel.

"It took a few years, but I earned their trust and now I run things for the Gulf in Monterrey. And things are good. We can barely keep all of those addicts in the States supplied with their nose candy. Yeah, it's gotten nasty with the competition between us and the other cartels, but that's just business. You have to fight for your share.

"But I never forgot about you, McCoy. You killed my father and put my brother in prison and I swore to make you pay for that. Four years ago I finally had a plan...and I started with your wife."

Jack's head snapped up at Jimenez's last comment and he glared at the narco boss with intense focus. "You killed my wife?" he asked in a low, tight voice.

"I have a source in Las Vegas who acquired the information I needed about you and your family," Jimenez told him, now pacing back and forth. "I sent a man there to kill your wife and make it look like an accident. Your friends were next, but then I was ambushed by the Sinaloas on a trip to Matamoros. Jesus rescued me, but I was badly wounded and spent the next several months in hospitals recovering. I had to put you on hold for a while.

"Last year I got things under control here and was able to get back to you. I sent Jesus to Vegas to continue executing the plan: breaking my brother out of prison and moving on the people close to you. And now here you are. Javier and I have waited a long time for this, McCoy.

"Our mother died a few years ago. She never remarried because she missed our father so much. It made me angry to see her hurt that way because of what you took from her. I swore on her grave that I would make you pay for that. Now it's time to keep that oath.

"This evening you will see what I have in store for you tomorrow. Right now you are going to your own room where you will eat and sleep. I want you rested for the test that will come."

"Patron, I want to know who helped the *gringo* ambush my men at the bar," said Jesus from behind the two brothers. "They're still out there and may be planning a rescue or these two as we speak."

"Whoever they are, they can't help him, Jesus," replied Fidel. "McCoy belongs to me now. It would take too long and too much force to get that information out of him and that would ruin our little show, and my revenge."

"However," he said, looking at Elena with a salacious grin, "Sergeant Cisneros will know and we have plenty of time to discuss that with her."

"Very well, patron, then I will prepare for the entertainment later," Jesus replied, then turned and walked out of the room.

Jimenez waved a hand and his gunmen stood Jack and Elena up and led them out of the room. Jack was taken one way down the hall and Elena the other. After two turns Jack and his guards came to another room with a barred door. They led him inside and removed his handcuffs, then left. A single guard remained outside.

Carpet covered the floor, but there were no windows in the room and the only furniture was a bed in one corner. A door on the far wall opened into a bathroom. What was once a real bedroom was now a prison cell.

Jack sat on the bed and leaned against the wall. He was tired and hungry, and a burning anger raged in his gut. He closed his eyes and tried to process everything that had happened in the last two days. It seemed incredible, but it was all too real. Now he was a prisoner himself and his future looked bleak. He didn't even want to think about what would happen to his daughter, or to Elena.

He thought about the Jimenez brothers and their vendetta against him for what had happened when they were only kids and he had been a young man. Slowly his thoughts turned to that time and place when this nightmare first began.

Chapter 19

Matagalpa, Nicaragua

March, 1979

The first light of dawn was just visible to the east when Sergeant First Class Jack McCoy left the mess hall and started for the officer's quarters on the other side of the camp. He stopped for a moment to put on his web gear and a rucksack. Earlier he'd done a three-mile run and a forty-minute workout with his Hapkido sparring partner. A plate of gallo pinto and some hot coffee gave him new energy for the day ahead.

Around him the camp was coming to life as civilian workers went to their jobs and squads of soldiers jogged by on their morning runs. The camp, two miles from the mountain town of Matagalpa, was two months old and still under construction. Wooden barracks had been constructed for the officer cadre and NCOs, but the enlisted troops still lived in tents. A new firing range was ready for use and several Huey UH-1 helicopters sat on a newly completed airfield just outside the camp.

Six months ago Jack's A-team from the 7th Special Forces Group at Fort Gulick in the Panama Canal Zone had been assigned to help the Nicaraguan National Guard form a new Special Forces unit. Their job was to hunt down the Sandinista guerillas who were trying to overthrow the government of President Anastasio Somoza, a right-wing dictator whose family had been in power since 1936.

The Somoza family ran the military and every government institution in the country. They had also acquired a great deal of wealth while most Nicaraguans lived in abject poverty. A Marxist guerilla group called the Sandinistas, with help from the Russians and Cubans, had begun a campaign of resistance against the government by urging rural villagers to rise up and overthrow the Somoza regime.

American businesses held a significant interest in Nicaragua's agricultural sector and the Carter Administration did not want to see the country turn communist. They had sent military aid to assist the Somoza government and Green Beret teams like Jack's were dispatched to help the National Guard.

The team recruited the best from the guard's airborne infantry unit and organized three companies of Special Forces troops. After four months of initial training, the guard commander was so impressed with their progress that he ordered one company be sent to a remote province in the northwest part of the country called Tuma La Dalia. Jack's team commander had assigned him to be the company advisor at their new location.

Tuma La Dalia was a mountainous area on the continental divide between the Pacific and Caribbean coasts. The largest town was Matagalpa, named after the Matagalpa Indians who inhabited the area. Some Indians lived in town, but most were found in remote villages scattered across the mountain slopes. They eked out a living growing small crops in jungle clearings, and some worked on the numerous coffee plantations in the region.

The military command staff thought the Indians were prime recruits for the Sandinista guerillas and ordered the company commanders to go after them hard. After talking to prisoners they had taken, Jack had reached a different conclusion: Except for an occasional convert, the Indians wanted no part of the Sandinista's Marxist ideology. They just wanted to be left alone to work their crops and raise their families.

However, the guard's commanders were convinced the Indians were conspiring against Somoza. Jack had witnessed brutal beatings of villagers on some of the operations he'd attended and the suspected guerillas had been whisked away to a military prison in Managua and not seen again.

Jack had complained about it, but his A-team captain told him his orders were to ignore what he'd seen and just do his job. They were there to train, not tell their hosts how to deal with their enemy. That didn't sit well with Jack. One thing he'd learned since arriving in Nicaragua was that the ruling class there looked down on the rural population with contempt and disdain and had little regard for their rights as human beings. Unfortunately for Jack, that attitude had come to Matagalpa with his company commander.

"Good morning, Sergeant McCoy," Major Jimenez de la Fuente said in Spanish as he opened the front door of the barracks apartment and motioned Jack inside. "Are you ready for another day?"

"Good morning, Major," Jack replied. "Yes, sir, ready to go."

"Very well, I'll just get my gear," Jimenez said then turned and disappeared into an adjoining bedroom.

The new wood barracks were small but comfortable. Through the door at the rear Jack could see Major Jimenez's wife in the kitchen. The smell of eggs, fried beans and rice drifted into the living room. As Jack waited the major's ten-year old son, Fidel, came out of the kitchen and greeted him.

"Hi, Sergeant McCoy," he said in English, a smile on his face. "I'm glad to see you."

Fidel was the youngest of the major's three children. An older brother and sister had returned to Managua to live with relatives, but Fidel had remained here with his parents. He attended school in Matagalpa and often accompanied his father and Jack around the camp or on trips to town. He was a bright kid who admired Jack and liked to question him about life in the United States.

Jack liked Fidel and enjoyed their conversations. The boy was well mannered and respectful of the adults around him, traits that Jack liked in a kid. He could see that Fidel adored his father and worried about him when he went on offensive operations against the guerillas. Jack did his best to ease the youngster's fears.

"Hey, Fidel, good to see you also," Jack told him. "Are you ready for school?" he asked, noting the boy's pressed shirt and pants and well-combed hair.

"Yes, sir. I have English this morning and I like that class."

"You should, Fidel. Your English is very good."

The boy's smile disappeared and Jack saw a worried look come over his face.

"Sergeant McCoy, my dad says you are going after the Sandinistas today."

Jack hesitated a moment, searching for the right words before finally replying.

"We're going to a village so we can talk to the people and find out if they need our help."

"My dad says there are guerillas there who want to fight."

"Fidel, the people there may just be villagers who don't want to fight anyone, but your father and I will be careful."

"Sergeant McCoy, can I ask you something?"

"Sure, what is it?"

"Will you watch out for my dad?"

"Of course I will, Fidel. Your dad and I always look out for each other in the jungle."

"He says you fought the communists in Vietnam and that you are a great warrior, but he thinks you don't want to fight the communists here."

Jack knew why Fidel's father had said that about him. The major came from a family that was part of the country's ruling elite. His father held a high-level position in Somoza's government and had helped the major acquire his position in the National Guard.

Jack had discovered that Major Jimenez held the rural Indians in utter contempt. He suspected they were all Marxist sympathizers and in collusion with the Sandinistas. Jack had watched him order the beatings and torture of suspected guerillas and had tried to intervene with little success. He knew the major tolerated him only because of Jack's knowledge and experience in jungle warfare.

Jack's fear was that Jimenez's bigoted attitude would be passed along to his impressionable young son. He hadn't noticed that so far, but the boy clearly wanted to emulate his father. Jack wanted to assure him without seeming to condone his father's views.

"Fidel, the communists are not good people," Jack told him, "but not all of the villagers are communists. Sometime it's hard to tell and I like to be sure who they are before we go after them. I promise I will do my best to see that the guerillas don't hurt your father."

"Thank you, Sergeant McCoy," Fidel said with a smile. "I feel better now."

"Fidel, don't bother Sergeant McCoy," said Major Jimenez as he came into the room with his gear and an Israeli Galil assault rifle, the standard issue for the guard soldiers.

"It's okay, sir," Jack told him, "I enjoy chatting with your son."

A knock at the front door revealed the major's senior NCO and driver, Sgt. Fausto Lucero, had arrived. Fidel's mother came out to see them off as Jack and the major went out the door and got into Sgt. Lucero's jeep. As they headed for the airfield, Jack looked back from the passenger seat to see Fidel standing in the door with his mother, watching them leave. Jack didn't know why, but an uneasy feeling in his gut told him he wouldn't see the boy again.

Chapter 20

The sun had fully risen when they met the four squads of soldiers already gathered at the airfield. Four Bell UH-1N Twin Huey helicopters sat nearby with pilots at the controls and the engines warming up. Master Sergeant Lucero stopped at the edge of the tarmac and they were met by Captain Cavazos-Molina, the officer assisting Major Jimenez on the operation.

Major Jimenez ordered the men to gather around him for a last minute briefing. A few days ago, an informant had told the major about a guerilla hiding in a village called Campo Verde about twenty miles north of Matagalpa. He was possibly wounded and being hidden by his family. There was little other information.

Major Jimenez had decided to search the village and, for the last two days, Jack had organized the forty troops into security and search teams and run them through a search exercise in a rough mockup of the village outside the camp. He felt satisfied that they were ready for the operation.

The teams already had their assignments and knew what to do when they landed at the village. Every man was armed with a 5.56mm Galil and wore web gear with extra magazines and other combat essentials. All of them, including Jack, wore camouflaged fatigues and boonie hats. On the right shoulder of the fatigue uniform was a white patch with the head of a black jaguar, its mouth open in a snarl.

Los Tigres Negros. The Black Tigers. An emblem the major had selected for the unit as a way to motivate and inspire them in battle. It seemed to work. The men were loyal and didn't hesitate to engage the guerillas when contact was made.

Jack watched the forty-year old major address his men. Tall with an athletic build, he cut a bold figure in his starched uniform. A nickel-plated Colt .45ACP with ivory grips rode in a holster on his web belt. *A gun to match his ego*, Jack thought. Jimenez was a competent officer, but his vanity and bigoted attitude made him more feared than respected.

Jack had far more respect for Master Sergeant Lucero and was glad the senior NCO was along with them. At six feet and two hundred pounds, the big Nicaraguan was a fifteen-year Army vet and was liked and respected by all of the men in the company. Mature and levelheaded, the sergeant was a counterweight to his more intemperate commander. The sergeant was also part Matagalpa Indian. His mother was from the tribe and he spoke the Indian language fluently. Sergeant Lucero would be a valuable asset on this operation.

The major finished his briefing and ordered the men onto the waiting helicopters. Jack and Sergeant Lucero rode with Jimenez in the lead chopper. Five minutes after takeoff they were flying low over the mountainous jungle, the wind blowing through the open doors and making conversation impossible.

Jack watched the landscape below and remembered the many helicopter rides like this he'd taken in Vietnam. Rides with his SOG team into the mountains of Laos to look for the NVA. With luck, tenacity, and boldness he'd survived those trips. Now he wondered if he would survive this one.

Thirty minutes later they reached Campo Verde, a small village of wood huts 500 yards above the La Tuma River. A dirt road led west through the jungle and a mountain stream flowed downhill past the houses on the southern edge. There were no vehicles, but Jack could see horses and cattle in pens around the houses. A few pigs roamed freely, rooting for food.

The helicopters separated and settled to the ground on all four sides of the village. The troops spilled out, with the security teams forming a cordon around the houses and the search teams moving to a clearing on the southern side where Jack's chopper came to rest. As they got out, Jack could see several adults moving among the houses and women yelling at children to get inside.

Major Jimenez and his radio operator moved to a high point near the stream and he issued instructions to the units around the village. Jack and Sgt. Lucero moved next to him and Lucero began speaking over a megaphone, telling the villagers why they were there and to cooperate with the search teams. Anyone resisting would be arrested.

The major spoke into his radio again and the search teams began moving through the village, searching each house they came to. As they did, a small group of older men moved down the slope toward the major. They were the tribal elders who made important decisions for the village. When they reached the small rise, Sgt. Lucero explained to them why they were there and told them to hand over any guerillas hiding in the village.

A man in his seventies replied that they were not hiding any guerillas. He said they did not like the Sandinistas and only wanted to be left along. Lucero related the information to Major Jimenez, but before the major could respond, a tense report came over his radio that a guerilla had been found. Jimenez keyed the mic and asked for confirmation. A moment later Captain Cavazos came on the radio and confirmed they had found a wounded guerilla. He had stabbed one of their men before he was subdued and they were bringing the suspect and the injured soldier outside.

A few minutes later Jack saw a group of soldiers emerge from between the houses. Two were carrying another man between them, his feet dragging on the ground. Two others walked at a fast pace next to them, their Galils pointed out at the crowd that was gathering around them.

Behind them walked Captain Cavazos with more soldiers and what appeared to be a family of villagers. Jack, Major Jimenez and Sgt. Lucero moved forward to meet them. The two soldiers carrying the wounded man laid him on the ground. His shirt had been removed and a thick dressing was wrapped around his upper chest.

A medic with bloody hands came from behind them and told Major Jimenez that the soldier, Private Armas, had been stabbed in one lung with a hunting knife and needed surgery or he would die. Jimenez ordered the private taken to one of the helicopters and flown back to camp immediately. As they carried the wounded man away, the major turned to Captain Cavazos.

"Sir, we found the Sandinista hiding under blankets in his parent's house," said Cavazos, pointing to a young, disheveled man dressed in a white cotton shirt, brown pants and sandals standing between two soldiers. His hands were tied behind his back. Jack guessed his age at about nineteen or twenty. He looked scared.

"He stabbed Private Armas with a large knife when they tried to take him into custody," added Cavazos, "but he has a bullet wound in his left leg and could not fight well. We arrested him and brought his family here as well."

Jack looked at a couple in their fifties standing next to the guerilla along with a teenage girl and a boy about eleven. Their hands were tied also.

"I thought you told me there were no guerillas here," Major Jimenez barked at the elderly man who had spoken to him before.

"Sir, I did not know the boy was here," the elder replied. "None of us knew."

"You lie," said Jimenez as he stood in front of the young man and his family. "Sergeant Lucero, ask these people why they were hiding this communist."

Lucero spoke to the man's parents in their native language for a few moments.

"Sir, they say their son joined the Sandinistas a few months ago. They didn't want him to go, but he was angry with the government because of the poverty here. One week ago he came back during the night. He'd been wounded in one leg and asked them to hide him until he recovered. They agreed to do so because he's their son. They didn't tell anyone else in the village that he was here."

"I don't believe them, Sergeant. They lie to us. They are part of the guerilla insurrection and now they have wounded one of our men."

Jack could see the major was angry as he stomped back and forth in front of the family.

"Sir, I think they tell the truth," said Lucero.

"Captain Cavazos," said Jimenez, ignoring his sergeant, "send a team to these people's house and burn it to the ground."

"Yes, sir," replied Cavazos, a startled look on his face as he turned and ordered six of his men to return to the village and carry out the order.

Jack knew the captain would not question the order. Hesitant and indecisive, he was easily intimidated by the major.

"Sir, are you sure that is necessary?" asked Sergeant Lucero. "We could take them all back to camp and question them until we are sure they are telling the truth."

Before Jimenez could reply, the voice of the helicopter pilot flying the wounded soldier back to camp came over the radio and told him that the man had died en route.

Jimenez turned and faced the soldiers around him. His face was twisted with rage.

"Private Armas is dead," he said. "These goddamn communists have killed him."

A groan sounded from the men and they turned on the villagers with angry looks. Sergeant Lucero translated for the elders and fear showed on their faces. In a trembling voice, the elder spokesman asked the major for mercy on his people.

Major Jimenez suddenly grabbed the young guerilla by his shirtfront and pulled him toward the stream. His wounded leg gave out and the major dragged him across the ground. At the edge of the water, he put the man in a kneeling position. He then ordered his men to place his family next to him.

By this time a large group of villagers had gathered behind the soldiers. They watched as the entire family kneeled on the stream bank and the major stood shouting at them. Soldiers from the search teams moved closer in case the crowd became violent. Major Jimenez pulled his .45 and turned to Sergeant Lucero.

"Sergeant, tell these people this is what happens to those who help the communists and kill our soldiers."

"Major, please don't kill them for this," Lucero replied. "They were his family. We can arrest them and put them on trial, but they don't deserve this."

"Very well, Sergeant. I will translate for them," said Jimenez. He wheeled around, leveled his pistol at the wounded Sandinista and shot him in the forehead. The .45 was loud in the quiet mountain air. The hardball round blew through the back of his head, spraying blood and brain matter, and his body toppled backward into the water.

The man's mother screamed out loud and his father moaned and asked the major to spare his family. The girl and young boy began crying and sobbing as Jimenez shouted at the villagers in Spanish that he would kill anyone who helped the Sandinistas.

"Sir, I beg you not to do this," shouted Lucero at his commander.

"Stand down, Sergeant, or I will have you arrested," Jimenez replied, then turned and shot the father in the head, dropping his body into the mountain stream.

"Major Jimenez, stop the killing!" shouted Jack as he stepped forward and confronted the officer face to face. He was shocked that Jimenez would actually commit murder in front of his men. Some of them had stunned looks on their faces and appeared unsure of how to respond to the major's behavior.

"Back off, Sergeant McCoy," Jimenez told him. "You are here to advise only, not tell me how to fight these goddamn communists."

"Major, these are simple mountain people. They're not communists and they aren't fighting your government. Don't do this."

"If you interfere, Sergeant, I will have you arrested."

Jimenez then turned and shot the sobbing woman in the head. She collapsed straight down and didn't move.

Jack had seen enough. Advisors weren't allowed to carry assault rifles, but side arms were authorized. Jack carried a Colt .45 ACP in a shoulder holster under his web gear. It was a customized civilian model he'd bought from a gunsmith and competition shooter in Arkansas. He pulled the pistol from its holster, flicked off the thumb safety and pointed it at Jimenez.

"Major, you are in violation of the Geneva Convention and the Nicaraguan Army Code of Military Justice. Stand down now or I will shoot you," Jack shouted at him.

By this time over a hundred villagers were shouting and trying to move forward. The soldiers blocked their advance but only slowed them. The situation was tense and about to get ugly. Captain Cavazos stood to one side, unsure what to do and unable to make a decision.

"Major, sir, please listen to Sgt. McCoy," Sergeant Lucero shouted at Jimenez.

"Sergeant Lucero, you are relieved of duty. Consider yourself under arrest."

Jimenez turned to Jack. "Sgt. McCoy, I will deal with you when we return to camp."

The major then stepped in front of the teenage girl, his .45 at his side.

"Major, I'm warning you," Jack shouted. "Put your weapon down and stop the killing."

Jimenez ignored him and pointed his pistol at the girl's head.

Jack put the front sight of his Colt on the major's temple and pressed the trigger. The .45 roared and Jimenez's head snapped back, a bloody mist flying out from the opposite side. His body dropped straight to the ground.

For a moment no one moved as shock settled over the crowd. Then some of the soldiers moved toward the stream bank, Galils raised. Captain Cavazos stood frozen in place. Jack prepared himself for battle.

"At ease, men!" Sgt. Lucero shouted in a loud voice at the approaching soldiers. "Sgt. McCoy is right. Major Jimenez was in violation of the law and our Code of Justice. He stopped the murder of more innocent people. There will be an investigation of this incident, but right now we will finish this operation and return to camp."

Lucero ignored the helpless Cavazos and began ordering the men to pull the bodies from the creek and turn them over to their families. He also radioed the team sent to burn down the guerilla's house and told them to cease the operation. While the men took Jimenez's body to the helicopters, Lucero told the village elders a detail from the army command staff would visit with them to discuss the incident and take their statements.

Jack rode with the sergeant in the lead chopper on the way back to camp. Some of the soldiers had given him hard looks, but most realized that what had happened was something to be resolved at a level far above their pay grade.

Jack sat by himself near the open door and stared at the green landscape rushing by below. He didn't regret what he'd done. Jimenez was an evil son-of-a-bitch who'd gotten what he deserved. The only problem he faced now was how to explain that to the ten-year old boy who had called him Dad.

Chapter 21

The chance for that explanation had never come, Jack recalled as he stared at his reflection in the bathroom mirror. Back at the camp, Sgt. Lucero had reported the incident to Guard headquarters in Managua and requested a transport plane for him. By nightfall he was standing in front of his A-team captain and the guard commander, explaining what had happened.

The National Guard did not want the incident made public and agreed not to press any charges against Jack, but insisted that he be removed from the country. Two days later he was back in Fort Bragg, North Carolina. The 7th Group commander was sympathetic and told Jack he'd done the right thing, but that his army career was effectively over.

Jack knew the commander was right and agreed to leave the army early with an honorable discharge. Four months later he entered the Clark County Sheriff's Department academy as a new recruit. One career had ended prematurely and a new one began.

Now that ordeal had come back to turn his life upside down. Jack's fear in Matagalpa had come true; the boy had become the father and had returned to exact revenge. He also faced another dilemma. Things looked bleak at the moment, but if a chance came to put down the monster the boy had become, would he take it or would the guilt he still felt stop him from doing the right thing?

Jack knew he had no answer for that as he finished brushing his teeth and drying his face. He hung the towel on the rack and returned to the bedroom. Earlier a guard had brought him a hot plate of food and the bathroom amenities he needed except for a razor. Now he waited for what came next from the Jimenez brothers.

That didn't take long. A group of guards appeared at the barred door and came inside. While three covered him with assault rifles, another cuffed his hands behind his back. He was led back down the hallway, up the stairs and through a series of rooms, each one more spacious and opulent than the one before. The drug life had been good to Fidel Jimenez.

Finally they went out a set of open French doors onto a large patio area. It was still light, but Jack could see it was late in the day. Heavy clouds lay on the horizon and the humidity was thick. The guards led him across the patio and around a high wall lined with palm trees. The sight that greeted Jack on the other side was not something he expected to see.

A crowd of nearly a hundred people was gathered on both sides of a large swimming pool. Most were cartel *sicarios* dressed in jeans, khakis and colorful western shirts. Scantily-dressed women accompanied many of the men and alcohol flowed freely. Lean, hard-looking men dressed in black fatigues roamed among the cartel gunmen.

The pool was sixty feet wide and over sixty yards long. The brackish water was fifteen feet below the deck. The far end sloped upward, the water ending at a sandy bank that was bare for twenty yards, then covered by bushes and small trees until it reached a high wall.

At the near end, just thirty feet from Jack, stood the Jimenez brothers and a smaller group of gunmen. One of them was Jesus, their murderous gun boss. He wore no shirt or boots and he looked at Jack with a wolfish grin. Elena, her hands cuffed, was also with the group. She still wore her black cargo pants, combat boots and green blouse.

Fidel Jimenez beckoned and Jack's guards moved him forward.

"Did you enjoy your meal, McCoy?" he asked. Now dressed in jeans, western boots and a white shirt, he still looked suave and dapper. His similarly dressed brother stood next to him and looked at Jack with undisguised hatred.

"It was fine," Jack replied in a noncommittal tone. He looked at Elena and she gave him a tight smile. He nodded slightly. "Where's my daughter?" he asked.

"She's safe and you'll see her soon." said Jimenez. "Now it's time for the after dinner show." He pulled his cell phone from his belt, punched a number in and said, "Bring him up."

"Come here," he said to Jack, walking to the edge of the pool. "I want to show you something."

Jack stepped forward and stood next to him. Twenty feet from the edge he could see three circular, concrete pillars protruding from the water. On top of them, stretching from each side of the pool, were two by six inch wood planks. A gang plank across the water.

Jimenez raised his head and began making a grunting, coughing noise from his throat. After a minute he stopped and pointed at the far end. Jack looked and saw three long, reptilian forms emerge from the brush on top of the bank and slither down to the water. They swam along the surface until they reached the pillars and began circling.

The crocodiles were huge. The largest was easily eighteen feet long. Jack guessed the two smaller ones measured around sixteen feet. Jack had a sick feeling in his stomach about

Jimenez's show.

"McCoy, you've probably heard stories about drug lords who like to keep exotic animals in their compounds," Jimenez said, staring down at the circling crocs. "It's said that Pablo

Escobar had more than a dozen lions, leopards and other African animals at his house in Medellin. I too share an affinity for wild creatures, but not the usual mammals. It's the reptiles that fascinate me.

"Three years ago I built this pool and had these saltwater crocs imported from Australia. They are more than just scaly pets, McCoy. I use these creatures to intimidate my enemies and settle scores with those who betray me. You are about to witness drug cartel justice."

To their left, another group of guards appeared with Lieutenant Colonel Benitez, the army officer who had sold guns to Jimenez and to the Sinaloas. They led him to the far side of the pool where the planking was attached. Benitez wore only his camouflaged pants. A guard uncuffed him and another came forward with a katana sword in his hand. He pulled the blade from its saya and, while the others covered Benitez with their guns, handed it to him, handle forward.

Benitez took the weapon in his right hand and looked at it a moment before moving his gaze to Jimenez. The look on his face was one of defeat and resignation. Jimenez returned his look with an arrogant chuckle and turned to Jack.

"The colonel is going to fight for his life on those planks. Jesus is a great martial artist and his favorite weapon in that art is the sword. He is very skilled with the long blade. Earlier I brought the Colonel here and told him that he will fight Jesus and, if he wins, he will go free. If he refuses to fight, my men will throw him into the pool alive.

"The colonel is a realist. He understands that he may have little chance against Jesus, but at least his death will be quick. It's far better than the alternative, so he will fight. One of my men will videotape it and I will send a disc to the Sinaloa boss here in Monterrey.

"It turns out the colonel's wife was that man's sister and he is thirsting for revenge. They will be coming for us in force very soon, so I want to get this done and show those bastards what happens to those who betray the Gulf."

"Sounds like you think there is only one outcome," Jack told him.

"Observe Jesus and you will see why," he said with a laugh, then turned and began issuing orders in Spanish to his men and the crowd.

The group moved closer to the edges of the pool. To Jack's right, Jesus held up his right hand and said, "Flaco."

The skinny gunman Jack had seen before came forward and handed a katana to his boss. Jesus pulled the long, curved blade from its elegant sheath and returned that item to Flaco. He clenched the sword handle in both hands and swung the blade in smooth, circular strokes. With a final look at Jack, he turned and moved to the plank walkway.

On the opposite side, Colonel Benitez stepped onto the plank and slowly moved forward to meet his opponent. He glanced nervously at the crocs below, but continued his advance, his bare feet searching for a firm grip on the plank surface. Jack turned his attention to Jesus.

The cartel killer moved out onto the plank, poised and confident, his katana by his right side. He paid no attention to the crocs and kept his focus on the nervous man inching toward him. At six feet and about 190, Jesus had a hard, muscular frame, but the most intriguing part of his physique was the large tattoo that covered his chest and stomach.

The tattoo was *La Santa Muerte*, the Mexican Goddess of Death, the female human skeletal figure dressed in a long robe and carrying a scythe in one hand. The fallen angel from Hell was popular with the drug dealers in Mexico because it was said she would forgive the most heinous of crimes committed by her devoted worshipers. Jack understood how a morally vacuous human like Jesus could murder his own sister; he had a protective saint watching over him.

The two men stopped about four feet apart on the planks. Jesus raised his katana to the basic fighting stance Jack recognized as *Chudan-gamae* in Japanese. A center-level posture with the right foot forward, the blade pointed forward at an upward angle, preventing the opponent from closing the distance.

Colonel Benitez adopted a similar stance, though not as precise. He waved the blade back and forth for a moment then lunged forward, swinging right to left at his opponent's midsection. Jesus deftly parried the blade with his and stepped back. He smiled then stepped forward and thrust his blade at the colonel's face, but at slow speed.

Benitez raised his katana and blocked the blow in time, but he was clearly alarmed at how easily Jesus could have cut him. The colonel was fit and healthy, but Jack could see that he had no experience with a sword. He recovered and adjusted his stance, bending his knees for better balance. After a moment he stepped forward quickly and swung low in a feint at Jesus's legs, then raised his blade and tried a downward cut at his head.

Jesus saw the feint and made no effort to parry. When Benitez brought his blade high to swing down, Jesus stepped forward and blocked the cut with his katana, then quickly stepped back and brought his blade down in a classic diagonal *Kesa-giri* cut across Benitez's left thigh. The cut wasn't deep, but bled profusely.

Benitez yelped in pain and stepped back, nearly losing his balance. He recovered and looked at his wound. His face was sweaty and his eyes were wide in fright. When the first drops of his blood landed in the pool, the crocodiles began thrashing and churning in the water, anticipating a meal. The scene sparked even more fear in his face.

Slowly he inched forward and made two clumsy swings at Jesus's head. The blows were easily blocked and Jesus made no effort to attack. It was clear he understood that this was an execution, not a fight. The crowd around the pool began booing and calling for Jesus to kill the Sinaloa traitor. There would be no mercy from these hardened killers.

"Jesus, *ya, basta!*" Fidel Jimenez shouted. Enough already.

Jesus said something that Jack couldn't hear, and the look on Benitez's face changed to one of anger, then rage. He lunged forward, swinging his blade back and forth while trying to keep his balance. Jesus parried each wild swing then brought his katana down in a *Gedan-gamae,* or low stance, to present his opponent an opening.

Benitez swung his blade in a wild horizontal cut at Jesus's chest. Jesus leaned back and, as the Colonel's blade swung past him, he swept his sword up in a vertical sweep, edge up, and the tip sliced Benitez's stomach from navel to thorax. Blood gushed and entrails protruded through the gaping slit. Benitez froze in place, looking down in shock at the wound.

For a moment he stared wide-eyed at Jesus, then dropped his katana into the pool and clutched his ruptured stomach with both hands. He stumbled but caught himself and stayed on his feet. Jesus studied him as wild cries from the crowd called for more blood. After a moment he stepped forward, swung his blade in a low horizontal slash, right to left, and severed Benitez's right foot above the ankle.

The army officer teetered right, arms flailing, and fell sideways toward the water below. He didn't make it. Jack cringed as the largest croc lunged upward, jaws open, and caught Benitez around the hips. He dropped below the surface, quickly followed by his two mates, and the greenish-brown water roiled violently. Moments later blood, cloth and bits of human flesh floated on the waves. The crowd roared its approval.

Jack felt little sympathy for the colonel. He'd sold his soul to the devil and had now paid the price. But even he didn't deserve this. He looked at Elena and she shook her head slightly, recognizing the depraved evil they faced.

Jesus stepped off the plank and took a rag from Flaco to wipe down his blade before putting it back in the saya. He moved next to Jack and Jimenez, a taunting smile on his face.

"Now you see what happens to those who betray my trust, McCoy," said Fidel. "I once trusted you and it cost my father's life. Tomorrow morning you will face Jesus on that plank. If you win, you and your daughter go free. If you don't, I get the justice I seek for my father. Rest well tonight. You will need it. Jesus has heard much about you and looks forward to this duel."

Jimenez signaled and Jack's guards circled him and moved him back toward the house. Others did the same with Elena. Jack looked back at the pool and thought about the fate that awaited him tomorrow. Would he too end up in the water as croc food? What would happen to his daughter and Elena?

He remembered the advice from his first SOG team leader for if they were about to be overrun by the NVA. "Never stop fighting, Jack. Fight until you win or the lights go out."

Good advice that he'd followed all his life. Tomorrow would be no different.

Chapter 22

Marco poured more coffee into Gary's cup and set the pot back on the counter. He took a sip from his own cup, made a sour face and sat down at the kitchen table. Gary finished wiping down his G36 and inserted a 30-round magazine. Laying the rifle aside, he pulled his .45 from its shoulder holster and did a function check. Satisfied his weapons were good to go, he picked up his coffee.

It was 9:00 p.m. on Wednesday evening. When the two men had escaped the Gulf narcos earlier that morning, Gary had called Viktor and Brian and briefed them on the situation. The two hopped the first plane to Laredo, used their phony passports and driver's licenses to cross the border and bought a used car in Nuevo Laredo. Marco had given them directions to his house in Monterrey.

"They should be here anytime," Gary said, glancing at the clock over the stove.

As if on cue, there was a knock at the front door. Moments later Marco greeted Viktor Tarasov and Jack's son, Brian, with a hearty *abrazo*.

"It's good to see you again, my friend," Marco told Viktor.

"Same here, Marco," said Vik. "It's been too long."

"Brian, I can't believe how much you've grown since our last visit," Marco said, one hand on Brian's shoulder. "Taller than your father now. Army life seems to agree with you."

"I like it fine, Marco, and it's good to see you again. I just wish it were different."

"So do I," Marco replied, his tone becoming more serious. "I'm glad you're here. We have much to do."

In the kitchen, Vik and Brian shook hands with Gary and sat down for a briefing on all that had happened since he and Jack had arrived in Monterrey. Twenty minutes later the mood around the table was quiet and somber.

"This place where you think they took them," said Vik, "do you know it?"

"It's Ernesto Jimenez's home on the west side of town. It's a big compound about half a mile off the main highway. Very rural. I've been there a couple of times and I know the terrain around it. There are places we can set up and watch the entry. There's a high wall around it, but we might get a visual on anyone entering or leaving."

"But what do we do after we get there, Marco?" asked Brian, the concern for his father clearly etched on his face.

"Right now I don't know, Brian. We're outnumbered and outgunned. There might be a hundred *sicarios* in that place. All we can do is go prepared and hope we get a break."

"Are you sure your GOPES unit can't offer any assistance?" asked Vik.

"I don't know the new commander well, Vik," replied Marco. "I've heard things that make me unsure if he can be trusted. I trust the men in the unit. I've worked with them for years. But I don't know about him. If we find out for sure that Jack and Elena and Brigitte are in the compound, I may ask for his help, but only if we have no choice."

"So we play it by ear and be ready if we get a chance to move," said Gary.

"Keep the faith, Brian," said Marco, noting the look on the youngster's face. "I know your dad well and these narco bastards are going to find out that Jack McCoy is not an easy man to put down."

"I hope so, Marco, but I want to be there if he needs me."

"Me too, so let's get ready to bring him home."

The sun was high when Jack's guards brought him out to the pool. Puffy white clouds floated overhead and the humid air smelled of rain. It was 9:30 a.m. and a large crowd was already gathered. Narco corridor music blared from overhead speakers. The guards took him to the side where the army colonel had mounted the planks yesterday and uncuffed him. He was ordered to remove his t-shirt and boots and then the cuffs were put back on him.

Jack actually felt good. He'd slept reasonably well during the night and the guards had brought him a light breakfast two hours earlier. Afterwards he'd stretched and done some light exercises to limber up. Now he waited.

The Jimenez brothers and their gun boss were not there yet, but a few black-clad Zetas waited across from him. Jack noted the crocs were not in the pool yet. Nor was there any evidence in the water that a man had been torn apart there yesterday. *They don't leave much behind,* Jack thought.

At that moment Fidel Jimenez came around the high wall on the other side, followed by his brother and Jesus. Behind them came Elena and his daughter, Brigitte. Both were handcuffed and surrounded by guards, including the big one named Diego and one with a bandage over his nose. Elena's left check was bruised and her lower lip swollen. A white t-shirt had replaced her green blouse.

Jack's heart sank when he saw Brigitte. If he lost this fight, he didn't want his daughter to see him go into the pool. Apparently, Jimenez felt no such compunction. The group halted near the head of the pool and Fidel Jimenez and Jesus walked forward to meet Jack. Jesus wore only his black fatigue pants and his torso muscles rippled in the sunlight.

"I trust you are well rested, McCoy," said Jimenez. "I look forward to a good fight between you and Jesus." Dressed casually again in tan chinos and a white shirt, he flashed a bright grin.

"I'm fine," Jack replied, his face showing no emotion. "What happened to Elena and why did you bring my daughter here?"

"One of the lovely sergeant's guards tried to take advantage of her last night. She broke the fool's jaw and his friends roughed her up a bit before they were pulled off. She's as dangerous as your daughter.

"And I brought your daughter so she can see what happens to people who betray me," he added, his smile disappearing. "I will take great delight in watching her reaction when Jesus feeds you to my crocs."

Jack stared into the brown orbs of the man who hated him so much, looking for some sense of humanity. While not as dead and vacant as those of Jesus, the dark eyes held nothing but a latent cruelty. The cheerful, friendly expression of the ten-year-old boy was long gone.

"I brought someone else who wants to see you fight for your life," Jimenez added, raising one hand in a signal.

From the group of guards a tall, lean white man in a brown Polo shirt and jeans walked forward to join them. As he drew closer, Jack understood why he was here.

"Hello, McCoy," the man said in a raspy, smoker's voice. "Been a long time, huh?"

For a moment Jack only stared at Mace Reynolds, a man who'd once been a colleague and partner, a member of his sheriff's department narcotics team investigating the major drug dealers in the Las Vegas area. Jack hadn't liked him much because of his arrogant, abrasive manner, but considered him a good investigator.

Until the team's drug investigations began to go bad. Known drug safe houses were empty when the team arrived to serve a search warrant. Dealers who had sold drugs to undercover detectives disappeared when they were named in arrest warrants. Jack knew they had a leak and a close look revealed the common thread in each investigation was Mace Reynolds.

The Narcotics commander approved a wiretap and Jack inserted a listening device in Reynolds' portable radio. The drop-in transmitter could be remotely activated with high-tech equipment loaned to them by the DEA. Within days they recorded Reynolds conspiring with the Colombian drug boss in Vegas to protect his drug stash houses and provide him with information on the team's investigations into his drug dealing activities.

When the Colombian and his Mexican cohorts were taken down, Jack had personally handcuffed Reynolds and booked him into the Clark County jail. He'd pleaded guilty before trial and was sentenced to fifteen years in state prison. Jack knew he'd been paroled after nine years and returned to Vegas, but had lost track of him after that. Now he was back.

"Hello, Mace," Jack replied. "Looks like you found your way home."

"Fuck you, McCoy," Reynolds spat at him. "I did nine years in High Desert because of you and I swore I'd get even with your ass for that. Now it's my turn to laugh when those crocs tear you apart."

Jack knew Reynolds was in his early fifties, but he looked ten years older. His short hair, once blonde, was nearly white and receding in front. His blue eyes were rheumy and his skin pasty and blotchy. His tobacco-stained teeth were chipped and broken. At six-three he weighed about 170 pounds. A long fall from grace.

"I never laughed, Mace," Jack told him. "You sold your soul and your badge. That wasn't funny, just pathetic."

"Mace has been part of my team for six years now," said Jimenez. "He has to leave when this is over, but I wanted him to be here—sort of a reward for his service."

"Your team?" Jack asked.

"Mace handles our business in Las Vegas. He sets up landing strips in the desert for my planes that take product there for distribution to California and the Pacific Northwest. He takes it to stash houses for cutting and repackaging and arranges transportation to the final destinations. He even helps with our competition.

"Last year he discovered a stash house in Henderson used by the Sinaloas. He gathered information on it and Jesus sent a team to take them out. We got a ton of uncut cocaine and killed the five Sinaloa dogs guarding it. Those bastards still don't know who sold them out."

Jack remembered the incident. The Henderson PD had investigated but never found the suspects.

"He also gathered the information I needed about your late wife," Jimenez continued, his gaze checking for Jack's reaction.

"When Fidel told me what he wanted," said Reynolds, fishing a pack of Camels and a lighter out of his jeans pocket, "I followed your old lady around for a week and watched her routine. I gave the information to the man Fidel sent to Vegas and I watched from the corner when he ran her down. Most fun I'd had in a long time," he added as he blew smoke in Jack's face and laughed out loud.

It took tremendous self-restraint, but Jack made no move toward Reynolds. If he survived, a time would come for that.

"Enough of this," Jimenez said. "It's time to make things right for my father." He signaled and a man with a katana joined them from the crowd. Jimenez and Reynolds then returned to stand with the others at the far side of the pool.

"Mace told me about the outlaws you killed in Vegas last year," Jesus told him, "and the professional gunmen you and your friends took down. He also says you are a good martial artist. I haven't had a challenge like you since the one who put this scar on my arm. I put him in the water, too. I've fed seventeen men to those crocs, *gringo*. Will you be number eighteen?"

"You talk too much, Jesus," Jack said, his hard blue eyes returning the killer's glare with equal intensity.

The Zeta boss took the katana from the *sicario* next to him and motioned with his head. The man unlocked Jack's handcuffs and stepped back. While the guards held their AK-47s on him, Jesus handed Jack the sword.

"Then I will let my blade speak for me," he said.

Chapter 23

As the Zeta boss moved to his side of the pool, Jack looked at the katana he held. It was his own, the one given to him by his martial arts mentor, Danny Kim. The one Jesus had used to kill Ana. He gripped the red and black leather-wrapped handle and pulled the blade from the black bamboo *saya*. The weight felt familiar and comforting. He held it up and sunlight glinted off the stainless-steel blade.

Jack thought about the hundreds of hours he and Danny Kim had spent sparring with their wooden *bokken* and bamboo *shinai* swords in Danny's Fighting Den studio. Kim had dedicated his life to the martial arts and held black belts in multiple disciplines. In his twenties he'd spent three years in Japan studying karate, jujitsu, and *Kenjutsu*, the art of the sword.

After opening the Fighting Den, he'd taught those skills to Jack and a few others in his martial arts circle. Jack had long admired the Japanese Samurai, the military nobility who fought for pride and honor. He'd begun studying *Kenjutsu* with Danny as a way to honor those great warriors. After twenty-five years of practice he was nearly the equal of his mentor.

Would it be enough to survive this battle? Maybe. He had more experience with the blade than the Zeta boss knew. He also had another edge: super-fast reflexes he'd inherited at birth. Fast-twitch muscle that had given him the ability to spar with heavyweight professionals and out gun the best marksmen in competition shooting. But there was one edge that outweighed all the others, he knew as he stepped toward the plank where the Zeta boss waited: the desire to save his daughter's life.

Fidel Jimenez stepped to the edge of the pool and uttered the series of grunts that told his pets it was feeding time. In a few moments the long, scaly forms slid out of the brush and down the sandy bank to the water. Slight ripples followed behind them until they reached the opposite end and began circling under the plank.

Jimenez smiled and signaled to the man operating the stereo. Showdown music from A Fistful of Dollars, his favorite Spaghetti western, filled the air. Liquor flowed and the crowd of *sicarios* began chanting for blood. Jimenez stepped back and stood next to his brother, savoring the moment.

"I love you, Daddy," cried McCoy's daughter from behind and to his right. Jimenez looked back as a guard smacked her on the head. Next to her Sgt. Cisneros cursed and kicked at the man. Jimenez shook his head sternly and the guard stepped back. Let the daughter encourage her father. It wouldn't help.

"You can beat this thug, Daddy." Brigitte cried out. "You're Jack McCoy. You have fools like him for breakfast. I believe in you."

"I love you, sweetheart," McCoy shouted from his position on the plank. "No matter what happens, remember that."

As McCoy moved forward, Jimenez studied the man he'd wanted to kill for so long. He was in great physical condition for a man his age. Broad shoulders and a wide chest sloped down to a flat, chiseled stomach. His arm muscles flexed and tightened. Weight training had clearly enhanced the muscular frame Jimenez remembered.

His short, brown hair was flecked with gray now and his nose had a slight bend. A two-day stubble of beard covered his cheeks. A short cut scar protruded from his hairline and an old bullet wound marked his right chest. His right side showed puckered, shrapnel scars and his left another bullet scar just above the belt. His left arm was heavily scarred at the elbow. Marks of a warrior's life.

Jimenez had been concerned his younger Zeta chief might have a lopsided advantage. Now he wasn't so sure. McCoy looked like a formidable opponent, a taller, stronger version of Jesus. If he had any skill with the sword, this contest might not turn out the way Jimenez had expected.

Jack paused to orient himself on the plank. The wood grain was rough and gave his bare feet good purchase. The six-inch width was sufficient, but allowed little room for error. Below the giant crocs circled menacingly. He flexed his leg muscles and stepped forward to meet Jesus at the halfway point.

The Zeta chief smiled and assumed the *Chudan-gamae,* or basic fighting stance. Jack took the same stance, his right hand behind the circular guard, the left closer to the end of the hilt. His attention was squarely on his opponent, not what lay beneath them. For a moment neither moved, then Jesus's smile disappeared and he stepped forward with a classic *Tsuki,* or straight thrust, at Jack's chest.

He was fast, but Jack raised his katana and parried the thrust with the side of his blade then leaned in and slashed right, and the tip of his sword opened a shallow cut across Jesus's chest, directly through the face of La Santa Muerte.

The Zeta boss stepped back, surprise, then anger, clouding his face. The fight barely started and first blood drawn by his opponent. Probably not what he had expected. His eyes narrowed and he went into a *Jodan-game,* a high-level, aggressive posture with his blade held backward over his head at a forty-five degree angle, prepared to strike at any angle.

Jack smiled inwardly and watched blood flow down the gunman's chest to soak his black fatigue pants. *Lesson learned,* he thought, knowing Jesus wouldn't underestimate him again. He assumed the *Hasso-gamae,* left foot forward, his katana held at face level slightly away from his body, ready to swing in any direction.

Footwork and positioning was the key to gaining advantage in *Kenjutsu,* but that was negated by the narrow bridge on which they fought. Now balance, reach and flexibility would determine the outcome. A weakness by one's opponent would also help, Jack knew, and he moved forward to find that link.

He aggressively closed the distance and swung his blade in a *Yoko-giri,* a horizontal side cut, left to right, at Jesus's chest. The Zeta boss stepped back, narrowly avoiding another cut, and came back with a *Kesa-giri,* a downward diagonal cut from right shoulder to left hip. Jack parried the strike with the back of his own blade and countered with a *Kiri-oshi*, a downward straight cut as his opponent leaned forward.

The cat-like Jesus leaned back in time to avoid the strike and Jack's blade cut thin air. Without pausing Jesus bent his knees, drew back to high guard position and came around in another *Yoko-giri* at Jack's legs. Jack was still raising his katana and Jesus's blade slipped under it. The tip caught Jack's forward left leg mid-thigh and opened a four-inch wide gash.

The pain was immediate and intense. Jack stepped back and his left leg buckled, throwing him off balance. He caught himself in time and straightened, his feet regaining purchase. He went back into *Chudan-gamae,* his blade forward to counter an attack as he re-assessed. Jesus was good. Even wounded he still worked his blade with skill.

Now Jack, too, was bleeding. He glanced down quickly and saw blood soaking his tan pant leg. The cut wasn't deep, but it would need stitches and the loss of blood would weaken him. The blood from Jesus's wound was already dripping into the pool and the crocs were churning the water. The crowd was calling for more blood. He needed to end this quickly.

"Did you think this would be easy, *gringo?*" Jesus asked with an open sneer, his katana at high guard. "You got lucky. Now that luck is over."

"You're still talking, Jesus," Jack told him. "You should be fighting."

The Zeta's eyes flashed with anger and he stepped forward, feinted with a *Yogo-giri* side cut from the left, then crouched and swung his blade in an upward diagonal slash from the right. Jack saw the feint and brought his katana down in a side block to deflect the upward cut. Jesus pulled back, looked hard at Jack, then crept forward and launched a flurry of slashes.

Jack parried, slipped and blocked in solid defense mode for a full minute, the clash of steel blades carrying above the background music. Finally, Jesus ceased his attack and stepped back, chest heaving, his open mouth sucking in air. He'd failed to penetrate Jack's defense and his face showed frustration.

Jack had not countered the onslaught of strikes, instead using defense to wear his opponent down and watch his moves. It had worked. Jesus had shown a preference to feint with a diagonal downward *Kisa-giri* from either side, then reverse to a *Yogo-giri,* right to left while leaning forward on his left foot. *Know your enemy, know his sword.* A classic quote in the Book of Five Rings by Miyamoto Musashi, the legendary swordsman of seventeenth century Japan. *Now to use that knowledge.*

Moving into a *Hasso-gamae*, Jack edged forward for his own attack. His leg wound had left the plank slick with blood and his left heel slipped, tilting him sideways. He righted himself in time, but Jesus used the distraction to lurch forward and slash at his neck. Jack caught the strike with the back of his katana, pushed it away and swung a reverse cut under Jesus's blade. The tip swept across both of his thighs just above the knees.

Jesus grunted loudly with pain and surprise as he stepped back and looked at the blood gushing from his legs. The cuts were deep and bleeding heavily. Time was no longer on the Zeta's side and for the first time Jack saw fear in his eyes.

Jack glanced down at the crocs, now in frenzy from the men's bloody wounds, then brought his attention back to his adversary. He stepped forward just as Jesus swung another diagonal, left to right *Kesa-giri* strike. This time his own bloody feet slipped under him and sent him off balance. He quickly righted himself just as Jack came down with an overhead *Kiri-oshi*.

Jesus leaned back in time to avoid having his head cleaved, but Jack's blade opened a long slash on the right side of his chest from shoulder to diaphragm. The Zeta grunted sharply and stepped back, his eyes wide in shock as lung tissue protruded through the slit.

"Not as much fun when they can fight back, is it?" Jack said with a taunting smile.

"I will gut you for that, *gringo*," Jesus replied, his voice wheezing and his features twisting with rage and hatred as blood flowed down his chest.

"You're talking again, asshole. You want my blood? Come and get it."

Jesus screamed a loud curse and lunged forward, slashing and cutting. Jack parried and blocked, deflecting every strike. After a minute Jesus pulled back. He was losing strength from the loss of blood and Jack could see desperation in his eyes now. He had one more attack in him and Jack was sure what it would be.

Jesus steadied himself and moved in with a left to right *Kesa-giri* diagonal downward slash with full speed. Jack parried with the back of his katana and pushed his opponent's blade to the side. Without stopping his momentum, Jesus swung to his right and up then reversed into a diagonal right to left *Kesa-giri*.

Jack knew this would be a feint and that Jesus expected him to raise his katana in a blocking motion as before. Instead, he leaned back and dropped the tip of his blade to the plank. Jesus had already turned the *Kesa-giri* into a *Yoko-giri* right to left side cut. When he realized Jack had not taken the bait, it was too late.

As the blade swept past him, Jack brought his katana up with all the strength in his upper body. The forward edge caught

Jesus's right arm between wrist and elbow and severed it completely. A geyser of blood gushed from the stump as the Zeta stumbled forward and released the grip with his left hand. The katana flew into the pool and one of the crocs lunged after the bloody hand still grasping the hilt.

For a moment Jesus simply stared at his right arm, now minus the hand, then grasped it just below the stump with his left and squeezed hard. The blood flow slowed to heavy ooze. Eyes wide he looked up at the man who'd beaten him. He found no mercy in Jack's hard glare. He twisted to look at the now silent crowd. The music had stopped and no one spoke, speechless at what they had just witnessed.

Jesus turned back toward. Jack. His pale face was beaded with sweat and his legs wobbled. "You win, *gringo*," he said weakly, dropping his right arm to his side, "but I go out my own way."

The blood began gushing from the stump again and Jack knew what he meant. In thirty seconds he would faint from loss of blood before falling into the pool and would escape the horror of feeling his body torn apart by the crocs.

"You don't get off that easy, you son-of-a-bitch," Jack snarled at him.

He stepped forward and raised his katana in a *Jodan-gamae*. "Ana Lopez sends her regards," he said and swung the blade low in a right to left *Yogo-giri*. The edge struck the Zeta's left leg below the knee and swept through it like soft butter.

Jesus's severed leg fell left and his body teetered right, his arms swinging wildly. He screamed loudly as he dropped into the pool. The largest of the three crocs lunged out of the water, clamped its jaws around his waist and dropped below the surface, shutting off Jesus's scream. The other two joined their mate and the water roiled and churned. In seconds blood and human tissue created a gory red soup in the pool.

Jack stared at the mess below him for a moment then looked across the pool at the man responsible for the bloody death. Fidel Jimenez's face showed no emotion. His calm expression gave Jack no indication whether he would keep his word to free him and Brigitte if he won the fight. Something in the dark eyes staring at Jack told him his fight for survival had just begun.

Chapter 24

"That should hold for now," the doctor said in Spanish as he finished taping the bandage over Jack's wound and stood up. "The painkiller I gave you will wear off in a few hours and you'll feel some discomfort."

A short, slender man around forty with wire-rim glasses and a bald dome, he had just closed the cut on Jack's left leg with a hand-held surgical skin stapler. He began putting his medical supplies back into his satchel as Jack stood up and tested the leg. The wound was numb and he could walk with a slight limp.

"That's okay, doc, thanks for your help," he told the man.

"In two weeks you should have those staples removed," the doctor said with a look that told Jack he doubted that would be necessary.

Jack simply nodded as the man turned and left the room, followed by the two armed *sicarios* standing at the door. Alone again, he removed his ruined BDUs and put on the worn jeans and red t-shirt the guards had brought him when the doctor arrived. The pants were a little large in the waist, but his belt kept them in place.

He sat down on the bed and wondered what was next. Jimenez had dismissed the crowd after the fight and ordered the guards to take Jack back to his room. He'd not even had a chance to say anything to Brigitte or Elena. The Gulf gunmen at the pool were in a foul mood over the death of their boss and Jack heard mumbles of revenge as he was led away. Was Jimenez keeping him alive to entertain his men?

That answer came quickly. The door was unlocked and Fidel Jimenez walked in with six guards. Five were armed with Galil assault rifles. The sixth, Diego, wore a Glock on his belt. All of them appeared alert and on edge. Jack stood up to greet his visitors.

"You're probably wondering why I sent my doctor to fix your wound," Jimenez said as he stopped in front of Jack. Dressed in jeans, hiking shoes and a tan canvas shirt, he looked ready to travel.

"I'm wondering why you haven't kept your word to free my daughter and me like you said," Jack replied. "Is a lack of honor just the Jimenez legacy?"

Diego, standing behind and slightly to the left of his boss, stepped forward and swung an open-hand strike at Jack's face. Jack's right hand caught his in mid-air and clamped down like a hydraulic vice. Bones cracked and the big gunman howled and buckled forward. Jack released him, put his palm against the killer's forehead and shoved him back. The other guards moved in, but Jimenez raised his hand and halted them.

"That was foolish, Diego," he said. "Don't do that again without my permission."

"*Si, patron,*" Diego uttered through clenched teeth, directing a murderous glare at Jack as he clutched his mangled hand.

"Diego handles my personal security and he's very protective," Jimenez told Jack. "He takes it personally when someone insults me. Remember that."

"I will," Jack replied.

"You knew I wouldn't let you go, McCoy. I'll admit that I thought you were dead and I wouldn't have to keep my word. I underestimated you. So did Jesus. But your debt to me is too great to let you go without avenging my father's death, and I want you in good health until then.

"Right now I have more important concerns. The Sinaloas are preparing to attack us in force. I have a man inside their organization and he sent word that they are bringing re-enforcements from Saltillo and Torreon. Their boss in Monterrey wants revenge for his sister and control of our smuggling routes.

"Most of my men are guarding shipments on the way to the border. I'm calling some of them back and moving to a more heavily fortified compound in the hills west of here. If they attack us there, we'll destroy them. I was planning to take you with me, but I have to meet some state police officials and find out if they can help us with the Sinaloa bastards, so I'm sending you and

Sgt. Cisneros with an escort. Your daughter and the others will follow. Don't worry, I'll be there soon and when these troubles are over, you and I will settle."

"I look forward to it," said Jack.

Jimenez nodded at Diego and the guards surrounded Jack and cuffed his hands behind his back. With Diego leading, he was taken back through the opulent residence and out a side door that opened to a long driveway. A red Ford F-250 Lobo model and three SUVs were lined up facing the front gate. The guards led Jack to a black Chevy Tahoe with its engine running and opened the door to the middle seat. On the passenger side sat a handcuffed Elena.

A guard shoved Jack into the seat and closed the door. A *sicario* behind the wheel glared at him but said nothing. Jack looked at Elena and gave her a tight smile. Her cheek was still bruised, but her cut lip was less swollen. She nodded and said, "I'm glad you survived."

"*Callate!*" the driver shouted, telling her to shut up.

Jack nodded and smiled again, but said nothing. Looking out the window he saw Jimenez talking to a gunman in black fatigues and carrying an M-4 assault rifle. After a minute Jimenez disappeared and the Zeta spoke into a portable radio. Shortly, several more gunmen armed with a variety of assault rifles appeared in the driveway.

Two entered the cab of the F-250 while two more climbed into the truck bed. Two more got into the rear seat of the Tahoe behind Jack and Elena while the black-clad Zeta climbed into the front passenger seat. Jack glanced back and saw at least a dozen gunmen get into the two black GMC Yukon Denalis behind them. They were taking the Sinaloa threat seriously.

The Zeta began issuing orders on his radio and the front gate opened. The pickup drove forward and the Tahoe driver followed close behind. Outside the gate Jack saw they were moving down a long, narrow dirt lane that led to a main road in the distance. On each side were cleared fields and scattered stands of trees and brush. Low hills rose a few hundred yards to their left and cattle and horses grazed near the bottom. The day was sunny and hot. Afternoon storm clouds were forming to the south.

Jack noted that neither he nor Elena had been blindfolded. Apparently, Jimenez didn't care what they saw now. Not a good sign. He looked at the hills in the distance and wondered if Marco and Gary were out there somewhere, watching them. He hoped his friends had survived. If so, they would be there, waiting for a chance to strike. Of that he was certain.

"We got more coming out," Gary told Marco as he peered through his Leupold 10x42s at the line of vehicles leaving the compound. The two men were on a low hill about 500 yards east of the intersection of the dirt lane and the paved road. They were hidden by thick oak brush and mesquite trees that covered the knoll. A hundred yards to their right, Viktor Tarasov and Brian McCoy were set up on another hilltop. It was just past noon and the sun was blazing hot.

The men had arrived there at four in the morning, driving to the rear of the hills across rough pastureland after leaving the paved road a mile from the compound. They'd driven there in the used Chevy Blazer that Vik and Brian had bought in Nuevo Laredo and a ten-year-old Jeep they'd purchased in Monterrey the previous evening.

Marco had used the two hills as observation posts a year ago while conducting surveillance on the Jimenez compound and knew the terrain. After setting up, the two teams kept in touch with a set of Motorola portable radios that Marco brought from the arms cache at his house. He also supplied Vik and Brian with side arms and assault rifles.

Marco had been napping under a thick bush a few yards away. On hearing Gary's warning, he picked up his Steiner binoculars and crawled next to his friend for a view.

"That's the second convoy in two hours," he said as the vehicles turned right on the main road.

"Yeah," Gary replied, "I just wish we were close enough to see who's inside."

"They could be in one of those vehicles."

"They could have been in the other ones, too."

"I know. What do you think?"

"I say we follow this one and find out. Vik and Brian can keep watch here. What's the range on the radios?"

"Ten miles, fifteen on high ground," Marco told him.

"I think it's worth the risk."

"I think you're right," said Marco as he unclipped the Motorola from his belt and depressed the transmit button.

"Vik, Brian, you there?" he asked.

"Yeah, Marco, go ahead," answered Tarasov a moment later.

"You see the convoy?"

"Yeah, we're on it."

"Gary and I are going to follow and try to find out if Jack and the girls are in it. You guys stay on things here and let us know if anything happens."

"Roger that."

Gary and Marco picked up their backpacks and rifles and hurried down the back side of the hill. Marco took the wheel of the Jeep and headed out as fast as the rough ground allowed. Fifteen minutes later they pulled onto the paved road and headed for the cartel caravan at full speed. The dented and rusted old white Jeep fit well in the local traffic.

Ten minutes later they were slowed by a cattle truck in front of them. Marco swerved left for a better view and saw a red sedan in front of the truck. Ahead of that car was the last Yukon Denali in the convoy. Marco settled in behind the livestock hauler and he and Gary prepared for the next battle to rescue their friends.

Jack could see they were moving in a northwest direction, away from the Monterrey metropolitan area. Looking back, he could see the Cerro de la Silla looming over the city's skyline several miles to the southeast. Traffic on the road was light. An occasional car or old farm truck passed them going in the opposite direction. The area was rural and the few houses in sight were set back from the road. As they moved ahead, the terrain on both sides of the road became more hilly and broken.

"Jesus was my friend, *gringo*," said the Zeta in Spanish as he looked back at Jack and Elena. "I will ask the patron for permission to make you pay for his death." The man was a near copy of his dead boss, just shorter with a leaner frame. His eyes had the same deadly look.

"Will my hands still be cuffed?" Jack asked, his own eyes returning the gunman's glare.

"Perhaps," he replied with no hint of reproach. He turned his attention to Elena.

"I will also take great pleasure in making your friend part of the patron's stable."

"Touch me, you pig, and it will be the last thing you do in this life," Elena told him in a cold, flat voice that left no doubt how she felt.

"We'll see," he said with a sinister grin.

Just then the Tahoe began slowing and the Zeta keyed his radio for a report from the *sicarios* in the F-250. A voice came back that an old pickup with a camper shell had pulled out in front of them from a side road. He was about to tell them to go around when a smoky, red streak flashed across the road to their right front and the Ford truck blew apart in a fiery explosion.

Chapter 25

The doors and hood blew off the big pickup and the frame bulged before it rolled over twice and came to a stop on the other side of the road. It was ompletely engulfed in flames. The two *sicarios* in the bed were blown skyward, their arms and legs flying in different directions. Those in the cab were no longer visible.

Jack realized they had driven into a Sinaloa ambush as automatic rifle fire erupted from the rocky outcrop on their right. The Tahoe driver slammed on the brakes and stopped at an angle in the middle of the road. The Zeta boss shouted orders into his radio and jumped out on the passenger side. He fired his M4 at the attackers as he ran to the other side of the truck, but a storm of bullets slammed him against the hood and dropped him to the ground.

"Elena, on the floor!" Jack shouted. They had not been belted to their seats and quickly dove to the floor, with Jack on top of Elena, as the two gunmen in the back seat scrambled out the driver side door. Rounds smashed through the windows and doors and Jack could feel the heat as they passed over his back.

The shooting shifted to their rear as the *sicarios* from the Tahoe and those in the Denalis returned fire. The battle roared on for a full minute before another explosion behind them rocked the Tahoe. Scattered shots continued for another minute, and then silence took hold.

"You okay?" Jack whispered to Elena as he raised his head slightly from her back.

"I think so," she replied, turning and looking up at him. Her eyes were wide, but Jack saw no fear in them. Outside they could hear shouts and the sound of engines moving close. After a minute the passenger door was opened by a young gunman with an AK-47. He looked at them a moment then shouted to someone behind him that he had prisoners.

A few moments later an older gunman carrying an M-16 assault rifle appeared in the door. He reached in and pulled Jack out by his t-shirt. He stood him against the side of the Tahoe, then did the same with Elena. The gunman told his young partner to watch them, then turned and walked to the rear.

The scene around them was one of utter chaos. Dark smoke rose skyward from the blazing F-250. The last Denali behind them had also been blown apart with a rocket-propelled grenade and was on fire. Jack could see the bodies of three Gulf *sicarios* who'd gotten out on the wrong side of the Denali behind them. The body of the Zeta boss lay near the front of the Tahoe.

Over twenty armed gunmen swarmed the area. Most were dressed in civilian clothes, but some wore camouflaged uniforms and they carried a variety of assault rifles and side arms. Some stood in the rocks where the ambush had been sprung. Others moved around the vehicles shouting commands at the surviving Gulf *sicarios* on the other side of the Tahoe.

Two Chevy pickup trucks had stopped across the road near the burning Ford. Two gunmen stood in the bed of each one. Next to them was a white Range Rover. Glancing to the rear, Jack could see three large black SUVs blocking the road behind the burning Denali.

Jack and Elena exchanged glances but said nothing to each other as the young gunman with the AK glared at them from a few feet away. Someone on the other side of the Tahoe shouted at him to bring the prisoners there. The youngster motioned with his rifle and Jack and Elena walked around the SUV to where most of the narcos were gathered.

Scattered on the pavement behind the bullet-riddled Denalis were the bloody bodies of seven Gulf soldiers. Nine still alive were being dragged and pushed to the side of the road by the Sinaloa gunmen. Four of those were wounded and bleeding heavily. The kid stopped them a few feet from a group of four older men. One of those was talking on a portable radio.

Dressed in jeans, a white shirt, western boots and a gray Stetson hat, he seemed to be in charge. Voices on his radio advised that they had the road blocked, but traffic was backing up and the police were coming soon. The man told them to hold the traffic until he had dealt with the prisoners. He clipped the radio on his belt next to a 1911 .45 ACP and turned to face Jack and Elena.

A little under six feet tall with a heavy build, he was in his mid-forties. His short, dark hair showed gray at the temples and he had a thick mustache. Heavy brows lay over a pair of mirrored Ray Bans. Jack wasn't sure why, but the man had a familiar look.

"You must be Jack McCoy," he said in Spanish in a deep voice, "and you would be Sergeant Cisneros," he added, looking at Elena. His teeth were a dazzling white against his dark complexion.

Neither Jack nor Elena said anything.

"Don't be surprised, McCoy," he said. "I run security for the Sinaloa boss in Monterrey and we have people in the Jimenez compound. I know about his feud with you and the fight with El Bruto at the pool. I wish you hadn't killed that bastard. I wanted to do that myself."

"Sorry to disappoint," Jack said in a dry tone.

"You didn't," he replied with a chuckle. "I'm glad that *hijo de puta* is dead, but now I have to deal with you. Jimenez knows we're coming for him after what he did to my patron's sister and her kids. He has a fortress in the mountains west of here and I thought he might be on his way there. We got you and the Sergeant instead. He probably went to see his friends in the Federales to try and save his ass."

"He told me the State Police," Jack replied.

"I like you, McCoy," the Sinaloa gun boss said, chuckling loudly. "Even now, facing death, you can still joke. It's too bad you're a goddamn cop." Before he could say anything else, a man came running from the direction of the Range Rover.

"*Jefe*, the state police and the military are on the way here," he said. "They're about thirty minutes out."

"I should just shoot you and this Federal bitch," the boss told Jack, "but I need to consult with my patron first and make sure he doesn't have any use for you. That means you get to live a bit longer."

He turned and looked at the Gulf *sicarios* lined up on the side of the road. "These assholes don't get that break," he continued and then shouted orders at his men. Those guarding the prisoners began pushing them into a kneeling position at the top of a bank a few feet from the pavement. The bank sloped down into a ravine full of brush.

The defeated gunmen offered no resistance. They seemed to have accepted their fate and stared blankly at their captors. A couple of the younger ones cried quietly. The Sinaloas, nearly twenty of them, stood in the middle of the road, assault rifles leveled at their enemies.

The gun boss moved Jack and Elena near the back of the Tahoe with three guards.

"Watch closely, McCoy," he said. "This is what happens to Gulf scum who try to steal our drugs and smuggling routes."

He moved forward a few steps and told his men to open fire. The tremendous roar of automatic rifles shattered the silence and a barrage of metal-jacketed bullets slammed into the kneeling men. The air behind them became a bloody haze as their heads blew apart and their chests and throats were riddled with dozens of rounds. Some fell straight down, but most tumbled backward down the embankment.

The firing stopped and the men went forward to check the bodies. A few more shots sounded at the bottom of the slope. A minute later a gunman appeared at the top and gave his boss a signal.

The Sinaloa chief gave more orders and his men began moving to the vehicles at each end of the ambush. Two brought cans of gasoline and splashed the liquid inside the Tahoe and the Denali behind it, then dropped matches through the broken windows. Jack and Elena were herded into the back seat of a Chevy Expedition with four guards and a driver. A moment later they were moving up the road in the same direction as before the ambush.

As they passed an old truck with a camper shell, Jack looked back at the mass of burning vehicles and bodies on the road. Somehow he and Elena had survived another bloody encounter with the narco terrorists. How much longer could their luck hold? Looking at the hard faces surrounding him in the SUV, he figured their time was about up.

"We need to follow them," Gary told Marco as the Sinaloa caravan drove away. Both men were crouched behind a large boulder twenty yards off the road and had just watched the brutal killing of the Gulf *sicarios* through their binoculars. Their Jeep was in a line of vehicles still stopped on the road where the gunmen had blocked their path, the drivers too afraid to move.

"I know, but it's going to be tough," Marco replied. "They can see us a long ways out here. We'll have to be careful."

"We can lay back and use the glasses to keep them in sight. Now that we know Jack and Elena are still alive, we've got to stay with them. They're probably taking them somewhere to get rid of them. We can't let that happen."

"I agree. I'd bet Brigitte is still in the compound, but I think something is going on. It looks like the Sinaloas are making a move on them and Jimenez is moving his people to new locations. If we can get Jack and Elena free, maybe they'll know where he's taking Brigitte. It's not much, Gary, but it's all we have. We're working blind here."

"I know, buddy. Let's do it."

The two men ran back to the Jeep and drove around the other vehicles. At the scene of the ambush, people were gathering to gawk at the bodies and burning SUVs. Marco steered around the crowd and moved on up the road in pursuit of the departing narcos. Gary used the Motorola to tell Viktor and Brian what had happened and to follow after them.

He told them the police would be at the ambush site and to use the four-wheel drive in their Blazer to go off road and move around it. Their plan was to follow the Sinaloas and hope for a chance to rescue Jack and Elena. His friends notified, Gary picked up his binoculars and watched the road ahead. Now the real work began.

Chapter 26

Fidel Jimenez closed his cell phone and uttered a loud curse. Not prone to losing his temper, he surprised the others in the room with a string of expletives. With him were his brother, Javier; his security chief, Diego; and Bernardo Huerta, the new Zeta boss. Huerta had been Jesus's *segundo* or second-in-charge, and, like his late boss, he wore a black t-shirt and black fatigue pants bloused in combat boots. The thirty-year old had also deserted the Mexican Army for a more lucrative career with the drug cartels.

They were gathered in a large room in the Jimenez compound that served as a place for entertainment and meetings to discuss cartel business. Diego had asked his boss to meet after receiving a distressed radio call from the caravan transporting McCoy and the female federal officer to Jimenez's fortress in the hills, which was called the Eagle's Nest. The meeting had just begun when Jimenez's phone rang.

"That was Fuentes, the state police captain on my payroll," he told them as he stopped cursing and calmed himself. "The Sinaloas ambushed the escort on the road outside of Villa de Garcia. All of our men are dead and they took McCoy and Cisneros. He put out patrols and a plane to try and spot them, but it's probably too late."

"*Patron,* how did they know about the convoy?" asked Diego. "We told no one."

"One of your men is a Sinaloa, Diego. We put spies in their camp, they do the same with us. Find out who he is and deal with him."

"I will, *Patron, en seguida.*" At once.

"Can Fuentes help us find McCoy?" asked Javier.

"Maybe. If they can find the Sinaloas and they haven't already killed him. I want McCoy back, but we have to deal with our immediate threat first. My source tells me they will have over one hundred fifty men when their re-enforcements arrive. We have forty at the Nest and about thirty here. Bernardo, how many are you bringing back?"

"Just over forty, *Jefe,*" replied Huerta. "I had to leave some men on the loads coming up from Vera Cruz and we have crossings at the river tonight in Nuevo Laredo and Reynosa. We also have planes leaving Nuevo Laredo tomorrow tonight for Las Vegas and Albuquerque. They need protection until they leave. It's the best I can do for now. Those returning should be here by tomorrow night."

"Good. If they hit us at the Nest, they'll need a thousand men. I want everyone there by tomorrow evening. We'll leave twenty here for security and our friends in the Federal Police will increase their patrols around the compound. Diego, Javier and I need to visit some friends and we'll go straight to the Nest tomorrow."

"I'll get a detail together right away, *Patron.*"

"Bernado, make sure the women get there and that we have sufficient weapons and equipment if they come for us."

"The Nest is well stocked, Boss, and I can bring more from our cache in Agua Blanca if necessary. I'll transport the women this afternoon."

"Very well, let's get to it."

While Javier and Diego organized the departure for Monterrey and the Eagle's Nest, Jimenez opened his cell phone and began dialing. The loss of McCoy was a setback, but only a temporary one. Jimenez had friends in high places who could help him find his old nemesis. He and his brother had waited over twenty years for their revenge. They could wait a bit longer.

It was late afternoon when the Expedition in front of the white Range Rover rounded a curve on the dirt road and Jack saw what appeared to be their destination through the windshield: an abandoned farmhouse in a grove of oak and sycamore trees. High weeds surrounded the house and two outbuildings with caved in roofs. An old stone corral sat to one side.

The route there had been long and circuitous. The Sinaloa caravan included the security boss's Range Rover, the two Expeditions and a red Chevy Silverado pickup carrying six *sicarios*. Two other Chevy pickups had left in another direction. After leaving the ambush they had passed through the small village of Villa de Garcia and then turned off on a dirt road and crossed over the Rio Vesqueria, or Vesqueria River.

The Range Rover carried police scanners and the security boss told the driver in Jack's vehicle that they were being hunted by the military and state police. For a while they stopped under a thick stand of pine trees while a plane flew overhead. After an hour they continued another few miles and returned to the main highway.

The convoy drove through another small village called Icamole. As they passed a Pemex gas station, Jack saw a police car and a green Chevy Blazer at the pumps. The officer looked up at the passing vehicles, but made no attempt to follow the obvious cartel caravan. *Smart move*, thought Jack.

A few miles past Icamole the lead Expedition again turned south on a dirt road and fifteen minutes later came to the old farm. A shallow stream crossed the road sixty yards from the house and the Silverado stopped on the bank after crossing. The other vehicles continued on and stopped in the weed-filled front yard.

The guards piled out of the Expedition first then pulled Jack and Elena out the side doors. The security chief got out of the Range Rover, but his driver remained inside. The gunmen in the other Expedition also stayed inside the vehicle. Jack's guards pushed him and Elena forward when their boss motioned them to go inside.

The old house was built of stone and concrete. The wood shingle roof was still in place but in disrepair. The two front windows were broken out and the front door was missing. Inside Jack saw that the front room had served as a living area with a small kitchen off to the right side. An open door at the back wall led to another room. A rusty wood stove stood along one wall and an old brown cloth sofa against another. Dust covered everything. "Your new home, McCoy," said the security boss as he took off his Stetson and wiped his forehead with a handkerchief. "For the time you have left."

"So, what's next?" Jack asked, glancing first at Elena standing next to him.

"I'm waiting for a call from my boss in Monterrey. I spoke to him on the way here, but he's distracted with the Gulf assholes and said he would call me back. Cell reception is spotty out here so he'll call on my car radio. Your fate is whatever he says it will be."

"This seems like a long ways to come just to dispose of us."

"You and your lady friend are cops, McCoy. If he has no use for you, he doesn't want your bodies found. There's a deep well

out back for that. We've used it before so you'll have company,"
he added with a vicious grin.

Before Jack could reply, a horn sounded outside and the
Sinaloa boss went out the front door. When he left, Jack took a
moment to size up the four guards standing around them. Two
were six footers and heavy while the other two were average size.
All were in their thirties and dressed in jeans, t-shirts and western
boots. One wore a blue Houston Astros baseball cap. Two were
armed with AR-15s, one with an AK-47 and the fourth with an
H&K MP5 submachine gun. All wore side arms and carried extra
magazines for their assault weapons.

They were alert and focused on their prisoners. Jack had
hoped he and Elena might find an opportunity to overcome one
of them and take a weapon, but handcuffed and against four, that
seemed unlikely.

Through a front window Jack could see the men in the
Silverado standing at the edge of the stream. They appeared
relaxed but observant. He looked at Elena and she smiled tightly,
fully aware of their predicament. Jack regretted bringing her into
his personal quagmire.

Ten minutes later the security chief came back inside. He
didn't look at Jack or Elena, and seemed to be in a hurry. He told
the guards he had to leave immediately and how they should
return to Monterrey to avoid the police and military patrols. He
then headed for the door.

"Boss, what do we do with the cops?" asked one of the bigger guards.

He stopped and looked back at them, his face impassive.

"*Mátalos,*" he said. Kill them.

Chapter 27

"The boss is leaving," said Marco as Gary crawled up beside him after retrieving his G-36 from the Jeep. On Marco's other side, Viktor and Brian, AK-47s at their sides, trained their own binoculars on the old house.

The four men lay under a thick stand of oak brush fifty yards from the stream. To their left front six Sinaloa gunmen lounged around the red Silverado parked on the far bank. As Barnes peered through his Leupolds, the man in the gray Stetson got into his Range Rover and that vehicle and one of the Expeditions pulled out of the yard, across the stream and back up the dirt road, passing them sixty yards away. The Jeep and Viktor and Brian's green Blazer were hidden in the thick brush between them and the road.

It was pure luck that had brought them here. From the ambush site Marco and Gary had followed the Sinaloa convoy until it turned on a dirt road that led north into the countryside. Both knew they would soon be spotted if they followed through

the deserted area. They turned back to the road and continued on
to a village called Icamole to wait for Viktor and Brian.

Ninety minutes later the green Chevy Blazer pulled into the
Pemex station where they waited. As Viktor and Brian filled up
at the pumps, the Sinaloa caravan drove past the station. Marco
and Gary alerted their friends and all four started after the
Sinaloas.

They soon caught sight of the last Expedition in the convoy
just ahead of two other vehicles. They slowed just enough to
maintain a visual and a few minutes later the lead Expedition
turned south on another dirt road. Marco and Gary, in the lead,
slowed and waited until the vehicles were out of sight before
turning onto the road to follow.

They stayed well back and followed the plumes of dust
raised by the convoy. The terrain was more broken and covered
with stands of pine and mesquite. At each curve Marco stopped
and Gary approached on foot to ensure it was safe to continue. At
the last curve they saw the narcos arrive at the house and pulled
off the road into the timber. A few minutes later the four men
were hidden under the brush watching and waiting to see what
came next.

The sound of the departing vehicles had barely faded when Jack and Elena came out of the house surrounded by four gunmen. They walked around the corner and disappeared from sight.

"That's not good," Gary whispered to Marco.

"No, it looks like they're about to get a firing squad."

"Marco, what do we do?" asked Brian in a strained voice on Marco's left.

"We go help them," Marco replied, rolling over to check the magazine in his Galil SAR.

He quickly whispered his plan to the others. Twenty yards ahead of them was a shallow draw that ran in the same direction as the creek. They would crawl through the low brush, drop into the draw and use it as cover to open fire on the six narcos by the truck. The shots would distract the killers with Jack and Elena and hopefully give them a chance to run or fight back.

The setting sun was a bright, orange ball over the hills to the west as Jack and Elena walked into the backyard area of the house, their guards close behind them. Cumulus clouds floated overhead like big cotton balls. *A nice final day,* Jack thought, taking in the peaceful country setting around them.

Twenty yards ahead an old stone wellhead rose four feet above the ground. A rotted pine post jutted up on one side. When they reached the well, Jack could detect the odor of rotting flesh drifting from the top. Circular in shape and about four feet across, he suspected there were a lot of bodies at the bottom.

He and Elena turned to face their killers. Jack had always suspected he would die by the gun, but not like this. Not handcuffed and helpless. Shot down with no chance of fighting back. His biggest regret was leaving his daughter in the hands of the criminal scum who were going to kill him. He hoped his friends would have better luck finding her.

The two bigger guards with the AR-15s stood closest to them, the smaller ones slightly behind them. The one in charge shifted his AR to one hand and drew a blue-steel revolver from his belt holster with the other.

"On your knees, *gringo*," he growled in Spanish.

"I'll die on my feet," Jack told him.

"On your knees or I'll shoot you in the gut and drop you down the well alive," the killer said with a malicious smile under his mustache.

Jack knew he would and slowly dropped to his knees.

"You too, bitch," the gunman said, pointing his revolver at Elena.

"*Pinche basura*," said Elena, calling him trash and spitting at his boots before dropping to her knees. Jack smiled inwardly. He really admired this woman's courage.

"Any last words?" the Sinaloa asked with a sneer, leveling his weapon at Jack.

At that moment two things happened at once. A loud muzzle blast sounded behind the two front gunmen and the executioner's face exploded outward in a burst of brains and bloody tissue, some of which splattered on Jack and Elena.

His body was still falling when two more blasts sounded and the man next to him spun to the ground next to Elena. Jack saw the Sinaloa in the Astros cap slam the butt of his AK-47 into the forehead of the third *sicario*, knocking him unconscious. He picked up the man's MP5 then turned back to Jack and Elena.

"Kevin Delgado, DEA, Houston office," he said in American-accented English as he helped Jack up by one arm and then Elena. "I've been in deep cover with the Sinaloas for the last five months," he added as he pulled a key from his pocket and unlocked their handcuffs. He then used one set to cuff the unconscious gunman.

Jack was nearly speechless as he rubbed his wrists and studied the man who had just saved their lives. In his early thirties, five-ten and one-eighty, he had an athletic frame and moved with efficient ease. A dark mustache and goatee matched his short hair. The hazel eyes were friendly but guarded. A chest pouch with AK magazines covered his white t-shirt and a Glock 19 rode his right hip.

"Jack McCoy, Clark County, Nevada Sheriff's Department," Jack told him then added, "This is Sergeant Elena Cisneros, ATF Division of the Mexican Federal Police. She doesn't speak English."

"No problem," replied Delgado. He introduced himself to Elena in Spanish and told her to call him Kevin. "Can you handle this, Sergeant?" he asked, handing her the MP5.

"Absolutely, and call me Elena," she told him, taking the submachine gun and doing a magazine check. She then secured three more magazines from the unconscious former owner.

"We can do more introductions later," Delgado continued, "but right now my friends at the truck are expecting me and these dead ones to come back around the house. We need to deal with them first."

Before Jack could reply, gunfire erupted at the front of the house.

"You guys take this corner, I'll take the other," Delgado shouted then turned and ran to the far side of the house.

Jack grabbed the AR-15 and ammo pouch from the dead Sinaloa who had planned to shoot him then ran with Elena through the back door of the house and into the front room. He kneeled down at one front window, Elena at the other, and took in the scene.

Three narcos stood on this side of the Silverado firing across the hood and bed at gun flashes just above the ground on the other side of the creek. The bodies of two others lay in the water and one on the near bank. Jack couldn't see the shooters on the far side, but he knew who they were.

"Let's take them, Elena" he shouted as he put the front sight of the AR on the gunman at the hood, flicked the selector switch to semi-auto and opened fire. To his right Elena did the same as the sound of Delgado's AK-47 came from the far corner.

A hail of bullets slammed into the Sinaloas beside the truck and sent them reeling to the ground, guns falling from their lifeless hands. A moment later the firing on the far side of the stream stopped.

"Marco, Gary, you out there?" Jack shouted through the window.

"Yeah, Jack," Marco shouted back in a relieved voice. "We're here."

Jack and Elena went out the front door and across the yard. Delgado joined the from the corner of the house. At the truck they saw Marco and Gary checking the bodies in the creek. A moment later Viktor and Brian stepped around the tailgate. After ensuring the narco gunmen were dead, the group had a welcome reunion with quiet smiles and relieved faces all around.

In Spanish, Jack told his friends what Delgado had done and that elicited another round of thanks and backslaps for the DEA agent. Delgado told them he was a former Marine who had worked for the Houston PD for five years before moving to the DEA. Six months ago an informant for the agency had introduced him into the Sinaloa cartel. The DEA prepared a phony ID and criminal record for him under the name Francisco Delgado. Since then he had been collecting evidence to be used for indictments against the leaders and extradition to the States.

"What do you have so far?" Jack asked him.

"I'll show you," he replied and headed for the Expedition in which he and Jack had arrived.

"Excuse me, guys, I have to pee really bad," Elena said and took off for the rear of the old house. Jack smiled, said he needed to do the same and stepped around the truck.

Minutes later all were back and Delgado was holding a blue backpack. He reached in and took a small, plastic bag from an inner compartment. Inside the bag were four computer flash drives about three inches long.

"These are audio flash drive recorders," he said, holding up the bag. "Each one has a microphone activated by a switch at the bottom. It took a while, but after a few fire fights with the Gulf forces, I gained their trust and felt confident enough to start using them.

"I have the Sinaloa narco boss in Monterrey, Armando Cruz, and his security chief on these along with some state and federal police officials. I also have some Nuevo Leon politicians incriminating themselves, including one in the governor's office. Now that I'm burned, I'll have to try and get these drives back to the U.S. Attorney in Houston.

"Jack, I couldn't let them kill you and Elena. That guy in the hat is the Monterrey security chief and I've been part of his personal detail for the last three months. I've seen him murder fourteen people. Most were Gulf narcos, but a few were just ordinary citizens who got in his way and two were state police officers doing their job. I was sick of hanging with these assholes and wasn't going to let them gun down two more good cops."

"And you have my and Elena's everlasting gratitude," Jack told him. "That guy struck me as a real piece of work. What's his name?"

"Miguel Leon-Valenzuela," Delgado told him.

On hearing the name, Jack remembered that he had thought the man had looked familiar. He looked at Marco and his friend returned the look with a painful grimace on his face.

"Do you know him, Marco?" Jack asked.

"I should. He's my little brother."

Chapter 28

Darkness had settled over the abandoned farm. All was quiet except for the chirping of crickets and the call of night birds. The air was cooler now and lightning flashed across the sky to the south. Everyone except Brian was gathered inside the old house. Jack's son had gone up the road a hundred yards to watch for any Sinaloas returning to the scene.

Jack noticed that Brian had been quiet and pensive since the gunfight and pulled him aside near the Silverado before he left for guard duty.

"You okay, son?" he asked, already knowing the answer.

"Yeah, I guess," Brian replied in a low voice, "considering what just happened."

"I know this is hard for you," Jack told him. "Killing men for the first time is never an easy thing, no mattered how justified it might be. We did what we had to do, Brian, and you did your part just fine."

"I shot one of the men in the creek, Dad. I saw my bullets hit him and he went down. I guess I'm just not sure what to think now."

"You don't need to think anything. You did what was necessary. These are vicious, brutal men, son, and it's going to get worse. We'll have to do a lot more killing to get your sister back from these people. And some of us may not make it. You understand that, right?"

"Yeah, I understand."

"Good. Remember, you've had some good training and you can shoot with any of us. I should know, I taught you. But a target range is not a battlefield. Vik, Gary, and Marco have a lot of experience with this. Stay close to them and follow their directions. It's okay to feel fear, son, but don't let it control you. Keep your head and you'll be okay."

"I will, Dad. I'll do whatever it takes to find Brigitte and bring her home."

"That's what I wanted to hear," Jack said, clapping his son on the shoulder before he headed off into the darkness.

Gary had built a fire in the old stove and passed out snacks and bottled water that he and Marco had brought in their backpacks. They'd also found food and water in the narcos' Silverado. A duffle bag in the Expedition yielded towels and toiletries and

Jack and Elena had cleaned up at the creek. They felt almost normal again.

As they ate, Jack explained to Delgado what he was doing in Mexico. He began with the events in Las Vegas and everything that had happened since his arrival in Monterrey, including his and Elena's capture by Jesus and the fight at the pool staged by Jimenez as revenge for his father's death in Nicaragua. He ended with the ambush on the Gulf convoy by the Sinaloas and their arrival here.

"Leon told us about the convoy," said Delgado. "His informant in the compound sent word this morning. We just had time to set up the ambush. He knows where Jimenez's fortress is and the route they would take. I was able to stay with him and didn't have to do any of the killing you saw, but that's what I've been dealing with the last six months."

"Do you know where this place is?" Jack asked.

"No, I've never been there, but some of the guys with me have been there on observation details. Leon sends them to watch the place and keep tabs on who comes and goes. I think the guy out back has been there."

"So he could tell us how to find it?"

"Why don't we ask him?" said Delgado.

The group went out the back door and gathered around the gunman whom Delgado had knocked out with his AK. He was cuffed by one hand to a rusty water pipe that protruded from the house close to the ground. Gary and Viktor shined their tactical flashlights on him. In his mid-twenties, he wore jeans and a tan work shirt. A scraggly beard covered his cheeks and a large, purple bruise with a gash in the middle rose on his forehead. He looked up at them through blurry eyes.

"Can you hear me?" Jack asked him in Spanish as he kneeled down next to him.

"*Si,*" he answered.

"I'm going to ask you some questions. If you refuse to answer, I will do to you what your boss was going to do to me if I refused to kneel down. Do you remember that?"

The young man glanced away momentarily before looking back nervously at Jack.

"Yes, I remember," he said quietly.

"I will put a bullet in your gut and drop you down that well. You will die on top of those rotting corpses screaming in pain. Do you understand?"

"Yes."

"Good, let's get started."

Fifteen minutes later they had a detailed description of Jimenez's stronghold in the hills and the route there. Using a notepad from the Expedition, Marco had taken notes and drawn a rough map of the area so any one of them could find it.

"Okay, that's good," Jack told the young gunman. "We're going to leave you here for now. In two days I will call the police and tell them how to find you and your friends we put in that shed." Jack pointed to a dilapidated out building nearby where they had put the bodies of the dead Sinaloas. "If we find out you lied, I will come back here and put you in that well."

The man nodded and remained quiet.

The group went back inside the house and Jack turned to Delgado.

"Kevin, I'm not leaving Mexico until I have my daughter. We're going to Jimenez's place and try to find out if she's in there. If she is, I'm going to get her out one way or another. My friends here are in this with me, but you don't have to be. I won't ask you to risk your life for someone you don't know. You should get those flash drives back to Texas and you can take one of our vehicles. The U.S. Attorney needs to hear what's on them."

"You don't have to ask, Jack," Delgado replied. "I've spent a lot of time and endured a lot crap to make this case against the Sinaloas. I want to get these flash drives back to the States so it's not a wasted effort, but your daughter is important. She's dead if you don't get her out of there and I wouldn't feel right just leaving you here.

"You can use another gun and I know the enemy well. There's a chance we can do this and if I don't make it, I'll count on one of you to get this evidence across the border. I'm glad to help. I owe these bastards some payback anyway."

"Okay, if you're sure. We're happy to have you with us and I'm grateful for the help."

"Not a problem, let's do it."

For the next half hour they discussed a plan to travel to Jimenez's fortress and try to determine if Brigitte was there. Marco and Elena knew the area, and it turned out they were only an hour's drive from the general location. They would get as close as possible in the Jeep and Blazer and then move in on foot for a careful recon of the Gulf fortress.

While the others went out to prepare for their departure, Jack asked Marco to stay and have a word with him. The fire in the old stove provided a faint light and Jack could see the pain and anguish in his friend's face. Now he knew why.

"I sensed something was wrong, Marco," he said, "and now I know. You want to tell me about it before we move ahead?"

His old friend sighed heavily and looked out the door for a moment before answering.

"I blame myself, Jack," he replied. "When I left our farm in Durango to live with my uncle in Brownsville, Miguel was only twelve. He fell in with some bad elements in the area and went down the wrong path. I should have been there to prevent that."

"Marco, you don't know that. He might still have turned out the way he did if you'd never left. You shouldn't blame yourself."

"Of six kids, he and I were the only boys. We were really close growing up. Our dad worked us hard in the cornfields and *zacate*, but we enjoyed it. If we weren't working on the farm or in school, we were riding our horses around the countryside pretending to be vaqueros."

"Sounds like me when I was growing up in Kentucky."

"I guess it does. We really liked the farm life. There was a big creek near our house and

  we used to swim and fish there in the summer. It was a good life. When I left for Texas, he asked me if I would ever come back. I told him that we were family and we would always come home."

"And when you did?"

"That was six years later. He was working for a local marijuana grower then. I tried to talk him out of it, but he wouldn't listen. He was making more money than he could at any honest job or even if he went to the States. I stayed home for a few months before I went to Guadalajara and signed up with the Federal Police, but I couldn't change his mind."

"Did he understand what he was getting into?"

"I don't think so. He thought dealing drugs was a harmless crime and he wouldn't do any violence against citizens or the police, but that didn't last. He got more involved with the Sinaloa cartel and moved up the ranks of the *sicarios.* When they took over from the Colombians and war broke out with the other cartels, he was in all the way.

"He's been arrested twice and has spent time in prison. The last time I saw him was at our mother's funeral three years ago. He told me he would never go after me or allow his men to hurt me, but he said I shouldn't get in their way. It was like talking to a stranger. Now he helps run a criminal empire and he kills people indiscriminately, even cops. He's not the kid brother I grew up with and it tears me apart. I'm glad our parents aren't alive to see what he's become."

"I'm really sorry, old friend" Jack said, placing a hand on Marco's shoulder. "That's a heavy burden. If there's anything I can do to help, I'm there for you."

"I appreciate that, Jack, but it's something he and I will have to resolve…one way or another."

"I understand."

"Don't worry. If he gets between us and finding Brigitte, as far as I'm concerned he's just another narco with a gun."

Jack nodded and headed outside to join the others. Marco put out the fire and followed.

Chapter 29

"That is one hell of a fortress," Gary said in Spanish as he handed the binoculars to Jack.

Gary, Jack, Marco, and Elena lay in thick brush atop a knoll about four hundred feet high. Ninety yards to their left Viktor and Kevin Delgado lay on another, slightly lower hilltop. At the bottom of that hill Brian guarded their vehicles, parked in heavy oak brush. Behind them the early morning sun illuminated the scene to their front.

Three hundred yards away on a flat stretch of ground was a long, high-walled structure separated by two lower walls on each side with wide metal gates in the center. The low walls were about eight feet high, but the walls of each structure were at least fifteen feet high on all sides. The roof on each was flat and a four-foot high parapet wall rose on all sides. The walls had a brown, stucco appearance and there were no windows.

The distance between the buildings was about eighty yards. The rear structure was about ninety yards long and fifty yards across. The interior appeared to be a collection of apartment buildings. From the view on top of the hill, a few pickup trucks and cars could be seen at the entrance and several men walked or lounged around the vehicles.

The front structure was sixty yards long and the same width as the rear half. At the rear, along the low wall on their side, was a parking lot with numerous SUVs, pickup trucks and sedans. There appeared to be a courtyard in the center at the rear that served as an entrance to the building. A dirt road lay along the southeast side of the building and led out to the main road one mile to the southwest.

The group had arrived at their location two hours earlier. Following directions given by the Sinaloa gunman at the abandoned farm, they had returned to the paved road, Highway 16, and driven west until they passed through a small village called El Milagro. Two miles past the village they crossed a wood bridge over the Rio Vesqueria.

One mile past the bridge was a dirt road that led to the fortress. However, the narco soldier had told them the road entrance was guarded by Gulf *sicarios.* He told them to look for another dirt road between two large boulders that lay just a hundred yards past the bridge. This was the route he and his friends had taken to reach the two hills from which they watched the Gulf stronghold.

Barely more than a goat path, the trail led through a low mountain range called the Sierra El Fraile, or Friar Mountains, about twenty miles northwest of Monterrey. The Jeep and Blazer inched over the rough ground for nearly a mile with headlights off. Fortunately, a full moon provided enough light to navigate until they came to the hills described by the gunman. Now, from their hidden positions in the brush, Jack wondered how they could ever rescue Brigitte from such a fortified location, even if she were there.

"Yeah, it's a big one," Jack replied as he scanned the buildings. "The kid didn't lie."

"Check out the tall hill over there," said Marco on Jack's left.

Jack focused his glasses on a much taller hill about four hundred yards to their right front. The hill rose five hundred feet high to a round knob no more than thirty yards long and fifteen to twenty yards across. Brush and low trees covered the slope but had been cleared away at the top. The incline on the fortress side was low and gradual, but the far slope appeared to fall away at a sharper angle. The bottom of the hill was two hundred yards from the gated entrance to the compound and a secondary road led from the gate to the top.

The structure on top of the hill was what caught Jack's attention. A wall of sandbags formed a square at the center of the knob. Several men could be seen moving around inside the defensive position and smoke rose from an unseen fire. A gray Ford pickup with roll bars in the bed was parked near the entrance.

The most prominent feature was the Browning .50 caliber machine gun on an elevated tripod in the center of the square. The muzzle pointed toward the road and a belt of ammunition fell to one side from the chamber. With a clear view nearly to the main road, the big machine gun was perfectly positioned to cover the entrance to the walled fortress.

"Now that is impressive," Jack said as he counted the guards inside the sandbags before handing the glasses back to Gary.

"Marco, how the hell do these narcos get their hands on a .50 caliber machine gun?" asked Gary in an incredulous voice.

"Welcome to the new Mexico, my friend," replied Marco, shaking his head. "They either steal them or buy them from crooked Army officers."

"Jack, it would take an army to break into that place," Gary told him as he eyed the hilltop fortification, "and we don't even know yet if Brigitte is in there."

"I know and we need to find out before we make any plans."

"How do we do that, Jack?" asked Marco.

"The best way is to talk to someone who's been inside the compound."

"And how do we get our hands on that person?" asked Gary.

"Guys, I have an idea," said Elena, speaking for the first time.

"What is it?" Jack asked her.

"Remember what the Sinaloa told us about the gunmen here going into El Milagro to gas up and drink at the cantina and buy stuff?"

"Yeah," replied Marco, "he said they go in trucks about every day, Elena, but we can't risk a shootout with a bunch of them just to try and capture one to question."

"That won't be necessary," Elena told him with a big smile. For the next ten minutes she laid out the details of her plan. When she finished the three men also had smiles on their faces.

"I think it might work," Jack told her. "Gary, Marco?"

"Yeah, it just might," said Marco. Gary nodded in agreement.

"Okay, tell Vik and Kevin."

Marco keyed his Motorola and told the two men on the other hill what they were going to do. Viktor acknowledged and said they would keep watch on the compound.

"Okay, Elena," said Jack, "let's get you ready."

El Milagro was a small village eight miles west of Icamole on the south side of Highway 16. The most prominent building was a Tienda Soriana, a combination grocery and retail store. Nearby was a Pemex gas station, a vehicle repair garage and a collection of small retail shops. The Cantina Dos Estrellas next to the

Pemex station was closed. Numerous small houses built of wood, cement blocks, and stucco lay scattered behind the town square. There were no traffic lights and only two paved streets were visible from the highway.

Marco pulled the white Jeep into the Pemex station and got out to fill the tank. Elena also got out and walked to the Tienda Soriana. Still dressed in her white t-shirt and black cargo pants, she drew stares from some of the customers at the station. While the tank filled, Marco went inside and bought cold drinks.

Jack and Gary sat low in the back seat and the Jeep's tinted windows also helped conceal them from passersby. Looking around, Jack saw three other vehicles at the pumps and several cars parked outside the market. A few shoppers could be seen around the nearby stores.

They had seen little traffic on the road into town: mostly farm trucks and older model cars common to the area. They had not passed any obvious cartel vehicles and Jack did not see any SUVs or pickups with roll bars around them now. He also noted there were no police vehicles in sight. As he and Gary maintained vigilance, Marco returned to the Jeep and handed sodas to them through the open window.

"Not much going on around here," he said after returning the hose to the pump and getting back in the Jeep. "That will help."

"Yeah, I don't want anyone to get hurt if things go bad for us," Jack told him.

Marco drove to the nearby Tienda Soriana, parked in a back row and went inside to join Elena. Thirty minutes later they came out carrying three large bags filled with items purchased with Jack's operational money. Two contained food and drinks and the third carried Elena's special purchases.

Back on the road, Marco drove west until he reached the location they had selected on the

way in: a clear, level spot on the south side of the road about sixty yards from a sharp curve. He parked the Jeep in the clearing with the engine facing the curve. Elena got out with one of the bags and hurried to a stand of sycamores twenty yards back from the road. Ten yards from the Jeep the clearing dropped fifteen feet into a rock-filled ravine. The top of the bank was lined with brush and high weeds.

"This should work fine," Jack said as he stood at the edge looking at the curve and back at the ravine. "If they stop, we'll be able to hear them from here and we're close enough to get the drop on them."

"I can't imagine them not stopping," said Gary, pointing at Elena who was emerging from the trees.

The federal agent now wore a pair of tight jean cutoffs that ended just below her buttocks, a white tank top that barely contained her full breasts, and a pair of open-toed sandals with heels that highlighted her long, shapely legs. With her hair brushed out and fresh lipstick, she cut a striking figure.

"Well, I hope this works," she said as she stopped at the Jeep and put the bag back inside.

"Don't worry, *hermana*," said Marco, grinning at her, "those fools will fall all over themselves when they see you."

"No doubt about it," agreed Jack, trying not to stare at the attractive policewoman. "Now, let's get ready."

Marco radioed Viktor that they were in place and ready to begin. Viktor acknowledged and said he would advise when anyone left the compound. Marco then gave the Motorola and his cell phone to Elena. Jack, Marco, and Gary took their weapons and dropped below the lip of the bank ten feet apart. Peering over the edge, they were well hidden by the thick weeds.

Marco and Gary were still armed with their G36s and .45s. Jack had the AR-15 and a 9mm Glock he'd taken from the dead Sinaloas at the abandoned farm. Elena's H&K MP5 was under a towel on the floor board of the Jeep and a Glock 9mm was stashed under the hood. All had extra magazines and were ready for battle. They just hoped it would not be a large force.

With the men in place, Elena sat in the driver's seat of the Jeep with the Motorola and a bottle of water and settled in to wait. It was now close to noon and the sun was high in a cloudless sky. Jack hoped they wouldn't have to wait long. As it turned out, he got his wish.

Chapter 30

Thirty minutes after the wait began Viktor Tarasov radioed Elena that a black Toyota Tundra with five *sicarios* was leaving the compound. He estimated their arrival at her location to be twenty minutes. Elena got out and relayed the information to the men below the bank as she raised the Jeep's hood. She then lit three road flares and placed them along the road in front of the vehicle.

Holding a white rag in one hand, Elena stood in front of the Jeep at an angle that allowed her to see vehicles rounding the curve from the corner of her eye. She hoped the narcos would think that her vehicle had stalled and stop to help.

Just then an old farm truck with an elderly couple came around the curve. As it came closer the driver pulled next to the Jeep and the female passenger leaned out the window and asked if they could help. Elena held up Marco's cell phone and told her thanks but that her husband was on the way. The woman took in Elena's appearance, frowned and motioned for the man to keep driving. As the truck disappeared down the road, Elena looked toward her friends, smiled with relief and resumed her stance in front of the Jeep.

She couldn't see him, but Jack smiled back at Elena and continued to watch her and the small portion of the road in his view. Five minutes later he saw her stiffen then turn and bend over the Jeep's grill. "They're here," she said out loud.

Jack pushed some weeds aside to see a black Toyota truck slowing as it approached and pulled into the clearing in front of the Jeep. Two men were in the cab and three more stood in the back with assault rifles in their hands. The letter G was written on the passenger door in large, white script.

As Elena straightened to look back at them, the driver and passenger got out and the three in the truck bed jumped down, rifles in their hands. One of the three whistled loudly and shouted at Elena. "*¿Oye, guapa, que' pasa?*" Hey, gorgeous, what's happening?

As Jack watched and listened, the truck passenger moved up close to Elena and asked with a lurid grin if she needed help, or anything else. His companions crowded around the front of the Jeep and leered at the attractive woman. Jack could see that the driver and passenger wore side arms and the passenger seemed to be in charge of the group.

Elena demurely stepped back and told them her Jeep seemed to be overheating and she had stopped to check it out. She asked if one of them could check the radiator and the driver volunteered to take a look. As the others stepped back, Elena stood on the passenger side of the front fender while the driver bent over the grill. The leader and the other three moved to the driver's side with their backs to the bank. Two had slung their AK-47s over their shoulders while a third held his Israeli Galil in one hand.

Jack saw Elena wipe the white rag across her brow in the pre-arranged signal that she was ready. He signaled to Marco and Gary and the three of them jumped up and over the bank.

"Manos arriba!" Hands up! Marco shouted as they quickly closed to within ten feet of the group, weapons leveled.

The five men whirled around with startled looks on their faces. The driver jumped back, pulling a pistol from his belt, and at the same time the man with the Galil raised it to his shoulder. Gary fired a three-round burst from his G36 into the chest of the driver just as Elena shot him twice with her Glock 9mm. As the gunman's body was falling, Marco shot the man with the Galil twice in the chest, blowing him back against the Jeep fender and dropping him to the ground.

"Si te mueves, te mataré," Jack told the boss in a cold, calm voice, his AR pointed at the man's head. If you move, I'll kill you.

The man and his two remaining *sicarios* raised their hands. Jack and Marco moved in and took their guns while Gary and Elena dragged the driver's body over the bank. When they returned, Jack told the three gunmen to pick up their dead friend and move down the bank. At the bottom they dropped his body next to the other one then moved a few feet away.

Elena went to the Jeep and returned with flex cuffs they had taken from the Sinaloa truck at the abandoned farm. She cuffed the three men's hands behind their backs then made them kneel and put ties around their ankles. Taking the dead man's Galil, she climbed to the top of the bank to watch the road.

Laying his AR against a rock, Jack studied the three Gulf gunmen kneeling on the ground. The apparent leader of the group was in his thirties, medium height and heavyset. He wore a dirty, white western shirt with silver snap buttons, blue jeans and brown western boots. His stomach bulged against a large silver buckle. His long hair curled over his shirt collar and a thick mustache made his fleshy cheeks look even heavier. He looked up at Jack with a sneer and hatred in his dark eyes.

His two companions were quite different. Jack guessed they were barely twenty. They wore jeans, work boots and t-shirts and had short hair. One wore a white Yankees baseball cap and a thin mustache. Both had scared looks on their faces and it was clear they were not yet part of the hardcore narco crowd.

"My name is Jack McCoy and I want to know if my daughter is in your compound," he said in Spanish to the leader.

"Fuck you, *gringo*. I not gon' tell you shit," the man replied in thick, broken English.

Jack exchanged glances with Marco and Gary then dropped to one knee so he was eye to eye with the defiant *sicario*.

"One of you will tell me what I want to know," he said, again in Spanish and glancing at the other two, "or you will wish you had never seen me."

"They not gon' tell you nothin'," he replied, laughing at Jack, "and you kiss my ass, you *gringo* shit."

Jack returned the man's glare for a moment before standing up and looking at his friends behind the three men.

"This asshole won't talk, Jack," Marco said in English.

"Yeah, I know."

"We should work on one of the kids?"

"Yeah," Jack replied, looking at the two youngsters whose heads hung down and who refused to look at him. "But they need some motivation."

"I'll be right back," Jack told them, then turned and walked over the bank toward the road.

Marco, Gary, and Elena exchanged puzzled looks. A minute later Jack returned carrying one of the road flares in his right hand. He stood in front of the leader, the flare spitting flame and sparks, and said in English, "Hold him down."

Marco and Gary grabbed him by the shoulders and hair and stood on his ankles.

"This is your last chance," Jack said in Spanish. "Tell me what I want to know."

"What you gon' do, *gringo*? Burn me?" he laughed, spitting on Jack's boots. "You go to Hell, you…"

Jack shoved the burning flare through his open mouth and into his throat. The Gulf soldier's eyes nearly bulged out of his head and a horrible screeching sound came through his lips, half scream and half gurgling wail. The smell of burning flesh filled the air as Marco and Gary struggled to restrain the terrified man.

The two young *sicarios*, horrified looks on their faces, threw themselves to the ground and tried to crawl away from the crazy *gringo* burning their boss to death. Jack broke the flare off in the gunman's mouth and pushed him back on the ground where he rolled and twisted, smoke and a shrill hissing sound coming through the black hole that had been his mouth.

Jack stood over him, pulled his Glock 9mm from his belt and fired a single round between the narco's eyes. The body stopped writhing and his wide eyes stared upward. Jack stepped next to the young gunmen a few feet away and looked down at them.

"Do I need to bring another flare?" he asked in Spanish.

Both shook their heads wildly, their eyes pleading for mercy. Jack looked at Marco and Gary and both nodded, acknowledging his plan had worked. He looked up at Elena and she, too, nodded. There was no condemnation in her eyes at what he'd done, only a look of resolute determination to see the job done. He returned her nod and looked at their hostages. Now the real work began.

Chapter 31

Jack watched from a front window as the green Blazer crossed the creek and pulled into the front yard of the abandoned farmhouse. The headlights went dark and Viktor Tarasov, Brian, and Kevin Delgado got out.

"Glad you made it," Jack said as he stepped out the front door to greet them. Elena came out behind him and Gary and Marco came from the corners of the house, assault rifles in hand.

"Yeah, I thought we might not once," said Viktor, "but it worked out."

"What happened?" he asked as the three greeted the others.

"On the road just past El Milagro, we passed a long convoy of Gulf vehicles. Must have been over twenty SUVs, pickups and a few cars. We thought they might stop us, but they just kept going. Probably headed for the compound and not concerned about the common folks on the road."

"That's a lot of troops," Jack replied, a frown across his face.

"Fifty to a hundred, I'd guess," Vik told him, "on top of the ones already there."

"Come on in and we'll talk about it,"

"Come on in and we'll talk about it."

Jack led the way inside and Gary and Elena handed out drinks and food to the three men as they gathered near the old stove where Marco had lit a fire.

"Okay, Jack," said Vik, taking a sip of hot coffee, "what did you find out?"

"A lot," Jack told Viktor. He, Marco, Gary and Elena had taken their captives back to the farm, separated them and spent the afternoon questioning them about the forces and the physical layout of the compound. When Jack was sure they had told all they knew, he handcuffed them to the water pipe next to their Sinaloa enemy.

"Brigitte is there along with ten other young women. They're kept in a room on the second floor. A woman guard is in charge of their security and they seldom leave the room."

"What about the forces inside?"

"There were over fifty when those five left to go for supplies in El Milagro. With the bunch you saw tonight, that means well over a hundred there now. They stay in the larger compound at the rear except for Jimenez's personal bodyguards. Some of the Zetas also stay with him, and the others stay with the main force.

"They're expecting a large force of Sinaloas to attack the place in the next couple of days, maybe by Sunday or Monday night. That doesn't give us much time. I want to get Brigitte out before that happens, but I don't know how we're going to do that. We have no way in and, even if we did, we can't fight that many."

"Jack, maybe we should bring in the law," said Gary from the old sofa along the wall. "The Gulf boys out back can provide enough information to get a search warrant for the compound. Marco can bring his GOPES men and an army unit from Monterrey. They surround the place and tell Jimenez to surrender with Brigitte. It's the only way to get her out."

"There's just one problem," said Elena. Now dressed in a full set of jeans, a red work shirt and her tactical boots, she sat next to the stove with a cup in one hand. "When we turn them over, they'll also tell how we killed their friends on the road. And we'll have to tell about the fight at the bar, what happened at Jimenez's home and the shootout here. If Marco and I tell them we didn't go to our bosses to help Jack because we didn't trust them, my ATF unit will investigate. We could all end up in jail while they figure it out."

"Elena's right," said Marco. "I think we did the right thing because there's just too much corruption among our own people, but it would be hard to explain that now. However, there may be a way to get some official help without giving up everything we've done."

"How do we do that, Marco?" Jack asked.

"I can call my replacement, Ayala, and tell him that Brigitte is in the compound and we need to ask the federal commander in Monterrey for a warrant and help from the military. I'll tell him what happened in Las Vegas and that you came down here to ask me for help in finding Brigitte.

"I'll say I suspected Jimenez was involved and we were surveilling his residence when he took her out of the compound and brought her to the fortress in the hills. We followed him and saw her taken inside. I'll tell him to bypass his boss, Beltran, because I don't trust him, and go straight to the Monterrey PF commander.

"They'll have to act or take the chance that the daughter of an American police officer was kidnapped on Jimenez's orders, brought here and killed because of something her father did to him years ago in another country. That would bring a lot of political heat from the States and embarrassment for President Caulderon. The bosses in Monterrey and Mexico City wouldn't like that."

"Can you convince him that will happen?"

"I don't know, but it's worth a shot. We're up against the wall and time is running out for Brigitte."

"How do you want to handle it?"

"I'll call him on my cell and ask him to come out here in the morning so he can meet you and we can give him the story. It has to be tomorrow because those bodies in the shed are getting ripe. In a couple of days, the stench will travel a hundred yards."

"What about the narcos out back?" asked Viktor.

"We'll hide them in the trees across the creek when Ayala comes. If he agrees to help, we'll leave them here until we get Brigitte back, then call the police station in El Milagro and tell them where they are."

"Should we all be here when he comes?" asked Gary.

"No. I think only me, Jack and Elena should meet with him. I'll tell him she's been helping us. If he sees the rest of you, he might get suspicious and not trust me. You guys can stay with the narcos in the woods. If this works out, hc never has to know you were here."

"Okay, it's worth a try," said Jack. "Like you said, we're running out of time." He looked at the others and everyone quietly nodded in agreement.

"Okay, Marco, make the call."

Jack, I think it's time you called in a favor," said Gary as Jack came back in the front door. He and Elena had just finished checking the three gunmen handcuffed to the water pipe at the back of the house. Marco was still outside on his cell phone with the GOPES commander and Viktor was on watch up the road in case a random group of Sinaloa or Gulf *sicarios* came to the farm. Brian and Kevin Delgado sat near the stove with drinks in their hands.

"What do you mean?"

"If the federal police agree to help, they need to know the layout of that compound in case they have to go in. It's a cartel boss's stronghold, so they may not have access to the blueprints. It would help if they had overhead photos, say from a satellite."

"Gary, how the hell do we get satellite photos?"

"You and I have a mutual friend in D.C. who could help with that."

Jack looked at his friend for a moment before smiling and nodding. "You mean Sam?"

"Yeah, Sam. If we tell him what we're up against, he'll tell his boss and you know he has the juice to get it done."

"I don't know, Gary. We're off the grid down here," Jack replied, glancing at Elena and Delgado, who listened intently. "They might not want to get involved and just tell us to let the Mexican police handle it."

"Not if I explain it to Sam. He'll understand and so will the Director. He can pull the right strings and get us what we need. He owes you, Jack. He'll do it."

Jack considered Gary's suggestion. Sam was Sam Coburn, the leader of a covert team of agents at the CIA that monitored Agency employees for treasonous or dishonest behavior. He reported only to the Director of the CIA. The year before, a Russian diplomat from Jack's past and a corrupt deputy director in the CIA's National Clandestine Service had tried to kill him with hired assassins. Jack had risked his life to help Coburn take down the diplomat and expose the CIA official for the traitor he turned out to be. Coburn had told Jack to call if he ever needed help with anything.

"We could use the photos, but how would we get them?"

"My burn phone has a SIM card for international calls. I'll call Sam and explain everything. He'll get the photos done for us, maybe by tomorrow. Marco's laptop is in the Jeep and it has an encrypted e-mail program. Sam can e-mail the photos to us and we give them to the Federal Police commander who handles the assault on the compound, if there is one."

"Okay, I guess it's worth the call. Go ahead."

"I'm on it."

A minute after Gary went out the door to make his call, Marco walked in. Jack did not like the look on his face.

"How did it go?" he asked.

"I'm not sure," Marco replied. "I explained what happened in Las Vegas and that you came to me for help to find Brigitte. I told him I asked Elena to help us and we went with you to the bar, but no one showed up. He doesn't know about the fight because Jimenez sent men to clean up the mess before the Monterrey PD arrived.

"I told him we surveilled Jimenez's residence and watched Brigitte and some other girls taken out and transported to the compound in the hills. We watched them go inside and they haven't come out.

"He sounded skeptical, but I think he bought it. He wants to meet us here in the morning at ten. He'll bring his assistant, a Lieutenant Chacon, and a small security detail. After he talks to you, he'll decide what to do."

"You're the one who sounds skeptical, Marco," Jack told him.

"His lieutenant, Chacon, was brought in by Beltran. He's not GOPES qualified and his duties are mostly administrative."

"You don't trust him?"

"I'm not sure. My gut tells me something just isn't right."

"Then trust your gut, Marco. It won't let you down."

"I think you're right."

"What do you want to do, Marco?" asked Elena.

Marco glanced at Jack, then back to Elena, a pensive look on his face.

"I think I want to follow the GOPES motto very closely, *hermana.*"

"And what's that?"

"Be prepared for anything."

Chapter 32

Fidel Jimenez hung up the phone and looked up at his brother, standing on the other side of his desk. "We got him!"

"McCoy?" asked Javier.

"Yes, that was Chacon, Ayala's lieutenant. That goddamn Leon has been helping McCoy look for his daughter. Apparently, they're old friends. He lied and told Ayala she's here in the compound. He wants him to go around Beltran and ask the federal police commander in Monterrey to obtain a warrant and bring a large force here to get her back. He warned there would be political repercussions if he does nothing and she gets killed and Leon would make sure of that, too. I should have killed that son-of-a-bitch before he retired."

"So what are they going to do?" asked Javier.

"Don't worry, it's taken care of," Fidel replied with a portentous smile.

"That's good, Fidel, but we still have to deal with the Sinaloas. If your sources are right, they'll be here in a couple of days."

Jimenez got up and walked to the wall on his right. A large detailed map of Mexico was pinned to a display board there. He thought about the coming battle as he studied the map.

He and his brother were in a large, secure room on the second floor of the main compound. The door that led out to the hallway was heavy steel and could be locked from the inside. Besides Jimenez's desk at the back wall, there was a large table with computers and telephones nearby where he and his cohorts planned strategies to fight the Sinaloas and move cocaine from entry points in the Gulf of Mexico to the border.

The room also contained a kitchen area with refrigerators, a stove, microwave ovens and an eating area. A door on the far side wall led to two bedrooms where the men slept. In one corner near the entry door was a ladder that led to the roof. The room was a mini-fortress inside a larger, virtually indestructible fortress.

"My spy in Cruz's house, Duran, sent me a text when you were outside with Diego," said Fidel. "He couldn't talk, but he says Cruz is still bringing men from Saltillo and Torreon to the west and from Vera Cruz and Tampico to the south. They'll arrive by late Sunday and attack us on Monday night. That gives us three days to get ready."

"He should know he can't beat us," his brother replied. "We have the Zetas and heavy guns. They can't penetrate this place. The walls are two feet thick, we can shoot from the roof and the only way in is the two gates. Cruz is a smart dude. Maybe he'll reconsider."

Jimenez made a circle on the map then turned and faced his brother. "No, after what Jesus did to his sister and her sons, he's intent on revenge. Besides, he wants our lanes across the river and our vehicle operation at the ports. We send twice as many cars and trucks across with loads as the Sinaloas and for every one *la migra* catches, two more get through. That's a good return, Javier, and Cruz wants it. He'll come. You can count on it."

"Fidel, we have over one-hundred forty men here now. Huerta is putting patrols at strategic points to warn us when the Sinaloas come. The basement has all of the weapons and explosives we need. What else can we do to prepare?"

"Yes, we have men and weapons, but my sources with the Sinaloas have heard rumors that Cruz has a new weapon."

"What do you mean? What kind of weapon?"

"They don't know. It's just rumors, nothing specific. Duran heard Cruz tell his security chief to get "the Eagles" ready, but he doesn't know what he meant. I'm just concerned, that's all."

"Fidel, we have the fifty on the hill and the one-thirty-four in the truck out back. That thing alone can wipe out a whole division. If those assholes are stupid enough to come here, we'll finish this once and for all. When we're done with them, Gulf will have the entire east coast and we'll own the border from Matamoros to Nuevo Laredo."

Before his brother could answer, there was a knock at the door, and a moment later Diego Galvan, the head of Jimenez's personal security force, came inside.

"Everything looks good, *jefe,*" said Galvan. "The men are settled in and ready to engage the Sinaloas. They look forward to the fight."

"What's the count, Diego?" Jimenez asked.

"One hundred forty-eight, not including the thirty on my force here and the detail on the hill. We can bring in more from the border if you want."

"No, that would slow the crossings at the river and ports and we have new shipments on the way north from Vera Cruz. I think we have enough for the job to come. How are we fixed for supplies?"

"We have enough food and drinks for five days, boss, but I hope this happens soon. Every room in the compound is filled and it's cramped. The men have their video games and porn flicks, but if nothing happens in a few days, they'll be hard to control."

"My source with Cruz says Monday night, Diego. Are the men well-armed?"

"Yes, they all have assault rifles and pistols with extra mags. The Zetas have some grenades and explosives."

"Good. On Monday we'll take the buzz saw from the truck and the machine guns from the basement and put them on the roof. We'll also pass out the RPGs and grenades, and make sure the men on the fifty have enough ammo, along with food and water."

"Will do, boss."

"Also, prepare a couple of the holding cells in the basement. Lieutenant McCoy and Sergeant Cisneros will be joining us again." Jimenez related what his police informant had just told him on the phone.

"That's great, boss. I look forward to seeing McCoy again," Galvan replied, rubbing the bandage on his right hand.

"They'll be here by tomorrow night or Sunday, and, Diego, I'll let you know when you can have your revenge. Understand?"

"Yes, sir. Understood."

"In return for your patience, you get first shot at Sergeant Cisneros."

"Thanks, boss," Galvan replied, a wicked smile on his face. "I'd like that."

"One more thing, Diego. Tell Camila to send the women over to the back for the night, along with beer and tequila. Let's try and keep the men entertained."

"Okay," replied the big, former Zeta. "I'll go tell her now." He turned to leave then looked at Jimenez, the smile back on his face.

"Does that include the McCoy girl?" he asked.

Jimenez looked at him for a few moments, then smiled and said, "No, not this time. When we get her father back, I'm going to arrange a special show for him with his daughter and a few of the Zetas. After that the men can have her."

"As you say, boss," Diego replied before going out the door.

"Javier, did you call my pilot?" Jimenez asked his brother as Galvan left.

"Yes. He'll be here tomorrow night."

"Good. My contacts in the PF and state police assure me we won't be bothered until this is over. We shouldn't after what I've paid for their cooperation. When Huerta returns we can finalize the plan for our guests on Monday night. I want to show the Sinaloas what great hosts we can be."

Javier looked at his brother and both men burst out laughing.

Brigitte McCoy walked out of the bathroom with her toiletries bag and returned to her mattress against the far wall. This room was much like the one at the other compound except there were no windows here and they had a small kitchen area where they could prepare their own meals. Since arriving the day before they had not been allowed to leave.

Their captors had brought their mattresses and Brigitte had arranged hers along the back wall with Michelle, Sophie, and Abella. The other girls lay along the side walls. Now dressed in a white, long-sleeved blouse with her black jeans and Nikes, she looked over at Abella as she sat down on the mattress. The young girl sat with her arms wrapped around her knees and her head down.

"¿Como te sientes?" Brigitte asked her. How are you feeling?

Abella raised her head and looked at her with red, teary eyes. "I'm scared," she replied.

Brigitte could tell the girl had not adjusted well to captivity. Last night she had cried for an hour before falling asleep. Brigitte had tried to comfort her without much success. Nearby, Michelle and Sophie looked at her with sympathetic eyes.

"We're all scared, Abella," Brigitte told her, "but if we stick together and watch out for each other, we'll be okay."

The teenager nodded and lay her head back down on her knees. Brigitte placed one hand on her shoulder in a gesture of support. Before she could say anything else, the front door opened and their overseer, Camila, came in with three men close behind her.

"Get up, ladies," she yelled, "and grab your bags. You're going outside for a while. And don't forget your condoms," she added. "You're entertaining tonight."

The three men moved around the room snarling at the women to hurry up. One of them was Paco, Brigitte's rapist. He'd removed the tape over his broken nose, but it was still bruised and swollen. He carried some kind of assault rifle as he and Camila, dressed in black fatigues, approached Brigitte and her friends.

"McCoy," she said, "you stay. The boss has plans for you later on."

"Don't take Abella," Brigitte pleaded. "She's just a kid. She's too young for this."

The young girl had cowered back against the wall and pulled a blanket up to her chin.

"Don't worry, *chica*, you won't be passed around," said Camila, extending her hand to the girl. "You're going to the Zeta chief's apartment. He'll take good care of you. If he doesn't, I will," she added with a sinister smile.

Brigitte stepped in front of Abella and shook her head. "No, you can't do this to her."

Camila grabbed Brigitte's right wrist and pulled forward. "Get out of the way, bitch," she growled, "you don't give orders here.

In a flash of movement, Brigitte rolled her right hand to the inside and up at a sharp angle. As Camila's hand lost its grip, Brigitte's left hand clamped the back of her fingers and her right grabbed the wrist. She rolled Camila's hand backward in a Hapkido reverse wristlock, then stepped back with her right leg and brought the woman to the floor face first.

Camila screamed as her wrist cracked loudly. From the corner of her eye Brigitte saw one of the gunmen moving in from her right. She quickly braced on her left foot and drove her right leg out in a hard side-thrust kick. Her foot landed in the man's soft gut, dropping him to his knees.

Brigitte turned to face the second gunman with her hands up when Paco stepped in from her left rear and drove the butt of his

Galil assault rifle into the back of her head. Brigitte dropped to her hands and knees, her head spinning from the pain. She tried to rise up, but Camila, now on her feet, stepped in and kicked her in the stomach, rolling Brigitte on her side. Cursing loudly, the enraged woman kicked her several more times before Paco pulled her back, warning that the boss would not be pleased if they hurt or killed McCoy's daughter.

On the floor next to her mattress, Brigitte watched through blurry eyes as Camila and the men herded the women, including Abella, out of the room. When they were gone, she reached up and massaged the knot on the back of her head. Her fingers were bloody when she lowered her hand. Slowly, she rolled onto the mattress, lay back and closed her eyes. As the darkness settled, she felt confident in one thing: her father was coming...and Hell was coming with him.

Chapter 33

The black, wrought-iron gates slid back and the white Range Rover pulled through the entrance to the elaborate Hacienda-style mansion in San Nicolas de la Garza, a stylish neighborhood on the north side of Monterrey. Armed guards on both sides of the gate waved as Miguel Leon-Valenzuela's driver pulled around the high, circular water fountain in front and stopped in the driveway.

Leon got out and moved up the stone walkway lined with bougainvillea flowers to the front doors where he was met by an aide to his boss, Armando Cruz. The man led him through the arched entrance and down a long hallway. Leon's boots clacked loudly on the porcelain tile floor. After two turns they came to an open door of a large den and office, where the aide left him.

Taking off his Stetson, Leon entered and found his boss sitting behind his elegant Caobilla wood desk, talking on his cell phone. Cruz waved at Leon and a minute later ended the conversation, closed his phone and got up to greet his security chief.

"Miguel, how are the plans going?" he said. Dressed in expensive white linen pants and shirt and brown Ferragamo slip-ons, the tall, lean Cruz was a dapper figure. With his dark, well-groomed hair, he looked ten years younger than his actual age of fifty and was a big hit with the ladies on the Monterrey social club scene. Very few in that club knew he was the leader of a small clique that ran the largest and most violent drug cartel in Mexico. Cruz had waded through a lot of blood to reach that position. His next goal was to eliminate his competition and be the sole narco power in eastern Mexico.

"Very well, *patron*," Leon replied. "Nearly all of the men are here and getting prepared in our safe houses around the city. The rest should be here by tomorrow night. Our scouts are checking the road to Icamole and El Milagro for Gulf patrols. We are well armed and supplied. If the PF and the military don't get in our way, this should go well."

"They won't be a problem. How about our new toys? Are they ready?"

"The armaments arrived yesterday and are being installed today. They should be ready to go by the end of the day tomorrow. The warehouse is well guarded. They'll be safe until we need them."

"Excellent!" Cruz replied as he walked to a nearby liquor cabinet and poured two glasses full of Aguardiente. He handed one to Leon.

"There is one thing bothering me," said Leon as he took a sip of the fiery liquid.

"What's that?"

"I left a detail to take care of the American cop and the ATF agent at the old farm. One of my men, Cervantes was in charge. His lieutenant, a guy named Delgado, called me later and said the job was done. He said Cervantes was busy and told him to call and ask for their next assignment.

"I told them to wait at their safe house until Sunday, but with things changing so fast I called Cervantes earlier today to tell him to go to Icamole and help with the road patrols. He didn't answer his phone and hasn't returned my messages. Delgado hasn't answered his phone either. I'm not sure what's going on with them."

"Do you think something happened at the farm?"

"If something went wrong, Cervantes would have called me. He knows better than not to answer my calls unless he's tied up with something. And he always gets back to me later."

"Maybe they were picked up by the police."

"We should know that by now. Tomorrow I'll send a team to their safe house and the farm. I'll also check their hangouts and alert the rest of the men to look for them."

"Okay, keep me informed."

"I will. Boss, have you heard from our man in the Jimenez compound?" asked Leon.

"He called just an hour ago. They've been told the attack will come on Monday night and are beginning initial preparations. That means Jimenez won't bring out his big guns until Monday. Of course, by then it will be too late."

"So the ruse worked?"

"That's right. They don't suspect a thing and took Duran's word. That was very astute on your part to check your men's phones. You caught him red-handed. Good work."

"Just routine, boss. I didn't really suspect him, but I like to play it safe in this business. There's always someone ready to sell out for the right price."

"Speaking of which, should we wrap up that piece of business?" Cruz asked, finishing his drink and setting the glass on the cabinet.

"Yes, we should," replied Leon, setting his own glass down.

Cruz led the way out of the room, down the hall and to the rear of the opulent residence.

Outside they crossed a large patio next to a swimming pool where several bikini-clad beauties lay soaking up sunrays. Tall palm trees towered over the green lawn along the high limestone walls on all four sides, and guards with assault rifles stood on parapets along the wall. After passing a large garage, they came to a small metal-frame building with a sloped roof and an armed gunman standing outside.

The interior of the building was one large room with a dirt floor. It was hot, and overhead florescent bulbs cast a bright light on a man tied to an old wood chair in the middle of the room. Cruz and Leon approached and looked down at their former employee.

Dressed only in jeans and old boots, Sergio Duran was a pathetic sight. Both eyes were swollen nearly shut. His nose was broken and both lips were cut and shredded. Dried blood had caked on his face and neck. Deep cuts and cigarette burns marred his chest. His head hung forward and air whistled through his open mouth. Blood spotted the floor under him.

"Have you had time to think about your crimes, Duran?" asked Cruz in a contemptuous voice.

The doomed man raised his head and peered through the slits in his eyes. The rickety old chair creaked with even that slight movement. "I ask your forgiveness, *patron*," he whispered.

"Only God forgives, Duran. You sold me out to the Gulf for ten thousand dollars. That scum who butchered my sister and nephews. Just boys, Duran. Hell, I would have given you ten thousand as a bonus this year. If Miguel had not checked your cell phone for recent calls and texts, you would have gotten away with it. But you were too stupid to use a throw-a-way and keep it hidden. Now you pay for that stupidity."

"I'm very disappointed, Sergio," said Leon. "I put you on my personal detail because you did good work and I trusted you. This is how you repay me?"

"I'm sorry, boss," Duran replied in a low, hoarse voice.

"So am I, Sergio."

"Miguel," said Cruz, extending his right hand.

Leon drew a Colt .45 ACP from a holster on his belt. The blue frame had gold inlays and the threaded tip of the barrel extended an inch past the muzzle. The ivory grips bore his initials in gold letters. From his rear jeans pocket, he pulled a custom-made suppressor, screwed it to the barrel and handed the weapon to Cruz. "There's a round in the chamber," he said.

"You want forgiveness, Duran?" Cruz asked. "I give you the chance to ask for it." He extended the .45, flipped off the safety and fired a single hard ball round through Duran's right eye. The bullet blew a hole in the back of his skull, the impact tipping the old chair backward onto the floor. Blood spread rapidly around Duran's shattered head.

"Have this thrash thrown out, Miguel," said Cruz as he handed the .45 back to Leon.

"Right away, boss."

"You have two days to get the men ready, Miguel. Jimenez thinks he's invincible in that compound, but he doesn't know about the surprise we're bringing. On Sunday night we'll blow that Gulf bastard and his goddamn Zetas straight to Hell."

Chapter 34

Jack glanced to the southeast as lightning flashed and thunder claps sounded in the distance. Dark clouds carrying heavy rain were moving in from that direction, but sunrays still poked through the nimbus clouds over the old farmhouse, and the air was heavy with humidity. Jack stood with Marco between the Jeep and Blazer they had parked sideways in the front yard, his eyes on the dirt road that led across the creek.

It was nearly ten o'clock on Saturday morning and the GOPES commander should arrive soon. Because of Marco's uneasiness, he and Jack had prepared defenses for a possible double-cross by Marco's boss. Thirty yards to the east of the house was an old stone and wood tool shed that had nearly collapsed. Two stone walls still stood with the rotted roof leaning to one side. Viktor Tarasov sat behind the walls with his G36.

The old stone corral on the other side of the house also provided good cover and Brian crouched behind the four-foot high walls with an Israeli Galil 5.56mm taken from a dead Gulf *sicario.* On the eastern side of the front yard, just past the tool shed, was a thick stand of Lacey Oak trees and shrub bushes. Gary lay at the edge of the trees with an AK-47 and several magazines. Behind him lay the three narco gunmen, gagged and hogtied.

Twenty yards across the fast-flowing creek on the east side of the road Elena and Kevin Delgado lay hidden behind a small rise covered with Redbud trees. Elena was armed with her H&K MP5 and Delgado his AK. The rise provided cover and a good view of the house sixty yards away. The creek was sixty feet across and a foot deep.

Marco had parked their vehicles in front in case things went bad and they needed cover. He now stood by the front fender of the Jeep holding his G36. To his right Jack stood near the front of the Blazer, his AR-15 cradled in his arms. On Marco's belt was one of the Motorola radios. He'd given the other three to Brian, Gary, and Elena. Marco had tied down the mic button on his unit so the frequency stayed open and the others could hear his voice. Vik Tarasov was close enough to hear Marco's voice commands.

"I hope I'm wrong, Jack," Marco said as he watched the road across the creek.

"Me too, Marco, but if you're right, at least we have a chance."

"Yeah, and now we wait."

The wait wasn't long. They heard the low rumble of heavy engines before the first black Chevrolet Suburban appeared around the curve just past the rise where Elena and Delgado were hidden. The big SUVs rolled along slowly until they reached the creek and then stopped momentarily. The tinted windows made it hard to see the people inside.

"He brought the War Wagons," said Marco.

"What?" asked Jack, glancing at his friend.

"They're armor plated," Marco replied. "We only use them on missions where we expect trouble. Ayala wouldn't use them just for a meet."

"A set-up?" Jack asked in a wary voice as the vehicles continued across the creek.

"Maybe. Heads up and safeties off, guys," Marco said in a loud voice. "If I say 'go,' open fire."

Marco and Jack stood up straight, rifles across their left arms, right hands on the grips as the Suburbans reached their side of the creek and parked at an angles left and right twenty yards away. The doors opened and black-clad figures wearing armored vests, balaclavas and carrying assault rifles poured out on both sides. *"Policia Federal"* in white letters adorned both sides of the armor. Two carried rifles with suppressors attached to the barrels.

Ten men lined up along the vehicles. A short, bald man in his thirties without a balaclava alighted from the driver's door of the left vehicle. He also carried an assault rifle. A taller man in his mid-forties wearing only a side arm and a black cap with the letters "PF" came around the grill from the passenger door. That made twelve.

"Something's wrong," Marco told Jack in English as he eyed the federal officers. "I'm not sure what, just follow my lead."

"Marco, good to see you again," said the older officer as he and the shorter one advanced a few feet. "I'm glad you're here."

"Director Beltran, I wasn't expecting to see you," replied Marco. "I thought it would just be Carlos, the lieutenant and a couple of aides."

"Lieutenant Chacon called me this morning," Beltran said, pointing to the shorter man next to him. "He told me Commander Ayala had a family emergency and couldn't make it. The lieutenant asked if I would accompany him to meet you. He said Lieutenant McCoy has some important information about his daughter's kidnappers and her location. I agreed to come with him."

"Emilio," said Marco, addressing Lt. Chacon, "I thought the commander's wife was in Texas visiting relatives."

"Uh, that's right," replied a nervous looking Chacon, his eyes darting around. "She got sick last night and her relatives called him. He left this morning."

"He's lying," Marco whispered to Jack. "Her relatives live in Chicago."

Lt. Chacon casually raised his rifle from his side and cradled it across his left arm.

"Aw, shit!" said Marco loudly in English. "They're Zetas! GO! They're armored up, head and waist shots."

Marco raised his G36 to his shoulder and fired a four-round burst that caught Beltran across his thighs and dropped him screaming to the ground. Three rounds from Jack's AR-15 hit Chacon in the throat and chin and sent him stumbling backward into one of the men behind him. Jack and Marco had barely made it behind the wheel wells on the other side of the Jeep and Blazer when the Zetas began advancing and loosed a barrage of automatic fire into and over the vehicles.

Suddenly, gunfire erupted from the corral, the old shed and the oak trees and the Zetas' advance was halted as their heads blew apart from high-velocity rounds. Blood, bits of skull, and black cloth flew as six of the Gulf killers spun and tumbled to the ground. Four of them, one limping, ran to the other side of the Suburbans and returned fire from each end.

Jack and Marco rose up and fired back and rounds from Brian, Viktor and Gary flew over the Suburbans. The four Zetas were in a bad position and turned to run across the creek toward the trees on the rise. That was a fatal mistake.

When the shooting started, Elena and Delgado could hear Marco's commands on the radio, but could not see the line of

Zeta commandos…until the surviving four ran to the back of the Suburbans, fired over the top then turned and ran toward them.

"Here they come," said Delgado from six feet to Elena's right as the black-clad gunmen hit the creek four abreast. "I'll take right."

"Roger that," replied Elena. "I've got left."

When the Zetas were ten feet from the bank, a burst from Delgado's AK-47 hit the one on the far right directly in the face, dropping him into the water. The man next to him continued forward, his assault rifle on full auto. High-velocity rounds cracked over the low rise as Delgado's next two rounds hit the killer low on his armored vest and spun him around and down.

Before the first Zeta dropped, Elena fired three rounds that hit the man on her left just below his chin, spinning him around and into the creek, blood spurting from his throat. The one next to him suddenly stopped and emptied his magazine at the new threat. Elena ducked as rounds tore up dirt on top of the rise and snapped overhead.

When the killer's magazine ran dry, he continued forward reloading on the run. His armor-hit mate stood up out of the water and began reloading as he advanced toward the rise.

"Now, Elena!" shouted Delgado, standing up and shouldering his AK. He walked forward down the slope and fired a long automatic burst that hit the Zeta on his right in the center of the vest just as he seated a new magazine. The rounds rose up his chest, punctured his throat and blew off the right side of his head. The dead narco dropped into the water.

Elena jumped over the rise, dropped to one knee and fired a five-round burst that caught the last man across his lower waist. He screamed and fell forward to his knees, blood staining the water around him. He tried to raise his rifle, but Elena triggered three more rounds into his masked face, and the fight was over.

"That was a close one," said Delgado as they stood on the bank and observed the four dead gunmen lying in the creek. On the other side, Jack and Marco had come around the Suburbans and asked if they were okay.

"Yeah, too close," Elena replied after shouting at Jack they were fine. "I'd like to have you on my team, Agent Delgado," she added with a taut smile at the DEA man.

"Likewise, Sergeant Cisneros," he shouted back over the ringing in his ears. "Now, let's go see what the hell just happened here."

Marco took a long drink from a water bottle and glared down at Ceasar Beltran, his former boss. The PF assistant director sat against the front wheel of one of the Suburbans, bloody bandages wrapped around both of his thighs. Three bullets had hit him, but had missed the bone and arteries and caused tissue damage only. He was in pain, but would live.

The dead Zetas had been stripped of their weapons and armor and taken to the old cattle shed behind the house where they joined the bloated bodies of the Sinaloas. The young Sinaloa gunman and the two from the Gulf truck ambush had been handcuffed again to the water pipe behind the house with water and snacks. Brian had gone up the road to stand guard and the others stood around the Suburbans.

"How did you know they were Zetas, Marco?" asked Jack as his friend handed the bottle back to him and they stepped away from Beltran.

"This," Marco replied, raising the assault rifle in his left hand for Jack to see. It was one

of the weapons used by Lt. Chacon and the Zetas. "This is the new Mexican Army weapon, the FX-05 *Xiuhcoatl* in 5.56mm, like your M-4s."

Jack looked at the black assault rifle with the raised carrying handle and integral, red-dot optical sight. It was a sleek-looking gun similar to the G36. He could see cartridges in the translucent, thirty-two round magazine.

"It's a Mexican-designed weapon that just came out last year and was issued only to the GAFE Special Forces units. The Army agreed to provide some of them to GOPES, but the shipment that was sent to us was hijacked by the Zetas last month and we never got them. My unit is still using the Israeli Galils. I was already suspicious because Chacon was lying about Carlos and when I got a good look at his rifle, I knew."

"You were right about Beltran, and it doesn't look good for the new commander."

"No, it doesn't. And it doesn't look good for Brigitte either. We just lost our only chance to get the Federal Police and the military to hit Jimenez's compound before the Sinaloas."

"Can you get the director of the PF in Monterrey to do something?"

"I don't know, Jack. If I go to him after what just happened here, I'll be on lockdown for a week. So will all of you. He won't move against Jimenez until he gets all of this sorted out and he knows who else is on the man's payroll. By that time, it will be too late for Brigitte."

Jack knew he was right. This would be a major investigation that could take weeks, and his daughter didn't have weeks. There had to be another way.

"What can we do now, Marco?"

"First we find out what this son-of-a-bitch did to my friend, Carlos, and then we find another way into that compound.

Chapter 35

"Please, Marco, I'm in a lot of pain," Beltran pleaded as Jack and Marco kneeled next to the wounded official. Sweat beaded his pale hatchet-like face and his thick mustache twitched as he spoke. His hands clawed at the top of his thighs in a vain attempt to stop the pain.

"There are medical kits in the Wagons with morphine," Marco told him, his hard eyes boring into the PF turncoat with no mercy. "You want the pain to stop, start talking."

"What do you want to know?" Beltran asked, glancing up at Marco with a look of defeat on his face.

"Everything, and if I think you're lying, even once, I'll put a bullet in each kneecap and leave you here. Then you'll know real pain."

"Okay, whatever you want, just get the morphine."

Marco signaled to Elena standing nearby, and she went into the rear of Beltran's Suburban. Moments later she emerged with a green canvas medical kit. Marco rummaged through it for a minute and brought out two blue and white syrettes containing a clear liquid. He removed the cap from each Duramorph ampul and injected ten milliliters of morphine sulphate into each of Beltran's legs above the bullet wounds. Within moments Beltran began to relax, and two minutes later he leaned back against the wheel, relief clear on his face. Marco tossed the empty syrettes away, turned on his cell phone's recording feature and leaned in close to him.

"Where is Carlos?" he asked.

"He's dead. Chacon shot him."

"Where's his body?"

"In a safe house in Monterrey." Beltran gave him the address.

"How did it get there?"

"Chacon called and told me you had called Ayala and what you wanted him to do. I told Chacon to kill him and take his body to the safe house. We were going to kill you, take you there and arrange it to look like you had confronted him because you thought he was in with the narcos. You killed each other in a shootout. It's Saturday so no one will look for him until Monday."

"No one is going to believe that bullshit," Marco replied in a low, angry voice.

"If we tell it right, they will," Beltran said, his eyes darting away from Marco's merciless stare.

"How long have you and Chacon been on Jimenez's payroll?"

Beltran hesitated a moment, his eyes glancing at the cell phone before looking at Marco.

"Two years for me. Chacon was recruited last year."

"And you've been providing him information on our operations ever since?"

"Yes," Beltran replied in a barely audible voice.

"Louder!" Marco shouted, slapping the side of Beltran's head.

The frightened man repeated his answer and cringed away as if he expected a beating.

"Have you seen my friend's daughter in Jimenez's compound?" Marco asked.

"No, but he told me she's there. He's going to give her to his men after he kills McCoy."

"What do you know about the Sinaloas hitting Jimenez's compound?"

"He has a spy in Cruz's house. The man told him they're attacking on Monday night. Cruz is using his sister's death as an excuse to wipe out his competition once and for all. The Sinaloa council agreed and he's brought in nearly two hundred men.

"I told Jimenez to leave the area for a while, but he says he has enough firepower to destroy the Sinaloas when they come. It's going to be a blood bath. I've diverted all PF missions in this area until next week. He has a colonel in the 8th Division working for him who's also suspended military operations until the attack is over. That's all I know."

A light rain had started and Beltran was moved into the farmhouse and placed on the old couch. The Sinaloa and the two Gulf soldiers were in an adjoining bedroom. Elena had replaced Brian on lookout duty and the others had gathered inside to eat. Gary was working on Marco's laptop and Jack stood near the door with Marco while they lunched on soft drinks and tortillas.

"After what Beltran's told us, do you think there's any chance the director would move on Jimenez before Monday?" Jack asked his friend.

"Not likely, Jack. His assistant is a sellout to the Gulf who ordered the new GOPES commander killed. A GOPES officer was also in the narcos' pocket and did the killing then brought a group of Zetas here to kidnap you and an ATF agent and kill me. It's a goddamn mess and he won't do anything until he knows what's going on. Even with Beltran's admission that Brigitte is there, it will be next week until he can get a warrant and convince the military commander to assist. That might be too late."

"There must be something else we can do," said a frustrated Jack.

"Maybe there is," said Gary as he joined them at the door.

"What do you mean?" Jack asked.

"Sam just came through."

Jack stood in the open doorway and studied the photographs carefully, scrolling down each page on the laptop. Marco and Gary looked over his shoulders at the screen. Sam Coburn had forwarded six satellite photos of Jimenez's compound to Marco's encrypted e-mail program. The detail was clear and sharp and included the nearby hilltop with the fifty-caliber machine gun nest. It also showed just how impregnable the fortress appeared to be.

"He built it well," said Gary in English. "Only way in is the two gates and those walls look thick. With that fifty on the hill, the Sinaloas will have a hell of a time taking that place."

"Yeah, it does look tough," agreed Marco, "and they have the chopper as a way out if things go bad."

The photos showed a walled square on the northwest side of the main compound that had not been visible from the hills. A gate in the low wall next to the compound opened into the square and inside sat a red and white EC 120 Colibri helicopter. The five-seat, Eurocopter model offered a quick escape from the fortress if needed.

Jack remained silent. After reviewing the photos twice, he looked at the two Suburbans outside and then stared off into the trees across the creek.

"What is it, Jack?" Gary asked after a couple of minutes.

"There might be a way in," Jack replied, "but it's risky and the odds aren't good."

"Okay, what are we talking?"

"Fifty-fifty…at best."

"Yeah, not great. How would it work?"

"Part of it means you have to go SOG again," Jack said, looking his old friend straight in the eyes.

For a moment Gary said nothing, then a knowing grin slowly spread across his face.

"What do you mean, Jack?" Marco asked. "Your Vietnam unit, the Studies and Observation Group?"

"He's talking about the fifty, Marco," said Gary.

"Can you do it?" asked Jack.

Gary looked again at the photo showing the machine gun emplacement before replying.

"You bet your ass I can do it," he said.

The rain was coming down harder and thunder clapped overhead as the storm increased in intensity. In Spanish, Jack had just finished explaining his plan to assault the Gulf fortress and now looked at the faces around him for feedback. Beltran had been handcuffed and placed in one of the Suburbans and Elena had come in from her lookout post to hear the plan. She was the first to speak.

"It might work, Jack," she said, "but you're right, it's risky."

"It is, Elena, and I want to make something very clear right now. I won't ask any of you to risk your life like this. We know the Sinaloas are going to hit that place the day after tomorrow. When they do, a lot of people are going to die in there and one of them could be Brigitte.

"I'm offering this as a way to get her out before then. But even if it works, some of us may not make it. I can accept that, but I have no right to ask the same from anyone else. You have lives and families to consider. If you think the risk is too high, tell me and we'll just go to the PF and hope for the best."

"Jack, I think the risk is too high that Brigitte will be killed if we don't get her out," said Marco. "I know these damn Sinaloas. They won't spare anyone when the killing starts. It's risky, but I think we have a good chance to succeed.

"I think Elena will agree with me that this is a chance to strike a hard blow at this damn cancer that's eating away at our country. If we can take out Jimenez and cripple the Gulf, it will be easier to beat the Sinaloas because we can focus our resources on one less enemy. It's worth the risk and I say we go for it."

"I agree, Jack," said Elena. "If we wait for the PF and the military, Brigitte will die. And Marco's right; this narco scum is a cancer and we should take the fight to them."

"You know how I feel, Jack," said Gary from his seat on the couch. "Enough said."

"I'm with Gary, Jack," said Viktor. "If it was one of my daughters in there, you would be right here, by my side, ready to lead the charge. I can't do any less for you. And my family would understand."

Jack nodded at his old friend and colleague.

"Jack, I've already told you where I stand," said Delgado as he warmed a cup of coffee on the stove. "I say we get your daughter out of there and I don't care how many of these bastards we have to kill to do it. As I said before, if I don't make it, one of you will and can get my flash drives home. This is my grandparent's country and I feel like I owe it to them to try and make things right."

"Dad, let's go get her," Brian told his father from the front door where he stood guard.

Jack looked at his friends and nodded his acceptance of their decision.

"I owe you all a debt I can never repay. You have my thanks and gratitude."

"You owe us nothing, my friend," said Marcos. "We all have a stake in this, so let's get it done.

Chapter 36

"There's the curve," said Marco, looking over the steering wheel to a curve in the dirt road just over a hundred yards ahead.

"Yeah, and there's the pine," replied Jack from the passenger seat, pointing to a tall white pine on the right side of the road.

"So far, so good," said Marco as he put the Suburban in park, picked up the Motorola on the seat and keyed the transmit button.

"Elena, we're here," he said.

"Roger that," came the reply from the GOPES SUV behind them.

Rain beat down on the windshield as Marco pulled off the muddy track and stopped thirty yards into the mesquite brush. Kevin Delgado drove the second Suburban and parked behind them. Jack and Marco checked their weapons and magazines. In the rear seat Viktor and Brian did the same. On the seat behind them lay Beltran, handcuffed with flex cuffs around his ankles.

It was late afternoon and they had left the old farmhouse two hours earlier. After agreeing to Jack's plan to hit the compound, they had discussed their options and the primary consideration was firepower. They now had the excellent FX-05 assault rifles they'd taken from the dead Zetas, but they needed more ammo and magazines. They also needed better radios and hard armor, not the soft ballistic vests they had found on the Zetas.

Jack remembered that the two Gulf *sicarios* had told them about a secret arms cache the Zetas maintained near a small village in the area. The frightened young narcos had been desperate to tell the mad *gringo* anything he wanted to know so he wouldn't shove a road flare in their mouths.

They pulled aside the young *sicario* who said he'd been to the cache twice, transporting weapons, ammunition and equipment bought or stolen by the Zetas. He described a block building on a remote piece of farmland about two miles from the main road that ran through a small hamlet called Agua Blanca. Marco pulled a map from the Jeep and found the village lay five miles due south of El Milagro. The closest route shown was a single-lane dirt road across the rangeland.

The narco said the arms were unloaded at the building and guards were posted there around the clock. They slept and ate in a small wood shack next to the arms building and were rotated on a weekly basis so they wouldn't get bored with the guard duty. A Gulf boss had told them the land was owned by the cartel and the local famers had been told to stay away. The young *sicario* described how the guards were positioned and gave them directions to the location.

It was likely the building had the arms they needed for the assault on the compound. They decided to raid the arms cache that afternoon, then find a place to rest overnight and hit the Gulf fortress on Sunday, right at dark.

Part of the plan included a soft entry into the compound, and for that they needed the help of Beltran. Jack and Marco explained to him that he needed to call Fidel Jimenez and tell him his team had found more Americans with McCoy and Leon. He wanted to take them to an interrogation site in Monterrey and question them to determine what they were doing there and what they knew. After the interrogation he would bring all of them to the compound on Sunday night.

With an unpleasant death his only other option, Beltran made a convincing call to the Gulf boss and set the plan in motion. The two Gulf soldiers and the Sinaloa were flex-cuffed by one hand to the old stove in the house and left with water and snacks. Marco would call the state police on Sunday morning and tell them where to find the narcos and the bodies of the Zetas and Sinaloas.

The group loaded into the GOPES War Wagons and drove out to Highway 16, turned left and drove toward El Milagro. The storm had become intense with rain coming down in torrents and thunder and lightning rending the dark sky. The weather worked in their favor as there was little traffic on the road and less chance of encountering police or Gulf patrols.

Two miles past El Milagro they found the faint dirt road leading south across the open rangeland. Water filled the tracks and the Suburbans moved slowly on the muddy road. The only life visible in any direction was an occasional horse and groups of Corriente cattle bunched together, tails turned against the wind and rain.

An hour later they came to a narrow asphalt road that was rutted and broken and barely wide enough for a single vehicle. Turning right they soon reached Agua Blanca, a collection of small houses, a Pemex station and a food market. Few people were in sight. Past the village a barbed wire fence paralleled the road on both sides and a short distance later they crossed a drainage tile filled with muddy water. On the left was the gate described by the Gulf narco.

Ignoring the "no trespassing" signs, they slid the unlocked gate back and proceeded along the muddy track past stands of pine and oak trees. Pinon brush covered the shallow draws and canyons and spruce trees dotted the low hills around them. The vegetation grew thicker as they advanced along the road.

One mile in they saw the curve ahead of them with the tall pine on one side described by the Gulf narco. Fifty yards around that curve would be the first guard post, a vehicle with four gunmen blocking the road. The arms' building was one hundred yards further on. There would be another truck or SUV with two more guards keeping watch and conducting random foot patrols around the building. Six more guards would be inside the adjacent wooden shack.

Everyone exited the Suburbans and gathered between them in the rain. They were quickly soaked to the skin. All wore ballistic vests they'd taken from the Zetas. Jack wore Beltran's cap and a dead Zeta's black uniform shirt. He also carried one of the suppressed FX-05s. Marco carried the other one.

"You know your jobs, but let's do a quick review," Jack told them. "Vik, you and Brian cover the shack with the off-shift guards. Gary and Kevin have the vehicle with the two outside the arms building. Gary, after Marco, Elena and I deal with the four around the curve, we'll radio and you take them out those two. Then we'll all join up and move on the shack.

"The rain works in our favor. You can get through the trees and brush pretty fast without much noise. The guards will probably be inside their vehicles and might even be sleeping. Let us know when you get in place."

Everyone acknowledged their understanding and moved off through the trees. In seconds Jack, Marco and Elena stood alone by the Suburbans, the cold rain dripping down their faces.

"Okay, let's do it," said Jack.

Twenty minutes later the three of them lay under heavy, wet oak brush fifteen yards from a beige Ford Explorer parked just off the south side of the road. Through the rain they could see two men in front and two in the back seat. They appeared to be smoking marijuana and drinking beer.

"Not a highly disciplined bunch, are they?" noted Jack.

"These are street thugs and gangsters the cartel hires, not the Zetas," replied Marco from his left.

"We need a way to get them out of the vehicle," said Jack as he looked up and down the road. The curve was thirty yards to their right. To their left the road disappeared in the rain and gloom. "Any ideas?"

"Let's try the same trick we used on the road," said Elena, lying on the other side of Marco. "I can go around the curve and come walking in alone. That should get them out. When I reach them, I'll move to this side of the road a little. When they bunch up around me, I'll hit the ground and you guys take them out."

"I don't know, Elena," replied Jack. "They'll be suspicious when they see you out here alone. They might just shoot you."

"Not if I'm unarmed and look lost. They'll check me out first. I can do it, Jack."

"Marco?" asked Jack.

"It's a bit more risky, but it might just work." Just then Viktor's voice sounded on the Motorola in Marco's hand.

"We're in place twenty yards north of the shack," he said. "No movement in sight."

Marco removed the plastic sandwich bag from his unit and replied. "Roger that, Vik."

A moment later Gary advised that he and Delgado were in the trees just west of a white SUV parked near the main building. Two guards were inside.

Marco acknowledged the transmission and turned to Jack. "Time to party."

"Not yet," Jack told him.

"What do you mean?"

"We've got company."

Chapter 37

Jack had a better view up the road and first saw the dark blue Ford Econoline van ease around the curve. He warned his friends and they watched as the vehicle advanced slowly and stopped next to the Ford Explorer. Two people were in the front seats. No one in the Explorer got out.

The side window of the van rolled down and the driver engaged in a short conversation with the occupants of the SUV. After a minute the van continued on down the road toward the buildings.

"What do you think?" Jack asked, looking at Marco and Elena.

"Hard to say," replied Marco. "Could be a re-supply or maybe more guards coming in."

"If no one was in the back, we still have two more to deal with," said Elena.

"Advise the other guys," Jack told Marco.

Marco keyed his radio and told Gary and Viktor to watch for the van. Gary acknowledged and ten minutes later came back. "We've got four guns pulling three girls out of the van and taking them inside the hut," he said. "They look young and their hands are tied. Probably snatched off the street and brought here for these punks' entertainment."

"Yeah, that's how they kill the boredom out here," Jack said, shaking his head.

"Jack, let's move before they hurt those girls," said Elena. "I'm ready."

"Okay, go. Try to get them together and closer to us. When you're ready, hit the ground and Marco and I will do the rest."

Elena rolled over, removed her vest and holstered Glock and lay them aside with her rifle. She unbuttoned the top of her red blouse and crawled backward through the brush. Jack and Marco nodded at each other and crawled forward a few more feet until they were at the very edge of the tree line. They now had a better view of the road and the men in the Explorer. They settled in to wait.

Twenty minutes later, Elena came around the curve, walking slowly, head down and hands clutching her arms against the cold. Her wet hair clung to her head and neck. She looked down at the ground, seemingly unaware of the vehicle in front of her.

The driver and front passenger stepped out of the Explorer, assault rifles at ready position. As they walked to the front, the two rear passengers followed. One held a pump-action shotgun; the other wore a sidearm. All were dressed in jeans, boots and short jackets. The driver wore a green and white El Tri ball cap. They stood at the front of the vehicle, talking to each other and watching Elena as she closed to ten yards.

The driver threw his joint to the ground and shouted at her, demanding to know what she was doing there. Elena looked up and stopped for a moment. She dropped her hands and continued forward, shouting back that she had jumped out of her drunk boyfriend's car on the main road and ran this way to escape from him. She asked if they could help her.

As Elena reached the men, their demeanor changed. They lowered their weapons and were now laughing and making lewd comments about helping the lost girl. They gathered around her and the driver grabbed her right arm.

"We can take you somewhere dry," he told her, a malicious grin on his face. Elena pulled away from him and stepped off the road toward the tree line, asking them not to hurt her.

"I'll take right," Jack told Marco. "On her cue."

"Roger that," Marco replied.

As Elena retreated the four *sicarios* followed closely, yelling at her to come back. Elena suddenly dove to the ground and covered her head, causing the gunmen to stop and stare at her.

Jack and Marco stood up in the waist-high brush and opened fire at ten yards. Jack's first three rounds caught the driver in the chest and blew him backward into the mud at the edge of the road. His next burst hit the man next to the driver in the throat, nearly decapitating him.

His body had not hit the ground when a long burst from Marco's rifle ripped the two on the left across their chests, sending them spinning and tumbling into the mud a few feet from Elena. The soft, whapping sound of the suppressed FX-05s did not carry far.

As the men went forward to check the bodies, the gunman with the shotgun rolled over and tried to rise. Elena shouted a warning and Marco fired a short burst into his face, ending the threat. Jack and Marco threw the killer's weapons into the Explorer then dragged the bodies into the brush. Elena recovered her equipment and waited for them.

"Marco, tell the guys we're good here and on the way," Jack told him. "We'll come in on Vik's side."

Marco radioed the information and they moved down the road to finish the job.

"We're good to go, Kevin," Gary told his partner as he clipped the radio back on his belt.

The two men were lying under a thick pinon tree twenty-five yards from the west side of a long cinder-block building with a low-pitched roof. Thirty yards long and twenty wide, the building could hold a lot of guns. The vegetation had been cleared on both sides and a small muddy stream flowed past fifty yards behind the building.

At the northeast corner stood an unpainted wood-plank shack with a sloped tin roof. The front door was blocked by the van, but a blanket-covered window was visible on the west side. Wires from a power line along the dirt road attached to the back of both buildings.

Straight across from Gary and Delgado was a white Envoy GMC with two *sicarios* inside. The driver of the blue Econoline had talked briefly to them before returning to help his companions move the three women inside the hut. The two in the SUV remained outside.

"You ready?" asked Gary as he handed Delgado his suppressed HK .45 USP.

Delgado nodded and stuck the pistol in the back of his belt, then crawled backward until he was out of sight. Gary continued watching and hoped their improvised plan would work.

Delgado moved quickly through the wet brush, around the rear of the building and to the other side. He made his way along the wall until he reached the corner where he could see the Ford van to his right. It blocked his view of the Envoy. The wood shack sat ten yards to his left front and he could hear loud rock music through the back door.

Crouching low, Delgado ran to the near side of the van and stopped to peek through the passenger window. The two Gulf soldiers still sat inside the SUV. He slung his rifle over his left shoulder and pulled his Astros cap low to shield his face and keep the rain out of his eyes.

Stepping around the front of the van he hurried toward the Envoy as though he wanted to get inside. As he neared the driver's door, the driver, a thin, mustached man in his twenties wearing a denim shirt and stained white cap, rolled down the window and asked Delgado why he was out in the rain. Over the roof Delgado saw Gary moving across the open toward them, FX-05 at high ready.

Through the open window he saw a sawed-off shotgun across the passenger's lap and a Ruger Mini-14 assault rifle between the seats. Delgado leaned over and asked the men if they wanted to come in and party with the girls. As the two laughed and said they'd like that, Delgado reached behind his back and pulled the HK.

Stepping back he fired two rounds through the window into the chest of the short, heavy-set passenger, the weapon making a low *pffff* sound. The man's eyes widened and he jerked upright in the seat for a moment before slumping against the side door. The driver reached for the Ruger, but Delgado swung the HK through the window and cracked him across the forehead, opening a gash above his left eyebrow.

Delgado opened the door and dragged the stunned man out onto the wet ground then quickly flex-cuffed his hands. He looked up to see Gary pulling the dead passenger out the opposite door. Taking the keys from the ignition, Delgado opened the rear compartment and they tossed the captured gunman inside.

"I shot the passenger because he was holding that sawed-off, but this guy might give us some information," he told Gary.

"Good thinking," Barnes replied. "I'll tell the others we're good."

A few moments later Marco replied that he, Jack and Elena were with Viktor and Brian in the trees on the other side of the shack. He asked them to try and get some information from the Gulf *sicario* about the interior of the wood building.

"Let's talk to our boy," Gary said to Delgado. "We need the inside layout."

They opened the rear trunk and pulled the gunman forward by his collar. Blood rolled down the left side of his face and his eyes widened in fright as he looked up at the two hard men standing over him with guns in their hands.

"Let's have a chat, asshole," Gary said in Spanish.

Ten minutes later he radioed the needed information to Marco.

"That's good feedback," Marco replied. "How did you get so much out of him?"

"I put the muzzle of my HK in his crotch and told him I'd blow his balls off if he didn't talk."

"That will do it," Marco replied with a laugh. "Here's what Jack and I want you to do."

Marco quickly laid out their plan to take down the group inside the shack. Gary acknowledged and said he would advise when he and Delgado were in place.

"You ready to help those young ladies out of a tight spot?" he asked the DEA man as they kneeled at the back of the SUV.

"Let's party, dude," Delgado replied with a wide grin.

Chapter 38

Jack held up one hand as the group gathered around him at the edge of the trees twenty yards from the corner of the guard shack. No one had come outside, but they could hear the low din of music through the covered window.

"Okay, a quick review," said Jack, turning to his friends. "The interior is one big open space. Just inside the door is a cleared area with chairs and couches, video games and a big-screen TV. Along both walls are the beds. The back part is a kitchen area and the bathrooms. We'll divide it right down the middle SWAT style. The right side is one, the left is two. The front door isn't usually locked. If it is, I'll kick it in.

"Elena and I will take one. Vik, you and Marco are two. Marco and I will button hook around the doors. Vik, you and Elena do a crisscross behind us. Brian, you've got the window on this side, Kevin has the other side and Gary has the back door. We'll probably catch them off guard. There are ten of them. Some might throw up their hands and some might gun up on us.

Just react as it happens after we get inside and remember that there are three young girls among them. There isn't time for a better plan. Any questions?"

Everyone acknowledged their understanding.

"Okay. Marco and I have the only suppressed weapons so it might get loud in there," Jack said as he tore small pieces from his t-shirt and stuffed them in his ears. The others did the same.

"Let's roll," he told them and sprinted toward the front of the shack, the others right behind him.

Brian and Kevin ran to the side windows Gary to the back door. Jack stood at the right side of the front door, Viktor behind him. Marco took the opposite side, Elena behind him.

"Go ahead," Jack whispered.

Marco grasped the doorknob, turned it slowly and the door cracked open. Jack nodded and raised his left hand. After a moment he dropped it sharply and Marco shoved the door back. Jack quickly stepped around the right doorjamb and Marco did the same on his side. Elena and Viktor ran through the opening to opposite sides of the door behind them.

The thump of loud rock music and the pungent smell of marijuana filled the air inside the shack. Eight feet to Jack's right front two *sicarios* in jeans and t-shirts sat on an old brown sofa holding video game consoles. A game was playing on the TV screen to his immediate right. Over their heads he could see two men struggling with a half-naked teenage girl on a bed against the wall, one holding her arms and the other dropping his pants.

The two unarmed gunmen sitting down looked up with startled faces for a moment then jumped up to confront the strangers who had just come through the door. Jack twisted on his left foot and his right leg shot out in a high sidekick that caught the man to the right on his chin and sent him flying backward over the sofa.

Elena swung the butt of her FX-05 into the temple of the other Gulf thug and dropped him to the floor. They quickly moved toward the two attacking the young woman on the bed. On the left side of the room they could see four more gunmen tearing the clothes off the other two girls and heard Marco shouting for them to get their hands up. At the rear of the large room were two more seated at a table.

Jack and Elena ran around the sofa and straight at the two rapists holding the girl on the bed. The man holding her arms shouted a warning and his partner dropped her legs, stood up and turned around. The short, skinny *sicario* wore only a dirty white t-shirt. His hard-on was still at attention and his face held a look of shock.

Her eyes flashing with rage, Elena glided forward and snapped a hard Taekwondo front kick into the man's groin. Her tactical boot crushed his testicles and dropped him screaming to the floor. His accomplice jumped off the bed and grabbed a blue-steel revolver from a nearby stand. As he brought the weapon around, Jack fired a three-round burst into his chest that blew him backward and through the sheet-covered window near the bed.

As Elena flex-cuffed the naked *sicario*, a blast of rifle fire shattered the silence and Jack watched the two gunmen in the kitchen area snatch AK-47 rifles from the table and run out the back door.

To Marco and Viktor's left front, four *sicarios* had two young girls down on narrow beds near the wall. On each bed one held the struggling girl down while the other tore off her pants and underwear. Focused on their victims, the gunmen didn't notice the new arrivals until Marco yelled at them to move back and get their hands up.

All four narcos jumped to their feet, stunned looks on their faces. The two closest to Marco saw his leveled FX-05 and threw up their hands. The other two made the fatal mistake of reaching for AK-47s leaning against the wall. Viktor triggered a short burst into the back of the first and two shots into chest of the second as he came around with his AK. Both were slammed against the wall and dropped to the floor.

Their two companions were quickly laid out and flex-cuffed. The terrified girls cringed on the bed and pulled sheets over them to hide their nakedness. Across the room Elena calmed the third girl and brought her to sit with the other two. Brian shouted through the broken window to ask if everyone was okay. Jack told him they were good and to come inside while he went to help Gary and Delgado with the two who had run out.

Gary was standing at the corner of the shack when the two *sicarios* burst through the back door with AK-47s in their hands. He shouted a warning at Delgado, standing a few feet along the opposite wall, before engaging the fleeing killers. Both spotted him as he shouldered his FX-05 and fired two rounds at the one closest to him.

Both bullets struck their target in the side and sent him sprawling forward into the mud. His friend returned fire with a long burst while still on the run. Delgado reached the corner and saw Barnes spin to the ground. As he ran forward to help, Gary rolled over, one hand clasped to his right hip.

"I'm good," he shouted. "Go get him."

Delgado nodded and turned to see the gunman run around the corner of the arms building. He sprinted after him and stopped at the corner to take a quick look. The man was running through the brush toward the rushing stream just yards away. Delgado ran to a nearby pinon bush, dropped to one knee and shouldered his rifle. He yelled at the man to stop.

The gunman stopped at the top of the bank, turned and raised his AK. Delgado lined the red dot sight of his FX-05 on the man's yellow t-shirt and squeezed off a single round. The high-velocity bullet hit the *sicario* at the base of the throat and blew him backward into the churning waters of the muddy creek. Delgado stood and watched the body float downstream.

"Let me take a look," Jack said as he kneeled next to Gary, now sitting up on the ground. He had come out just in time to see his friend hit the ground and Delgado chase after the fleeing *sicario*. He immediately ran to help his friend.

"Don't think it's too bad," Gary replied as he unbuckled his pants and pushed them down, "but I need to stop the bleeding." Looking down, they could see that a single bullet had hit the right side of his hip a few inches below the belt, punching a hole through the flesh but missing the bone.

"Let's get you inside," Jack said, putting one arm over Gary's shoulder and helping him get up. Barnes flexed his leg and was able to stand without any assistance. Jack stood close as they walked through the back door.

"Brian, Gary took a hit. We need the medical kit," Jack shouted at his son who was helping Viktor, Marco and Elena secure the surviving *sicarios*. Brian immediately ran out the front door and up the road toward the Suburbans.

Gary sat down on the sofa at the front of the room as Elena grabbed a sheet from one of the beds and stuffed it against the bleeding wound. Marco turned off the loud stereo and went outside to check the perimeter while Viktor stood over the subdued gunmen.

"Just those four?" Jack asked Elena, pointing at the men on the floor.

"Yeah," she replied. "The one you kicked has a broken neck."

"Are the girls okay?"

"Yes, just scared. We came in before these assholes could finish raping them."

"Good. Let's find out what happened."

Jack and Elena sat on the bed opposite the young women and in Spanish asked them how they ended up here. In scared, shaky voices they described how they had been kidnapped off the streets of Colonia Independencia earlier in the day. The two younger ones, sixteen and seventeen, had been walking home from a mercado. The older one, nineteen, had been waiting at a bus stop alone. They were told not to fight or they and their entire families would be killed.

Jack told them they were safe now and would soon be home. He radioed Brian to check the dead narcos on the road for any money they had and bring it with him. While Elena helped the girls get dressed, he and Viktor searched all of the bodies at the shack. Just as they finished Brian came in with the medical kit and a handful of peso bills. Elena counted the money while Jack and Viktor treated Gary's wound.

"There's morphine ampuls in here if you want," Jack said as he poured an antibiotic powder into the entry and exit holes. He then repeated the process with a Quik Clot hemostatic agent and taped a sterile combat gauze over the wound.

"It hurts some," Gary said as he buttoned his pants, "but I'd rather keep my mind sharp."

"Okay, that should hold for a while, but it needs treatment."

"When this is over, Jack."

Just then Marco came through the back door and joined them at the sofa.

"You gonna make it, buddy?" he asked Gary.

"I'm good, Marco," Gary replied. "Just a flesh wound, as they say in the movies."

"We might have a problem," Marco told Jack.

"What is it?"

"The door on the building has an electronic number lock. We need the code to get in."

"One of these guys might have it."

Marco looked at the four prone narcos, one of whom moaned loudly. "You're right," he said, looking back at Jack and Viktor. "Give me a minute."

While Viktor and Brian helped Marco, Jack rejoined Elena and the three girls at the beds.

"The cartels pay good wages," Elena told him, pointing to a pile of dollars and Mexican pesos on the bed. "There's over forty-seven hundred dollars here."

"Good. Divide it up between the three of them. A little compensation for their trouble."

"Can any of you drive?" Jack asked the young women.

"I can," replied the nineteen year-old.

"Okay, I want you to take the van back to your neighborhood and leave it on the street. Then just go home and try to forget this ever happened. Don't tell anyone about it. Understand?"

"This is yours," Elena said a few moments later as she handed each one her share of the narcos' money. "Now do as my friend says and just go home."

The girls nodded their understanding and Jack and Elena guided them outside and helped them load into the Econoline. When the van had disappeared up the road, they went back inside.

"Got it," Marco said as they came in. "One of the guys Vik shot was the team boss. He had the code on his cell phone. One of his buddies gave it up."

"Good work. I won't ask how.

"No need. Now, let's go see what we came here for."

Chapter 39

"This place is a special operator's dream house, Jack," remarked Viktor as he gazed at rows of weapons and equipment stacked throughout the large cinder-block building.

While Brian maintained a guard on the road, the others had filed into the arms cache and began opening crates of rifles, handguns, ammunition, uniforms, body armor, tactical radios and virtually anything else that could be used by a special ops or SWAT team. Gun racks along both walls held dozens of assault rifles in various models and calibers, some with attached suppressors.

Dozens of wood crates held magazines and ammunition in both handgun and rifle calibers. Along one section of the back wall military fatigues hung from clothes racks. On a nearby table were boxes containing body armor and ballistic helmets, rucksacks and combat medical kits. Under the table were boxes of civilian clothing. Other crates held Glock, Smith and Wesson, Kimber and other American-made handguns.

"Yeah, looks like we'll find everything we need for what's coming," Jack replied. He and Viktor stood in the middle of the building watching the others inspect the crates of equipment.

"Jack, we should get outfitted and test fire our guns," said Marco as he came back to stand with them.

"Good idea. Where the hell does all this stuff come from, Marco?"

"A lot of it is stolen from police departments and the military. The rest they buy from retailers or on the black market in the States. Remember, they have the money to buy anything they want. We should get done here and find a place to hide out until tomorrow," Marco added. "The Zetas might come back any time."

"Where can we rest up and stay out of sight?"

"I suggest we go back to El Milagro and get rooms at one of the motels there. We take the War Wagons to that side road we took to the back of the hill overlooking the compound. We can hide them there then take the Envoy and the Explorer to town. Elena and I will rent the rooms. I doubt anyone will notice us in this rain.

"We can keep Beltran with us as long as we keep a guard on him. Tomorrow afternoon we go back to the Wagons, gear up and make last minute plans before dark. I'll call one of my sergeants in GOPES tomorrow and tell him about this place. They can come out here and clean it up."

"Marco, assuming we pull this off and get Brigitte out of there, what are you going to do about Beltran and everything that's happened with him?"

"I don't know, Jack. He's on my cell phone recorder admitting what he and Chacon did and that should help. If he survives tomorrow night, he's going down hard. The PF chief in Mexico City will send a shitload of people here to investigate this mess. I'll have to put my retirement on hold and Elena and I will have to answer a lot of questions. But that's okay. It's worth it to get Brigitte out of that hole and find out who else is in bed with these damn narcos. I'm just sorry we lost Ayala. He was a good man."

"I feel bad about bringing you into this, Marco. If there's anything I can do to help, just let me know. I'm happy to come in with you and talk to the investigators."

"No need to feel that way, Jack. If this works, all of you should get back to the States right away. I'll let you know how it's going and if you can come back. Remember, even if you weren't here, we'd still be fighting this war. You just got caught up in it."

"Okay, then let's finish up here and move on to El Milagro."

The next two hours were spent selecting the weapons and equipment they would use in the attack on the compound. Each fired several magazines through their chosen assault rifles and handguns to ensure proper functioning, then cleaned and oiled them thoroughly. Combat fatigues and vests, first aid kits, armor, tactical radios, and personal items were carefully selected by everyone. They also found something that would give them a tactical advantage.

"Jack, come look at this," Gary shouted from a rear corner of the building.

Jack put down his FX-05 and cleaning rod on the other side of the room and moved to see what his friend had found. Marco and Elena joined him at a low shelf built into the wall where Barnes was standing.

"We just struck gold," he said, pointing to three wood boxes on the shelf. The lid of one had been removed and was stenciled with the words *"Ejercito de Guatemala."* Army of Guatemala. Inside the box were five rows of eight M67 Army fragmentation grenades. There were two layers in each box. Jack picked one up.

"These will definitely give us an edge," he said, eyeing the round, olive-drab explosive. "How do they get their hands on Guatemalan Army stuff, Marco?"

"We recover a lot of guns and explosives from El Salvador and Guatemala. Stuff left over from the terrorist wars in the eighties."

"Well, let's put it to use for our side," Jack replied, putting the grenade back in the box. "Let's take as many as we can carry."

While Gary and Elena packed the grenades into rucksacks, the others began loading the Suburbans with their guns and equipment. The rain still fell but with less force now, and night would soon fall. Everyone picked a set of dry clothes from the stack of civilian clothing and changed out of their wet garments before leaving. The five Gulf soldiers were flex-cuffed by one arm to the metal beds inside the wood shack and left with food and water. The bodies of their dead teammates were placed inside the arms building.

Marco and Elena drove the Suburbans with Beltran cuffed and stuffed in the back seat of one. The others piled into the *sicarios'* Ford Explorer and the GMC Envoy. They moved back up the dirt lane to the narrow paved road leading to Agua Blanca and returned via the rutted, muddy road north across the open rangeland.

It was dark when they drove west through El Milagro on Highway 16 and Jack noted that there was little activity. Traffic was light in the rainy weather and they had not encountered any police or military patrols. They soon crossed the wood bridge over the rushing Rio Vesqueria and found the side road between the large boulders.

A half mile up the muddy lane they found a stand of white pines on the left that would hide the Suburbans from view. They stashed the vehicles and transferred Beltran to the Envoy. Thirty minutes later Marco parked the beige Explorer in front of the

Posada Dos Piños in El Milagro. While the others waited outside, he and Elena went in to rent their rooms.

The Two Pines Motel was an old, decrepit looking building a half block east of the Tienda Soriana. The white paint on the stucco exterior was faded and the red tiled roof was chipped and broken. Four cars and a pickup truck occupied the parking lot. A few shoppers hurried in and out of the food market. One block west, a single car was gassing up at the Pemex station. A slow night in the small town, and that was fine with Jack.

"We got four rooms on the back side so we're out of sight," said Marco as he and Elena returned to the SUV. "Elena and I will take one and you guys can double on the others. One is for Beltran and his guard. We can take shifts on that."

"I'll take the first," said Jack as they drove to the rear of the motel. "I want to change his bandages and give him another shot of morphine so he stays quiet."

Minutes later, Jack guided Beltran into a room near the back corner of the motel. There were two sagging beds and an old desk with an armchair. An ancient Magnavox TV sat on a stand in one corner. The brown shag carpet was torn and stained and the curtains barely covered the window. The bathroom was small and smelled of mold, but everything worked.

While Marco and Elena went to the market for food and drinks, the others used the rainy darkness to bring in their weapons along with several cases of ammunition and rucksacks full of magazines they would load during the night. Gary stayed with Jack to help treat Beltran's wounds and stand guard while he used the bathroom.

"Gettin' tired, buddy?" Gary asked as Jack yawned and rubbed his face with both hands.

"Yeah, it's been a rough week," said Jack as he stood near the window and messaged the sword cut on his thigh. It hurt, but the bleeding had not started again.

"You know we're too damn old for this Rambo shit, don't you?" Gary said from the chair, an FX-05 on his lap.

"Yeah, not like 'Nam any more, is it?" Jack replied with a weary grin.

"Hell, Jack, we were kids then, still teenagers. We could fight all day, run all night and still find time for booze and women."

"Yeah, teenagers who killed men for a living."

"It's what we did, Jack. It was war. We didn't like it, but we were good at it and we learned to deal with it. Some couldn't."

"And here we are again, killing on a war time scale. Why us, Gary?"

"It's who we are, Jack. Someone has to stand up and tell the bad ones to stand down. If no one did, what the hell kind of world would that be? Vik says we're the sheepdogs. Who gave us that job? Damned if I know. I guess we were just born to it. Right now, I'm glad it's us because we're the best chance Brigitte has to get home alive."

"I hope we can pull this off, Gary. I can't stand the thought of losing her."

"Jack, we have a good team. You and me, Vik, Marco, Elena, we know this game well. That Delgado kid is a hell of a gunfighter. He would have made a great SOG man. And I think Brian is a better shot than you. If we can't do it, it can't be done."

"I hope you're right," Jack replied. "And you're right about Delgado and Brian."

Before Gary could reply, Beltran came out of the bathroom, shirtless, wearing fresh black fatigue pants and drying his hair. He sat down on one of the beds and looked at his captors.

"McCoy, you can't win an assault against the Jimenez compound," he said in a dry voice. "If you let me go, I will convince him to release your daughter. I can also make you a very rich man. Just name your price."

"You want to put a bullet in his sorry ass," Gary asked Jack, "or should I?"

"If we didn't need him, I'd be happy to let you do it. If you gave me money, Beltran, I'd burn it," Jack continued. "Now keep your mouth shut or we'll find a way to get in there without you."

Beltran was about to speak when there was a knock at the door. Jack opened it and Marco and Elena came in with sodas, bags of hot food and more towels.

"We just took dinner to the other guys," said Marco. "We also got more towels and told the manager not to send the maids around in the morning."

"Good idea," said Jack as he helped Elena lay out food and utensils on the old desk.

"Jack, I told Marco I'd like to go visit my brother in the morning," said Elena as Jack unwrapped a steaming hot burrito. "We don't hit the compound until tomorrow night. He lives in San Nicolas Hidalgo, which is a small place just north of Monterrey. I can take the Explorer and be there in an hour. It may be the last time I'll see him."

"That's fine, Elena, and I'll go with you."

"You don't have to do that, Jack. I'll be fine."

"It will be safer if there are two, and I don't mind."

"Okay, if you wish. I'd like that."

"I told her it was you or me, Jack," said Marco. "The Gulf and the Sinaloas will have patrols out tomorrow and the military may have roadblocks up closer to town. She needs the company."

"Then let's get some rest and see what tomorrow brings."

Chapter 40

The black Ford Expedition turned right on Avenida Jose Vasconselos and sped east at high speed, followed closely by two more SUVs. It stopped briefly at the next red light then plowed through amid blaring horns and shouted expletives from surrounding cars. One block later the convoy came to a halt in front of the ten-story Intercontinental Presidente Hotel.

Tall palm trees lined the entrance to the opulent hotel in Monterrey's Old Town district. Parking attendants drove luxury vehicles out of the entrance area as guests arrived and departed, but none moved to take the keys of the two Ford Expeditions and the white Range Rover between them. They knew better than to even approach those expensive wheels.

Miguel Leon-Valenzuela and three men in dark suits stepped out of the Range Rover and headed for the front doors. Four more exited the two Fords and trailed after their boss. Others remained behind to ensure the valets kept their distance.

Leon and his retinue swept across the marbled floor of the lobby, past ten-foot high potted plants and a towering waterfall, to the high-speed elevators on the west wall. On the second floor they moved down the carpeted hall to the Gran Chipinque ballroom. Outside the double doors stood Armando Cruz.

"This better be good, Miguel," snapped Cruz as Leon stopped in front of him and his men spread around them. Dressed in a black tuxedo, the Sinaloa boss glared at his security chief. "I'm about to introduce the next governor of Nuevo Leon state in there," he continued, pointing at the ballroom. "He works for me. Do you know what that means if he wins the election?"

"I'm sorry, *Jefe,*" said Leon, "but we have trouble. Is there someplace we can talk in private?"

Cruz looked up and down the hall then pointed to his right. "This way," he said, and led the group to a second set of double doors that opened to a small, empty conference room. Inside he flipped on a light switch and moved to a nearby table.

"I'm listening," he said as he sat down and folded his arms.

"I told you that I sent teams to look for Cevantes and his men when he didn't check in after killing McCoy and the ATF woman," said Leon. "They found them at the old farm, all dead except for one, a kid named Castillo."

"What the hell happened?" demanded Cruz.

"He said Cervantes picked him and two other men to take McCoy and the woman to the back. The others stayed out front to wait. When Cervantes was about to kill them, one of the team shot him in the back then shot the other two and hit him in the head with his rifle and knocked him out. When he came to, he was handcuffed to a pipe behind the house. McCoy and the others put the bodies of his team in an old shed. Later they came out and asked him where Jimenez's compound was located. He'd been there to watch the place and told them how to find it."

"Who's the turncoat, Miguel?"

"His name is Francisco Delgado. We called him Frankie because he's from the States, but it turns out he's a DEA agent."

"What?" shouted an incredulous Cruz. "I thought you had all your men checked out."

"I did, boss. Our private investigator in Dallas did a thorough background on him, but it was all a plant by the DEA. Castillo says he heard them talking in Spanish in the house and Delgado told them he has audio recordings of you and me talking about moving our product and other business stuff. He also recorded you talking to some of your people in the PF and the governor's office. One of them is probably the guy in the ballroom."

"Jesus Christ, Miguel!" Cruz shouted as he jumped up and began pacing back and forth. "How the hell did he get recordings of us?"

"He was good, boss. Very sharp, well-organized, capable. I put him on my personal security team and he was with us when you met those people and you were discussing business. He probably has a lot of details on those flash drive recordings."

"Miguel, if that information gets to the federal prosecutors in the States, do you know what that means? Indictments for us and Calderon won't hesitate to have us extradited. I don't want to spend the rest of my life in a *gringo* prison."

"Me neither, boss, but there's more."

"Go on," Cruz said, anger flashing across his face.

"There were three more *gringos* with McCoy and the woman, and another Mexican cop."

"Who?"

"My brother. Marco and McCoy are old friends and he's been helping McCoy try to get his daughter back from Jimenez."

"What else did Castillo hear?"

"Yesterday they were gone for a while and when they came back they had two guns from Jimenez's compound with them. They ambushed a Gulf vehicle and brought them back to the farm for questioning. They were still there and my men took care of them, but, boss, McCoy wants to assault the compound to get his daughter back."

"What! That's bullshit, Miguel. Seven of them against that place! No way!"

"I think I know how. This morning a group of Zetas and a high-ranking PF man came to the farm dressed like Marco's GOPES men. McCoy and his group killed them and took the PF guy prisoner. He's on Jimenez's payroll and I think they're going to use him and the PF vehicles to get into the compound. Also, they questioned one of the Gulf men about a Zeta arms cache in the area. I think they were going to raid the place for the arms they need to do the assault."

"That doesn't make any sense, Miguel. There's over a hundred men in that place with heavy guns. Even if they got inside, they'd never get out. Is Castillo sure what he heard?"

"He thinks so, boss. He didn't hear everything well, but he thinks they're going to hit the place tomorrow night."

"I don't believe it, but if they do, that's our chance to stop them before Delgado gets to the States with those recordings. Put some men in place to watch for those PF vehicles going in there. If they show up, that's when you move in and we take care of two problems at once. If they don't show, you still hit Jimenez like we planned.

"Also, put patrols on Highway 85 in case they go north and alert all of our men on the border from Matamoros to Nuevo Laredo. Send them pictures of Delgado and tell them to watch the ports of entry. We have to stop that son-of-a-bitch before he gets across the border."

"Will do, boss. I think McCoy might try it. He won't leave his daughter in Jimenez's hands. We just need to be there when he makes his move."

"Is your brother going to be a problem for you, Miguel?"

Leon hesitated a moment before replying. "No. I told him once not to interfere in our business. If he gets in the way, my men will take him down."

"Then go do your job."

Chapter 41

Brigitte examined herself in the bathroom mirror. She had a cut lip, a bruised cheek and a black and blue left eye. Her ribs also hurt. Still, she was in fairly good shape considering the beating she'd taken from Camila. The woman had brought the girls back to the room in the morning while Brigitte was still asleep.

The young captives were quiet and subdued after their night in the *sicarios'* compound. A few prepared lunch, but the others simply lay down on their mattresses. Abella was one of them and Brigitte asked her what had happened. The teenager told her she'd spent the night alone because the Zeta chief had not returned to his room. No one came for her until Camila brought her back to the room. Brigitte was pleased the youngster had been spared a humiliating ordeal. She consoled the teen and encouraged her to stay strong until they were rescued.

As she returned to the main room, Brigitte thought about the change she'd noticed in the behavior of Camila and her guards when they came to the room. They seemed hurried and more concerned about something other than the women. They had barely spoken and now Camila carried a Glock on her belt.

Brigitte knew what had them worried; her father was coming. She didn't know when, but soon. Of that she was certain. And she had to be ready. She went to the kitchen area and looked around for a weapon. They had been allowed only plastic knives and a few pots and pans. One was a heavy iron skillet on the stove. It would make a good club.

Finding nothing else she returned to her mattress and began mental plans for the confrontation she knew was coming. When her father arrived, she would do her part to save herself and the other girls from these monsters. *I can do no less*, she thought, smiling inwardly. *I'm Jack McCoy's daughter.*

"We're close now, Jack," said Elena as she turned the Ford Explorer onto a dirt street called Calle Vista Verde.

It was eleven o'clock on Sunday morning and they had left El Milagro nearly an hour ago. It was a beautiful sunny day. Large white clouds dotted the cerulean sky and a slight breeze cooled the air. Jack had remained under a blanket in the back until they reached Monterrey and the narco vehicles Elena had passed paid her no attention.

Dressed in old jeans and a red Polo shirt, he felt better after a night's rest at the motel. He'd showered and shaved off four days of beard with a razor Elena had bought at the market. Still, he could feel the accumulated fatigue lingering just below the surface.

Little sleep and the stress of nearly constant combat the last few days were taking a toll. Soon he would be running on pure adrenaline. But he could rest later. Right now his daughter needed him and he would keep moving and fighting until she was safe...or the lights went out.

San Nicolas Hidalgo was a semi-rural community just north of Monterrey. The homes had large lots and small fields of corn and beans were scattered about. The houses were modest, but appeared neat and tidy. Families dressed for church gathered in some of the yards. Jack felt a sense of peace and tranquility here.

They topped a low rise and were met with a magnificent view. The Sierra Madre Mountains towered in the south and the low hills of the Sierra El Fraile lay sprawled in the distance. Pecan and avocado trees grew in abundance everywhere.

A hundred yards down the street Elena stopped in front of an older adobe-style single-story house with a pink tile roof and a small front porch with concrete steps. A fresh coat of white paint made the house stand out from its neighbors, and a green Chevy van was parked in a detached wood garage.

The house was set forty yards back from the street and three old cars were parked in the dirt front yard. A man with only one leg leaned under the hood of one. Two wood crutches leaned against the fender. A girl about five and a boy of seven or eight stood watching him.

"This is where I was born and raised, Jack," said Elena as she turned off the Explorer. Dressed in jeans and a white shirt from the Zeta's cache, she looked happy to be there. "I love it here when the sun is shining like today. It's so beautiful."

"It's a nice neighborhood," he told her. "I like the view here."

"It was more rural when I was small. My parents bought the house before I was born. We used to have cows and chickens, even horses. It was a nice place to grow up. When my father died ten years ago, my brother and his wife moved in to help my mom. My mom passed two years later and he stayed on."

"Is that him working on the car?"

"Yes, he's a very fine mechanic and people bring their cars here so he can fix them."

"Looks like he's seen a little misfortune of his own," Jack told her.

"Another reason I hate these damn cartels so much. Three years ago he had a garage in Monterrey and five mechanics working for him. He also had three tow trucks and he made a good living. Then one day he got caught in a gun battle between the military and a truck full of narcos on Highway 40.

"A bullet smashed his left leg and the doctors couldn't save it. He couldn't work for a long time and lost his garage and all of his tow trucks. He works here now and his wife works part-time.

I help them as much as I can, but they struggle. He needs a prosthetic, but he wants to save his money for another garage. That will take time, but he won't give up."

"Somewhere in my country last night some Hollywood starlet or Wall Street banker was shoving cartel cocaine up their noses for a quick high," Jack said in a quiet voice as he stared out the window at the man working on the old car. "I wish I could grab them by the neck and rub their faces in the blood and misery their selfish attitude has brought to so many people."

"I wish the same thing sometimes, Jack, but we can't fight human nature. Some people will do what they want and others will help them no matter the cost. All we can do is hold them accountable and protect the innocent. Now, let's go meet my brother."

As they walked down the gently sloping driveway, the young girl shouted "Aunt Elena," and ran forward to embrace Elena, followed closely by her brother. Elena hugged and kissed them both and Jack could see the affection they had for each other.

Elena's brother looked up then put aside his wrench and wiped the grease from his hands with a rag. Putting the crutches under his arms, he hobbled forward to greet his sister. "It's good to see you again, little sister." he said as they embraced warmly.

"Likewise, big brother, " Elena replied. "It's been too long."

"And whose fault is that?" he said in a scolding voice but with a smile.

"I know I don't visit enough. But I'm here now and I want you to meet someone. Jack, this is my brother, Ramiro," she said, continuing the conversation in Spanish. "Ram, this is Jack McCoy from Las Vegas, Nevada."

"A pleasure to meet you, Mr. Cisneros," said Jack as he shook hands. About forty years old, Ramiro Cisneros was above average height and lean and wiry. His gray t-shirt showed muscular forearms and the left leg of his jeans was tied off under his stump. Brown, intelligent eyes showed friendly warmth and his lips parted in a welcome smile. His short, black hair was showing the first tinges of gray.

"A pleasure to meet any friend of Elena's," he replied, "and please call me Ram."

"And I'm Jack."

Just then a woman came out the front door and saw the visitors in her yard. She gave a squeal of delight, and hurried forward to hug Elena. Ram introduced his wife, Lola, to Jack. About the same age as her husband, Lola Cisneros was a slim, attractive woman with medium-length brown hair and bright, hazel eyes. She wore an apron over a yellow dress and white sandals. After introductions, she insisted they come inside and have lunch with them.

The interior of the house was bright and well furnished. The tile floors were clean and little dust showed anywhere. The kitchen was large and had a small, attached dining room. There

Lola introduced Jack to two more of her children, two girls, ages ten and twelve.

While Jack and Elena sat down with Ram, Lola and the kids served hot tacos and iced Aguas de Jamaica, Mexican tea. The family caught up on news and Jack learned that Elena had a brother in Vera Cruz and two sisters on the border. Elena told them that Jack was a SWAT officer visiting with Marco and she was helping them with some police training issues at the GOPES office.

When lunch was finished, Lola served Ram and Jack a cup of *champurrado*, a hot chocolate and cinnamon drink then she took Elena into a rear bedroom to show her a new dress.

"I know my sister well, Jack," said Ram as he looked at his guest and sipped on his drink. "She won't tell me when there is trouble, but I can tell."

"It's complicated, Ram," Jack said, looking away for a minute. "I'd say more if I could."

"I understand. I know her work and the problems she's had there. She's not the same woman since her husband was killed. The suspension is tough for her. She is more obsessed with making the cartels pay for their crimes. I admire that, but I don't want to see her hurt."

"Neither do I. She's a capable, intelligent woman and you can trust her to make sound decisions."

"And I trust her colleagues will look out for her," said Ram.

"You can be sure of that," Jack told him.

Their conversation was interrupted by the return of the women and kids. After another half hour of casual chatting, Elena told them she wanted to stop at the neighborhood church before they returned to Monterrey.

Outside, Elena said goodbye with hugs and kisses and Jack saw tears in her eyes as she embraced her brother. Jack thanked Ram and Lola for inviting him into their home.

"Stay safe, Jack, both of you," Ram said. The look in his eyes said more than his words.

"I will, Ram, and you as well," Jack said, then turned and joined Elena at the Explorer.

Elena pulled into the lot of the San Hidalgo Catholic Church and parked near the entrance. A bell in the tower was still ringing and parishioners were coming out the double oak doors. The church looked old but well maintained and a large cemetery spread behind it.

"Would you like to come inside, Jack?" asked Elena, turning and looking at him.

"No, you go ahead. I'll wait here."

"All right, I'll only be a few," she replied, then opened door and got out.

When she disappeared through the oak doors, Jack noted that his was the last vehicle there. The others had left for home or other Sunday activities. He wished he could return to a peaceful evening at home, but that was not to be. In a few hours he would return to a world of violence and death. He just hoped that he and his friends would live to see another Sunday.

"That was comforting," said Elena as she slipped back inside the Explorer. "I attended this church when I was little and it feels like home."

"It's good to have something like that," agreed Jack.

"Are you a religious man, Jack?" asked Elena.

"No, not really," he replied, gazing at the mountains. "I'm more agnostic than religious, but I think religious faith is a good thing. It can make you a better person."

"Do you think it's wrong to kill someone and then go to church and ask forgiveness?"

"Not if you do so for the right reason, Elena. We both know that some of our fellow humans are just pure evil and sometimes people like you and I have to make that hard choice. I think a just God understands that."

"You're a wise man, Jack McCoy," she said as he looked back at her. In the afternoon light he could see small flecks of gold in her brown eyes. She truly was a beautiful woman.

"If I were such a wise man, I wouldn't be here trying to save my daughter from a beast." He continued. "Elena, I have a suggestion."

"What is it?"

"Let me drop you off at your brother's house and I'll tell the others you couldn't make it. His family needs you here. You owe them far more than you owe me."

"You're very kind, Jack," she said. "Marco told me you were a good man and I know now what he meant. But I have to do this. I owe it to my country and to my late husband. I can do no less than he did to fight this disease that's tearing our people apart. I can't stop now."

"Mr. Lozada was a lucky man. He'd be proud of you."

"I was the lucky one, Jack. It was a privilege to be his wife. Now I want to honor his memory."

"Okay, let's go do that."

Elena started the Explorer and drove out of the church parking lot.

Chapter 42

Marco stopped the Envoy behind the last car in the line and left the engine running and the lights on. Several more vehicles were lined up in front and people were standing in the road talking to each other.

"What do you think?" asked Jack from the passenger seat.

"I have a bad feeling about the bridge," Marco told him. "You guys wait here while I check it out."

While Marco walked forward to find out what had happened, Jack keyed the Motorola and advised the rest of the team in the Explorer behind them. In the back seat, Cesar Beltran squirmed uncomfortably between Barnes and Delgado. His last shot of morphine was wearing off and the pain was returning.

"Yeah, what I thought," said Marco as he opened the door and got back inside. "The heavy rain weakened that old bridge and it collapsed. We'll have to find another way across."

"We passed some brush and timber on this side a quarter mile back," said Jack. "We can pull in there and hoof it across the stream. The side road is just a hundred yards ahead and the Suburbans a half-mile in. It won't take long."

"You're right," said Marco. "Let's go."

He turned the SUV around as Jack advised the others and they drove back up the road past other cars stopping for the traffic jam. Five minutes later, they pulled into a thick stand of timber fifty yards off the road. With Marco in the lead, the group carefully paralleled the road toward the Rio Vesqueria. Twenty minutes later they reached the rushing stream and Jack shined a tactical flashlight across the water.

"Not as fast or deep as before," he noted. "We should be okay."

With boots strung across their shoulders and rifles above their heads, the group moved slowly into the dark water and inched their way toward the other bank. Elena slipped once and fell to her waist, but Jack quickly pulled her up. They reached the other bank with no further mishap, put on their boots and headed away from the river.

A few minutes later they found the side road and quickly made their way to the hidden Suburbans. With Beltran secured inside one, they pulled their equipment from the large SUVs and suited up for combat. Thirty minutes later Jack pulled them together for a weapons and equipment check.

Dressed in black from head to toe, their jackets were covered with PF tactical vests over plated armor. The Protech polyethylene plates would stop multiple hits from 7.62mm rounds. The vest pockets carried extra magazines, grenades, and combat medical aid. Everyone carried two side arms. Jack, Gary and Viktor were armed with Kimber CDP II .45 ACPs in Blackhawk Serpa holsters strapped to each thigh.

The others had chosen Glocks and everyone carried a Cold Steel tanto combat knife. The Delta 4 ballistic helmets on their heads would stop any handgun round. Under the helmets were low-profile earmuffs with UHF radio receivers and a short boom mic transmitter. The SWAT-TAC I muffs could be switched from voice activation to push-to-talk and provided good hearing protection. The transmitter was in one of the Suburbans and had a range of ten miles.

Jack was confident that everyone was ready. They were well equipped for the battle to come, courtesy of the men they would be fighting. The irony wasn't lost on him as he drew a diagram in the muddy road and shined his flashlight on it.

"I gave you a rough outline of the plan at the farm," he said, "but let's go over it again." He paused a moment, looking at the six faces around him.

"When Beltran makes his call, Gary will head out on foot. He'll radio when he reaches the hill and we move out for the compound. There'll be a checkpoint just off the highway, but they should just wave us on. The tricky part is at the compound. The rear compound is where most of the *sicarios* will be and there's about eighty yards of space between the rear and front sections."

Jack pointed to the diagram with a long stick. "An eight-foot wall connects them on each side with a sliding gate in the middle of each wall. The sat photos showed four guards on each gate. Just to the left of the entry gate is a parking area with about twenty trucks and SUVs. It backs up to a six-foot wall that runs from the side of the compound to the inner courtyard. The courtyard is a small area that leads to the front door.

"Vik and Brian will park the Suburbans in the opening near each wall and stay there. Elena, Marco, Kevin and I will get out with Beltran to meet our guests. They may meet us outside and that's where things will get dicey."

Jack paused again to look at Elena, Marco and Delgado. "I'd like to get inside before the shooting starts. That will make it easier for Vik and Brian to take out the gate guards and get ready for the main force. But we might not make it. They'll get suspicious because we're wearing balaclavas when there's no reason to have them on and because the people they expect to see, us, are still inside the vehicles. Let's hope Beltran can get us through the front door, but we'll do what we have to.

"The front section has two stories and the stairs are just inside the front door. The Gulf boys told us to expect twenty to thirty guns in there, Jimenez's personal security and some Zetas. They'll have side arms and rifles, but nothing heavy and probably not armored up. The *sicarios* also told us there's a cellar that has big guns, ammo, explosives. Marco, the ones on the lower floor will try to get down there. You and Kevin will have to stop them before they can get to the heavy stuff or we're in trouble."

Marco and Delgado nodded their understanding.

"Our edge in there is the grenades. We can blow the hell out of that place because the only innocents are the women in the corner room on the top floor. Elena and I will fight our way up there and bring them down. I don't care if we don't get Jimenez and his brother. My only concern is Brigitte and the other girls. We'll stay in radio contact and if anyone needs help we try and get to them.

"Vik, you and Brian have the yard. After we go inside you take out the guards at both gates and anyone else still outside with your suppressed FXs. Use your knives to flatten the tires on the Suburbans so ricochets can't get under. Those vehicles will be good cover. You can also use the low walls on each side of the courtyard. When the shooting starts, the guns in the back section will come running. You have to hold them until we can get out.

"This compound is a great defensive position, but its weak point is there's only one way out. The men in the rear have to cross the open ground between the structures to reach us or escape. If we can hold them inside, we have a chance to do this. They'll probably use some of the vehicles back there as cover to cross that space. And that brings me to the most critical part of this operation.

"Gary, if you don't get control of that fifty, we don't have a chance. Vik and Brian can hold them for a bit, but there's over a hundred guns in there. They'll overwhelm two men. If you have the fifty and they come out in the open they're dead meat. That's our edge. When the shooting starts, the guards at the checkpoint will head for the compound. You'll have to take them out, too. You, Vik and Brian can hold the others until we reach the women and get out."

"I hear you, Jack," Barnes told him in a confident voice. "Consider it done."

"I will. When we get out, we take some of their vehicles and head for the hill. You hold them until we get there, then we'll pick you up and head north across the desert toward Highway 85 and Nuevo Leon. That's about it. I told you this was fifty-fifty at best, but it's probably worse.

"We have good weapons, grenades, and armor. We have Quik Clot to stop bleeding, bandages, and morphine if we take a hit. Most of the men we're facing are street thugs, not hard-core troops. If we hit them fast and hard, we have a chance. Still, it's just a chance.

"Brian and I have the most at stake. I'd rather he not be here, but he loves his sister and he won't have it any other way. I've accepted that. But I have no right to ask the same from the rest of you. We can call this off right now, go back to Monterrey and turn it over to the PF."

For a few moments no one said anything. Then Marco turned to Jack. "Too late to turn back now, Jack. Let's get this done."

The others added their concurrence as Marco pulled Beltran from the Suburban and brought him to stand with the group. The PF official could walk better after another shot of morphine. Marco handed him his cellphone. "Make it good, you son-of-a-bitch, or I'll gut shoot you and leave you here," he told him.

"Marco, this is insane," Beltran pleaded. "You can't possibly do this. They'll kill all of

you."

"Not your problem, asshole. Make the call and don't fuck it up."

Beltran dialed the number for Fidel Jimenez and put it on speaker phone as instructed. The cartel boss answered on the second ring. Beltran told him that he and his men were coming to the compound with McCoy and Cisneros. He also had valuable information they'd obtained from the other Americans with McCoy. Jimenez acknowledged and said his men would meet them at the front door.

"Okay, game on," Jack told them. "Gary, check in when you reach the hill and we'll head out. Let's try to time it so you have the gun just as we get inside."

"Roger that," Barnes replied as he threw a rucksack across his shoulders along with a spare FX-05. A second later he disappeared in the darkness.

Jack looked at the others and nodded his thanks and appreciation for their efforts to help rescue his daughter.

"Now what, Dad?" asked Brian.

"Now we wait, son. Now we wait."

Chapter 43

"Beltran is on the way with McCoy and Cisneros," said Fidel Jimenez as he closed his cell phone and looked up at his brother sitting across the table from him. His security chief, Diego, sat next to him and the Zeta commander, Bernardo Huerta, stood next to Jimenez. The men were studying maps and diagrams on the table, preparing for the coming battle with the Sinaloas.

"What about Leon and the other *gringos*?" asked Javier.

"They didn't survive the interrogation. Beltran said he obtained important information for us. Diego, advise the checkpoint that two PF Suburbans will arrive shortly and to send them through. Also, tell the gate guards and the detail on the hill."

"Right away, boss," the big narco replied, reaching for a portable radio on the table.

"Bernardo, who's on the first floor?"

"My lieutenant Santos and three of his men, and about twelve of Diego's men."

"Tell Santos to take some men and meet them out front and escort them up here. I want to keep going over these plans." Huerta pulled a small radio from his belt and issued the orders.

"I like your plan to hide teams in the trees on the perimeter," Jimenez said, pointing to one of the maps. "Do we have enough men for that?"

"Yes, *Jefe*," Huerta replied. "Enough to cover all sides."

"And all our weapons are ready?"

"The men fired their personal weapons today and we test fired the one-thirty-four behind the hill. We'll mount it on the roof tomorrow and hand out the RPGs and grenades. The fifty is also ready."

"Good. Tomorrow morning we go on full alert. No booze, no weed, guards on the roof, patrols on the highway. "

"Done, boss. Let them come. We'll kill them all."

"What I wanted to hear," Jimenez told them. "Now, let's have a drink and review while we wait for Beltran. I'm anxious to see McCoy again."

Gary stopped and kneeled beside a mesquite bush, his eyes scanning the dark terrain, his ears tuned to the night noises. The only sounds he heard were a coyote howling in the distance and an owl somewhere behind him.

He'd made good time over the rough ground and was at the base of the hill. Starlight and a three quarter moon showed the back slope had a twenty-five degree angle and was covered with low brush and scattered trees. An easy climb. Gary took a long drink from a bottle of Aquafina then pulled out his prepaid cell. His call was answered on the first ring.

"Sam, we're about to go hot and I wanted to find out how it's going on your end...Can he get it done?...I understand...Okay, I'll try to keep you advised...roger that. Out."

That morning Gary had called Sam Coburn again, explained what they were about to do and asked if he could persuade his boss, the director of the CIA, to provide some assistance. Coburn agreed to try and had just told Barnes that he was at Laughlin Air Force Base in Del Rio, Texas in case the director got a green light from the president to run a rescue operation.

The president would hesitate to authorize a covert action in Mexico, but the director had worked for him when he was the governor of Texas and they were longtime friends. He also knew about Jack's help in uncovering a CIA mole and a Russian spy operation the year before. Sam was confident he would come through. Gary just hoped it wouldn't be too late.

Barnes put away his cell and hit the push-to-talk switch on his left headphone.

"Jack, you there?"

The answer was immediate. "Go ahead, Gary."

"I'm at the bottom, about to head up. If you don't hear from me in thirty minutes, you'll be on your own, and good luck."

"You, too, buddy. Out."

Barnes adjusted his rucksack and checked his pants over the bullet wound on his hip. It throbbed a little, but the Quik Clot was still holding. He moved up the slope in a zigzag pattern, slipping through the damp brush like a wraith in the dark. His boots made no noise on the sodden ground and he paused periodically to listen and adjust his bearings. *Like old times in Laos and Cambodia,* he thought, smiling to himself as he continued uphill.

Twenty minutes later he reached the edge of the brush line. In front of him was the top of the hill and the sandbagged gun emplacement. The brush and small trees had been cleared away for thirty yards on all sides and the cleared ground was soft dirt. Kneeling under a low pine tree, Barnes could see a glow of light over the sandbag walls and hear faint voices. About thirty feet to the rear was a portable toilet. No guards were in sight around the position.

Gary rose to a crouch and sprinted quietly up the low incline to the near side of the sandbag fortress. His back against the wall, he could smell smoke and hear the voices more clearly. A poker game was in progress and someone was losing badly. He needed to know how many there were and their positions inside the enclosure.

With slow, deliberate moves, he made his way to the corner and peered around. Light from the fire shined through an opening in the front. Barnes removed his helmet, then unslung his rucksack and spare FX-05. He set aside his suppressed weapon and prepared to crawl around to the front. As he moved forward, a man with an AK-47 in one hand stepped around the corner.

The narco held a cell phone to his right ear. His conversation indicated he was talking to a girlfriend. He stepped forward a few feet, slung the rifle over his shoulder then unzipped his pants and began urinating. He never noticed the dark shadow against the wall of sandbags.

Gary knew the man might see him when he turned to come back. As the narco continued talking and emptying his bladder, Barnes drew his Tanto from its sheath on his hip. Slowly, he inched forward until he was only an arm's length from the man's back then stopped in a crouch on the balls of his feet.

The Gulf *sicario* laughed at something, zipped his pants up and ended the call. Barnes lunged upward, closed his left hand over the narco's mouth and pulled him back against his chest. As expected both of the man's hands rose and clutched at the hand over his mouth, leaving his sides exposed.

Barnes brought his right hand around in a powerful swing and drove the blade of the Tanto sideways between his victim's ribs a few inches below the armpit. The seven-inch blade penetrated to the hilt. The man's body stiffened and bucked wildly as his killer pulled him backward to the ground, a muffled scream never getting past Barnes' hand. Thirty seconds later he stopped moving.

Glancing over his shoulder, Gary dragged the body back and dropped it next to the sandbag wall. After cleaning and re-sheathing his Tanto, he picked up his suppressed FX-05 and flipped off the safety. Dropping prone he crawled around the corner and toward the entrance. The sandbagged emplacement was about twenty feet long and fifteen wide. The walls were five feet high and had a door-sized opening in the front.

Barnes reached the opening, paused a moment, then raised his head and peeked over the top sandbag. Five feet away was the tripod mounted .50 caliber Browning on top of a wood pallet, barrel pointing out the opening. A shirtless narco leaned back against the spade handles of the big machinegun, watching six of his friends playing cards on a small table in the center of the enclosure. A battery-powered lamp provided light and a small fire burned behind them.

The men were seated on boxes and buckets in a circle. Empty beer bottles were scattered around them and the smell of marijuana was strong. *You boys wouldn't have lasted one night in the jungle,* Barnes thought, taking in the scene. More boxes, rucksacks, sleeping bags and other items were stacked along the walls. There was no one else in sight.

Barnes crawled back until he reached the high section of wall and rose to one knee. In one fluid movement he rose up, leaned over the wall and fired a three-round burst into the head of the narco leaning against the Browning. The slapping sound of the suppressed FX-05 broke the night silence as the top half of the narco's head blew away, flinging blood and brains across the card players.

The dead *sicario* had not hit the ground before Gary stepped into the opening, FX-05 tight to his shoulder, and opened fire. The gunmen were still looking back at the sudden intrusion when the first bullets hit them. The three facing him were slammed backward to the ground with one landing in the fire. The three with their backs to him were rising when a dozen rounds plowed into their torsos, spewing blood and sending them spinning and tumbling to the ground.

The slide locked back and Gary ejected the spent magazine, reloading as he moved forward to check the bodies. No survivors. He pulled one body from the fire then kicked the shirtless narco off the pallet and checked the cartridge belt in the chamber of the Browning. Ten hundred-round belts had been linked together to provide a thousand rounds of continuous fire.

Gary pulled the headspace and timing gauges from the side of the Browning and quickly adjusted the bolt and recoil group. With a round in the chamber, the big gun was ready to rock and roll. He went outside to reclaim his helmet and spare rifle then returned to the machinegun. Down below he saw the Suburbans inside the compound. *Time to go loud,* he thought. As he reached up to activate his boom mic, a tremendous blow struck the side of his head. The last thing Barnes remembered was the ground rushing up to meet him.

Chapter 44

Brian steered the Suburban off the pavement and up the dirt road toward the headlights. "Okay, Beltran," said Jack from the rear seat next to Elena, "this is your first test. If they stop us and you want to live, get us through."

The PF official was in the front passenger seat, his right wrist handcuffed to the door. He was the only one not wearing a balaclava. The Glock in his belt holster was unloaded. He glanced nervously at Jack. On Jack's left Elena glared at Beltran through the eyeholes of her balaclava, causing the man to turn back.

Five minutes later they reached the blockade on the road. Two pickup trucks were parked on one side and a Jeep Wrangler on the other. Their headlights pointed down the road. Behind them were sandbagged emplacements with several *sicarios* standing inside. A gunman stood on each side of the road and one waved his arm at the Suburbans to continue ahead.

So far, so good, Jack thought as Brian sped on. He looked at Elena and she nodded, their luck holding. Jack looked at the low hill on their right, able to see only the top against the starlit sky. Gary should be checking in any time now...if things went well.

Ten minutes later they reached gates of the compound. Floodlights mounted on the roof illuminated the area in every direction. As they slowed, the gates slid back and four guards with assault rifles appeared to wave them through. Brian pulled through the opening and turned left toward the entrance of the front building.

The space between the compound structures was well lit and to their right Jack could see narcos moving around between the apartment buildings. Several vehicles were also parked there. Three more guards stood in front of the opposite gate fifty yards away.

To their left more than twenty trucks and SUVs were parked in two rows from the gate to the near wall of the structure. As they turned around the vehicles, a pickup truck in the outside row caught his eye. Two men were standing over a large machine gun mounted in the bed of the pickup. They appeared to be loading the weapon and Jack's alarm bells rang loud when he recognized the gun.

"Vik, you see that?" he asked as he hit the PTT button on his headphones.

"Yeah, Jack, I got it," Tarasov answered from the Suburban behind them. "I'll take care of them and the four guards on the gate. Brian can handle the other three."

"Roger. If they turn that thing on us, we're done."

"You're right. I won't let that happen."

Jack turned to Brian. "Pull in front of the courtyard and stop close to that low wall. Vik will stop behind you. You can use both the vehicles and the walls for cover."

"Okay," Brian replied.

"Son, before the fireworks start, Vik will give you some advice," Jack said as he leaned forward and placed a hand on Brian's shoulder. "If he tells you to do something, listen to him. He's an old hand at this game. Remember your training and follow his lead and you'll be okay."

"I will, Dad."

Jack patted his shoulder then pulled a handcuff key from his pants pocket, leaned around the front seat and unlocked the handcuff on Beltran's wrist. "Remember, Beltran, as long as we stay alive, so do you," he told the nervous PF man. Beltran glanced back at him but said nothing.

Jack looked over at Elena and she nodded. He couldn't see it, but he was sure the gritty, courageous woman was smiling. He smiled back, feeling confident with her and the others at his side.

As they reached the front of the building, Brian turned right and drove forward. Two six-foot high walls ran fifteen yards from each corner, leaving a twenty-yard opening directly in front of the entrance. Low steps led to a concrete porch in front of the building's double doors. Above the porch was a balcony with an iron railing. A group of armed men stood below the balcony. Jack switched his headphones to voice activated.

"We have a welcoming committee," he said softly into his boom mic. "Let's try to get inside, but Gary hasn't checked in so be prepared for anything."

Brian pulled to a stop a few feet from the low wall and Viktor stopped behind him. Jack and Beltran got out on the passenger side and Elena and Brian on the driver's side of the Suburban. Brian remained near the door with his FX-05 at high ready while the others walked to the steps of the porch. Behind them Viktor stood near the door of his SUV while Marco and Delgado joined Jack and Elena.

Jack and Beltran led the way up the stairs toward the six men waiting for them. One was dressed in black fatigues while the others wore jeans, khakis and casual shirts. The narco in black wore a side arm; the others carried assault rifles.

Jack and Beltran stopped a few feet in front of them. Elena moved to Jack's right while Marco and Delgado stood to the left of Beltran, all at modified attention, rifles raised to the ready position, the way GOPES men would do.

"*Comandante* Beltran, I am Santos," said the black-clad Zeta. "Señor Jimenez sent me to escort you and your men inside. Where are your captives?"

"They are inside my vehicle," Beltran replied in a stiff voice, pointing back at the Suburban. "I'd like to speak to your boss before I bring them in. It's important."

"I don't understand, *Comandante,*" Santos replied, an alert look appearing on his face. "My orders were to escort all of you inside."

"There is something I'd like to discuss with your boss before I bring McCoy and Cisneros inside," Beltran said, his nervous voice alarming Jack.

"*Comandante,* why are your men wearing their balaclavas here?" the Zeta asked, clearly suspicious now.

Before Beltran could reply, the faint sound of a rifle shot came from the hill top gun emplacement. Santos reached for a portable radio on his belt and requested a situation report from the gun crew. He glanced from Beltran to the hilltop with nervous eyes and his men became more wary. After a moment a loud, frantic voice came over his radio.

"*Jefe* Santos, all the men are dead! We're under attack!"

"¡*Ahora!*" Now! Jack shouted as Santos looked back at them and reached for his pistol.

Jack, Marco, Elena and Delgado lowered their suppressed FX-05s and unleashed a barrage of fire into the group of men barely six feet from them. The high-velocity rounds sent the narcos sprawling backwards to the porch floor, blood spurting in all directions. Only one was able to return fire before falling, but a three-round blast from his AK-47 caught Beltran across the chest and dropped the crooked cop to the floor.

"Vik, Brian, the gate guards," Jack shouted into his boom mic. "Elena, Kevin, go with them."

Tarasov and Delgado sprinted around their Suburban toward the entry gate as Elena ran with Brian to the opposite gate. The guards had heard the AK-47, but couldn't see what had happened because the Suburbans blocked their view. All four guards from the entry gate were running toward the entrance, assault rifles raised, when Viktor and Kevin dropped to kneeling positions and opened fire on full auto. The gunmen were running close together and the blast of rounds slammed all four to the ground in a lifeless heap.

"Kevin, the truck!" shouted Viktor.

The two narcos in the truck bed with the large machine gun had stood watching as their friends ran toward the building. When the two GOPES men appeared and shot them down, they lunged for their own rifles. Before they could engage, Viktor and Kevin each fired a long burst from twenty yards that blew the two men over the truck gate to the ground. While Viktor covered, Kevin went forward to make sure they were dead.

Elena stopped at the corner of the low wall and dropped to one knee as the three guards from the opposite gate ran toward the entrance. To her right, Brian leaned around the rear fender of his Suburban. At just ten yards, both opened fire with three-round bursts and sent the three narcos spinning to the ground. One tried to rise, but Elena fired another burst into his side that dropped him for good. They ensured all were dead and returned to the building entry.

From behind the Suburban Jack watched some narcos moving around in the far part of the compound, but none seemed alarmed. The loud rock music blaring from between the buildings told him they hadn't heard the AK gunshots and had not noticed the other guards running toward trouble.

He turned back as the others rejoined him. While Marco stood guard they dragged the bodies of the dead *sicarios* to the open areas behind the low walls.

"Gary, are you there?" Jack spoke into his boom mic as he stood with the others near the door. No answer. "Gary, come in, over." Still no answer.

"He may be down," Jack told them, "but we still have a chance. Vik, you know that gun on the truck, right?"

"Yeah, Jack. We both fired it once, if you remember?"

"I do, and it's even better than the fifty. You take it and Brian will work from here."

"Roger that."

"We'll check on Gary when we're done here," he told the others. "Right now let's finish the job."

As they moved toward the front doors, Jack hoped the turn of bad luck hadn't ruined the only chance of rescuing his daughter.

Chapter 45

"Santos, come in!" Bernardo Huerta shouted into his portable radio. There was no answer. He tried again with the same result.

"*Jefe,* I need to get out there and see what's going on," the Zeta boss told Fidel Jimenez. The Gulf chief stood behind his desk, alarm on his face. His brother sat at the map table. Across the room, Jimenez's helicopter pilot had turned from the big screen TV to watch his boss.

The men had heard the faint echo of rifle shots out front. The gun detail had not answered Huerta's radio call and now Santos was not responding. Jimenez knew there was trouble.

"Yes, Bernardo," he replied. "Find out what's going on. Keep trying to raise the hill crew. They may be in trouble. And tell your Lieutenant in the rear to send more men to the gates and a detail to the hill if they don't answer soon. And alert the road guards."

"I will. Diego, you stay with the boss until I tell you it's safe," Huerta said as he picked up his folding-stock AK-74 and magazine vest. "I'll send some men here to assist in case there's trouble," he added as he disappeared out the door.

"Javier, tell Camila to lock down the women," Jimenez told his brother. Javier grabbed his portable and issued the order, then joined his brother at the desk.

"Fidel, what the hell is going on out there?" he asked.

Fidel Jimenez looked at him. A group of PF GOPES men had just entered his heavily fortified compound and, moments later, it seemed they were under siege. Had Beltran turned on him? Was the military outside? As he considered the options, it dawned on him. It seemed incredible, but he was sure.

"McCoy!" he replied, a dazed look on his face. "It's that goddamn McCoy."

Brigitte told the others to be quiet as she listened by the door. There was no sound. After a few moments, she turned back to them. They had all heard what sounded like faint gunshots outside the building, and the girls began whispering in frightened voices. What was going on? Were the Sinaloas attacking?

There had been no further shots and no one had come to the room, but Brigitte knew what was happening: her father was here! She had no doubt. She also knew the guards would come to lock them up somewhere.

"Michelle, Sophie, it's time," she said in English to the two European girls standing behind her. "My dad is here. Let's get ready."

Brigitte had told her friends that her father was coming for them and that they had to act when it happened. The two had been skeptical, but agreed to help. They knew this might be their only chance to escape this nightmare.

They had rummaged through the rooms looking for weapons to use against the guards. Brigitte had chosen the heavy cast-iron skillet from the kitchen while Sophie picked a large metal pot. They'd found a broom with a cracked handle and had broken it off, leaving a sharp, pointed end. Michelle wielded the three-foot stake.

Brigitte told the other girls to remain on their mattresses so everything would look normal when the guards entered. Then she, Michelle and Sophie secured their weapons and took up positions by the door. She was certain it wouldn't be long. Brigitte didn't want to hurt anyone, but she would do whatever was necessary to fight these monsters.

As Jack and the others disappeared through the front door, Vik Tarasov turned to Brian. "We need to hurry, Brian," he said. "If one of them comes out of the back and sees the guards are gone, the fight is on. Go do the tires on your ride and I'll do mine, then get your rucksack."

Both men ran from the porch to the Suburbans they had parked out front. Brian grabbed an extra FX-05, a rucksack with grenades and extra magazines from the rear seat, then pulled a Tanto from his belt sheath and began slashing the tires on the big vehicle.

The self-sealing run-flat tires would quickly close a bullet hole, but couldn't defeat the slash of cold steel. All four were quickly deflated and the Suburban rested on its chassis. Brian then ran to the other SUV where Viktor had done the same.

"Listen close, Brian," Vik told him as they kneeled behind the driver's door. "Things are about to get bad here. A lot of guns are going to come across that open ground shooting. This vehicle is good cover. Fire over the hood or around the fender, then move to the rear and fire from there.

"Don't shoot twice from the same spot or they'll home in on you and pop you when you come up again. You can move behind the wall and shoot from there. Keep them guessing where you are. This place is well lit, so use snapshots when you come up and grenades and full auto if they get close. Understand?"

"Yeah, Vik. Where will you be?"

"You saw that big gun on the truck over there? That's our backup. If Gary's down we won't have the fifty, but that gun is just as good. I'll work it and with you here, we should be able to hold them until your dad and the others finish inside. And keep this," he added, handing his rucksack to Brian. "I won't need it. Any questions?"

"I don't think so," Brian replied in a tentative voice.

Tarasov placed a hand on his shoulder. "You'll do fine, kid," he said with a tight smile. "Remember your training and why we're here. Let's get the job done and go home."

"I'm ready," Brian replied.

Tarasov nodded and disappeared around the rear of the Suburban, leaving Jack's son to prepare for the fight of his young life.

Viktor climbed over the tailgate of the Toyota Tacoma and began inspecting the big machine gun mounted in the bed. The M134D Minigun was a 7.62mm, six-barreled, electrically-operated machine gun manufactured by the Dillon Aero Corporation. Capable of firing 3,000 rounds per minute, it could deliver a virtual rain of fire on its target.

This gun was mounted on a steel tripod bolted to the truck bed. The electrical motor drive was connected to the truck's battery, and a linked belt of ammunition flowed from the gun's receiver to a large metal ammo box on the floor. The box held 4,000 metal-jacketed rounds. Two more boxes sat nearby. A large steel plate with a narrow opening for the barrels protected the gunner from incoming rounds.

Two years previously Viktor and Jack had attended a Special Operations weapons expo at Nellis Air Force Base near Las Vegas and had fired the gun for practice. It was a devastating weapon. He could only wonder in amazement at how a drug cartel got its hands on such arms, but, at that moment, he was glad it was there.

He quickly checked that the ammunition belt was secured inside the feeder module and flipped the switch on the electric control box mounted over the barrel assembly. The big gun was ready for action. And just in time.

Viktor looked up and saw a dozen narcos emerge from the back compound, rifles in hand, then split up and head for the two gates. He switched his radio headset to voice activated.

"Heads up, Brian," he said. "We got company."

"I see them," came the reply.

The gunmen had advanced only a few yards when they saw that the gate guards were not in sight. Shouts of alarm arose, and then a group of seven began running toward the entry gate. The others headed for Brian's position.

Tarasov grabbed the spade handles of the M134D, turned the barrels toward the charging narcos and pressed the push triggers with his thumbs. A ripping sound like a high-powered chainsaw blasted from the big gun and a storm of red tracers tore into them. The effect was a virtual explosion of human flesh as arms and legs flew off, heads blew apart and torsos were shredded.

In an instant, seven men became little more than bloody clumps of meat on the ground. To his left Viktor heard Brian firing single shots and saw three of the *sicarios* in his group lying on the ground. The last two returned fire as they ran back toward their compound. Before he could turn the mini-gun toward them, the two men spun to the ground and lay still.

"Good job, Brian," Tarasov said in his boom mic, "but the fun is just starting. Let's put a few rounds through the entrance to keep their heads down."

Two eight-foot walls ran from each side of the rear compound, leaving a thirty-yard opening in the middle. Armed gunmen were gathering at the entrance and looking over the walls to try and determine what had just happened to their friends. Noise and commotion came from the rear as leaders shouted orders and organized the men.

Tarasov pressed the triggers again and swept the concrete wall and entrance with a long blast of 7.62mm. Dust, chips and a man's head went flying from the top of the wall and two gunmen caught in the opening blew apart like rag dolls. Brian emptied a full magazine from his FX-05 through the entrance.

Viktor knew that would hold them temporarily, but they would eventually try to cross the open ground and close on the invaders. There were over a hundred Gulf soldiers in there and, even with the mini-gun, the odds were against them. Hopefully, Jack and the others could get out fast. Viktor looked at the hilltop gun nest and wondered if Gary had made it. *Where are you, buddy?* he thought. *We need you now.*

Chapter 46

A wide, empty hallway led down the center of the building's lower floor. Just in front of them a stairwell rose to the second floor. Jack and his friends stopped at the bottom to remove their balaclavas and reset their helmets.

"Good luck, guys," he said to Marco and Delgado. "Stay in contact."

"Roger that," replied Marco as he and the DEA agent headed down the hallway.

Jack and Elena looked at each other and headed up the stairs in a crouch, FX-05s at shoulder level. As expected, the landing at the top opened into a large recreation area with furniture, TVs and game machines scattered about. On the far left wall, a door led into another large room. Straight ahead, a wide hallway that led toward the rear drew their immediate attention.

A large group of armed men was halfway down the hall and headed toward them. A few were dressed in black fatigues, but most wore street clothing. All carried assault rifles and side arms.

"Elena, corners!" Jack yelled as he dropped to the floor at the left corner of the hallway in a prone position, followed closely by Elena to the right. Both leaned around their corners and fired a burst into the mass of gunmen, sending four of them spinning to the floor.

The roar of gunfire filled the hallway as the narcos returned fire, blowing chunks from the corners and causing Jack and Elena to duck back. Someone shouted orders to withdraw into the adjoining rooms for cover.

"Elena, grenades!" Jack shouted. Both grabbed a grenade from their vests, pulled the pins and tossed the explosives around the corners. Three seconds later screams of agony followed the explosions that sent dust and debris flying through the air. Jack leaned around and fired an entire magazine down the hallway. As he pulled back to reload, Elena did the same.

For the next moment there was silence. Reloaded, they peered around the corners to survey the damage. The hallway was filled with dust, and the floor and both walls were peppered by shrapnel and bloodstains. The shredded bodies of six narcos lay sprawled about.

Jack knew their best chance to prevail was to hit their opponents with fast, hard and overwhelming violence. Take the offensive and not let up.

"This room first," he told Elena, pointing to the door on his left. She nodded and crawled behind him to the open doorway. He rolled to the opposite door frame and glanced inside. The room was a large gymnasium filled with machines and weight equipment. Several narcos were crouched behind machines guarding their door and another one that opened into the hallway.

Gunfire erupted and bullets came through the door and punctured the walls over their heads, causing Jack and Elena to flatten and pull back. They each pulled another grenade and tossed them through the open door. More screams followed the ear-splitting explosions. A moment later, Jack and Elena crisscrossed through the door into the dust-filled room.

The grenades had knocked over machines and equipment and pockmarked the walls with metal fragments. Three gunmen lay dead in front of them and several others stumbled around, dazed and stunned, across the room. Jack was raising his FX-05 to further reduce their odds when he was tackled from behind and taken to the floor. From the corner of his eye, he saw the same thing happen to Elena.

Stacked along the wall behind them were several leather-bound punching bags. Four of the narcos had hidden behind them and were protected from the grenade shrapnel. Though stunned by the blasts, they had recovered enough to react when their attackers came through the door. Not firing to avoid hitting their friends across the room, two had taken Jack down and two more had acted on Elena.

A black-clad Zeta, bleeding from both ears, wrapped his arm around Jack's neck and tried to place a carotid chokehold. Another gunman in jeans and a white t-shirt punched at Jack's face from his left side. Though face down, Jack released his rifle and put his hands on the floor. With all his power, he pushed up and rolled to his right, putting the Zeta under him. As T-shirt leaned over to punch him in the face, Jack pulled both knees in to his chest and kicked up and out. His heels caught the narco under his chin and sent him flying backward.

The Zeta's chokehold had loosened slightly and Jack brought his head forward then slammed it back into the man's face twice. The arm fell from his throat and Jack rolled over and rose to his knees. The Zeta also rose, his face bloody and twisted with rage. He launched a side kick at Jack's face, which Jack deflected and then returned with a roundhouse kick that caught him on the side of his head and sent him sprawling over a rack of barbells.

Fifteen feet to his left, Elena was rolling on the floor with two *sicarios.* As he moved to help her, a scream from behind caused him to turn and see white T-shirt charging him with a Gerber dagger held high. The man's broken chin drooped obscenely and blood flowed from his shattered mouth. As he closed and brought his arm down, Jack stepped in, twisted under and caught the man's wrist with both hands. He raised his right knee and brought the man's arm across it, snapping the elbow like a dry stick.

The killer's scream was cut short as Jack pulled the dagger from his hand and brought the six-inch blade down into the hollow of his throat. He pushed the gurgling, dying narco away and turned to face the Zeta running toward him. From the corner of his eye, he saw the *sicarios* temporarily stunned by the grenades were now moving toward them.

When the two narcos took Elena to the floor, her fifteen years of martial arts training kicked in to high gear. She rolled to her right and out from under the one on her back. As the one on her right leaned in and punched her in the face, she brought her knee up into his chin and sent him sprawling backward.

His partner came back with another punch that made her see stars before she rose and brought her right foot around in a spinning heel kick. Her combat boot crushed his temple like a tin can. As his body hit the floor, two more narcos tackled her, screaming curses and punching at her.

Elena rolled with the tackle, hitting the floor on her back with both men straddling her. As the tall one closer to her raised his fist, she slammed her right elbow into his eye socket, making him scream and roll away. She twisted her head as his six-foot, two-hundred-pound partner brought his fist down and caught a glancing blow on her cheek.

As the man drew one leg across her and raised his fist again, she reached down, grabbed his testicles and squeezed with all her might. The big man screamed and rolled away from her. As she rose, the man she had kneed in the chin slammed into her and both fell to the floor near a rack of barbells. He grabbed her throat with one hand and landed blows with the other.

Elena wrapped her left arm around his clutching arm, rolled into him and pushed him to the floor. She brought her knee up into his crotch, making him scream and push back from her slightly. She grabbed a twenty-pound barbell from the rack and brought it down on the man's forehead with all the power in her body. His eyes rolled up as his forehead split and blood and brain tissue pushed through the crack.

As Elena rose to her feet, the big, mustached narco grabbed her by the helmet and threw her across the floor, ripping off the helmet and headphones. She landed head first against a butterfly weight machine and was momentarily stunned. Before she could recover, the big man grabbed her feet, pulled her back and sat across her waist. Screaming curses at her, he wrapped his hands around her throat and began squeezing the life out of her.

Jack slipped under the Zeta's right cross and grabbed his throat with a right-hand C-clamp. Pushing back, he swiveled inside, hooked his right ankle behind the man's left calf and slammed him to the floor. Before the dazed killer could recover, Jack raised his right foot and brought his steel-soled Blackhawk down on the man's throat with over two hundred pounds of force.

As the Zeta lay choking to death, Jack turned to meet the onrushing narcos. They were still a bit rattled from the grenade blasts and moving more slowly. He front-kicked the first man in the chest and sent him stumbling into a bench-press machine. Spinning on his heel, he delivered a side kick to the chin of another Zeta closing in on him. The powerful kick broke the man's neck and dropped him straight down.

The remaining three tackled him and pushed him into a stack of heavy bags. As they rained blows on his face and kicked at him, Jack pushed up and went Muay Thai on them. He slammed his right elbow into the face of the one directly in front of him twice then brought his knee up into his chest three times. Face bones crushed and ribs shattered, the narco slumped to the floor, dying of internal bleeding.

The Zeta on his left reached back and drew a Glock Model 19 from his belt. Jack stomped his right boot on the instep of the narco on his right, shattering his foot. As the man dropped to the floor screaming, Jack grabbed the Zeta's gun hand and pushed up. The gun went off, sending a bullet into the ceiling.

Jack retained his hold on the man's wrist and took him to the floor. The Glock slipped from his hand and landed a few feet away. As Jack straddled him, he saw a large narco choking Elena ten feet to his right. She was struggling under the big man, his knees blocking access to her holstered Glocks. Jack saw the Zeta's Glock just three feet from him. He rolled over and kicked the gun, sending it skidding across the floor to Elena's side.

"Elena!" he shouted. "Gun!"

Elena looked at him, her eyes wide, her battered face red, fighting to breathe. She grabbed the Glock with her right hand, placed the muzzle against the big narco's side and fired three fast rounds. The man jerked to his left and dropped to the floor, blood spurting through the holes in his blue shirt. Elena rolled over and sucked in gulps of air.

Before Jack could regain his position, the Zeta pushed him to one side and jumped to his feet. Jack rose with him and launched a series of combination kicks and punches that sent the professional killer sprawling back against a punching bag. Jack followed and put the man's head in an arm-bar hold. Spinning to his right, he swung the Zeta across a low rack holding several barbell plates. With his arm-bar still in place and the man's back arched over the rack, Jack dropped straight down. The Zeta's cervical vertebrae snapped with a loud crack and his body slumped to the floor.

"Jack, look out!" shouted Elena in a hoarse voice.

Jack turned to see the narco with the shattered foot limping toward him with a knife in his right hand. Jack grabbed a forty-pound barbell plate from the rack and smashed it down on the man's head as he closed in, dropping him with a shattered skull. Turning back, he quickly returned the favor.

"Elena, behind you!" he shouted.

Elena turned to see the tall narco, with his left eyeball bulging from his eye socket, holding a long barbell over head as he staggered toward her. Blood and eye fluid ran down his face as he stopped three feet from her and prepared to strike. Elena, still on one side, rolled to her back and opened fire with the Glock.

Bullet after bullet thudded into the killer's red t-shirt and sent him stumbling backward, the barbell dropping to the floor. The seventh and final round slammed him against the shrapnel-scarred wall where he slid down, leaving a long bloodstain on the white paint.

The room was suddenly silent. After a moment Elena looked back at Jack and the two warriors nodded at each other, knowing they had just survived another deadly encounter...and the fight had barely started.

Chapter 47

"They're here! Get ready!" Brigitte said softly. She'd heard the voices outside and raised a finger to her lips. She motioned for the other girls to sit on their mattresses and look normal. On the other side of the door, Michelle and Sophie raised their weapons. Brigitte flattened against the wall, her body tensed for action.

There was a clicking sound as a key was inserted into the lock and turned. The door swung open and Camila stepped through, her eyes on the girls against the back wall. Behind her Paco and an older narco named Roldan followed.

"Get up, bitches, it's time..." was all Camila said before Brigitte's heavy skillet struck her in the face with a sickening thud. Before the two men could react, Sophie hit Paco on the forehead with her pot. Blood flew and the narco fell to his knees. Roldan swung his fist at Sophie and went for a pistol on his belt.

As he brought it up, Michelle lunged forward and drove the sharp end of her broomstick into his throat. The tip of the wood spear penetrated six inches out the back of his neck. Roldan dropped his gun and staggered back, his hands clutching at his bleeding throat. A horrible whizzing sound came from his mouth.

Brigitte spun on her heel with a side kick that sent him against the far wall, where he slid to the floor and lay choking as blood pooled around his head. She turned back to see a dazed Paco rising to his feet and brought the skillet down on his head, knocking him unconscious.

"Bring the strips," she shouted in Spanish. Two of the girls jumped up and hurried over with strips of sheets they had torn off to use as ties on their captives. They would not be necessary for Roldan or Camila.

The female narco lay on her back, sightless eyes staring upward. Her forehead was split open and her face was crushed. Brigitte looked at her with no pity or compassion. Against the wall, a gurgling sound came from Roldan's mouth and his body relaxed. Brigitte took Camila's Glock Model 19 from her belt then helped drag the two bodies into the bathroom.

She pulled the unconscious Paco to a far corner then returned and gave Roldan's Beretta 9mm to Michelle. Now they had good weapons. When her father came, they could help. Feeling more confident now, Brigitte locked the door and settled in to wait.

Fidel Jimenez keyed his radio again. "Bernardo, come in! Bernardo!" No answer. He gave Diego and his brother a worried look. They had listened as gunfire and explosions shook the building and screams echoed down the hallway. Now all was quiet.

Before the fight started inside, they'd heard assault rifles and the M134D blasting outside. The Zeta commander in the rear compound came on the radio and shouted that the GOPES had taken over the machine gun and were firing on them. He said he was organizing a counterassault and requested Bernardo's assistance. Then his radio went dead.

Jimenez tried to contact the hill top gun crew again with no success. He wanted to bring the road guards to the compound, but he didn't want to leave the main road unguarded unless they were under a serious attack and needed the help.

"Diego, go and find out what's happened to Bernardo," he told his security boss. "He may need your help. I'll keep trying to raise the rear compound and the gun crew. If we're in real trouble, I'll call in the road guards."

"Will you be okay, boss?" Diego asked.

"We'll be fine. We're armed and we'll keep the door locked."

"Okay," Diego replied. He picked up his Israeli Galil and motioned to the seven narcos with him. Jimenez hit the button that unlocked the automatic steel door and the armed men went out into the hallway. The door slammed shut and Jimenez sat down. *That damn McCoy! I should have killed that son-of-a-bitch.* Now it was too late.

Just past the stairway Marco and Kevin Delgado found two large rooms on each side, one a game and recreational space with TVs, game machines and computers. On the left was a dining room with tables, chairs, a stove, refrigerator and other kitchen amenities. Ahead, down a short hallway, they could hear a man shouting orders to go check on the shots fired out front.

Marco and Kevin moved to the nearest corners of the hallway just as a group of eight narcos rounded a corner at the far end. All were armed, but appeared unconcerned, laughing and joking about some idiot accidentally firing his AK. A single Zeta led the bunch.

Marco nodded at Kevin, then both leaned around and emptied their magazines down the hallway. The storm of bullets cut into the densely packed gunmen, sending them jerking, twisting and spinning to the floor, spurts of blood turning the walls crimson. Only the two at the rear survived the fusillade and made it back around the corner.

"Kevin, grenade!" shouted Marco in English.

Delgado plucked an explosive from his vest, pulled the pin and tossed it down the hall where it exploded just past the corner. A high-pitched scream erupted from the connected hallway. Stepping over the bodies, both men ran to the corner and found a disemboweled narco gasping for breath on the floor. Marco ended his pain with a round between the eyes.

Three doors down the hall opened to the right. A loud voice there shouted orders to take the elevator to the basement and get the heavy weapons. Marco and Kevin moved ahead cautiously, stopping at each room to open the door and toss in a grenade before moving to the next one after each explosion.

When they reached the opening, they found a large freight elevator leading down. Marco shook his head. "Let's find a stairway," he told Delgado.

The two men moved on down the hallway, clearing two more rooms with grenades, and found a staircase where it ended. Inside the stairwell they took positions on the outer edge of the stairs and proceeded down, FX-05s trained on the landing at the bottom. There they found a steel door with a small window that showed a cavernous room on the other side.

"Here we are," Delgado muttered. "How many do you think are in there?"

"Only one way to find out," Marco replied. "You open the door and I'll toss two in, then we buttonhook around. Engage as required and look for cover. Not a great plan but all we have. You ready?"

"I was born ready, Marco," Delgado replied with a big grin. "Let's do it."

As his partner pulled the door back, Marco mumbled something about crazy drug cops, then threw two grenades into the large space in front of him. Delgado slammed the door shut then jerked it open again after the explosions. FX-05s shouldered, both men darted around the doorjambs to confront their enemy.

Fifty feet to their right was the open door of the freight elevator. To their left front, seventy feet across the room, was a large plastic-covered pallet. Along the wall to the right were stacks of military equipment, weapons and boxes of ammunition. Just sixty feet to their right front, six narcos were rising and stumbling around a large table where a machine gun lay.

Some were bleeding from shrapnel wounds and holding their ears. A single Zeta, blood flowing from his ruptured eardrums, shouted at them to find cover. The Zeta and two others dodged to their right behind a stack of ammunition boxes. The remaining three turned to their attackers.

"Kevin, the table!" shouted Marco.

Twenty feet away was a large steel table covered with automatic rifles and magazines. The two men rushed forward, grabbed the edge of the table and flipped it on its side just as gunfire erupted. Bullets thudded into the tabletop but didn't penetrate. Marco and Kevin leaned around each end and returned fire on full automatic. Their bullets hit the three standing narcos and slammed them to the floor dead.

Thunder filled the basement as a blast of rounds from behind the ammo fortress peppered the table and ricocheted around the room. Marco pulled back and shouted at Kevin to throw a grenade. He pulled an explosive from his own vest, then looked to his right and saw his partner lying still on the floor.

Chapter 48

Elena retrieved her radio headset and helmet from the floor and sat down on a bench next to a high stack of barbells. Twenty feet away, Jack, his FX-05 in one hand, finished checking the bodies of the narcos to make sure they were dead.

"There could be more up here," he said to Elena as she buckled on her helmet. "We should move." He cradled his rifle and moved to pick up hers where it still lay on the floor. At that moment a rifle blast came from the side door that led into the hallway. Jack felt a hard thud as a bullet struck the receiver of his FX-05, knocking it out of his hands and sending him stumbling backward over a metal stand loaded with plates.

He looked up in time to see the big, long-haired security chief named Diego coming into the room with an Israeli Galil in his hands. Behind him came more armed narcos. As gunfire filled the room and bullets pinged off the bench and plates, Jack's hands flashed to the Kimber .45s still secured in their thigh holsters.

One in each hand, he leaned around the end of the bench and saw eight gunmen gathered inside the door shooting or moving into position to open fire. The metal stand was wide but not solid, and Jack knew he was in trouble.

Before he could return fire, shots sounded to his right. He looked over to see Elena standing behind a stack of barbells with a Glock Model 17 in each hand, pouring bullets into the group of hired guns. Her first shots hit Diego in the chest and stomach, pushing him back and turning his white shirt red.

More bullets hit the others and their attention was diverted to the new threat. When they turned toward Elena, Jack leaned over the bench and opened fire with his Kimbers. Thunder filled the room as the two sides exchanged shots.

The narcos had become unnerved and were shooting in panic. Jack was shooting on pure instinct; more than three decades of experience in close quarters combat helped him focus on his targets with deadly precision. The big .45 rounds from his Kimbers sent the narcos spinning and twisting to the floor. He felt a thud against his chest then a thump and burning pain on his left calf; a moment later he felt the same sensation on his right bicep. Still, he returned fire.

From the corner of his right eye, he saw Elena's head snap back and a moment later she staggered and drop to one knee but continued firing. The slides on Jack's Kimbers locked back as the last narco dropped to the floor and lay still. In the end, superior marksmanship, nerve under fire and protective armor prevailed.

Jack looked at Elena as she rose to her feet and shook his head, showing his disbelief that they had survived the deadly shootout. She concurred with a nod and reloaded her Glocks. Jack did the same as he stood and noticed blood on his right hand. Then he saw the bullet hole in the muscle tissue of his bicep. His arm still worked so it could wait.

He turned to pick up his FX-05 and felt a sharp pain in his left leg. Looking down he saw blood pooling around his boot. With his Tanto he cut open the pant leg and saw another bullet hole through the outside of his calf just below knee. More patching to do.

He picked up his rifle and saw that the receiver was dented from a 5.56mm bullet and the bolt would not retract. He tossed the useless weapon aside, deciding he would grab one of the spares in the Suburbans if they made it back out. A groan from where the narcos had fallen drew his attention. He looked over and saw Diego rising to his knees near the door.

A Kimber in one hand, Jack limped over and stood in front of the dying narco. His white western shirt and denim jeans were drenched in blood. His eyes were wide and blood dripped from his open mouth. He raised his bandaged right hand toward a pistol on his belt.

"*Por mi hija, cabron,*" Jack said. For my daughter, asshole. He pressed the Kimber's trigger and blew the life out of the cartel killer.

Jack saw a Remington Model 1100 semi-automatic shotgun in the hands of a dead narco. He picked it up and took the ammo belt from the man's shoulder. The magazine was full of double-ought buckshot rounds. The short riot gun was a deadly close-range weapon and would do until they he could get another FX-05.

Jack joined Elena where she sat on a weight bench rubbing her chest. "You okay?" he asked.

"My boobs hurt, but I'm good," she replied. "The vest stopped a Galil round and I took a pistol bullet on my helmet. Kevlar works."

"You're bleeding," he said pointing to her right leg.

"I took a hit on my thigh. Will you look at it and see how bad?"

She twisted sideways and Jack used his Tanto to cut open her pants leg. A pistol round had punched a hole through the outer muscle of her thigh just below the hip.

"It needs to be clotted, but we should finish clearing the floor and find the women first," he told her. "Are you good?"

"I'm good, but we're a mess, aren't we?"

In addition to the bullet wounds, their faces had taken a beating during the fight. Blood ran down Jack's face from a gash on his left cheekbone and his right eye was bruised and swelling. Blood dripped from his nose and both lips were cut and bleeding. His chest burned from the hit on his armor. Elena's nose looked broken and she bled from cuts to her lips and both cheeks.

"Yeah, but we look better than them," he said with a grin, pointing to the dead narcos.

"We sure do. Let's go find your daughter," she replied through her own smile.

Jack paused at the corner of the hall and looked back at Elena. Her FX-05 was pointing down the hall behind them, guarding their six. Bloody footprints on the tile floor marked their progress and so far they had encountered no one else.

They had reached a dead end. According to the young Gulf soldiers they'd interrogated, the room on the left was Jimenez's fortified retreat. On the right was the room where the captives were held. Jack eased around the corner and moved to the door ten feet away.

"This should be it," he told Elena as they took positions on each side with Elena watching the hallway. She nodded for him to continue.

Jack turned the doorknob and found it was locked. Considering the situation for a moment, he decided to take the direct approach and called out her name. "Brigitte, it's Dad, are you in there?"

A moment later he heard running footsteps inside the room and the lock clicked. The door swung open and in front of him stood the reason he'd come to Mexico and risked his life over and over again. His beautiful daughter flung herself into his arms, weeping and hugging his neck.

"Daddy, I knew you'd come for me," she sobbed. "I knew it. We heard the shooting and I knew it was you."

Jack relaxed his arms for a moment and looked down at her. "Of course I came for you, sweetheart," he told her. "You're my baby girl. I had no choice."

She hugged him tight again and after a few moments, he pulled back so they could move further into the room. Elena remained by the door to watch the hall. Just inside, a group of young women stood looking at them in amazement. In Spanish Brigitte quickly explained why they were there and that she wanted to take them with her.

"*Pinche hijos de putas.*" Damned son-of-bitches, Elena uttered in disgust at the cartel narcos for what they had done to the girls.

"Sweetheart, this is Sergeant Elena Cisneros of the Mexican Federal Police," Jack said, continuing in Spanish and introducing the two. "She and Marco Leon helped me find you. Marco is downstairs and your brother, Gary Barnes and Vik Tarasov are outside."

"Thank you so much, Sergeant Cisneros, for helping my dad," said Brigitte. "I'm indebted to you forever."

"No thanks necessary, Brigitte," Elena replied with a smile. "I'm very happy we found you, and call me Elena."

"Looks like you didn't cooperate with them," Jack continued in Spanish, noting Brigitte's bruised face and bloodstained hair.

"I tried to help one of the girls," she replied, pointing to Abella, "and took a beating for it. It was worth it."

"Daddy, you and Elena are beaten up and you're bleeding," she added, looking at his face and bloody shirt and pants leg.

"We took some hits in the gunfire you heard and we need to bandage up. But tell me who that is," he said, pointing to Paco sitting against the rear wall, his hands behind his back.

"That's the bastard who raped me and hit me on the head with his rifle butt," she said as they moved to stand over the prostrate narco, and she explained what had happened when he and Camila came to lock them up.

Jack pulled Paco up by his hair and looked at him with a hard glare. "You have a lot to answer for, boy," he said through clenched teeth. The Gulf soldier looked away from the icy blue eyes, fear clearly engraved on his face. The women had moved in closer, making it clear they wanted revenge.

"First, Elena and I need to patch our bullet holes, "Jack said, lowering his Remington and pushing Paco back against the wall. He turned to move toward a nearby chair.

"Daddy!" Brigitte shouted in alarm.

Jack turned to see Paco had grabbed a girl holding a Beretta in one hand, and now held the pistol against her head as he backed up to the wall. Somehow he had worked his hands out of the bed sheet ties and kept it hidden, waiting for a chance to strike.

"Drop your gun or I'll kill this bitch," he shouted then pointed the gun at Jack. That was a mistake. A loud blast sounded and Paco's head snapped back. He dropped like a dead weight, an ugly smear of blood and brain tissue on the wall behind him.

Michelle shrieked and ran to stand with the other girls, who pulled her close to offer comfort. Near the door, Elena lowered the smoking muzzle of her FX-05. "He won't rape anyone else," she said.

While Elena maintained a guard, Jack dragged Paco's body into the bathroom. Back in the main room he began pulling bandages and packets of blood clot from his vest pockets.

"Yours is worse," he told Elena. "You go first. Brigitte and the girls can help. I'll stand guard and check in with Marco and Vik."

Brigitte quickly bandaged Elena's wounds and had started on her father when a voice came over Jack's radio that sent a chill up his spine.

"Dad, Vik is down! I need help!"

Chapter 49

It didn't take long for the narcos to organize. Over shouts from the Zeta bosses, Viktor heard the sound of engines starting and moments later he saw the front of three SUVs slowly moving through the entrance. The heads of the drivers were barely visible over the dashboards and others could be seen at the rear of each vehicle.

"You ready, Brian?" Vik asked over his boom mic.

"Yeah, Vik, ready," Brian answered in a tense voice from behind his Suburban, glancing at Tarasov in the truck bed.

"On my mark," Viktor told him.

"Roger that."

Tarasov watched and waited as the vehicles crept forward. Gunfire suddenly erupted as shooters leaned over the wall and fired at the truck and Suburban. Bullets pinged off the protective plate and punctured the truck body as the SUVs came closer.

"Now!" Viktor shouted as he pressed the triggers on the M134D. A stream of red metal swept across the vehicles, delivering death and destruction. Hundreds of rounds shredded bodies, blowing tires and puncturing the engines. They stopped in their tracks, their drivers ripped and torn. As Viktor raked them again, tracer rounds found the gas tanks and each one exploded, sending flames and smoke into the air.

The narcos at the rear ran back to the compound, but were blown apart before they could reach safety. From behind the Suburban, Brian emptied magazine after magazine into the compound's entrance. Viktor released the triggers and looked over the barrels to survey the damage.

A group of narcos suddenly popped over the wall and sent a concentrated barrage of rounds at the truck. As Viktor turned the machine gun toward the group, several bullets hit the guard plate and came through the narrow opening. He felt a severe blow on his helmet and the brightly lit compound went dark.

Marco grabbed Delgado's ankle and pulled him back as more rounds hit the table and glanced off the concrete floor. He pulled the pin on a grenade and tossed it toward the three guns behind the ammo boxes. The explosive fell short, but the concussion temporarily stunned the shooters.

A quick exam revealed a shallow furrow across the top of Delgado's right shoulder with minor bleeding. Another round had glanced off the side of his helmet and knocked him unconscious.

Marco rose up and fired off a full magazine to keep their heads down while Delgado regained consciousness. As he ducked and reloaded, return fire came back at him but less than before.

Marco knew he had to do something fast or the gunmen would try to move on both sides of him. Without Delgado's gun, he would be in trouble. He prepared two more grenades and shouted into his boom mic.

"Jack, Elena, are you there? I need backup!"

"Brian, come in," Jack shouted. Silence. "Brian, answer me!" Again, silence.

"Hurry, sweetheart," Jack said as Brigitte finished wrapping a bandage over the clotting agent in his calf wound. "Your brother needs help."

"You're good, daddy," she said, tying off the bandage. "That should hold for a while." His bicep was already wrapped. Elena stood by the door, bandaged and ready to go.

As Jack stood up and grabbed his Remington 1100, Marco's voice came over his headset requesting help. Jack knew they were in a bad situation.

"Marco, Vik is down and Brian needs help," he shouted. "Can you hold?"

"Not for long. We cornered some rats in the basement, but Kevin got hit and he's unconscious. I'm outnumbered and about to get flanked. I could use a hand."

Jack was torn because his son needed help, but so did his good friend, who was much closer. He tried to raise Brian again and this time he answered.

"Dad, Vik got hit and went down in the truck," he said in a desperate voice. "He's not answering me. I've got hostiles coming across the compound behind vehicles. I can't hold them much longer."

"Jack, go help Brian," said Marco. "We can't let them get in here."

"Okay, Marco. We'll drive them back then Elena can stay with Brian and I'll come down to you."

"Roger that. Good luck."

As Jack turned toward the door, another voice came over his radio and changed the entire situation.

"Jack, you and Elena go help Marco. I'll take care of these assholes outside."

Gary was back.

"Roger that, buddy," Jack said, grinning through the pain in his face.

"Keep this, sweetheart," he told Brigitte, taking a prepaid cell phone from his pants pocket and handing it to her. "I'll call you when it's safe to come outside."

"Okay, Daddy. Be careful. I love you."

"I love you, too."

"You ready, partner?" Jack asked Elena as he joined her at the door.

"Ready," she replied through bloodstained lips.

"McCoy has his daughter, Javier," Jimenez told his brother. He'd not been able to raise Camila on the radio and Diego wasn't answering. They'd heard the single shot in the room across the hall where the women were held and outside a battle raged in the rear compound. McCoy was winning.

"Are you sure, *hermano?*" his brother asked.

"I'm sure," Jimenez answered as he moved to a large safe across the room and removed a briefcase and another item. "I underestimated McCoy. He's more formidable than I gave him credit for. We need to evacuate."

"How do we do that now?"

"Mario, is the chopper ready?" Jimenez asked his pilot who stood nearby. A forty-year-old dressed in a light green pilot uniform, the man looked nervous and queasy.

"Yes, boss," he replied, "we're ready to go."

"Javier, tell the road guards to move in and assist the men in back," Jimenez told his brother. Cedillo raised his portable radio and issued the order.

"Fidel, how do we get out of here with all the fighting out there?"

"We wait until there's a lull in the shooting. Then we move fast."

"But what about our money in the basement? That's over fifty million dollars."

"We have to leave it. There's more in other locations and we can earn it back. A small price to pay for saving our lives."

"Maybe so, but I hate to see that goddamned McCoy get it."

"McCoy doesn't want our money. He has what he came for. Now we just need to get out of here alive so we can come back for him later on."

Jimenez took two folding-stock AK-74s from the safe, placed them on his desk and sat down to wait. He was a patient man. He'd waited this long for revenge against McCoy. He could wait a while longer.

Chapter 50

Gary Barnes finished checking the ammo belt and closed the lid on the Browning's receiver, then worked the bolt to seat a round in the chamber. Down below he could see four vehicles slowly crossing the open space toward the entrance. Over two dozen narcos walked behind them, firing over the tops. Brian was returning fire as quickly as possible, but he could only slow them. That was about to change.

Just minutes before, Gary had regained consciousness as a long-haired *sicario* in a green t-shirt was rummaging through his vest pockets, removing grenades and magazines. He'd already taken Barnes' Kimbers and FX-05.

His helmet was still on and his aching head told Barnes that he'd probably taken a glancing round that had knocked him out, but hadn't penetrated the Kevlar. A bulge against his right hip told him he also still had a chance to get out of this predicament alive.

The narco finished pilfering Barnes' vest then grabbed him under the shoulders and began dragging him to the rear of the enclosure. The dim light gave Gary cover to move his right hand to his hip and pull his Tanto from its sheath.

When the gunman reached the rear and was about to release him, Gary reached up with his left hand, grabbed the man's long hair and flipped him forward onto his back. Rolling to his knees, Barnes plunged the seven-inch blade into the center of the narco's chest to the hilt. The man gasped loudly and started to tremble and convulse while Gary sat on him. After a few seconds he went still.

Back on his feet, Barnes looked around and saw how he had missed the man. He'd been asleep under a serape in the corner between stacks of boxes and rucksacks. He'd looked just like part of the equipment. *Damned Murphy's Law.*

Gary made sure his dented helmet was secure then recovered his two FX-05s and Kimbers where the narco had placed them against the sandbags. As he moved to the .50 caliber, he heard Jack and Marco describing their situations inside the compound. He quickly told Jack to help Marco while he handled things in the compound.

Now he was back in the game and some bastard was going to pay for his headache. He trained the Browning's sights on the vehicles four hundred yards away and pressed the triggers between the spade handles. The big gun thundered and a stream of bullets poured from the long barrel. Every tenth round was a tracer and the stream quickly turned red.

In the compound the huge bullets tore into three SUVs and a pickup like a tornado. Hoods and fenders blew off and tires exploded. The shooters behind them were blown apart like melons under a sledgehammer. Tracer rounds found the gas tanks and all four vehicles exploded into flame like the other three already burning.

The surviving shooters ran to the back, but only two made it inside the entrance as Gary raked the open space with rounds. The compound was littered with body parts and burning vehicles.

"Brian, you there?" Gary asked.

"Yeah, Gary. Go ahead."

"I'll hose down the area again and you get to the truck and pull Vik back to your location. Can you do that?"

"Yeah, I'm ready. Let's do it."

Barnes pressed the triggers again and sent another storm of bullets into the compound. Back and forth he swept the open area with a hail of lead no human could survive. After three minutes of continuous fire, the Browning's barrel began to glow red. He fired another hundred rounds before releasing the triggers.

"Brian, you there?" he asked in his boom mic.

"Yeah, Gary, I've got Vik behind the Suburban."

"How is he?"

"A round went through his helmet and cut a groove along his head. He's bleeding some, but he's coming around. I need to clot and bandage him, but I think he's okay."

"Do what you need. I'll keep their heads down."

"Roger that."

Just then a string of headlights appeared down the road heading toward the compound. *Road guards to the rescue. Okay, boys, bring it on.* Barnes swiveled the barrel left and sighted on the first of the three vehicles to reach the front. The 700-grain bullets hit them while they were still moving and sent them careening on their sides. Bodies flew from the back of a Jeep Wrangler and within seconds all three were blazing heaps of metal.

Gary ceased fire and grabbed a spare barrel for the Browning from a stack of parts next to the tripod. Using rags to protect his hands, he quickly removed the hot barrel and attached the spare. He was ready for more action and he still had over 500 rounds in the link belt.

Gary turned his attention back to the compound just in time to see an explosion blow a hole in the near wall of the rear section. When the smoke cleared, he saw men pouring through the hole and running toward the hill. He swiveled the Browning right to meet the new threat and discovered the tripod mount would not move far and low enough to cover the advancing enemy.

Shit! Goddamned Murphy's Law again! he thought. *Hurry up and kick ass, Jack. I'm gonna need help.*

Jack and Elena followed Marco directions to the basement and had just reached the landing at the bottom of the stairs. Jack peered through the small window, but couldn't see his friend or the Gulf shooters. Gunfire echoed inside the large room.

"Marco, we're here."

"I'm pin downed, Jack," Marco shouted. "I scrambled their brains for a minute with a grenade, but they recovered and I'm taking fire. They're about to move on me."

"Can you toss another grenade?"

"Yeah, when you're ready. They'll be to your right front behind a big stack of ammo boxes. You can move straight ahead and flank them behind all the equipment there."

"Okay, go!"

A moment later an explosion ripped the air and Jack flung the door open. He and Elena darted through the opening and ran straight toward a table covered with clothing and rucksacks. They upended the table and looked over the top. Sixty feet away Marco and Delgado lay behind another table. Just forty feet in front of them was the stack of ammo boxes where three narcos fired at Marco. It appeared they hadn't noticed the arrival of Jack and Elena.

"If we can make it to that over there, we've got them," Jack told Elena, pointing to a table with a stack of boxes underneath, just thirty feet to the right of the narcos.

"Yeah, there's enough stuff scattered around so we can crawl below their sight," she replied.

"Marco, put out some rounds. We're going to flank them."

"Roger that," Marco replied. A moment later he emptied a magazine around one end of the table.

Jack and Elena started their crawl, their heads low to the floor. The room was a cauldron of thunder as Marco and the narcos exchanged fire and rounds ricocheted off the floor and walls. Slowly, Jack and Elena made their way to the table, using the scattered military equipment to stay out of sight. A minute later they reached their target.

Elena peered over the top and quickly ducked back down. "We've got them. When you're ready."

"Go!" Jack shouted.

At that same moment the narcos made their move to flank Marco. Two of them, one a Zeta, jumped up and ran directly toward Jack and Elena. The third one ran to the far side.

As he stood, Jack leveled his Remington and fired a single round at the Zeta. At ten feet the load of buckshot blew a big hole in his face. He was still falling when Elena dropped his partner with a three-round burst to the chest.

To their right, the third narco halted, surprised by the new threat, and raised his AK-47. Before he could fire, a round from

Marco's FX-05 caught him in the throat, cut through his cervical spine and dropped him dead. The shrapnel-ravaged room was suddenly silent.

"That was close," said Marco as Jack and Elena joined him at the table where he was helping Delgado sit up. The DEA agent rubbed his head, but seemed to be okay.

"You gonna make it, buddy?" Jack asked him.

"I'll be fine when the bells stop ringing," he replied with a slight grin.

"I'm glad they didn't get that thing going," Jack said, pointing to the machine gun on the nearby table. The weapon was an M249 Squad Automatic Weapon, or SAW. Like their assault rifles, it fired a 5.56mm round, but in linked belts at a high rate of automatic fire. It was a deadly weapon in close range combat.

"They were trying to when we came in," said Marco. "I'm glad they didn't get to these, either," he added, walking to a nearby wooden crate and pulling out a green tubular object. The M72 Light Anti-tank Weapon, or LAW, was powerful rocket-propelled grenade used by military forces around the world.

Before Jack could reply, Gary Barnes' voice came over his headset. "Jack, those boys had some explosives back there. They just blew a hole in the rear compound and about twenty of them are coming up the hill at me. I can't get the fifty on them. The rest are starting to move on Brian again. Get out here if you can."

They all heard the transmission. Delgado tried to stand, but fell back to one knee and blood flowed from his nose. Marco helped him lie down and turned to Jack and Elena. "Go ahead. I'll make sure he's okay then come up."

"Roger that," Jack replied, then spoke to Barnes. "Gary, can you hold until we get there?"

"I'll do my best. Gotta run, buddy. I've got dopers to kill."

"Looks like it's just us, partner," Jack told Elena.

"No problem," she replied with that familiar grin. "Let's go kick some cartel ass."

Chapter 51

Miguel Leon-Valenzuela stood outside his Range Rover and fumed. In front of him was the washed -out bridge over the Rio Vesqueria. On the other side, in the distance, came the faint gunfire of a raging battle. And all he could do was wait until the scouts he'd sent up both sides of the river found a place they could cross.

Behind him were thirty trucks and SUVs filled with *sicarios* ready to do battle with the Gulf. Leon knew he'd been right about McCoy hitting the compound tonight. Now if he could just get there before it was over. As he considered his options, the portable radio on his belt squawked.

"*Jefe,* it's Maldonado. Come about half a mile west of the bridge—the water is shallow enough to cross. I'll wait here with the lights on."

Leon turned to his lieutenant. "Pablo, tell the men to start up. We're on the way."

As Pablo issued the order, Leon got into his SUV and his driver started the engine. He might just get there in time after all. In time to clean up after McCoy and finish off his hated enemy.

Jack and Elena stopped and kneeled behind the first floor stairwell and Jack radioed Brian.

"Brian, you there, son?"

"Yeah, Dad, I'm here."

"We're about to come out. Give me a sit rep."

"I'm with Vik behind his Suburban. He's coming around, but he has a nasty head wound. I'm trying to dress it while I put some rounds out. The narcos are gathering at the front of the rear compound. There's over fifty still back there. They're probably waiting for their friends to hit Gary before they close in."

"Okay, keep firing on them. Elena and I will be there in a minute and I'll try and get to the one-thirty-four."

"Will do."

"You have a brave son, Jack," Elena told him from her side of the stairs. "Your daughter, too. You should be proud."

"I am," he said, looking at her with a tight smile. "Thank you for helping me get her back."

"It's been an honor to fight by your side, Jack."

"Likewise, my friend. Now, let's go finish this."

They moved to the front door and paused to look out. They could see Brian behind the Suburban on the right, firing single shots at the entrance to the back compound. Next to him lay Vik Tarasov. The open ground between the compounds was a nightmarish scene. Seven bullet-riddled vehicles burned brightly, sending smoke and flames high in the air. Bodies and parts of bodies lay strewn on the ground all around them.

"You join Brian and I'll make my way to the truck gun," Jack told Elena. "We should be able to hold them until Marco gets here."

"Roger that," she replied.

Jack pushed through the door, Elena close on his heels, and started across the front porch. He was nearly to the stairs when Elena shouted, "Jack, look out!" and he felt her push him forward. At the same time he heard a three-round blast from her FX-05 and a single shot from above. A moment later, he heard the thump of a body landing on a hard surface. Jack caught himself as he fell to one knee and turned to see what had happened. The sight rocked him to his very core.

Elena lay on her back, gasping and choking, blood flowing from her mouth. A few feet away, under the second-floor balcony, lay a narco, stunned and bleeding from his upper legs. An AK-47 lay next to him.

In an instant Jack was kneeling next to Elena, one hand under her head as he removed her helmet and radio. The narco's single bullet had hit her between the top of her vest and the hollow of her throat, angling down through her torso. It had missed her heart, but had certainly destroyed her lungs. Jack knew instinctively that the wound was fatal.

"Jack, I'm sorry," Elena gasped through blood-soaked lips, her chest heaving and her eyes blinking wildly.

"It's okay," he told her, taking one of her hands in his. "You don't need to be sorry for anything."

"*¡Mátalos!*" Kill them, she said, squeezing his hand tightly.

"*A cada maldito,*" he told her in a choking voice. Every damn one.

Elena's lips parted in a smile and more blood flowed from the corner of her mouth. Her head rolled to one side, her eyes turned glassy and her grip relaxed in Jack's hand.

For a moment Jack couldn't move, his eyes moist and his mind frozen. The noise of the battle behind him was a dull roar. Then a dark, malevolent force began building inside him, deep in his soul, a black cloud of visceral hatred that drove every thought from his mind except one: complete destruction of the forces that had caused him such pain.

Jack raised his face to the sky and unleashed a scream that was more animal than human. When he couldn't scream any more, he remained on his knees, tears flowing down his cheeks. A noise behind him made him turn his head. He saw the prone narco trying to sit up. Jack rose, his Remington 1100 in one hand, and walked to where the man lay. He ignored the bullets pounding the wall around him.

The black-uniformed Zeta had somehow escaped their fight on the second floor and had hidden on the balcony. Elena's bullets had shattered both of his legs. He lay back and looked up at Jack.

"*Ayudame!*" Help me, he mumbled.

"Okay," Jack said in English. He lowered the muzzle of his shotgun to within six inches of the man's face and began pulling the trigger. The 12-guage bucked and roared and Jack stared impassively as the man's head disintegrated. Eight rounds later the gun went silent and there was nothing left to shoot.

"Dad, they're coming," Brian shouted from the Suburban. "I need help."

Brian's words brought Jack out of his trance.

"Keep shooting, son," he yelled. "I'm going to the gun."

Jack ran around the SUV and down the row of narco vehicles until he reached the Toyota with the M134D. High-velocity rounds cracked over his head like loud, angry bees as the gunmen in the rear opened fire on him. He climbed into the truck bed and checked the big machine gun. The ammo can was over halfway depleted. Jack unhooked the belt from the receiver, then pulled a full can from the side and put a new belt into the feeder module. He closed the receiver and fed a round into the chamber. Another 4000 rounds ready for action.

Bullets ricocheted off the guard plate and truck bed as the advancing narcos concentrated their fire on Jack's position. Behind him he heard Brian firing on full automatic and watched as narcos spun and fell to the ground. As he turned the rotating barrels toward the enemy, a burst of rounds came through the plate opening and hit him in the chest.

The impact sent him sprawling against the truck cab window. Jack lay there, stunned, unable to move. His chest burned with pain and he fought to breathe. He felt unconsciousness closing in on him. As he struggled, a voice in the back of his mind shouted at him.

When they come, Jack, fight! Fight until you win or the lights go out. His SOG team leader from long ago. Advice that had served him well. *Get up and fight, you son-of-a-bitch!* he shouted at himself. *Elena gave everything. Don't let her down. Do it for your kids! Do it for her!*

With a great heave, Jack gulped air into his lungs and the cloud lifted from his vision. He sucked in more air and slowly climbed to his feet. To his right he saw green and red tracers flying over the hilltop gun emplacement. As bullets thudded into the Tacoma, he heard Brian's voice in his headset.

"Dad, are you there? They're closing in!"

Jack looked over the M134D and saw dozens of narcos emerging from between the burning vehicles, assault rifles blazing. He quickly grabbed the handles and swung the barrels to the near end of the line.

"You goddamned sons-of-bitches wanted war with me!" he screamed at the top of his voice. "Well, by God, you've got it!"

He pressed the thumb triggers and the big gun spewed out a red storm of destruction. At just thirty yards, a tidal wave of steel-jacketed metal slammed into the line of cartel gunmen like a sledgehammer of death. Bodies blew apart and heads, arms and legs flew in all directions. His face contorted in a killing rage, Jack swept the line from one end to the other.

The air filled with dust and became a dirty red mist. Bodies piled on one another until the advance stopped in its tracks. The ones still standing in the rear turned to run, but Jack was having none of that. He turned the gun's sights on the fleeing killers and sent more red death into their ranks. Screaming at the top of his voice, he hosed the entire field until the belt ran dry and the only sound was the gun's electric motor still whirring as he kept the triggers pressed down.

Finally, the rage died and the red haze was gone. Jack released the triggers and stared at the scene in front of him. The ground between the compounds looked like the floor of a slaughterhouse. There was no movement anywhere and a strange silence had settled over the location. Brian's voice came over his earphones.

"Dad, are you there?"

"Yeah, son, I'm here. You good?"

"I'm good, dad."

Jack released his hold on the machine gun and looked at the hilltop where another battle raged. "Give'em hell, buddy," he said softly.

Chapter 52

Over the sandbag wall, Barnes could see the heads of the narcos as they plunged uphill through the brush. In the moonlight he counted at least twenty. In fifteen minutes they would be at the edge of the clearing. He tried again to adjust the pivot mount on the fifty without success. He couldn't get the range of fire he needed.

At two places in the wall, he quickly kicked sandbags out until he had openings he could use as firing ports. He then placed an FX-05 at each window and placed grenades from his rucksack next to the rifles. He just hoped the shooters didn't have grenades.

In the compound, a firefight raged between Jack and the narcos. A heavy machine gun that Gary recognized by sound was pouring fire into the rear compound. He smiled, knowing that Jack had control of the cartel's weapon. *Good job, buddy.*

Voices down the hill brought his attention back to his own problem. He could now see the narcos at the edge of the clearing. They spread out in a line and advanced across the open area. An idea formed and Gary began placing his grenades in a row along the sandbag wall.

He then grabbed his suppressed FX-05 and fired off a magazine through the right opening in the wall just as the gunmen moved forward. He saw four go down. Following a Zeta's commands, those on one side dropped prone and opened fire while the others ran forward ten yards.

Bullets blew through the opening and Barnes let out an agonizing scream as though he'd been wounded. The firing stopped and more commands were shouted. Gary picked up a grenade and pulled the pin. He needed to time this just right if it was going to work. He counted off seconds until he figured the distance was right then threw the grenade over the wall.

He quickly pulled the pin on another and threw that one. The first grenade exploded as he tossed the fourth on over the wall. The explosions continued in a series as Barnes finished throwing eight grenades into the clearing outside. Screams of pain followed the explosions.

Picking up his FX-05, Barnes looked out the left opening. Through the dusty air he could see over a dozen bodies on the ground, some still moving. Six narcos were still advancing toward him. Leaning forward he opened fire and dropped the two closest on his right. Before he could pull back, return fire raked the window. One bullet hit the stock of his FX-05, knocking it from his hands and another struck him in the chest.

The impact staggered him back and he stumbled over an ammo box, landing on his back near the opposite wall. His chest hurt, but he could still move and breathe. Gary knew he couldn't reach his rifles in time and drew his two Kimbers just as the first narco stepped through the left opening.

He extended the .45s and triggered four rounds into the killer's chest that blew him back through the opening in the wall. Before he could move, a second gunman came through the opposite window and leveled his HK-33. Gary was faster, firing three rounds into his face and dropping him to the ground.

He caught movement to his left and quickly twisted around behind an ammo crate just as two Zetas came through the front opening. The one in front carried a Galil and he and Gary opened fire at the same time. Four hollow-point .45s hit the killer in the center of his chest, staggering him back against his partner before he dropped to his knees and fell face down.

Dirt and wood chunks flew into the air and Barnes felt a thump against his right forearm. The limb went numb and the Kimber fell from his hand. He quickly rolled left behind the fifty tripod and extended his left-hand pistol. As the second Zeta straightened and raised his Galil, Barnes fired one round that hit him under the chin and blew out the top of his head.

Right arm by his side, Gary quickly reloaded his Kimbers while checking the perimeter for additional threats. Finding none, he examined his arm wound. A bullet had hit the muscle on top of his forearm, cutting it to the bone. He needed to clot and wrap it before he weakened from blood loss. A shot of morphine would help with the pain when the numbness wore off. As he started that process, he checked in with Jack.

"You there, buddy?" he asked.

"Yeah, Gary. You okay? I heard grenades up there."

"That was me. They saved my ass. I took another hit, but it's not bad. When I finish wrapping, I'll take their truck up here and meet you at the bottom of the hill."

"Roger that. Let me know when you're down."

Gary recovered his FX-05s and rucksack and stashed them in the narcos' truck parked nearby. The Ford F-250 was a diesel, 4x4 extended cab with a large grill guard. Just what they needed for the run through the desert. One fight done, another about to start.

Jack climbed out of the Toyota and headed back to the Suburban. There he found Brian tying off a bandage around Viktor Tarasov's head. His friend leaned against the rear wheel with a bottle of water in one hand.

"How you feeling, Vik?" Jack asked as he kneeled next to his friend.

"Head hurts, but I'll make it," he replied, holding up his helmet.

A rifle round had penetrated the Kevlar and gouged a crease along Viktor's scalp under his headphones, just above his right ear. Jack had suffered a similar wound the year before and knew the effects.

"Yeah, that was a close one," Jack said, examining the helmet.

"I'm really sorry about Elena, Jack," Viktor added, glancing at her body on the porch.

"Yeah, so am I," Jack responded, handing the helmet back to his friend.

He noticed movement along the courtyard wall to his left. Turning his head he saw three men easing along the wall toward a small side gate that led to the helicopter enclosure.

"Stay with Vik," he told Brian as he grabbed an FX-05 leaning against the vehicle. Jack sprinted up the steps, across the porch to the corner and leveled his rifle.

"Going somewhere, Fidel?" he asked in a loud voice.

Fidel Jimenez, his brother Javier and their pilot stopped and turned to face him. The two brothers were dressed in jeans and polo shirts and carried assault rifles in their right hands. Fidel Jimenez held a briefcase and a long object in his left hand. In the flickering light from the burning vehicles, Jack could see fear on his face.

"Looks like you win, McCoy," he said in English, dropping his AK-47 to the ground. Javier did the same. "I congratulate you. I underestimated your ability and your tenacity. My mistake, and now I pay for it."

Jack looked over his sights at the man who had caused him such pain and grief and willed himself to pull the trigger, but his finger wouldn't cooperate. As hard as he tried, he could not complete the act. His face contorted with the anguish roiling through him and Jimenez seemed to sense his conflict.

"I understand, McCoy," he said. "When you look at me, you still see that ten-year-old boy who asked you to look after his father. If you pull that trigger, you'll kill the boy, not the man he's become. Your conscience won't allow you to do that."

Jack said nothing, his gun sights still fixed on Jimenez's chest. After several quiet moments, he let out a breath and lowered the muzzle.

"You better leave, Fidel," he said. "Before I change my mind."

Jimenez shifted the long object in his left hand to his right and tossed it across the porch. Jack caught it with his left hand. It was his katana.

"I was going to take that as a souvenir," said Jimenez, "but you've earned the right to keep it." He turned and headed for the side gate, followed by his brother and their pilot.

Jack slung the katana over his back and tried to sort out the conflicting emotions going through his mind. Nothing seemed to make any sense. A minute later he was joined by Brian and Viktor.

"It's okay, Dad," Brian told him as they heard the helicopter motor in the enclosure. "He'll get justice eventually."

"I hope you're right, son."

They waited, and the red and white Colibri rose over the side of the compound then turned and hovered three-hundred feet above the side gate. The three men were clearly visible in the cockpit. Fidel Jimenez raised a microphone to his mouth and his voice sounded over a speaker mounted outside.

"Don't worry, McCoy," he said, "this is just a setback. I'll recover and come back to give you another chance at me."

Just then a look of alarm crossed Jimenez's face and he motioned wildly at the pilot. At the same time, Jack heard a metallic clacking sound behind him. He turned to see Marco with an M72 LAW anti-tank rocket mounted on his shoulder and looking through the flip-up sights. Marco's fingers closed on the trigger on top of the tube and flame and smoke shot from both ends of the long tube.

An instant later a 40mm rocket grenade slammed into the helicopter as it turned to flee. The chopper exploded in a fiery red ball, sending its blades and other parts spewing across the compound. The remaining hull dropped to the ground and a secondary explosion blew that section apart. Jack and the others had ducked under the balcony to avoid flying debris and now returned to the edge of the steps to look at the destruction.

"I understand why you couldn't shoot, Jack," said Marco. "That's because you're a good man. But I owed that Nicaraguan son-of-a-bitch for what he's done to my country and to my friend lying there."

"You did the right thing, Marco," Jack replied. "Thank you."

Marco nodded and added, "There's something in the basement you should see. You, too, Vik."

With a last look at the burning helicopter and the end of a long saga, Jack turned to follow his friend.

Chapter 53

"How much do you think is there?" Viktor asked as he stared at the huge stack of money in front of them.

"Millions," Jack answered. "Tens of millions."

In one corner of the huge basement was a stack of U.S. currency four feet high, ten feet wide and fifteen feet long. The twenty and hundred dollar bills were wrapped in clear plastic bundles that weighed at least sixty pounds each.

"The wages of sin," Marco observed. "A lot of people died for that money. We should make sure the Sinaloas don't get their hands on it and I know how. Come over here."

He led them to a corner at the other end of the room and pulled a green tarp from another large stack. Long tubes of red plastic the size of a fire hose lay packaged in bundles of ten tubes. The word "*peligro,*" danger, was stenciled on each tube.

"That's Tovex, isn't it?" commented Jack. Tovex was a water-gel explosive composed of ammonium and other nitrates. The powerful blasting agent had replaced dynamite in commercial applications and was widely used in Mexican mining operations.

"It sure is," replied Marco. "Close to a thousand pounds, I'd guess. Enough to bring down this entire compound, and there's more over here."

On a wide wall shelf a short distance away hung coils of a detonation cord called PETN, boxes of blasting caps and electric detonators. A car bomber's dream.

"Can you rig this, Vik?" Jack asked. Tarasov had been SWAT's explosives expert.

"Yeah, Jack," Tarasov replied. "There's enough det cord and caps here to go around the whole stack. I don't see any fuse for a manual detonation, but these electric detonators will work."

"I can help with that," said Delgado. "I had EOD training in the Marines and used to blow roadside bombs in Iraq."

"Good, you two get started. Marco, Brian, let's grab some of those rucksacks over there."

"How many, Dad?" Brian asked as they moved to the table where the rucksacks and other equipment were stacked.

Jack thought for a moment, then replied, "Ten. One for each of the women upstairs." He paused, then added, "No, make that eleven, and just take the hundred bills."

He led them back to the stack of money and they quickly ripped open bundles and filled the rucksacks with American currency. Jack borrowed Marco's cell to call Brigitte and told her to lead the women down to the front of the building.

"Good move, Jack," Marco told him. "Those girls deserve something for what they've suffered. Let's take some of this heavy stuff, too, in case we run into more trouble."

"Good idea. The money won't make up for everything, but it will give them a new start."

"Come on up when you're finished," he told Viktor, and then he, Marco and Brian carried the rucksacks and other items out to the front porch.

"Let's pick some rides for our exfil," Jack said and led the way out to the trucks and SUVs parked along the wall. They selected two black Ford Expeditions and a blue Chevy Silverado extended-cab pickup. All were 4-wheel drive with full tanks and keys in the ignition.

They lined the vehicles up in front of the entry gate with the engines running and the rucksacks stashed inside, then returned to the courtyard. Brigitte, her arms around her brother, and ten young women waited on the porch. Jack explained what was happening and told them to split up between the two Ford SUVs. Brian would drive one and Delgado the other.

As the women hurried to the vehicles, Gary Barnes' voice came over their radio phones.

"Jack, Marco, we got trouble."

"What is it, Gary?" Jack asked.

"I'm about to head down and I see headlights on Highway 16 coming this way. Must be thirty vehicles and I'd bet they're Sinaloas coming a day early. We've got maybe thirty minutes."

"Okay, we'll meet you at the bottom of the hill in ten."

"Roger that."

"Let's get Vik and Kevin and get out of here," said Jack. As he turned toward the front door, Viktor and Delgado walked out.

"We got a problem, Jack," said Viktor.

"What is it?"

"We rigged the det cord and caps, but this detonator won't work," Viktor said, holding up a remote control device with a blinking green light on one end.

"What do you mean?"

"The max range for this thing is about two-hundred yards if everything is above ground. I didn't see that until we rigged the charges and I checked the control box on the detonator. With the charges in the basement, this is only good for fifty yards or so and when that Tovex blows, this whole compound and everything a hundred yards out will go sky high."

"Can I see that?" asked Marco.

Viktor handed him the remote detonator and Marco held it up for examination.

"And you couldn't find any manual caps or fuses?" Jack asked.

"None, they're all electrical."

"Well, I guess the damn Sinaloas get it all," Jack said, a look of frustration on his face.

"No, they don't," said Marco.

The others looked at him with puzzlement on their faces.

"You guys load up and get out of here. I'll handle this part."

Jack's mouth dropped and he stared at Marco with a look of shock.

"No, Marco, no, you don't need to do that," he said. "We can just leave it and get out of here before they arrive."

"We won't make it, Jack. There are over a hundred of them. They'll chase us down and we can't fight that many. Elena's gone and Vik and Gary are wounded. They probably have units on the highways to the north. We won't get very far. If I can stop most of them here, you can fight your way through the rest and get to the border."

He reached into his pants pocket, withdrew his cell phone and handed it to Jack. Reluctantly, Jack took it.

"Make sure the federal prosecutors in the States get that audio recording of Beltran. With that and Kevin's flash drives, they have a strong case to extradite Cruz."

"Marco, for God's sake, please, we can all get out of this. Come with us and you can come back when we put the heat on Cruz."

"It's more than just Cruz, Jack. That's my brother leading those Sinaloas. He's brought nothing but shame to my family and our people. It's time that ended, and it's up to me to do it."

Jack just looked at Marco, the anguish straining his face and voice.

"Marco..." was all he could say before his friend cut him off.

"It's okay, Jack. I understand, and I love you like a brother for feeling that way. But this is something I need to do. Please, take the others and go. Fast. I'll hold them as long as I can."

Jack looked at his old friend for a long moment then slowly nodded and turned to the others. "Let's load up and meet Gary."

"Vik, do I press the green light?" Marco asked Viktor.

"Yeah, Marco," Viktor replied, his voice tight with emotion. "Press the green light button and the one next to it turns red. Press that one when you're ready."

"Okay, got it."

"Marco, I really…"

"It's okay, Vik," Marco cut in. "Take care of yourself. It's been an honor to know you."

"*Igualmente, mi amigo.*" Likewise, my friend.

Viktor turned and headed for the vehicles. Brian and Delgado, their faces grim, nodded at Marco and turned to follow. Jack looked at his old friend once more.

"You don't need to say anything else, Jack," Marco said before Jack could speak. "Between us it's all understood. That's who we are."

"*Vaya con Dios, viejo amigo.*" Go with God, old friend, Jack said softly.

"And you, as well," Marco replied.

Jack walked to where Elena lay and kneeled down. He placed a hand on her cheek and said quietly in Spanish, "I wish I could have done more, Elena. I hope we meet again in a better place."

He rose and hurried to the Chevy Silverado parked in front of the Ford Expeditions. Viktor was in the driver's seat. Between them lay the radio transmitter from the Suburban so they could stay in touch on their headsets. Two FX-05s leaned against the seat.

Jack nodded at him from the passenger seat and Viktor gunned the big engine. They roared through the open entry gate, followed closely by the Expeditions. Two minutes later they reached base of the hill and found Gary in front of a dark Ford F-250 talking on his cell phone. He closed the phone as Jack got out and explained what had happened at the compound.

"Goddamn it, Jack, that shit sucks," he said, his voice rising with anger. "Both of them? I wish we could stay and kill more of those bastards." He shook his head and spat on the ground.

"Me, too, but we have to get those young women to safety. You good to go?" Jack asked, looking at Gary's bandaged forearm.

"Yeah, just a ding. I'm good."

"Was that Sam on the phone?"

"Yeah, he's at Laughlin with assets standing by. He's waiting for a go from his boss."

"What kind of assets?"

"He didn't say. I told him we're heading north and we might have hostiles on our tail. He said to keep him informed and he'd do what he can."

"Okay, you lead. We'll stay close. You ready?"

Gary looked at him for a moment. "Yeah, let's go."

Chapter 54

When Jack had formed the plan to hit Jimenez's compound, he'd looked for a route they could follow to the border if they were successful. The area to the north was mostly desert, open range and farmland with small farms and villages, but no towns of any size. After studying Marco's maps, Jack decided they would drive northeast across country to Highway 85, the major highway that would take them to Laredo, Texas.

They would cross two local roads and the Rio La Negra before reaching Highway 85. Before leaving the hilltop, Gary had used a compass he'd found at the Zeta cache to set an azimuth for the route he would follow. Now he held the compass in one hand and steered with the other to stay on course. His headlights, on high beam, alerted him to ravines and rough ground ahead of time. Still, the going was rough, even for the SUVs. He hoped the rough ground would be their only worry.

Marco stood in front of the courtyard and watched as the headlights of the first vehicle came through the open gate. The white Range Rover veered left to avoid the bodies strewn across the center of the compound and stopped twenty feet in front of him. Six other vehicles followed and parked close behind. Others stopped outside and armed *sicarios* fanned out to look for their Gulf enemies.

Miguel Leon-Valenzuela got out of the passenger door and walked toward Marco, followed closely by his lieutenant. His men in the other vehicles began moving around the compound to look for surviving Gulf soldiers. Many stopped to stare at the hideous scene. Smoke and fire rose from the burning vehicles, and helicopter parts were scattered everywhere. It was impossible to walk without stepping on parts of bodies. The smell of burning flesh made some turn and vomit.

"Hello, Miguel," said Marco as his brother stopped a few feet away to face him. Wearing his gray Stetson and dressed in a white western shirt, jeans and boots, the big Sinaloa security chief with a pistol on his belt cut an imposing figure.

"Hello, Marco," he replied, "I figured you'd be here. It looks like you and your friends were successful. Did you help McCoy get his daughter back?"

"I did. My friend is on his way home now. I hope you won't interfere."

"I can't allow that, Marco. A DEA agent with him has information that will hurt the people I work for. I'm guessing they headed northeast for eighty-five. Is that right?"

Marco remained silent.

"That's okay. I admire your loyalty."

"Pablo, send ten trucks after them," said Miguel, turning to his lieutenant, "and tell the units on eighty-five to head south and look for them in the desert. Take them alive if possible. I want that son-of-a-bitch Delgado."

"*Si, jefe,*" replied Pablo, raising a portable radio to his mouth and giving the orders.

"And Pablo, send the birds," said Miguel.

"How did we come to this, little brother?" Marco asked, his voice tinged with sadness. "You on one side, me on the other."

"We took different paths, Marco," his brother replied. "I don't know why. It's just who we are, I guess. Different people."

"We weren't so different when we were kids on the farm. We were close then. We shared everything. We looked forward to a good life. What happened?"

"That was a different time, Marco. A different life. We were kids then. We're not kids anymore."

"No, but we're still brothers."

"I told you at our mother's funeral not to interfere in our business and I wouldn't let my men hurt you. Why didn't you listen?"

Marco looked down for a moment then back up at his brother, a sad, painful expression on his face.

"Miguel, do you remember what you asked me when I left to go live with our uncle in Brownsville?"

"I asked if you would ever come back and you said family always comes home."

"That's right. It's time you and I went home, Miguel" said Marco as he raised the detonator in his right hand. He pressed the green light and another one turned red.

Leon looked at his brother in puzzlement before realization set in. As he raised one hand and started to shout, Marco smiled and pressed the red light.

Brian's Expedition, the last one in line, crossed State Road 1 and quickly caught up with the other vehicles as they headed into a low range of hills called the Sierra Milpillas. Jack sat back in the Silverado and tried to relax. The only remaining obstacle between them and Highway 85 was the Rio La Negra.

He suddenly felt the Silverado begin to tremble as the ground under them shook and rolled. The big truck veered slightly as Viktor struggled to hold it steady. Jack thought he knew the cause. He looked over the horizon above Gary's truck, fifty yards ahead of them, and spoke into his boom mic.

"Gary, there's a low hill just ahead to the right," he said. "Pull up there."

"Roger that," Barnes replied. Then a moment later, "I felt it, too."

The Ford F-250 led the way up the hill and stopped at the top. The other vehicles pulled alongside and Jack got out with a pair of binoculars in his hand. Through the glasses he could see a large cloud of smoke rising in the night sky above the compound nearly fifteen miles away.

"Adios, viejo amigo." So long, old friend, Jack said softly as Gary and Viktor joined him.

"Jack, look over there?" said Gary, his own binos still raised to his eyes.

Jack looked to the left and, between the scattered lights of farmhouses in the distance, he saw nearly a dozen sets of headlights moving north toward them at high speed. The Sinaloas were in hot pursuit.

"Five miles or so, you think?" asked Gary.

"Yeah, about. Let's hit it; we still have a river to cross."

They piled back in and set out as fast as the ground permitted. The river was still five miles ahead and they needed time to cross before the narcos got there. Gary's Ford plowed through brush and high grass, around large rocks and pinon trees. A herd of Corriente cattle appeared in front of them and quickly scattered as the trucks barged forward.

"Jack, I just told Sam where we are and what's going on," said Gary's voice in Jack's earphones. "I think he said he has approval to come get us, but I'm not sure. I lost the connection and couldn't get him back."

"Roger that," replied Jack. "Let's hope he can find us."

After a pounding twenty-minute ride, they arrived at the bank of the Rio La Negra.

"Can we make it?" Viktor asked as he studied the water. The river was a muddy channel sixty yards wide. It flowed smoothly but not fast. It didn't look deep, but they couldn't be sure. All the men had gathered at the bank and the women had remained inside the Expeditions.

"I think so," said Jack. "It doesn't look too bad. You go first, Gary. Slow and easy, and we'll follow."

Back in his truck, Gary eased the Ford into the water and pushed forward. The water turned out to be shallow, only rising halfway up the wheels.

"You're looking good," Jack told Gary as he and Viktor followed twenty yards behind. The Expeditions brought up the rear. The two trucks and Delgado's Expedition reached the other bank first. The one driven by Brian was still mid-stream when the right front wheel slid into an underwater hole. Despite his best attempts, Brian could not right the big SUV.

"Okay, Brian, get everyone out," Jack told him from the far bank. "Make sure they hold onto their rucksacks."

As Brian and the five women unloaded into the muddy water, Gary pointed at the other bank and said, "We got more trouble, Jack."

Chapter 55

A flood of headlights swept across the brush-lined far bank as three narco-filled pickup trucks pulled up to the edge of the stream. Shouts erupted as eight of the gunmen ran into the water and waded toward the Expedition. Ten others lined up on the bank and began firing at the three vehicles across the river.

"Gary, come with me," shouted Jack. "Vik, Kevin, give us some cover."

As Jack and Gary charged down the low bank and across the river, Viktor and Kevin dropped prone and returned fire at the narcos on the other bank. Brigitte and the five girls with her ducked behind the Expedition.

As they closed in, Jack saw three of the women outside the Expedition, rucksacks on their backs, and Brian was helping the last two out through a passenger door. The narcos were now just thirty feet from them and closing fast. Jack heard one yell at his buddies that their boss wanted them alive. Rifle rounds cracked overhead and tracer rounds lit up the night.

As the last two women exited the vehicle, Brian turned and shot the leading narco in the chest, dropping him into the water. Two others quickly returned fire and Jack saw cloth fly from the top of Brian's shoulder as he stumbled back against the open door of the Expedition. The women began screaming and struggling through the knee-deep water as the narcos swirled around them.

Unable to fire for fear of hitting the women, Jack screamed out loud as he and Gary plowed into the melee. A gunman holding Michelle by the hair raised his AK-47 and Jack slammed him in the face with his FX-05. That man dropped and two more lunged at him, one grabbing his rifle.

The knee-deep water made it difficult to fight, so Jack released the weapon, reached behind his back and drew his katana from its *saya*. In a smooth, continuous movement, he brought the blade down in a diagonal slash that opened the man's chest from neck to sternum. He fell back and disappeared under the water.

To Jack's left, he saw Gary take two narcos down into the water as two others continued pulling at the women. The man who grabbed Jack's FX-05 threw it at him and raised his M4 carbine. Jack deflected the thrown rifle with his katana then raised one foot out of the water, twisted right and brought his sword down at a sharp angle. The blade caught the killer's left arm at the elbow and severed it cleanly.

The man screamed loudly as his arm dropped into the river and the stump gushed blood. As the man dropped his M4 and grabbed his left bicep, Jack whirled right, his katana fully extended, and swept the blade through the man's neck. For a moment the Sinaloa's wide eyes simply stared at him, then his head fell forward and dropped into the river, followed closely by his body. The water around them turned red.

Three of the women were wading quickly toward the far bank. The other two were being dragged backward by the Sinaloas. Jack saw one of Gary's opponents floating on the surface, blood spurting from his neck. Barnes was on his knees with one arm around the other's neck, plunging a Tanto into his chest.

Jack shouted at the retreating narcos and splashed toward them, his katana held high. A big one with a bald head and a bulging stomach shoved the woman he was holding against Jack, sending them stumbling backward into the water. The woman pushed away and the Sinaloa rushed forward, his AK held high.

As he closed Jack rose to one knee and swung his katana one-handed right to left under the plunging rifle stock. The butt glanced off his left shoulder, but the tip of his blade disemboweled the big narco, dropping his entrails into the muddy water. The man unleashed a guttural scream and fell back into a sitting position, hands clutching his gaping stomach.

To Jack's left front, the last narco shoved aside the woman he was holding and aimed his HK-36 at Jack. Before he could fire, a rifle blast sounded from behind and a bullet struck the Sinaloa in the mouth and blew through the back of his head. The gunman dropped straight down.

Jack look back and saw Brian standing next to the Expedition, smoke rising from the muzzle of his shouldered FX-05. The son he'd thought might have been dead had just saved his life. With bullets snapping all around them there was no time for triumph. He yelled at Brian to help get the women to safety as he sheathed his katana, and he and Gary recovered their rifles from the river bed.

With Viktor and Delgado providing cover fire, they waded back to the bank, where they shook the water from their rifles and handguns. On the far bank, more Sinaloas arrived in SUVs and began firing across the river.

"Vik, get everyone loaded up and move out," Jack shouted at Tarasov. "Gary and I will cover and follow."

Viktor, Brian and Delgado helped the women load into the remaining vehicles and Viktor sped out in his Silverado with Delgado following behind in the Expedition. Brian was in the driver's seat of the F-250.

Over thirty Sinaloas now lined the far bank, pouring fire across the river. Jack and Gary dropped prone, pulled spare magazines from their vests and returned fire as fast as possible. Gary had lost his helmet and radio headset in the river, but Jack heard Brian's voice in his earphones.

"Dad, I have Brigitte and two girls in the truck. Jump in the bed when I pull up."

Jack looked around and saw the Ford slide to a stop fifty feet behind them. He yelled at Gary, ten feet to his right, and pointed. He and Barnes ran for the truck. Just as they reached the tailgate, Gary spun around and fell to his knees. Jack grabbed him by one arm and threw him into the bed then jumped in beside him.

Brian floored the big diesel and sped away as bullets pinged off the bumper and tailgate. Two smashed through the rear window but missed the occupants inside. In seconds they caught up with the others speeding across the desert floor. Jack looked back and saw the Sinaloa vehicles crossing the river.

"How bad is it?" Jack asked as Gary clasped his right shoulder.

"Hurts like hell, but I think it missed the bone."

The truck bounced across the rough desert ground and Jack knew the jarring ride had to be painful even though they lay on a pile of rucksacks. He could see blood running down Gary's right arm.

"Okay, no time for patching. Hang in there."

Jack felt the truck move down an incline then level off across smoother ground. A minute later, he heard Viktor's voice in his earphones.

"Jack, we got a problem."

"What is it, Vik?" he replied as the Ford came to a stop.

"We got a ravine in front of us and it's a four-foot drop. We'll have to find a crossing point."

Jack pulled a bandage and packet of Quik Clot from his vest and handed it to Gary. "Wait here and fix that. I'll see what we got."

Jack walked around the Expedition and stopped next to Viktor and Delgado in front of the Silverado. In the glare of the headlights was a dry gully, sixty yards across. The near bank over four feet high. There was no way to get down. Fifty yards to the right it curved back toward the low hill. To the left, the banks became ten feet high as far as they could see.

"Okay, we go back over the hill and downstream," Jack said, pointing left. "Vik, you lead, Gary, Brian and I will take the six."

Viktor nodded and all of them returned to their vehicles. When Jack reached the Ford, he looked in at Brian and saw that his left shoulder was blood-soaked. "You okay, son?" he asked.

"Yeah, Dad, I'm good. Just a notch on top. The bleeding's stopped now. My chest hurts, but I'm glad I had the armor."

"Me, too, and thanks."

"Just glad I was there, Dad."

Jack smiled at his son and climbed into the truck bed. The Silverado turned and moved across the low ground, the Expedition and Ford following behind. They were halfway to the hill when headlights appeared at the top and six pickups crested the top. To their right, two more trucks and two SUVs came around the side.

"Jack!" Viktor shouted in his boom mic.

"Yeah, I got'em. You and Kevin park sideways here, get everyone out and move back to the ravine. We'll take cover there."

"Brian, pull over there," Jack shouted through the truck cab window, pointing right.

Brian drove the pickup fifty yards to the right and stopped just a hundred yards from the narcos on the side of the hill. Brigitte and the women scrambled out the driver's door while Jack and Gary unloaded the rucksacks from the bed and they all ran for the ravine behind them.

The women got out of the Expedition and Silverado and ran for safety while Viktor and Delgado covered them from behind the vehicles. They were slowed by their money-filled rucksacks, but all made it to the ravine and dropped over the bank. The Sinaloas now poured a heavy volume of fire down the hill and from the side. Viktor and Delgado returned the fire.

When he saw the women were safe, Viktor shouted at the DEA agent. "You ready to evac, buddy?"

"Not yet," Delgado shouted back, pointing up the hill.

Three pickups were advancing down the hill with Sinaloas walking behind them and firing around the sides. Delgado opened the passenger door of the Expedition and pulled out two long tubes. "Let's try these," he shouted, throwing one of the M72 LAWs to Tarasov.

Both men quickly activated the rocket launchers, leaned over the front of their vehicles and picked a target. A second later the 40mm HEAT rounds slammed into the two trucks on the left. Metal and bodies blew into the air amid fire and smoke and gas tank explosions added to the flames. The truck on the right began backing quickly up the hill.

Delgado reached back inside the Expedition and withdrew one more item.

"You first, and I'll cover with this," he shouted with a wide grin as he tossed his FX-05 to Tarasov. In his hands was the M249 SAW from the compound basement. A five-hundred round belt of ammo hung from the receiver and curled over his shoulder.

Viktor gave him a thumbs-up and sprinted for the ravine as Delgado leaned over the hood of the Expedition and triggered a long blast at the hilltop. The Sinaloa fire slowed under the withering barrage. Delgado ducked below the hood and prepared to run when a trail of fire and smoke shot out of the sky and the Silverado to his left blew apart in a fiery explosion that sent him flying backward to the ground.

Chapter 56

"Jesus Christ, Jack, these bastards have gunships!" Gary shouted from his position six feet away.

Jack looked over the bank at the two helicopters hovering at the top of the hill. The UH-1 Iroquois models were painted black, and one had M75 40mm grenade launchers mounted above each skid: the weapon that had just destroyed the Chevrolet pickup. The other one had an M60 machine gun mounted at the door with a gunner on the trigger.

"They're old Hueys," Jack shouted back. "Military surplus from 'Nam. You can buy them anywhere. They probably stole the guns or bought them on the black market."

"So what the hell do we do now?"

Jack looked around to assess their situation. To his left, Viktor had just dropped over the bank on the other side of Gary. To his right was Brian, and on the other side of him were Brigitte and the young captives. They clung together below the lip of the bank. Some were crying and all were terrified.

All except Brigitte. Jack's daughter held a spare FX-05 in her hands and was firing at the narcos on the side of the hill. A rucksack with grenades and magazines lay by her side. Jack smiled as he watched her. He was proud of his kids. Now if he could just get them home safe.

Sixty yards to their front, Delgado lay immobile behind the Expedition. The Silverado burned fiercely to his left and the Sinaloas continued sporadic fire from the hill. The helicopter with the M60 turned and circled to the left.

"Gary, that Huey is going to come around behind us," Jack shouted. "You and Brian concentrate fire on it when it gets close enough. Vik and I will go for Kevin. If we can get his SAW, we might have a chance. Brigitte, keep firing on the shooters over there," he added. "Try to keep their heads down."

"I will, Daddy," she shouted back at him.

"Gary, Brian, cover!" Jack shouted as he and Viktor climbed over the bank and sprinted toward the Expedition away.

The night sky was lit up by the burning vehicles, and bullets cracked by their heads and kicked up dirt all around them as they ran in a zig-zag pattern. Behind them, Gary and Brian poured rounds at the hilltop while Brigitte fired at the gunmen on the side of the hill. Those had dismounted from their SUVs and were advancing on foot toward the pickup. When Brigitte's bullets dropped three of them, the others scurried behind their vehicles.

Jack and Viktor reached the Expedition just as Delgado sat up and crawled behind the front wheel. He still cradled the SAW in his arms. A piece of metal protruded from his left leg just above the knee and blood ran down to his boot.

"You're hit, Kevin." Jack said as he dropped next to him. "Can you move?"

"Probably not too fast," Delgado replied with a tight grin.

"Okay, give me the SAW and I'll cover. Vik will help you on the run."

"Let's do it," he said, handing the machine gun to Jack in exchange for an FX-05.

Viktor helped Delgado to his feet and began a fast hobble for the ravine as Jack leaned over the front of the Expedition and opened fire on the hovering gunship.

"Brian, he's coming in low," Gary shouted. "Let's spread out. I'll fire on the pilot, you focus on the gunner."

"Roger, that," Brian shouted back over the gunfire. He and Barnes ran to the center of the ravine and moved twenty yards apart as the Huey came toward them from the far bank. Behind them, Brigitte fired on full automatic at the approaching Sinaloas.

The gunship swept in at three hundred feet and the door gunner fired a long blast at the two figures in the dark creek bed. The 7.62mm tracer rounds tore up a line of dirt just twenty feet from Gary. Barnes ignored the incoming rounds and fired a full magazine across the plexiglass shield of the cockpit as Brian fired from his position.

The chopper suddenly swerved and banked to the right. The cockpit shield was riddled with bullet holes and the door gunner had ducked back inside. As Barnes watched, the Huey climbed and flew back to the far side of the ravine. It stopped and hovered three hundred yards away, barely visible in the dark.

"We popped him good," Gary shouted at Brian, "but he's not down. He'll be back. Let's give your sister a hand."

The two men ran back to the bank and resumed firing at the narcos on the side of the hill. A quick check revealed they were nearly out of ammunition. Gary and Brian had three spare magazines and Brigitte only two. They divided the remaining grenades and prepared to sell their lives at a high price.

The SAW spat out empty casings and a line of red tracers climbed skyward toward the Huey. The bullets pounded the bird just as both grenade launchers fired and the round's impact rocked the helicopter. The M75 grenades struck the ground ten feet from the Expedition. The big SUV bounced and Jack fell back to the ground.

He rolled to his knees, stunned and slightly deafened. Shaking his head, he peered around the Expedition, now on flat tires, and saw over two dozen narcos moving down the hill behind their vehicles, assault rifles blazing. Rounds thudded into the vehicle and snapped overhead. The gunship still hovered above the hill, but did not fire any additional grenades.

Jack looked toward the ravine. Viktor and Delgado had stopped to look back at him and a moment later a burst of rounds hit the two men. Blood and cloth flew and both went spinning to the ground. Jack jumped to his feet and ran toward them. He'd almost reached them when an impact on his back slammed him face down on the ground.

"They're moving again," Brian shouted, pointing at the narcos who'd risen and walked toward them around the side of the hill behind the cover of their trucks and SUVs.

Gary looked toward the hillside and knew they were in trouble. Over twenty Sinaloas were now just seventy yards away. To their front, over thirty were advancing down the hill, guns blazing. Jack, Viktor and Delgado lay on the ground between the ravine and the burning SUVs.

"Brian, Brigitte, keep firing on them," Gary shouted, pointing at the gunmen to their right. "Single shots only. Save the grenades until they're close. Brian, if the chopper comes back in, use your last mag on full auto. I'm going to help your dad."

"Okay, Gary, good luck," Brian replied.

"You, too," Barnes replied, looking at Jack's kids and wishing he could save them.

He was getting weak from his shoulder wound, his hip throbbed and his head hurt from the hit on his helmet, but his friends needed him. And that's all that mattered.

He climbed over the bank and ran toward them. The advancing Sinaloas had almost reached the SUVs and the Huey was now moving closer. Gary dropped between Viktor and Delgado and began a wound check. Both had taken more hits to their armor and had been stunned, but were still breathing and beginning to recover.

Bullets had ripped through Viktor's right deltoid and bicep, but didn't appear to have hit bone. Another had punched a hole just above his left hipbone. Blood soaked his shirt and pants. Delgado was worse. A burst had caught him chest high. His armor had saved him, but both arms were hit and the left one was smashed just above the elbow.

"You take Kevin and I'll drag Vik," said Jack as he rolled over just ten feet away, saw Gary and began crawling toward them. The back of his vest was ripped, but he was still alive.

"Roger that," Gary replied. He rose on one elbow to grab Delgado and a bullet creased his right cheekbone while another struck him in the chest and knocked him on his back.

"Gary!" Jack shouted as he crawled to his friend and rolled him over. His face was covered in blood and he gasped for air. Jack pounded on his back and he sucked in a big gulp.

"Thanks, buddy," Gary said in a raspy voice.

An explosion rocked the air behind them and they looked up to see the Expedition blown apart by a burst from the gunship's grenade launcher. The narcos had dropped thirty yards on the other side so anyone around the SUV could be dispatched. Now they moved forward again.

"Here," said Jack, handing Gary Delgado's FX-05. "If these bastards want us so bad, let's make them pay a price."

"Roger that," said Gary as he lay prone and shouldered the rifle. To his right, Viktor rolled over and looked at his friends. "Yeah, let's take some of that scum with us," the big Russian said with a wicked smile. He pulled the blood-soaked bandage off his head, threw it aside and sighted his FX-05 toward their enemy.

Jack lay flat behind his SAW as more rounds kicked up dirt in front of him and one clipped his left shoulder. He barely felt the hit as a killing rage burned through his veins. He placed his katana and Kimbers on the ground next to the machine gun.

"Come and get it, you sons-of-bitches," he snarled over the sights.

Chapter 57

The gunmen on the side of the hill were now just fifty yards away. Their bullets cracked across the lip of the bank as Brian and Brigitte returned fire. The line halted momentarily when one of the trucks came to a stop, its engine spewing steam. The driver jumped out and tried to run, but Brigitte blew him to the ground as Brian reloaded.

"Good job, sis," he shouted from ten feet away. He tossed her a full magazine. "I have one more for the chopper. Keep shooting until they reach us, then toss the grenades. Stay with the other girls and they'll take you alive. Keep fighting, Brig."

Before she could reply, he ran to the middle of the ravine and took a kneeling position as the Huey began moving toward him. The chopper came out of the dark at full speed. At one hundred yards the door gunner opened up and walked a line of steel-jacketed death across the gully floor toward Brian.

At seventy yards, Brian sighted just below the cockpit, flipped the selector switch on his FX-05 to full auto and pulled the trigger. The rifle bucked against his shoulder and he smiled as the bullets smacked into the plexiglass shield. He was halfway through the magazine when the helicopter exploded in a fireball that lit up the night and spread parts across the ravine.

Brian stared at the sight in amazement, knowing his bullets couldn't have done that. As the smoke and flame cleared, he saw the shape of a large, black helicopter a hundred yards behind the Huey and moving his way. When it reached the ravine and hovered above him, he recognized it as a Sikorsky UH-60 Black Hawk, the warhorse of the American helicopter fleet. The cavalry had arrived.

"What the hell was that, Jack?" Gary shouted as the explosion sounded behind them.

"Looks like Brian got lucky," Jack shouted back as he looked at the burning helicopter dropping to the ground. "Let's see if we can do the same," he said as he triggered a long blast at the narcos' gunship hovering over the approaching narcos.

The bird moved forward and more grenades burst from its side-mounted launchers. The rounds went high and exploded on the ground twenty yards behind them. Shrapnel hissed through the air over their heads. The pilot turned the aircraft for a better line of sight, but before he could fire again, the Huey blew apart in a fiery explosion that showered flame and metal down on the Sinaloas underneath.

Jack and Gary looked at each other with stunned expressions. "We didn't do that," Gary said.

"No, he did," Viktor said, pointing behind and to their right. The Black Hawk now hovered just behind them, its rotors thundering, and they watched as fire and smoke flew from the 70mm Hydra rocket launchers mounted on each side. The rocket grenades hit the line of Sinaloas in front of them and blew men and vehicles in all directions.

Jack and Gary looked at each other, grinned and said at the same time, "Sam!"

The first explosions were still thundering when the Black Hawk fired another string that ripped into the narcos and decimated their ranks. It then banked right and sent a burst into the group on the side of the hill. Bodies and vehicle parts flew into the air. Gas tanks exploded and sent more flame skyward.

The Black Hawk moved behind them and two more helicopters came in from the north. Jack recognized them as Sikorsky HH-60 Pave Hawks, transport models used to insert and recover special ops teams behind enemy lines. One of the Pave Hawks hovered sixty feet above them and Jack watched as men in desert-camouflaged uniforms fast-roped out the doors.

In seconds twelve men were on the ground with five headed toward the narcos on the side of the hill and the others advancing on the ones to the front. They wore Kevlar helmets and tactical vests over armor, and all carried M4 carbines and side arms. One of the men left the others and ran toward Jack and his friends.

"Sorry we're late, buddy," said Sam Coburn as he dropped between Gary and a barely conscious Delgado, "but the president was a little slow giving us a go ahead. You know, political bullshit he had to deal with, but he finally came through. And the director sends his regards."

"No problem, Sam," said Gary. "You made it and we're damn glad to see you. This is Delgado," he added, pointing at DEA agent, "he's been giving us a hand. I'll explain later."

The CIA man nodded and said, " Jack, Vik, good to see you again. Looks like you boys took a beating."

"We're shot all to hell, Sam," said Jack, "but we're still alive."

They turned as gunfire echoed to their front and on the hillside to their right. Among the burning vehicles they could see Sam's team cleaning up the remnants of the Sinaloa force.

"Don't worry, those guys are good," said Sam. "They'll take care of things."

Behind them dust whirled as the Pave Hawks settled to the ground.

"We have medics on both birds," Sam shouted over the thumping rotors. "They'll start working on your wounds."

More gunfire crackled to their front and, moments later, a figure came out of the smoke and walked to their location. With Sam's help, they all struggled to their feet.

"My guys are about done, Sam," the man said as he stopped in front of them and slung an M4 over one shoulder. "No survivors and we'll leave the mess for the Mexican police."

"Guys, this is Captain Dan Churchwell," said Coburn. "He's with the U.S. Border Patrol BORTAC unit. They're the Border Patrol's SWAT team."

"I'm familiar with them," Jack said, extending his hand, "and thanks for the help, Captain."

Churchwell was a muscular six-footer in his late forties and spoke with a slow Montana drawl. His straw-blonde hair was showing gray at the sides and he had a tough, competent look.

"Call me Dan. Just happy we could help," Churchwell told Jack. "And kick some narco ass in the process," he added.

Just then, two men in Air Force uniforms ran up to them from the Pave Hawks with medical kits in their hands.

"Dan, let's get everyone on board and get out of here before the Mexican police come to see what these fires are all about," said Coburn.

"Roger that, Sam," Churchwell replied with a grin and began issuing orders through a boom mic on his helmet.

While Coburn helped Jack and his friends to one of the Pave Lows, Churchwell and his men went to the ravine and brought Brian, Brigitte and the women to the big choppers. The Black Hawk hovered nearby, watching for any hostile forces that might appear. None did and within minutes the helicopters lifted off the desert floor and headed for the border.

Jack sat near one of the open doors and watched the medics working on Gary and Delgado. Brian and Brigitte sat against the opposite wall, Brigitte with her head on Brian's shoulder, her eyes closed. Jack could not even describe the relief he felt that his kids had survived the ordeal and were going home safe. But the cost had been high.

He looked through the door at the night sky and thought about the events of the last week. Countless time he'd risked his life to try and find his daughter and dozens of people had died, although he felt no regret for most of those deaths. And all because one man had never known what a monster his father had been.

The worst part was the death of two people who had given all to help him. One an old friend who'd made the ultimate sacrifice to help them escape and to erase the shame from his family legacy. The other a woman of tremendous courage and integrity who was determined to fight the plague sweeping her country. Jack hoped their fellow citizens would recognize their effort and appreciate their sacrifice.

He would never forget. And he would ensure their lives had not been lost in vain. This violent saga had started for him over four years ago when Jimenez had killed his wife, and it wasn't over yet. He still had one act of justice to complete. Only then could there be a sense of peace for him and his friends.

Chapter 58

Las Vegas, Nevada

Four months later

Mace Reynolds steered his white Toyota Highlander off Bruce Woodbury Beltway and headed north on Tenaya Way. Mace sat back and drummed his fingers on the steering wheel to Sonny and Cher's *Gypsies, Tramps and Thieves*. He felt good tonight. He'd picked up some items he needed for the run tomorrow night and had stopped for a drink before heading home. His fortunes were looking up now that he was back in business with the Gulf.

Mace feared his lucrative deal with Fidel Jimenez was over when he saw news reports on CNN about the destruction of a major Gulf cartel stronghold in Monterrey, Mexico. He'd tried to reach Jimenez with no success and the planes had stopped arriving. He wondered if Jack McCoy had somehow turned the tables on his captors and destroyed Jimenez's compound. Highly unlikely, he'd thought. The attack was probably just part of the ongoing warfare with the Sinaloas or another cartel.

Then two months ago he'd received a call from an old contact in Monterrey telling him the Gulf was still in operation and wanted to resume sending loads of product into Vegas. Mace quickly agreed and began searching out viable airstrips in the remote desert area of northern Clark County. Since that phone call he had landed four planeloads of meth and cocaine. Good times were here again.

Mace turned down Iguana Lane and, ten minutes later, pulled into the attached garage of his gray stucco ranch home. He parked next to the Ford F-350 diesel pickup he would use to bring home the load tomorrow night. Mace liked his new house in this vacant area of the county. His closest neighbor was two hundred yards down the street, giving him the privacy he preferred for his business.

In the kitchen he dropped his purchases on the counter and pulled a Budweiser from the refrigerator. He was thinking about a snack for the TV room when he realized he didn't hear his dogs barking and clawing at the back door. The pit bulls loved to come inside when he got home. He set the beer down and turned on the outside light. The dogs were nowhere in sight. He opened the sliding glass door and stepped outside. The last thing he remembered was a shock to the back of his neck and then darkness.

"They're on the way in," Jack said as he closed the prepaid cell phone and looked into the dark sky to the south.

On his left, Gary Barnes and Viktor Tarasov performed a last-minute check of their Colt M4 carbines and side arms. Jack did the same with his own weapons. All three men were dressed in black military fatigues and watch caps. They felt good against the October night air.

Their gunshot wounds had nearly healed now, but they were still sore and stiff. Jack felt some lingering pain in his chest and back from the blunt trauma of the hits he'd taken to his armor. The other wounds were now fresh scars that itched at times. He knew Vik and Gary had the same problem. While Gary and Vik kept watch, he thought about the last four months as he watched the steady light of the small plane approaching them half a mile away.

The rescue choppers had taken them to Laughlin Air Base near Del Rio, Texas where Sam Coburn had ambulances waiting on the runway. Brigitte and the young women captives had been taken to an administrative building while the men went to the hospital. Gary and Delgado were admitted overnight due to their more serious wounds. Jack, Brian and Viktor were treated and then joined the women.

After a long debrief with Sam, the base commander and the CIA director via a video conference call, the director agreed to help return the Mexican women captives to their homes in

Monterrey. The two European women were taken to their embassies in Washington D.C. for repatriation home.

Jack explained the rucksacks full of cash and the director agreed they should be allowed to keep it and offered assistance in setting up bank accounts for them to legitimize the drug money. "It's the least we can do for them given what they've suffered," he said. Jack told only Sam about the eleventh rucksack and Coburn helped him keep it safe until they left the base.

Gary was released the next day and returned to Las Vegas with Jack, Viktor, Brian and Brigitte. The doctors could not save Delgado's badly wounded left arm and it was amputated above the elbow. After a short recovery, the rugged DEA agent decided to stay on the job and was re-assigned to work in Miami, Florida.

After taking some time to deal with the emotional trauma of her rape and kidnapping, Brigitte was back in law school in California and Brian had returned to West Point. A call from the CIA director helped ease his way back without having to explain the fresh gunshot wound to his shoulder.

Frank Martines had placed Jack and Viktor on leave until their wounds were sufficiently healed. After two months, Jack felt ready to work again, but he had one more task to complete first. Gary flew in from Bend, Oregon to join his friends at Jack's house and, after a long discussion, they all agreed on one thing: it was time Mace Reynolds paid for his sins.

Some computer research revealed Reynolds' current residence in the north part of Clark County. Using rented vehicles and portable radios, they surveilled him for several weeks and discovered he was back in business, receiving planeloads of drugs in the desert north of the city. Two weeks earlier they had seen him setting up a new runway in a remote area and decided it was time to act.

Jack contacted Kevin Delgado in Miami and secured the phone number he needed to get the plan moving. He called the number and, two days later, received a return call that set things in motion. They resumed surveillance and when Reynolds left his house earlier in the evening, they moved in for the takedown.

An open side gate took care of the pit bulls and a stun gun to the base of the skull rendered the disgraced narc unconscious when he stepped out of the house. Now he lay flex-cuffed, gagged and blindfolded in the rear of a nearby Cadillac Escalade.

"You can get him out now," Jack said as he watched the incoming plane.

Gary and Viktor opened the rear of the Escalade and pulled a shaking, groaning Reynolds to the ground. They dragged him to where Jack stood then stepped back to watch. In front of them was a three-hundred-yard long stretch of level desert ground that had been cleared of large rocks and brush. Along both sides solar LED walking lights were stuck in the ground every fifty yards to provide the pilot guidance on landing.

At the far end, a Cessna T207A Turbo Skywalker with special tires hit the ground and began coasting toward them. The plane pulled up thirty yards away and sat idling, its lights still on.

The passenger door opened and three men climbed out. The pilot remained inside. The passengers walked forward through the settling dust and stopped fifteen feet away.

"Is one of you McCoy?" the one in the center asked in English.

"That's me," Jack answered.

"I am Gomez," he replied. "These are my associates."

Gomez was in his thirties, medium height and weight. He wore a green western shirt, denim jeans and western boots. His companions were older, taller and dressed in black fatigues and combat boots. None were armed, but they all had the hard look of cartel killers.

"Is that the dog who helped steal our cocaine and kill our men in Henderson?" Gomez asked.

"He is," Jack answered, his face impassive.

"May we see his face?"

Jack reached down and ripped the blindfold and gag from Reynolds face. He looked up, his eyes blinking as he took in his surroundings. After a moment he looked at Jack with a stunned expression.

"McCoy, what the hell is going on? I thought you died in Mexico."

"No, Mace," Jack told him. "Things changed after you left and your boss didn't make out so well. Now it's your turn."

"What do you mean? Who the hell are they?"

"Think about it for a minute."

Reynolds looked at the three men and the plane. After a few moments, realization set in. Sinaloas!

"Aw, shit, no, McCoy," he said, looking up at Jack with terror on his face. "No, man, you can't do this. This ain't right. You know what they'll do to me?"

"Yeah, Mace, I know."

"No, man, don't do this. Just shoot me. Right here, just put a bullet in my head. I know I got it comin'. Don't let those bastards take me, please!"

Reynolds voice shook with panic and tears streamed down his face.

Jack kneeled down and looked him directly in the eyes.

"Mace, it's going to be a long, hard death. One you've truly earned. But if you scream really loud, maybe God will hear you and give you a quick release."

Reynolds looked into Jack's icy blue eyes and realized there would be no mercy tonight. He hung his head and sobbed loudly. Jack stood up and faced Gomez.

"He's yours."

"This is very generous of you, McCoy," Gomez told him as he shook a cigarette from a pack of Marlboros and lit up. "Perhaps we can continue this temporary relationship."

To Jack's left, Gary and Viktor made a subtle shift in their stance. Jack fixed the cartel gunman with a stony gaze and said, "This is a one-time, mutually-beneficial arrangement. If I ever see any of you in Clark County again, I'll kill you on sight."

After a moment Gomez blew out a puff of smoke, smiled and said, "Understood."

He signaled with his left hand and his two associates walked up to Reynolds. One of them took a compact case from his fatigue pocket and removed a syringe containing a clear liquid. He grabbed a struggling Reynolds by the hair and plunged the needle into the back of his neck. In a few seconds the struggles stopped and he lay back on the ground.

The two narcos dragged their unconscious captive back to the plane and loaded him inside. Gomez gave Jack a salute and climbed in with his men. The Cessna turned around and taxied back down the impromptu landing zone, lifted off and disappeared into the night.

When the plane had disappeared into the darkness, Jack felt like an old, heavy burden had been lifted from his shoulders. He looked up at the star-lit sky and said softly, "That was for you, Gabrielle."

"Time to go home, Jack?" asked Gary as he and Viktor stood on either side of him.

Jack looked at the two men with whom he shared a bond nearly as strong as that which he shared with his children.

"Yeah, buddy," he said, putting his hands on their shoulders. "Time to go home."

The three men walked to the Escalade, got in and drove out of the desert.

EPILOGUE

Mexico

A large crowd was gathered in front of the San Hidalgo Catholic Church when Jack pulled into the parking lot. The Sunday morning mass had just finished and people had gathered to chat with friends and neighbors before going home. Jack parked his silver Ford Explorer in a space at the rear and sat for a moment watching the sprinkle of rain on the windshield.

He'd crossed the border early that morning, before daylight, and had driven straight to Monterrey. Using his own passport and a tourist card in his own name, he'd had no problem and was quickly passed through by Mexican Immigration. That was good because he would have had a problem explaining the rucksack full of American hundred-dollar bills on the floorboard had they wanted to inspect his baggage.

On the drive down he'd thought about all of the events that had happened since he was here last. The Gulf cartel had recovered since the fight at the compound and was once again at war with the Sinaloas and the Mexican police and military. No surprise there, Jack knew. New bosses always stepped in to take over and continue the enterprise. The money was too big to ignore. Still, there had been small victories.

The audio recordings on Marco's cell phone and Kevin Delgado's flash drives had resulted in the U.S. attorney in Houston indicting Armando Cruz along with several other cartel chiefs. Numerous politicians in the Nuevo Leon state had been arrested by the Mexican Federal Police. Cruz was now in a Monterrey prison awaiting extradition to the United States.

After the battle at the compound, the Mexican military had recovered more than two hundred bodies from the blast site. Among the remains were those of Marco and Elena. Kevin Delgado had given a statement to the Mexican PF that the two officers had assisted the DEA in an undercover operation that resulted in the rescue of several captives and the destruction of a large amount of drugs and weapons.

The Mexican government recognized Marco and Elena as heroes in the war against the cartels and awarded them the highest medals they could bestow for their bravery. Their families were given pensions in their names and high-level politicians and officers attended their funerals.

Jack felt a melancholy sadness as he watched the crowd break up and move out of the parking lot. He picked up a bouquet of roses off the passenger seat and got out. The light rain and cloudy sky matched his somber attitude. He approached a priest who was waving good-bye to parishioners from the front steps.

Jack nodded as the short padre looked up at him. He seemed suspicious of the big American dressed in Wranglers, a white shirt, cowboy boots, a brown bomber jacket and tan cap with a military emblem, but after a moment of conversation he complimented Jack's fluent Spanish and directed him toward the cemetery.

Jack walked between the rows of well-maintained graves until he found the one he had come to see. The low mound of dirt was still fresh and flowers lay near the modest headstone. Jack took off his cap and dropped to one knee. His eyes became moist as he remembered the beautiful Mexican cop who had battled so fearlessly by his side to help rescue Brigitte. She was a rare individual and he considered himself lucky to have known her for even a short time.

"I wish things had not ended this way, Elena," Jack said in Spanish. "You still had a lot of life to live and I wish you had stayed with your brother. But I understand your passion for justice. Something we shared. You did well and you can be proud."

After a few moments Jack placed the roses on the grave, then stood and put his cap back on. Looking up, he wished the sun was shining. She would like that.

"Descansa en paz, mi amiga. Tu la ganaste," he said softly. Rest in peace, my friend. You earned it.

Jack raised his hand in a sharp salute then turned and walked back to his Explorer.

Jack stopped in front of the white house with the pink roof and watched two men talking near an old blue Pontiac in the front yard. After a moment the men shook hands and one got into the Pontiac. He drove up the driveway, turned right and disappeared down the street. The other man picked up his crutches and walked to a nearby green pickup, opened the hood and looked underneath.

Jack drove down the driveway and stopped behind the truck. The rain had stopped now, but the clouds remained. He picked up the rucksack from the floorboard, got out and approached the man under the hood. Ramiro Cisneros looked up at him, a curious look on his face, and dropped the rag he was holding.

"Jack, this is quite a surprise," Cisneros said as he put the crutches under his arm and walked around the truck. "What brings you back to Monterrey?"

Dressed in jeans and a blue jacket over a white sweatshirt, his eyes held a look of sadness. Jack could tell the loss of Elena had been hard for him.

"I just came from the church," Jack told him. "I wanted to visit her grave, and I also wanted to see you before I leave. I have something for you, but I didn't call first because I wasn't sure you would see me."

Ram looked at him for a moment; then his lips cracked in a knowing smile.

"It's okay, Jack," he said. "I don't blame you for her death. Elena died doing something she believed in and wanted to do. Sometimes I think it was just her destiny."

"That may be, but I still feel guilty. Like I should have done more to save her."

"Jack, when you came with Elena, she told my wife why you were really here and that she admired how you were trying to rescue your daughter. She had no children and she felt it was her duty to help return your daughter to you. She also wanted to strike a blow against the criminals who had killed her husband and who are causing such destruction in our country.

"She later sent my wife a text telling her how you wanted to leave her here and not risk her life. She admired you even more for that, but she couldn't turn back. She was committed to seeing justice done. I appreciate that, too, Jack. That was very gracious of you. But don't blame yourself for what happened. She wouldn't want that."

"I feel privileged to have known her, Ram, but it was only for a short time. I know how she died, but I don't know anything about her before we met."

Ram looked at him for a moment, nodded and said, "Then come inside, Jack, and I will tell you how she lived," he said. He turned on his crutches and walked toward the house.

Jack followed and, as he neared the front door, the clouds overhead suddenly parted and a warm breeze swirled around him. He stopped and looked up at the brilliant sun now shining down. In the distance, the Sierra Madre Mountains loomed large. Over his right shoulder, he saw a V-shaped flock of geese flying over the Sierra Fraile foothills. It was going to be a good day after all.

Jack looked back up, smiled and followed Ram inside the house.

End

Made in the USA
Lexington, KY
22 March 2015